Praise For The Thrillers Of Mark Nykanen
The Bone Parade, Hush, Search Angel, and now, *Primitive*

"Primitive captures the raw and rugged high alpine environment, a powerful, emblematic setting for this furiously-paced thriller about a mother and daughter, and the radical environmentalists who want to use them to deliver a desperate message to the world."
— **Christopher Van Tilburg, author of** *Mountain Rescue Doctor*

"[The Bone Parade is] the creepiest page turner since The Silence of the Lambs."
— **US Weekly**

"An irresistible suspense thriller . . . "
— **Kirkus Reviews (starred)**

"[The Bone] Parade goes down easy. Really easy."
— **Entertainment Weekly**

"You won't be able to stop reading."
— **Salem Statesman Journal**

"The novel is deeply unsettling and exciting—a testament to the author's skill as a storyteller."
— **Booklist**

"A thrilling page-turner."
— **The Oregonian, about** *Search Angel*

"Artful and well-written."
— **Ridley Pearson,** New York Times best-selling author

"Fans of [Thomas] Harris and other dark thriller writers may eat this one up."
— **Publishers Weekly, about** *The Bone Parade*

D1565372

Primitive

by

Mark Nykanen

Bell Bridge Books

This is a work of fiction. Names, characters, places and incidents are either the products of the author's imagination or are used fictitiously. Any resemblance to actual persons (living or dead,) events or locations is entirely coincidental.

Bell Bridge Books
PO BOX 30921
Memphis, TN 38130
ISBN: 978-0-9821756-4-4

Bell Bridge Books is an Imprint of BelleBooks, Inc.

We at BelleBooks enjoy hearing from readers. You can contact us at the address above or at BelleBooks@BelleBooks.com

Visit our websites – www.BelleBooks.com and www.BellBridgeBooks.com.

10 9 8 7 6 5 4 3 2

Cover design: Debra Dixon
Interior design: Hank Smith
Photo credits: Shack - "© Saraberdon | Dreamstime.com"
                  Woman - "© Sophiesourit | Dreamstime.com"
                  Blood Spatter - "© Alexandr Labetskiy | Dreamstime.com"

:Lo:01:

For Anika Taylor Nykanen

Prologue

Sonya Adams froze. The sight of the cougar left her as rigid as the little girl sitting in the snow. For eternal seconds the triangle of animal, child and woman remained unmoving. *I don't owe these people anything*, Sonya told herself. *They kidnapped me to get media attention. They may kill me.* Then with no more thought than she'd give to breath itself, Sonya began to inch toward Willow, keeping her eyes on the huge lion, at least seven feet from its reddish nose to the tip of its twitching tail. Its teeth were bared, its ears pinned back.

My God, it's going to spring.

The girl started to sob.

"Willow, it's okay," Sonya said in a deliberately loud voice. "It's just a big old cat. Please don't cry, and I want you to stay really still. Do you know how to play freeze tag?" The whole time she talked, Sonya moved closer to her, saw the girl nodding her answer, and said, "Good. I want you to stay frozen right now. That's really important."

Four more steps and she could stand in front of her. As she eased forward, she slowly slipped off her bearskin coat, then raised it high above her head, making herself look as large as possible.

One more big step and she'd be standing between Willow and the cougar. But that's when her leg post-holed in the snow, all the way to her thigh. She almost toppled over, and felt a stabbing spasm in her lower back when she righted herself.

To her horror, the lion's hind feet pumped, ready to leap.

*

All over the world, people were riveted to their televisions for another glimpse of kidnapped fashion model Sonya Adams, held captive in what appeared to be a survivalist encampment somewhere in the wilderness of the Pacific Northwest. Passengers for an American Airlines flight from Chicago O'Hare to Miami crowded closer to a screen tilted down toward the departure lounge.

A blue-suited gate attendant announced that boarding was about to begin. "Quiet!" snapped a tall man in a dark overcoat. He and the other passengers had their eyes trained on CNN, which was airing the latest Terra Firma podcast. This one, however, did not feature

Sonya.

Only a document stamped *Top Secret* filled the screen, as the altered voice of the podcast's female narrator—an environmental hero or a lunatic terrorist, depending on one's perspective—announced, "On Christmas day, Terra Firma will post this highly classified CIA report on the Web. It will be our gift to the world. But we are sorry to say that it is far more frightening than any act ever contemplated by any terrorist anywhere. 'Methane: Global Warming and Global Security' was authored by scientists with the highest security clearances in our government."

The podcast showed a close-up of the title. "The report reveals that officials know that massive deposits of methane that had been frozen in the seabed of the Arctic Ocean for millions of years are releasing into the atmosphere in amounts far greater than has ever been recorded—or revealed—publicly."

"Oh, my God," a woman said.

"Methane," the podcast narrator continued, "traps heat at more than twenty times the rate of carbon dioxide. For eons the frozen seabed, like the permafrost on land, has sealed billions of tons of methane under the Arctic Ocean. The methane was stabilized by cold temperatures and the pressure of the water above it.

"But temperatures have increased dangerously in the Arctic, and the methane is now releasing from the seabed over thousands of square miles in what scientists are calling 'methane chimneys.' *Huge releases of methane in the past have been linked by renowned scientists to the hothouse conditions that gave rise to dinosaurs.* We will give the government till Christmas, just ten days, to publish this report first and explain why it has hidden these terrifying developments from the world's people. We say to the government: break your ties to Big Oil, Big Coal, and big money."

The screen went blank.

People everywhere turned to one another in alarm.

At O'Hare, the crowd stood in stunned silence.

"Dinosaurs?" A young man with an iPod pulled out an earbud. "Did she say '*dinosaurs*?'"

Chapter 1

Finally, some down time, was Sonya's first thought on the day she was abducted, as she awakened to the last hours of simple, sweet normalcy that she would ever know.

She rolled away from the light leaking through the mini-blinds of her heritage home in a historic Denver neighborhood. Sonya had been booked solid for the past two weeks, and this morning offered the rare luxury of sleeping in after working until ten thirty last night on a major magazine ad for Nordica ski boots. She snuggled the comforter around her neck as the phone began to ring softly.

Dutifully, she picked up the receiver and checked caller I.D. *Chatwin Modeling Agency*. Then she did her best at nine a.m. to sound awake, alert, and, most of all, young and energetic. Sprightly.

Her voice cracked on, "Yes?"

"Sorry-sorry-sorry, but I gotta wake you up because you *are* the flavor of the month."

Jackson, Jackson, Jackson, she thought, *turn down the flattery.*

"Are you up for Bozeman, Montana, honeypants? It's a last-minute thing. The art director says he's gotta have *you.* "

"Hold on." She sat up, covering the mouthpiece to clear her throat, trying to sound if not youthful, at least alive. "How last-minute is it?"

"Not *that.* " A pause. "Say an 8:40 flight tonight?"

"Sure." She rose from the bed, arched her lower back, and heard a distinct pop that felt good.

"You still having trouble with your email? Because I tried sending you the shoot schedule and it came back."

"Yes." Waking up. "I'll just come by." Downtown Denver was only ten minutes away. "I've got to drop off my laptop anyway."

"The shoot starts early tomorrow."

"How early is 'early?'"

"Oh, you'll definitely be catching the sunrise."

Sonya hadn't seen that for a while. She opened the blinds, and noticed that the last of the red and orange leaves had fallen on her quaint, snow-dusted street. That's when the memory of her daughter's birthday jolted her, as if it had been hiding in the back of her mind waiting for the right moment to leap out. Much as Darcy herself had been known to jump out of her shadowy life with a suddenness that had been shocking to her mother.

Sonya sighed. Twenty-three years ago, to the day, she'd given birth to her only child, an extraordinarily difficult daughter, but also an amazing—and passionate—young woman. On Sunday, she'd left Darcy a phone invitation to a birthday dinner. Now it was Thursday, and she hadn't heard back from her. No surprise there, which was the saddest part of all—realizing that even though her expectations of Darcy had sunk to heartbreaking depths, they could still be exceeded by reality.

So at 8:40 tonight Sonya would hit the road again. *Grab the work while you can*—the model's mantra. You never knew when you'd hit a dry patch that would turn into an endless professional desert. Always a worry when you're a middle-aged model. Forty-four, to be precise. Advertisers needed mature faces to sell products to aging baby-boomers, but not *too* mature.

She hadn't asked about the client. Most likely a catalogue shoot or a newspaper ad. Maybe a billboard. Or a new product. Her smiling face had also adorned packaging for everything from yoga mats to orthopedic pillows (the two were not unrelated, in her experience).

She fixed a cup of chai tea and settled at her vanity to do her face, studying the fine lines that had formed above her lips.

And here you thought you were getting too old for pleats. You just didn't know that they'd show up on your face.

She saved her lips for last, smoothing on a sienna-colored gloss, and strode back into the bedroom to slip on a silk and rayon jacket with a jacquard vine pattern. Fall colors. Then she gave herself a strict once-over before a full-length mirror, straightening the mandarin collar on her crisp white shirt before judging herself fit enough to walk in the door of the agency.

Chatwin Modeling Agency occupied a spacious suite on the fifth floor of one of Denver's oldest and most distinguished buildings. With its stone-and-mortar, ornamental turrets and tall, mullioned windows shimmering in the snappy, late autumn sun, it looked as much like a fortress as any castle Sonya had ever seen. A broad band of stained glass depicting Saint George slaying the dragon arched over the red brick entryway.

The elevator opened to Jackson pacing behind an elegant black-enamel reception desk that swept away from the far wall of a brightly lit lobby, appointed with teal leather chairs, brushed steel end tables, and fuchsia walls. Jackson remained on his feet most of the day, working the phone and pausing only to tap away at a keyboard or to direct the work of his two young female assistants.

Aspiring models waited on both sides of the lobby, balancing portfolios on their laps and flipping through magazines, bringing Joni Mitchell to mind, singing about lots of pretty people

"... *reading Vogue, reading Rolling Stone* ... "

Lots of pretty faces on the walls, too. Hers was sandwiched between photographs of a *Sports Illustrated* swimsuit star and a plus-size model famous for her three brief lines in an ad for a popular ice cream bar: "This is *real* pleasure. And I won't deny myself. *Ever!*"

Both of them had moved on to New York agencies. Sonya had seen other models come and go, less illustriously in most cases. Her own photo had been updated yearly for the past two decades. She wondered how many more times she'd sit before Ms. Katie Chatwin's camera before her features disappeared from these walls forever. If adulation of youth really was the cold hard face of fashion, then every month saw more of her future melting away.

Jackson flaunted his own brand of eye candy: Tall, lean, handsome in an overtly angular manner that suited him at twenty-nine, but cursed with an upper lip so sparse that his head shots had never landed him a reputable agency. Now he directed the daily flow of models and tended to Ms. Chatwin herself, who referred to him as her Girl Friday, a tired moniker that he embraced fully.

"Here you go, honeypants."

Sonya skimmed the travel arrangements to make sure there were no surprises (that's the last thing you wanted on a shoot).

Bozeman. Alaska Air. 8:40 p.m. Return tomorrow 6:25 p.m.

Flipping the page, she noted her day rate: $1,500. Pretty much the top of the food chain for a middle-age model in these parts. Scanning further, she saw that the client was *The Frontier Ahead* catalogue (buckskin jackets and western skirts, Navajo blankets and silver bracelets). They'd plucked her from the cyberspace cattle call on the agency website. All the particulars for all the world to see: *Sonya Adams. 5'10". Size 6. Bust: 36 inches Waist: 27 inches Hips:*

36 inches Shoe: 8. Eyes: Brown. Hair: Brown.

A near-perfect figure, but she thought she'd probably nabbed the job with her smile. Sonya wasn't coy about her assets and liabilities. The smile made her appear healthy, wholesome, "Bright as a peppermint Altoid," in the memorable words of her favorite art director.

"Katie busy?" As long as she was down here she'd like to slip in and see her agent.

"She *is*. New girl. *Hot*. But don't worry, she's a petite. Name's Taffeta. Don't you just love it? Mobile, Alabama." Said as if that explained everything. "Why? Is there something *I* can do for you?"

"I just wanted to talk to her about my daughter." Katie Chatwin called Darcy, "A diamond in the rough." Sonya still held out hope that her girl might try the modeling business. Maybe even end up liking it. "It can wait."

She spotted the smile starting to creep across Jackson's face, but he stopped short of using his pet name for Darcy, "Little Miss Makeover."

Bizarre to have a daughter so notorious for her appearance that she'd earned a slew of unflattering nicknames over the past several years, especially when you made your living with your looks. And not just looks. Sonya had achieved this success by having a predictably cheerful demeanor, while Darcy had gained her reputation by using harsh means—and behavior—to create a much starker image.

As chance would have it, her daughter rang her cell as she stepped back onto the elevator.

Take a breath.

Which she did, *twice*.

"Happy birthday, sweetheart."

"You still want me over for dinner?"

"Yes, of course . . . "

"But?"

"The only uncertainty you hear is that a job just came up. I've got a flight tonight, but if you could come over at five we could probably do it?"

"Four"

Sonya had been negotiating with this kid since she'd learned to talk, but four o'clock would never be enough time to get ready. "I'm sorry, it's got to be five."

"Remember what I'm eating."

"I know." She tried to keep impatience from bubbling over. And almost told Darcy to forget it, that you don't call *me* at the last minute. But a big part of the challenge she'd always faced in parenting Darcy had been knowing where to draw the line. Sonya still wasn't sure of the answer so she tended to err on the side of kindness, and often felt like a fool. "Okay, five," she said.

Look, you'll do dinner, she told herself. *It'll be quick, and you'll be on your way to Bozeman. It'll be what it'll be. What it's been for too long now.*

She stared at her watch as the elevator opened to the ground floor, already gripped by panic.

Forget the laptop. Get a move on.

By the time she got home she had three bags full of produce and a bouquet of flowers. A gift for Darcy was always problematic, but maybe she'd like the lilies. They were truly lovely.

Two hours later she'd worked the food processor so furiously that she expected to see a spike in her utility bill. But this was Darcy's birthday, so it would be a raw food fest: mock salmon pate, which bore as much resemblance to the real thing as it did to Milk Duds; carrocado mush, a blend of carrots, avocados, and *dulse* (basically seaweed, but "harvested from virgin tidal pools") and sprouted quinoa, which appeared a little *too* alive when she globbed it into a serving bowl.

Sonya wiped up the pits and peelings sliming every surface, loaded the dishwasher, and drew herself a bath, spritzing it liberally with lavender oil.

After lighting a scented candle and turning the Jacuzzi on low, she lay back, relaxing into the padded headrest.

And fell asleep.

She woke with a start at twenty to five, rose from the tub like Glenn Close in *Fatal Attraction,* and dried off so fast she left a towel burn on her bottom.

Sonya dashed into the bedroom and threw her clothes back on. Looked herself over in the full-length mirror and checked her face. *It'll do.* Stage one of Darcy triage was complete.

Stage two came when she packed her carry-on. She'd had to do this too many times in the midst of a hellacious argument with her daughter, and been left having to buy a hairdryer, eye makeup, underwear, or some other overlooked item on the road. Pack now, pay less later.

Sonya wished that she could have reacted less harshly, but Darcy had never seemed to understand that her mom was supporting her with no help from her feckless father.

Stage three came when Sonya fortified herself with a glass of wine.

The front doorbell sounded as she took another sip of sauvignon. Her hand froze with the glass inches from her lips.

More, she barked at herself with the kind of urgency normally associated with a 911 call. She took a mouthful, then smoothed the front of her slacks and headed calmly to the door as the opening notes of Pachelbel's *Canon in D Major* rose for the second time.

"It would help if you'd give me a goddamn key."

In response, Sonya managed a greeting and a hug, reaching out in word and deed to put aside Darcy's profane and familiar complaint, and received in return a stiff whiff of alcohol, tobacco, and firearms.

"Look at you, twenty-three. Happy birthday."

"Thanks, pork chop."

A term of endearment at one time. Now? Sonya honestly had no idea. Maybe it meant Meat Eater. Maybe, "You're a pig, Mom." *Don't ask.*

Darcy shrugged off her mother's hand and a dark wool jacket, then whipped her knitted cap across the room, where it landed with handsome accuracy on the arm of a tufted blue couch.

Her hair fell in clumps to her shoulder. Sonya found herself reaching for the tangled mess.

"Don't," Darcy warned. "I'm letting it go. I want dreads."

Dreadlocks. Of course. As predictable as her tetchiness. Dreads, like the ones festering on that white guy's head at a most unforgettable shoot two months ago. He'd had a bone handle knife, of all things, poking out of his locks of hair like an accessory. It had been a newspaper ad for McFaddins Fashions, a shot that had turned into an increasingly popular poster well beyond and outside of the original ad. The full-page spread had featured Sonya in a linen pants suit and pearls casting her most censorious look down at the *neo-primitive*, as he'd described himself, crouching at her feet in a loincloth . . . and that's all, unless you were inclined to include the tattoos and piercings that had covered his entire upper body, from his neck to his navel, his deltoids to his derrière.

"Darcy, I wish you wouldn't get dreadlocks—"

"Not now. I'm not in the mood. I'm majorly PMSing."

"—because you have such lovely hair." W*hen it's not a tangled, unwashed mess and dyed all colors of death.* But again, those most chosen words remained unspoken, as they often must for a mother.

Darcy might not have heard them anyway, because she'd followed the flight of her hat to the couch before veering into the kitchen to root through the refrigerator for a Corona (she ate raw food *except* for beer and tequila). It was her birthday, so Sonya had stocked up.

"Lime?"

Sonya pointed to the fruit basket.

Darcy fondled three of them before slicing up the ripest with such professional dispatch—she bartended nightly at a place named *Rio deGenerate*—that for the first time in Sonya's life she actually felt sorry for a piece of fruit. Her daughter stuffed the wedge into the bottle and took a swig that lasted several seconds, then eyed her mother.

Her mother eyed her right back, the better not to notice the piercings: eyebrows, nose, ears (half a dozen in each . . . at last count), tongue and, reportedly, breasts, labia (major and minor), and the worst, by far, two tiny titanium barbells through the bridge of her nose, which gave Sonya's beautiful child the unmistakably deranged look of a bride of Frankenstein.

"I'm gonna do it," Darcy said.

It, in this context with this girl at this time was as loaded as two simple letters could possibly get. Did *it* refer to dropping the seedy job, the "art" classes (held in a squatter's loft), and the druggie friends, including her boyfriend, Kodiak, and their housemate, Lotus Land?

Or did *it* mean she'd finally return to school to get a Masters in Fine Arts?

If only, Sonya would think moments later, though Darcy's revelation wasn't absent of all artistic considerations:

"I'm gonna get inked. Finally."

"Inked," Sonya said in a tone that spoke more of incredulity than ignorance.

"Yep." Darcy pulled off her sweater, unveiling a ratty, "recycled" sleeveless camisole, once peach, perhaps, but now broadly stained and washed-out. "I'm gonna get a big tattoo for right here," stroking the whole of her bare shoulder like it was a pet.

Don't, Sonya warned herself. *Not a word, not a single word.* She knew in the pre-dawn of her emotions that even a lone critical note would buttress her daughter's decision to further disfigure herself, for that was the only view Sonya had on this subject. Piercings? Ugly as they were—and here her eyes rose to those belligerent-looking barbells in the bridge of Darcy's pert nose—the holes would eventually seal up. But a tattoo?

"A snake in the grass." Darcy said, "with its head coming up right here." Her thin, graceful fingers circled a patch of skin right below her ear.

"You'll be in turtlenecks the rest of your life," flew from Sonya. Dismayed not so much by Darcy's huge smile as by her own inability to restrain herself.

"I'll wear my apple earrings with it."

Sonya, still in shock, added bewilderment to her ever-expressive face.

"The Garden of Eden. Don't you get it?" Darcy grinned.

*

Dinner went as well as Sonya could have expected, given Darcy's opening gambit and her dietary demands.

Now it was time for the cake, a mound of raw carrot clippings with almond "icing."

Sonya planted the candles in the concoction and watched them immediately begin to lean over, Tower of Pisa-style, so she jammed them in another half inch before firing them up. She carried the gleaming, orange and brown mass to the table singing *Happy Birthday* in French, a family tradition since Darcy had entered the third grade of the Denver International School. The girl's facility with her second tongue far surpassed her mother's, but the last time Sonya had tried to get away with singing *Happy Birthday* in English, Darcy had been sixteen and had screeched, "No, Mom, you *ruined* it." (But in French, of course, not that a translation had been necessary.) And, well, that had been the end of *that. Bonne Fete A*

10

Toi it would be, *qui-qui.*

"Thanks," Darcy said as Sonya set the cake down in front of her.

She closed her eyes and could have been a pre-teen again for all the simple delight she squeezed into her face while making a wish.

As she blew out the candles, Sonya's hand settled lightly on her bare, blank shoulder, and Darcy squeezed it gently, an act of kindness so unexpected that it left her mother startled, shaken, and more wary than ever.

What's that tell you? Sonya asked herself later as she backed down her driveway. *She was so nice to me there for a while, even thanked me for the flowers. It's like she'd just heard I had cancer or something.*

And then she'd wanted to talk. *Of all the days.*

Sonya glanced at her watch and moved rapidly from surface streets to the freeway, darting through the last of Denver's drive-time traffic. One more quick turn took her into the airport's long-term parking, where she retrieved her carry-on from the back of the car.

Is that snow?

The cold damp spot on her cheek turned out to be rain. She hadn't noticed the clouds moving in, or the terminal up ahead, which bore the unlikely appearance of a tent, as if it might have rambled nomadically across the Front Range before settling here.

The strange design no longer shocked her, and she wondered if there'd come a time when a snake on Darcy's lovely neck would seem as normal.

Less than an hour after boarding, she landed in Bozeman. As she rolled her carry-on past security, she spotted her driver, a young woman in a white shirt and dark tie with a chauffeur's cap pulled low on her forehead. She held a plain piece of cardboard with *Sonya Adams.* It looked like a flap torn from the top of a packing box that had been scribbled on with red crayon.

Never a good omen when the client's penchant for penny-pinching begins with the modest cost of a neat sign.

What gives? Sonya wondered. Major catalogue companies had never been this cheesy.

At least they'd assigned a driver to her. And they certainly hadn't scrimped on the car: a white stretch limo. Town cars were much more typical, so no complaints there. A chance to stretch her long legs after the cramped seating on the plane.

Fat, cold raindrops pelted the dark windows as they pulled away from the terminal. Sonya checked her watch and figured she could be in bed by ten-thirty.

Several minutes later the driver pulled onto the shoulder by a stand of conifers, their wet bark shiny in the headlights.

"A warning light," the chauffeur said after lowering the vinyl privacy panel that separated them. "Got a phone? "

"Sure, but don't they give you one?"

"Yeah, but I forgot it."

Sonya dug out her new Nokia and scooted up to the opening. The driver took the cell with her eyes on the rearview mirror, never bothering to thank her.

As Sonya sat back down the electronic lock sounded for the front passenger door. She looked up to see a man racing from the trees to slide in beside the driver. With a start, Sonya realized that she recognized him.

He spoke without turning around. "You're locked in and you're not getting out. Don't try a thing or I'm coming back there."

"What's going on?" Sonya tried to sound outraged, but her hands, arms, her whole body had begun to shake.

The privacy panel rose, isolating her as the driver sped back onto the road.

Sonya lunged for the door. *Locked.* She stabbed the lock button with her finger and yanked on the handle again, then spun around when she heard a truck coming up behind them. She waved frantically, mouthed "Help, help," before realizing that the driver couldn't see her through the limo's smoked glass.

And no one would miss her at the shoot because this wasn't a modeling job. This was a trap, and she'd flown right into it. And the driver had duped her into surrendering her only means of calling for help.

But why me?

She hit the switch to lower the privacy panel. Nothing happened. In a sudden fury, she pounded the black vinyl. It started down, and she backed away, wishing she'd left it alone.

The young man stared at her. He looked the same as when she'd seen him before: bone-handle knife rising like a hair stick from his balled-up dreadlocks. The last time, he'd been crouching at her feet, posing for that McFaddins ad, affecting a feral taunt on his face.

He looked deadly now. And then he pulled the blade from his hair.

Chapter 2

"Didn't you hear me the first time? Sit back in the seat and don't make me come back there."

Horrified, that's exactly what Sonya did. The privacy panel rose.

An hour and twenty-four minutes later, it remained in place. She'd checked the panel almost as often as she'd checked her watch, trying to track how far they'd gone. She thought they might be driving north on a state highway, but she'd always had a lousy sense of direction, a shortcoming she'd never experienced more cruelly than tonight.

She wished she could see whether he'd put the blade back in his hair. It frightened her almost senseless to think of the weapon in his hands, and him coming back after her.

The heater fan hummed relentlessly, making the back of the limo uncomfortably hot, and the switch to turn it off didn't work. Sweat streamed from her scalp, down her brow and back and neck, dampening her blouse and bra and leaving her limp and feverish.

She'd shed her leather trench coat and a cashmere sweater, and now undid the top two buttons on her blouse, discreetly fluffing it to try to get some air. Feeling watched, even though she didn't know how they could see her back here.

Her throat and mouth burned as if they'd been scoured with sand. Dizziness and a dreadful feeling of sickness finally forced her past her considerable fear. She knocked meekly on the panel. It lowered less than an inch.

The guy with the dreadlocks turned, showing a face that had become as well-known as her own from the McFaddins poster.

"Could you turn down the heat? Please*?"* Sonya's voice croaked, a sound so weak it scared her. "Water?" she managed.

The young man whipped the knife up from his lap and smacked the vinyl by her face, making her jump back.

The panel closed.

She could have wept in fear and frustration. Why hadn't Jackson checked, called *The Frontier Ahead* to make sure it was they who'd requested Sonya Adams? But why would he? It was so routine. No one ever checks. Who thinks abduction?

They did.

The heater fan never faltered, and she grew so furious she wanted to pound the panel again; but she didn't have the strength even to sit up properly. And then her eyes landed on the vinyl where he'd smacked his knife, and she couldn't stop imagining what he could do to her, what he might have done to other women. At the shoot Sonya had considered the knife a prop, not a harrowing fixture of some insane life.

Miles and miles went by. Nobody passed them. They didn't pass anyone else. Few headlights appeared. She checked her watch again: one hour fifty-seven minutes.

This heat is killing me.

She edged back up to the dark panel and used what felt like the last of her strength to tap it. She felt on the verge of passing out. When it cracked open, she caught the driver's eyes in the rear view mirror, and pantomimed drinking water.

Dreadlocks glanced at the clock on the dash and leaned forward, retrieving a water bottle from a pack. The window opened two more inches, barely enough room for him to slip it to her.

"What's going on? Tell me, please."

The window closed once more without a response.

The heater fan suddenly fell silent, and in that first instant she imagined a degree of cooling. *Thank God.* She ripped the cap off the bottle and drank greedily, downing half of it before finding the harsh metallic taste repugnant, like water from the rankest desert well.

That was her last thought before melting to the carpet.

*

Waking was like coming out of a coma. Her thoughts were sluggish, and only the most basic elements of her surroundings registered: blanket, cold, movement.

The limousine hit a pothole and her head bounced. When she settled she felt the carpet on which she lay. Rough. Grimy. Smelled like a dog. And the blanket covering her was bristly as a brush. Then she heard the rapid metallic rhythm of studded snow tires.

Not the limo.

Her eyes opened to darkness so blank she blinked to check herself, but still she saw nothing. The scratchy blanket covered her head too. And her mouth wouldn't shut. It hurt. She tried to work her jaw. Couldn't.

Christ, they've gagged me.

Another bump. She bounced again. Her neck ached. She was on her side. She tried to brace her head, but couldn't: Her hands were tied behind her back. Her feet were tied too.

She sank into herself, so aghast she didn't feel it at first. A chilly dampness. And then she realized she'd wet herself.

Oh God.

Another jarring bounce made her neck hurt worse. She must have been sleeping in an awkward position. Not sleeping, *drugged,* she told herself.

Wet.

She shifted the coarse blanket off her face, then let her eyes travel as far as they could. This was the back of a big vehicle. A Suburban or the like, with the seats in the back taken out.

Two people, a driver and passenger, sat up front. Sonya started when her eyes fell on a guy sitting near her on the raised platform that filled the rear compartment. No, there were two people back here too. The second was the woman limo driver, but without the chauffeur's cap. Sonya looked at the guy again: Dreads, with that knife rising from the back of his head. Both of them staring at her in silence. Like zombies. More than any threat, this terrified her.

She grunted, trying to speak. He drew the knife from his hair, his face still blank as he crawled toward her.

She tried to roll away. The blanket fell off as he grabbed her, his fingers long and hard. Steely tentacles. He pressed the blade, still warm from his scalp, against her face. Then he cut the cloth and jerked away the gag.

"Where am I?" Her words came as if from a broken dream, stumbling across stepping stones of consciousness. No answer, but he understood her. She could see it in his eyes as he sat back still staring at her, crossing his arms, the knife casually pointing toward her.

"You drugged me." The accusation came on a cloud so thick her voice sounded more of wonder than anger.

"She's hammered," the young woman said to him. "She won't be able to do anything for a while."

Still nothing from him. Just that stare, the silence now complete but for the steady drumming of the snow tires.

The next time she awoke her mouth and throat were as parched as they'd been in the limo when she'd torn open the water bottle. But her head felt clearer.

The road had changed. Rougher, jarring her every few seconds, and the sound of the snow tires had been replaced by gravel or rocks clattering against the chassis. She tried to look at her watch before remembering that her hands were tied behind her back.

It's not there.

She rubbed her wrist against her lower back to check. Her Movado was definitely gone.

"Where's my watch?"

"You won't need it." Dreads' eyes had never strayed from her.

Won't need it? Only the dead don't need time, she thought immediately.

She looked closely at him. "You took it?" Her Movado bangle watch? She'd paid more than a thousand dollars for it.

No answer.

"You're stealing from me." But even as she accused Dreads for a third time, she told herself not to antagonize him over a watch, no matter the cost.

She took a steadying breath, riveted again by his familiar face. It had startled her when she'd first met him on the set at McFaddins, his striking facial features, so handsome in contrast to a body riddled with tattoos and piercings. She'd shaken his hand and wondered where McFaddins had found him.

Now, she realized with a fresh infusion of fear, she was likely to learn the answer.

Dreads nudged her with his boot. "Change your wet clothes."

She shrugged off his touch. Furious at his effrontery, and embarrassed that they knew she'd wet herself. But, yes, she did want to change, desperately so.

He waved the knife in front of her face. "I'm going to cut you loose so you can do it. Don't try anything stupid. Now roll on to your belly."

She felt the knife by her wrists, the delicious release of rope. By her feet too. She sat up stiffly.

The woman, who looked very young, maybe twenty with a round face and tiny eyes, handed her clothing. Soft leather, all of it.

Deerskin, Sonya thought. "Can you look away?"

They both shook their heads.

Sonya put the deerskin clothing aside. "Where's my carry-on? I've got clothes in there."

"You won't be needing them." Dreads.

"The trench coat? My sweater? What did you do with them?" Testing him. Gently. Trying to understand her situation. He shook his head.

"You threw everything away?"

Dreads pointed to the deerskin. "These are your clothes now."

She grabbed the blanket, thinking she could cover herself with it; but now that she'd fully awakened, the fabric felt weird, unlike anything she'd ever touched. And it had an odd smell.

"What is this thing?"

"A blanket." Dreads.

"I know that, but what's it made of?"

"Hair."

"Hair?"

"Human hair."

Her stomach lurched and she kicked the blanket away as she would have a spider or snake, revolted by its touch, the abrupt mingling of anonymous history with personal odors and colors and oils, curls and waves and kinks: the visceral memory of so much hair from so many people so close to her face. Where had they gotten that much hair? All she could think of were Nazi death camps and the shaved heads of thousands of starving prisoners.

She sat there stunned, weakened by the drug and chilled by temperature and circumstance. She absolutely could not take her clothes off in front of them: *People who make blankets out of human hair.*

"I'll stay like this."

"No you won't. You stink." Dreads pushed her with his boot again, harder this time. "Do it or we'll do it for you."

She didn't doubt him. With that bone-handle knife back in his hair he looked like a caveman killer.

"Would you hold it up so I can have some privacy?" She addressed the young woman, thinking she would understand. No reply.

Sonya took a bracing breath and draped the blanket over her head, cringing as the weight of all that hair settled on her skin again.

She pulled off her clothes and used a leg of her slacks to dry herself, dropping them by the rear door.

When she unfolded the deerskin, she found a pair of pants and a skirt, along with a top. They felt like they'd fit. Why not? They'd thought of every other detail.

"Underwear?" she asked, already knowing the answer.

They didn't bother to respond.

She pulled on the deerskin pants, not gracefully, but she managed to tug them up to her waist without putting herself through too many contortions. The fly buttons felt as if they were made of bone. Still covering herself with the bristly blanket, she took off her blouse and had begun to ease the deerskin top over her head when Dreads offered another command:

"Bra."

"No."

"We'll make you."

She threw it on the growing pile.

Sonya paused over the fringed skirt, then realized it would give her an extra layer of warmth. As she tied it on, she thought it was not unlike the western wear sold in *The Frontier Ahead* catalogue.

She pushed away the creepy blanket. "Could I please have my coat?"

Dreads leaned over the wide front seat and turned back to her with an armful of fur.

"What is it?" The experience with the blanket made her hesitate.

"Bear fur." He also handed over a pair of wool socks and hand-tooled, fur-lined books.

"Can someone please tell me what's going on?"

Still no answer from any of them.

She put on the coat, snugging the fur collar around her neck. That's when she noticed that her opal earrings, like her watch, had been taken from her.

"They were my mom's," she said softly. "She gave them to me right before she died." Feeling abandoned, utterly alone, she shook her head, fighting tears. They spilled anyway.

Dreads nodded at her coat, boots. "There's something else we're going to give you."

She wiped her eyes. His voice had lowered, sounding more frightening than ever before.

"What?" Her question came out in an unintended whisper.

He hesitated—his first hint of indecision—and then sat forward, eyes burning, "We'll tell you when we're ready."

Maybe he knew she was still drugged. Within minutes of lying back down, she fell asleep.

When she awoke the third time she noticed the slightest graying of the sky before realizing that they'd tied her up again. At least they hadn't bothered with the gag. Who'd hear her anyway?

The young woman had dozed off, but Dread's eyes remained fixed on her. Sonya wondered if he'd stalked her after the McFaddins shoot, if this was the culmination of some sick obsession, but she felt far too fearful to ask.

She risked propping herself against the wheel well. He didn't stop her. She noticed snow in the trees and the softer sound of the tires on the road.

If this were the pre-dawn, then they'd been driving at least six hours. *Don't they need gas?* Maybe they'd filled up while she was asleep, covered her up again. That would have been a risky move, especially without a gag. But if they hadn't stopped yet, and they pulled into a service station, that's when she'd scream, do whatever she could do to save herself.

What service station? she asked herself sourly, a half hour later. Nothing but trees crowded the country road. Unplowed, just wide enough for two cars. No towns, not even a road-side sign since she'd awakened. In the headlights she saw what looked like half a foot of snow. They were moving through it cautiously.

She kept her eyes on the white world ahead of them, still dazed but less so by the minute.

The driver grunted, said they'd be pulling over up ahead for a bathroom break. It was the first time she'd heard him speak. Gruff.

She could use a bathroom right about now, but it was a figure of speech. He turned onto a two-track and drove through the woods for another couple of miles before stopping. She spotted snow falling in the stillness, so lightly that she hadn't noticed it in the headlights.

"Don't try to get away," Dreads said as he freed her. "We'll run you down, but even if you made it into the woods, which is *not* going to happen, you'd die from exposure before anyone would find you. It's ten degrees."

The most he'd spoken. Every word boiled down to another

threat.

"I'll watch her, Akiah." The young woman wiped the sleep from her eyes.

Akiah. Sonya hadn't been able to remember the name he'd used at the shoot, but she was certain it wasn't Akiah. That would have stuck with her.

They climbed out of the vehicle, joined by the driver and the guy in the passenger seat.

Sonya was no outdoorswoman, but she skied and knew this was pure Rocky Mountain powder. The fresh snow brushed off her deerskin pants as easily as dust as she and the young woman trudged behind the nearest tree.

They returned to the car, trailed by the burly driver, who'd maintained only a discreet distance. The others stood waiting, large fuel cans strapped to a wooden cargo carrier right above their heads.

The sky had paled enough to see that they were all dressed in deerskin, heavy fur coats, and the same style of boots. She looked like she belonged. To what? Some crazy cult?

They piled back into the old Suburban. She cursed herself for not noting the license plate but she was greatly relieved when they didn't tie her up again. Where would she go?

They stayed on the same narrow road as it rose slowly through a thick forest. No oncoming traffic, which she hoped for frantically. They'd have to slow way down, maybe pull over. She could scream, raise a huge ruckus. But all they encountered was more snow.

About forty minutes later they turned on to a rougher path draped with huge drifts, and started getting jounced so hard that Sonya had to steady herself with her hands.

The vehicle slowed and the driver navigated carefully.

Her first glimpse of the sun came through the pines to her left. It made the snow in the trees sparkle, and she felt a wrenching sense of loss for the mountains of Colorado, even for the nature walks her parents had forced her to take with them until she hit her teens.

They were still climbing, only now the ascent grew steeper and the snow even deeper. A logging road, she realized when they came upon a vast clear-cut. The stumps rose only inches above the snow, dark circles in a field of white.

She turned around and saw only the slightest depression from the tires; the feathery snow had settled back into the tracks as quickly as it had been pushed aside, a trail that would disappear with the next snowfall or breath of wind.

The clear-cut ended and the vehicle trundled for another hour through a forest that never thinned.

Her ears popped, her first notice that they were descending into a valley, rolling toward the dull, flat face of a frozen waterway. She remembered another line from Joni Mitchell, singing about a river— *to skate away on*—and wondered if they were in Canada, Mitchell's homeland. They'd been driving long enough on these unmapped logging roads to have slipped across the largely unguarded border.

In the distance she spotted two dogsled teams.

This is it.

After all these hours and miles of back roads, she knew without question that this would be her only chance to escape. There hadn't been any service stations. There hadn't even been any people until these two with their sleds.

She got ready to scream, to raise that ruckus, the biggest commotion these crazies with their deerskin and knock-out pills had ever seen.

The driver slowed as they approached the dogsleds. She read a bearded man's face for any familiarity with her abductors, drawing a blank.

As soon as her driver stopped and opened his door Sonya shrieked "Help. They're kidnapping me. Please stop them. Help!"

"They're with us," Akiah snapped.

She fell against the wheel well, shaking with terror, hope a shattered vessel.

The driver talked briefly to the bearded man before returning to the truck and opening the door next to Sonya.

"Get out."

"Get out?" A fresh flood of panic set in: *new* abductors? Dogsleds? *The middle of nowhere?*

"You're going with them." He gripped her arm so hard it hurt.

"What's going on?" As scared now as she'd been in those first few moments after Akiah had ducked into the limo, right before they drove her away from the life she'd known to this throbbing nightmare.

She wanted to fight back, kick and punch and pound her way free, but there were six of them.

Akiah seized her other arm, and they forced her to the bearded man's dogsled. He was big, wore glasses.

"Get in," he said. "We're gonna be mushing for about three hours."

"Three hours?" She could hardly believe this.

"You need to go to the bathroom, better do it." He looked at her closely. "What about food? Water?"

"Feed her," Akiah said as if she were animal stock. "And give her some water."

The dogsled driver handed her a wineskin.

She looked at it warily. "What's in there—"

"It's fine," Akiah said impatiently.

She was so thirsty she almost didn't care.

"I've got some biscuits soaked in bacon grease," the dogsled driver said as she handed back the wineskin.

She was starving and stared as he unwrapped a white cloth with two bundles the size and approximate shape of iPods. At the same time, she had the eerie feeling that she'd time-traveled into some twisted Jack London story.

He handed them to her. "Eat them while we move." Turning to Akiah, he added, "I feel too exposed out here."

"She probably won't be reported missing till tonight, at the earliest," Akiah told him. "But get in the sled," he said to Sonya.

The dogsled driver spread open a pile of thick furs and looked at her. She didn't move.

"Don't make us tie you up," Akiah said. "You don't want that. Not out here."

She looked at the men who surrounded her and knew she had no more choice than the sled dogs in their chains and harnesses a few feet away. She climbed in, dizzy with disbelief, vaguely aware of the big bearded guy covering her with the furs.

Akiah waited till he was finished, then crouched next to her. She drew away from him, fearing yet another threat.

"You think you've had it great, don't you? Silly watches, cashmere sweaters, all that crap." His eyes burned into hers again and he leaned forward, bracing himself on the frame of the dogsled. "Remember what I said about giving you something else? All I'm going to tell you is it's something you never could have imagined, even if your life depended on it."

23

My life?

My life depends on you, she thought as he stood. *On all of you in your bizarre hides and fur.* She couldn't compromise this gritty understanding with hope, not out here in this frozen, unforgiving land.

Who are these people? she asked herself once more. *What do they want with me?* She was desperate for answers, but all the gathering questions fled before a sudden sense of the savagery ahead.

Chapter 3

The huskies tore through the snow, panting and pulling fiercely on their reins and leaving whispery white puffs in their wake. They towed Sonya's sled at the speed of a strong long-distance runner all the way down a daunting slope to a frozen river.

She figured they'd fly across the ice and that Edson—she'd overheard his name as they took off—would stay this course as long as he could, but the dogs slipped on the bare patches and the sled no longer tracked as surely.

"Steady, steady," Edson said to himself, but the worry in his words made her clench the sides with her furry mittens as it began to fishtail.

The lead sled, driven by a woman named Juno, headed directly toward the forest dwarfing the far bank. Sonya glanced at the glittery ice and wondered if it was thick enough to support two dog sleds and three humans this early in the season; but it showed no signs of cracking, and Juno and her team were already climbing toward the trees.

When Edson's first two dogs leaped up on the bank the others lunged after them, eager for the snow's sure footing; but the angle still slowed them.

"Mush, mush!" Edson cracked the whip over the dogs' heads as they clawed up the last of the rise.

"Yeah," he yelled in triumph once they headed into the woods, and she recalled his desire for "cover," the way he'd worried aloud about standing in the open with the others.

She looked around at the icy river and forest, and felt as if she'd been swept into a strange and scary movie. Then the dogs raced into the shadows and her sense of eeriness darkened even more.

"What river was that?" She had to shout over the sound of the dogs and the constant creaking of the wood sled.

"The—" Edson caught himself before naming it.

She'd almost eked it out of him, though the payoff might have proved marginal at best: Her knowledge of geography was no better than her sense of direction. He could have tossed out the name of any river and it wouldn't have meant much to her, unless it was one of the huge ones, like the Columbia, or had a place name that would have made their whereabouts obvious.

The pines and firs rose at least fifteen stories above them with trunks six, eight feet across. Sonya realized they'd entered an ancient forest, trees so dense with boughs that a sylvan green blocked out most of the robin's-egg blue sky.

They raced along a trail that might have been pounded down when they came to pick her up, but any thoughts she had of following it back out were quickly crushed by the memory of the long drive through those huge snow drifts. She doubted she'd even find that logging road once the blizzards began their blinding march across the mountains.

Ten degrees, that's what Akiah had said when they stopped to relieve themselves. It felt colder now. She'd pulled the wool hat down over her forehead, and scrunched the fat collar of her fur coat up to her eyes.

Dry air, dry snow. She trailed her mitten out to check its consistency. Light enough to fly away, sparkling in a rare treat of sunlight.

Most of the journey became a blur of snow-crusted bark and boulders, and brooks frozen so fast that they still appeared to be bubbling. After the first hour Sonya lost all interest, knowing she'd never find her way back; and though jumpy and worried, her fatigue and the soft fur finally lulled her to sleep.

She didn't awaken until Edson and Juno halted the dogs on top of a hill about five hundred feet above a settlement that spread out over roughly a hundred acres. At its heart lay a large circle of attached, stucco shelters with chimneys made from stones that might have been dredged from the ice-bound river that bordered the far side of the outpost. Shake roofs poked through the snow where the wind had blown the hardest. Rising up in the broad open area inside the circle of homes was a large building with the round shape and sloping roof of a yurt.

She stiffened when she saw big, half-butchered creatures hanging from uprights near the building's exit. Bones and frozen blood. *But where are the people?* And then with a sickening fear she prayed—*Oh dear God no*—that she wasn't looking at human remains.

A barn stood way off to the left, set apart from the houses by a copse. Through those trees she thought she could see another structure, but it was hard to be sure from here.

"Is this where you're taking me?" Sonya asked.

"You'll find out soon enough," Juno said.

Sonya's eyes drifted to the natural hot pools along the river, currents of steam vanishing over this primitive outpost in the backcountry. Of *what* country? She didn't even know if she was still in the U.S.

Edson mushed the dogs and they moved on. The sun had disappeared behind a steely scrim of cirrus clouds. The landscape looked as grim as she felt.

Moments later they passed under one of the three covered openings in the circle of homes. Edson halted the sled by the fourth door to their left. It creaked open.

A woman stood before them in long underwear. About Sonya's height and age, maybe a few years younger, with shoulder-length pigtails, each one strangled by a rawhide strap. She had arctic blue eyes and a body so brittle-looking that Sonya thought she'd snap if she sneezed. Even her face appeared rigid enough to rupture. The lack of makeup didn't help. And the long underwear seemed like a peculiar getup for greeting someone for the first time. After Sonya's exposure to the biting cold, the outfit didn't appear capable of keeping her warm.

"You got her," the woman said as they stepped into the warm entryway. "I'm Andromeda." A name, but not a hint of friendliness. "Take off your boots and leave them here." She pointed to two identical pairs lined up against the wall.

Sonya, dazed by the sudden warmth, pulled them off, along with her coat, mittens and hat. A large man stared at her from the shadows.

Edson and Juno remained just inside the door, though Juno did edge forward when she spoke.

"You're going to be staying with Andromeda and Desmond. They'll be watching you. Don't try to escape. He'll get you." Eyes on Desmond, the man in the shadows. "Or you'll die. Do you understand that? Shake your head yes or no."

God, you're obnoxious.

Sonya glared at her and refused to respond.

Juno stared back. "I'll tell you what'll happen if you do get away. The cold will kill you, or you'll get eaten by cougars. They're hungry this time of year and we've had a plague of them. We don't even let the kids in the forest anymore without at least two adults. And if you try to take the dogs, they'll turn on you, and that would be worse than being eaten by a starving cougar."

Sonya didn't buy that business about the dogs—they'd seemed plenty comfortable around her—but what Juno said about the cougars could be true. Every so often she'd seen stories about mountain lions killing a jogger or poaching family pets at one of the many new home developments encroaching on their territory in the high country. The reports usually included the tips her father had given her as a child on how to ward off an attack: Don't run, and make yourself look as big as possible. Which had always made Sonya glad that she'd made *her* home near downtown Denver.

Juno took Edson's arm and they walked out.

When the door closed, Sonya noticed that the only light in the cottage came from candles, metal sconces on the walls and fat, artless balls of wax burning on the table and above the stone hearth. There was also a window, but it was fogged-up and small, no doubt to conserve heat. Probably the reason for the thick walls too. Straw bale, she guessed.

The floor felt plenty warm. She wondered how they did it. Radiant floor heating hardly seemed likely.

Desmond stepped from the shadows in nothing but his long underwear, which stretched across his sharply muscled body.

Sonya thought he could have modeled gym wear, then quickly corrected herself. *Not with that face.* It wasn't the straggly beard so much as the flinty appearance of his features. Handsome but ugly was how she immediately thought of men like him, good-looking guys who always appeared on edge, tense, terminally frustrated. A lot of them, she'd sensed, felt like failures in some fundamental way, as if they'd never lived up to their good looks, and were old enough to know they never would.

Her two warders stood before her, so clearly resembling each other that it was spooky. Both were blond and tall with icy blue eyes. And both sported red, yellow, and black tattoos of a vaguely Aztec design. And of course their identical cream-colored long underwear.

"We're having tea," Andromeda said. "Do you want some?"

Offered as an obligation.

Sonya nodded, and Andromeda led her to a simple wooden table, then moved to an old-fashioned wood cook stove. A kettle sat steaming, and she served a cup of amber tea in a mug that looked like it had been shaped by an amateur potter: The sides were three times thicker than they needed to be and the handle felt as bulky as a baseball bat. The tea proved no more pleasing, like a bitter root boiled in water.

Without warning, Desmond began to stroke the nape of her neck. She shivered and yanked her head away.

"Don't you *dare* touch me."

He stared at his hand, as if the offending instrument were not his own, then pulled a chair so close that she could smell him when he sat. His odor wasn't offensive but his touch had left her whole body feeling violated.

"*You* don't give orders. You're *our* prisoner." Words like slaps.

She shifted her chair away, but he filled the fresh divide with his face, breath, hard eyes.

A predator, she thought. *And he's doing this right in front of her.* But Andromeda seemed to pay no attention.

Desmond smiled as if he'd read Sonya's thoughts and were amused by them. "Are you scared?"

"*Don't* do it again." She'd jerked back so far that the rungs in the chair were digging into her spine. *Who the hell are these people?*

Andromeda nodded at Sonya, who thought, *Why's she doing that? Because I tried to make him back off? Or because she approves of what he's doing?*

Sonya looked at Andromeda again and realized that the reason didn't matter. It was such a clearly practiced pose that it looked no more real than makeup. Sonya had used similar expressions of approval in dozens of ads for laxatives, contraceptive creams, anti-inflammatories, and the like.

"We'll be watching you," Desmond said. "And we're going to be living *very* close to each other."

"Not like that we're not. Not with me. Stay *away.*" Sonya felt caged, the small room like the back of the limo, but worse: now she had *him* sitting inches away.

He leaned even closer. She couldn't back up anymore, his moist heat coming over her in a sickening wave.

"You're really scared, aren't you?" Not a drip of compassion in his voice.

"I'm telling you—"

But she couldn't finish—Andromeda was suddenly behind her, working the tight muscles on the back of her neck.

"Stop," Sonya shouted, jumping to her feet, her own hands out. *What are they, a team?*

"You'd better calm down before you meet the council," Andromeda said sharply.

"What 'council?' What are you talking about?"

"Get back there." Andromeda stabbed her finger toward a green door to the right of the hearth.

"What's that?" Pulses of panic again.

"Your room."

"Where do you guys sleep?"

"For the time being, we'll sleep out here."

"When you see we don't bite, we'll move back in with you," Desmond added in an oily voice.

Never.

He reached up to a shelf and pulled down a set of long underwear, thrusting it at her. "Wear them."

She tensed when his hand brushed hers and retreated with the bundle past the green door, her breath coming in anxious bursts. Andromeda barged in with a bowl of water, sponge, and a round of pale soap, ordering her to "clean up."

A sharp insult. No one had had to tell Sonya to "clean up" since her early childhood. But she did feel dirtied by the abduction, and the bowl made her long for her bath.

"Make yourself look decent for the council." Andromeda set the bowl on a night stand and lit a stubby candle, revealing a room the size of a walk-in closet, Dickensian in its dimensions and darkness.

"What council?" Sonya asked again.

"The Council of Consensus."

"Who are they? Are they going to explain all this?"

Andromeda left without answering, closing the door behind her.

Sonya looked in vain for a lock, but at least there was no keyhole to spy on her either.

She stared at the bowl and realized that she did want to wash up. But as she started to untie the fringe skirt she froze and peered at the door again. No way could she undress with those two only a few feet away. Especially him.

She settled for washing her face. After patting it dry she looked for a mirror, bewildered when she couldn't find one. Panicky too. No mirror? No makeup? *Nothing* of the life they'd taken from her?

She couldn't remember the last time she'd performed this ritual without inspecting herself carefully, eyeing the lines, wrinkles, assessing the latest setback of age and the possible costs to her career.

Again she searched, casting candlelight on the walls, alert for a reflection.

As she lowered the flame at last, the answer to her question came to her, stark as a steel spike: Nothing remained of the life she had known. *Nothing.* Not even the familiar contours of her own face.

Shaking, she held the burning wick over the water, staring down at it like Narcissus. The soapy surface yielded only the glow.

She plunked herself down on the bed, drained by eighteen hours of the worst fear she'd ever known. The mattress felt as uneven as an old futon.

Sitting soon led to lying down and wrapping herself in the blankets. But a second later she kicked them away, trembling before she saw that they were woven from wool, not hair.

She lay back down and stared at the door. The candle burned beside her, sputtering in its spent wax and throwing shadows around the room. In an instant she fell asleep, dreamless and defeated.

Chapter 4

A bony hand shook Sonya from a deep sleep.

"Get up," Andromeda threw the blankets off her, "*now.* "

As she left the room, Sonya groped around in the dark for her new clothes before remembering that she'd never taken them off . . . and why.

Steeling herself, she walked out to the dimly lit living area, determined to meet with this "Council of Consensus" and find out why she'd been kidnapped to this bizarre place. Her tall roommates waited by the front door, sinewy figures in the shadows.

She threw on her boots, coat, and hat, and followed them into the stream of people walking toward the large, yurt-shaped community center. As they neared it, she noticed the smell of roasting meat and felt her gnawing hunger.

"Where do you get your food?" she asked Andromeda.

"We hunt," Desmond said without looking at her, as if he couldn't bear the sight of Sonya after being rebuffed.

"With what?" She wondered if they had a cache of weapons. *Guns.*

"Bows, arrows," he said as they approached a large bronze gong hanging from posts near the entrance to the center. "Spears."

Sonya glimpsed a pair of six-foot torches burning on either side of a big, open wooden door, illuminating the people inching by. She felt their stares but kept her head down, stealing only peeks at those closest to her, their fur-crowded faces vacant and scary.

When she did glance up she caught Edson's attention, but he looked away. Juno, by his side, had her gaze fixed firmly on the family in front of them.

Inside, torches high on the walls threw ample light on the large round tables that filled the center, the smell of their smoke oppressive in the still air.

Thick, foot-high candles squatted on the tables, each of which had room for ten rudimentary wooden chairs. A quick count indicated seating for upwards of a hundred.

But the floor in the very middle of the room had been reserved for a seven-foot, inlaid quartz mandala that reflected the shifting light. A row of smaller mandalas extended from both sides of its center axis.

"Don't step on this," Andromeda said. *"Ever."*

The members greeted each other warmly, *very* warmly in some cases. Sonya saw not only hugs and pecks on the cheek, but women kissing each other openly; a handful of men did too. The kissing itself didn't bother her—she worked in the fashion industry, after all —but seeing it after being kidnapped to such a rough-hewn place felt extremely strange.

What struck her most, however, were the children. Wherever she looked they appeared remarkably well-behaved, and she wondered if they'd been smacked into submission.

Andromeda veered toward a table at the front of the hall as Desmond grabbed Sonya's arm and marched her to a lone chair facing the growing crowd.

"Sit." He pushed down on her shoulders, and then stood right behind her like a sentry.

People stared at her. She looked down, wiping her sweaty palms against her pants.

To her right stood a rectangular table, the only one in the hall, with eight empty chairs.

A door banged open behind her. She jumped and turned, and saw kitchen workers in wool tights and tops pouring out with huge platters of roasted venison, potatoes, parsnips, and beets.

"Don't *move.*" Desmond seized her head and forced her to look straight ahead.

Sonya watched the crowd fill their plates, hunger twisting her belly. It was twenty-four hours since her abduction, and all they'd fed *her* were two greasy biscuits. Fear alone kept her from fainting.

A woman in a long, forest-green robe stepped onto a wooden box the size of a milk crate and began to wave a flag that contained elements of the Stars and Stripes, Union Jack, Maple Leaf, and Rising Sun, along with features of flags Sonya couldn't identify.

The assembled quieted. Only now did Sonya's eyes rise high enough to notice the banners hanging from the high ceiling. Each one depicted a different activity: hunting, candle and soap making, farming, flint-knapping, weaponry, weaving . . . . There must have been a dozen or more of them.

"All rise," the woman said, and everyone stood amid a shuffling of feet and chairs and the outcries of the smallest children. Sonya remained seated until Desmond jerked her upright.

Furious, she listened as they chanted:

> "We pledge ourselves to Aboland
> and the vision we hold dear,
> to build a new life in a new land
> and struggle without fear."

Everyone joined hands above their heads—Desmond tried to take hers; she refused—and then clapped exactly three times, reciting, "Earth, air, water."

As she sat, still fuming from Desmond's manhandling, the entire scene—banners, furniture, the heavily laden platters of wild food and the plain manner of dress—began to feel eerily medieval.

The kitchen workers swept by a second time to fill mugs with icy water from gray ceramic pitchers. None for her, and she felt her thirst too.

The crowd ate the meat with their hands and used crudely carved spoons to scoop up their vegetables, pausing only to eye her. No one smiled. No one nodded. Hunger, thirst, and the fury of strangers.

As they finished eating, the kitchen workers swooped down for their plates.

Minutes later men and women moved to the rectangular table.

The explanation. Maybe it's coming. At this point, that's all Sonya cared about.

"Stand," Desmond said to her.

Rather than risk his touch, she rose immediately. He turned the chair so she faced the council, the crowd now to her left. She felt his hands forcing her shoulders again and sat right back down.

The last person to take his seat at the table was Akiah, joining the three men and four women now before them.

What proved more arresting was a large screen wheeled into the room by two young men. They placed it behind the Council and raised it above their heads. For a rough outpost, it appeared incongruously high-tech, even more so when a woman placed a laptop computer on the Council's table. Cables ran from its ports across the floor and under the bottom of the nearest door.

"The Council of Consensus will now come to order."

No more than twenty feet from Sonya, a stout man in a purple robe stepped onto the same small platform that had been used by the woman who'd wielded the flag. He looked like he was in his late fifties or early sixties, though Sonya was fast losing her ability to judge age: The absence of makeup, hair product, or clothes other than furs and skins made everyone in Aboland appear older, tougher. Like the pictures she'd seen of sod-busters weary from years of cracking the hard shell of wilderness.

"Tonight we've called a special council."

The screen filled with the famous McFaddins poster of her and Akiah.

"Sonya Adams," the man said, "you stand convicted by the Earth's Court of Justice."

Earth's court of what?

If she'd any doubts about the lunacy of this group, any lingering hope that in the end sanity would prevail in their narrow slice of Siberia, they vanished with this last remark. Whatever this place was, whatever these people had become in its grip, would not be subject to reason. Then she looked at their serious faces and knew without question that the whole lot of them were a few degrees off axis and spinning way out of control.

The man turned to a white-haired, shriveled old woman seated near the center of the council table. Unlike him, she wore no robe, only her deerskin clothes; and rather than gaining stature when she stood, she appeared more shrunken than ever. Tattoos extended from both sides of her neckline and sprouted from under her sleeves down the backs of her hands.

The woman nodded to the crowd and lifted her arm, as if in benediction, movements that looked pained and tender. Sonya thought she could easily be in her eighties, and that if the woman spoke as slowly as she moved, she'd be here most of the night explaining why Sonya had been abducted. And "convicted" by the earth's court of whatever. *Don't forget that. Jesus!* But the woman's voice sounded surprisingly strong, and the look she directed at Sonya felt piercing.

"We did not choose you for this poster, Sonya Adams. In a very real sense, *you* chose yourself." She used a long stick to point to the image of the poster. "Your entire career made you the perfect person to look down upon Akiah, to pass judgment symbolically upon him."

Her pointer moved up to Sonya's greatly enlarged face. The censoriousness so evident in the ad and the standard-sized poster appeared overweening here.

"You accepted the pearls, the pants suit, the hair so carefully drawn back from your perfectly constructed face, as you have accepted the accouterments of your trade for so many years."

A flurry of Sonya's ads flashed on the screen, all of them easily downloaded from the Web, showing her in everything from silk slippers to mink coats, with gorgeous male and female models as her companions in many of them. A pair of stately Russian wolfhounds even flanked her in a series of vodka ads.

Sonya watched herself age as the photos jumped from one to another, and saw that they'd been arranged chronologically. The products she posed with became noticeably less valuable after she hit her thirties.

"You have been a champion of *rampant* consumption. That is why you stand convicted of crimes against the earth."

She paused as more photos appeared of Sonya smoking in tennis whites, cradling a bottle of scotch as if it were a baby, even resting her hand on the shiny parts of an F-16 fighter jet.

"And then there was this—" the poster reappeared—"among your very last efforts. So while you ask, 'Why?' we ask, 'Why not?' Or to put it another way, 'How could it have been otherwise?'

"Sonya, you might say, 'But I'm not the biggest fish in the sea. Why not take Cindy Crawford or Gisele Bündchen or Kate Moss . . .'"

You'd never have gotten close enough to snatch them.

" . . . but it was you, Sonya Adams, who brought your gaudy career, with all of its absurdities and obscenities, to the ad with Akiah. You could say that this poster—" she pointed the stick emphatically at the screen—"is your biggest achievement because *this* is the reason you're here. Have you ever looked at it closely?"

She stared at Sonya, who decided not to dignify this Star Chamber with a cued response.

"*We* have. And we know why it's become the fastest selling poster in history . . ."

What?

She must have caught Sonya's look of incredulity because she nodded at the woman at the computer and said, "Bring up Poster Retailing dot com."

Sales figures for *Neo-primitive and Primster* were superimposed over the mock-up. Under *Units Sold* Sonya saw the startling number: 1.2 million.

"The poster sales started doubling five weeks ago, but those numbers were still not outstanding. Then, look here . . ." A chart appeared, also courtesy of *PosterRetailing.com*. A line shot upward at almost ninety degrees. "In the past two weeks sales have skyrocketed. You were very busy working during that time, and these sorts of phenomena often occur below the radar screen of the dominant culture. And why would you have cared anyway? You got your money up front and signed away your rights like you always do. But this," she pointed to the sales chart, "is news now, and not just to you. *People* magazine."

The *People* website jumped on screen. A box in the middle of the homepage framed the poster under the headline, *The Primster and the Primitive*.

"This, conveniently enough, just showed up this afternoon. But we expect that tomorrow, certainly no later than the day after, it will change to something like this." A new headline replaced the old one: *The Primster Kidnapped to Terra Firma*.

"In a moment we'll tell you why you'll be getting a lot more attention than this, but first let's look closely at the poster itself." Her pointer rose once more. "Look at the way you could cut it right down the middle and cleave the culture of fashion into the prim, proper domain of the privileged and the teeming, subterranean world of those who reject the standards and sanctity of your unmarked skin."

The old woman's voice rose, chilling Sonya as she looked once more at her wrinkled tattoos and imagined what these lunatics might do to her own "unmarked skin" with their ink and needles.

"The reason this poster has become so popular with the tribal young all around the world, why it's broken the barriers of language, is the power of irony, the way it turns the message of the ad upside down. McFaddins wanted it to say, 'Shop here and you'll avoid these sorts of unseemly encounters. You'll maintain your *dignity.*'" She said this last with open disdain. "But the tribal young see a very different message. They see themselves rising to challenge the whole idea that anyone should ever sell the illusion of wealth and privilege with a product. Akiah crouches at your feet, but he towers over you in influence."

The woman stared at Sonya. An ominous silence fell over the room, as if it had been rehearsed.

"Sonya Adams, stand up. I want to make sure you get a good look at what you're about to see."

Sonya shook her head, refusing to move as she'd also refused to respond to the woman's question about the poster. The screen switched to a younger Sonya reclining in a shiny black Cadillac. Sparking diamonds hung from her ears, and she wore a silvery fur very different from the bear skin draped across the back of her chair now.

Desmond gripped her arm so hard she gasped. "Stand *up.*"

Before he could jerk her to her feet, she rose, shaking off his arm.

More ads followed: Sonya in large SUV's, all a-smile; holding a plastic bottle of motor oil as if it were an heirloom; playing pump jockey in a tiger costume. Even beaming on an offshore oil-drilling platform with her arms held wide, as if to embrace the whole enterprise.

"Crimes against the earth," the old woman intoned in her harshest voice yet.

As her words trailed off, Sonya's ads were displaced by iconic photographs of tsunamis; typhoons; devastating floods; hurricane Katrina; dead and bloated bodies; blizzards; cracked lake beds; wildfires; headlines about heat waves, thousands dying.

"It's not just global warming. It's not just climate change," the woman said. "It's climate *chaos* because the one painful truth we've learned for certain is that computer studies have vastly underestimated the effects of the greenhouse gases that *you* championed with your highly paid efforts. *Till now.*" Her eyes bored into Sonya. "You're done with all that, Sonya Adams. You'll be sentenced soon . . . "

Sentenced? To what? Sonya froze as she thought of those horrifying pictures of westerners beheaded by Islamic fundamentalists.

" . . . the Council of Consensus will decide your fate. While we deliberate, we'll podcast your life in Aboland to the rest of the world."

As she spoke a young woman walked up to Sonya, shooting her with a video camera. Yet another choreographed move.

"We'll use your face as it's never been used before: to drive home the catastrophe of climate chaos, and to advocate a way of life that doesn't assault the earth, that doesn't rape Mother Nature. That doesn't commit *murderous* crimes against a dying planet."

Her last words hung in the air. They felt like a noose swinging right above Sonya's head.

"You probably think we're crazy. We're not. We're the most rational people you'll ever meet. Rational people do not commit slow suicide, as most of the world is intent on doing with its deadly use of oil. We're inspired by aborigines who make everything they can by hand, from a simple spoon—" she held one up—"to the weapons they need to survive." A man on the Council lifted a spear above his head, pumping it up and down like a warrior. "And we're guided by the double-bind theory of the late anthropologist and interdisciplinary scientist, Gregory Bateson. He was among the most eminent thinkers of the twentieth century. Are you familiar with him?"

A photo of a tall man with a shock of white hair filled the screen.

Sonya shook her head, not at all eased by the old woman's invocation of an "eminent" thinker. She stared instead at the man wielding the spear and knew they wouldn't be the first group to use rational ideas to justify irrational actions. Old as history.

"I'm not surprised that you haven't heard of Bateson. Let's try something simpler. I'm sure you'll recall the Bread-and-butter fly in Lewis Carroll's *Through the Looking Glass.* It lives on weak tea and cream . . . "

What the hell is she—

"Don't you dare shake your head like *you're* disgusted. This is why you're here." The woman glared at her. "If you have any sense of self-preservation, you'll listen. Now do you want us to go on, or do you want to be taken away right now?"

"Answer her," growled Desmond.

"Go on."

The woman hesitated, still infuriated, then continued in a voice that steadied as she spoke. "When Alice asks what happens if the Bread-and-butter fly can't find any weak tea with cream, the Gnat tells her it dies, and this *always happens.* What Bateson's work tells *us* is that the Bread-and-butter fly is a singular metaphor for our civilization because *if* the Bread-and-butter fly were to drink its tea, what would happen to its wings, which are thin slices of bread and butter? Or its head, which is a lump of sugar? It would turn into a soggy mess. It would be destroyed by the very thing it needs to survive. But if it doesn't get the tea, it starves. It's trapped in Bateson's 'double-bind,' as we are in our use of oil. We're consuming billions of barrels of the tea that's destroying us, that's causing climate chaos.

"So first and foremost, Aboland has rethought the use of our toxic 'tea.' Second, as soon as our first podcast announces that we have you, there will be a massive outpouring of attention, as there always is when an attractive white woman is abducted, especially when pictures of her are so readily available. You'll be the 'star' of these podcasts. Every day we'll put out a new one, and we fully expect that every one of them will be rebroadcast on major media worldwide because no one's ever done this before. But even though the interest in this experiment will be intense, they won't find you." She shook her head. "We've worked this out very carefully. The podcasts will be protected by multiple Internet connections with a series of firewalls. Not even the electricity can be traced—it's all powered by solar fuel cells. So don't hold out any hope for some heroic rescue, because when we need to we're more than willing to move from the primitive to the post-industrial. And we absolutely need to make the world understand that we, as a species, have become the Bread-and-butter fly. We'll also make the world understand that your crimes against nature, deadly as they are, are not unique." She drew a long, labored breath. "And neither will be your fate."

Chapter 5

Darcy stormed off the elevator, tore her mother's portrait from the lobby wall, and shoved it at Jackson, who froze in his headphones right below the sterling silver letters that spelled out *The Chatwin Agency*. His thin lips pursed into a pencil line as he started backpedaling.

She blocked his escape, and in less than three seconds had him pinned against the elegant black enamel desk. *You're not getting away, you son of a bitch.* Eye to eye.

"Try hanging up on me *now*, Jackson. Try blocking my calls *now*, Jackson."

She seized him by the collar of his Armani jacket, and now gave him a quick shake, shouting, "What the *hell* did you do to her?"

She thrust her mother's photograph toward his face once more, then slammed the whole thing down on the desk, shattering it.

The lobby had been teeming with wannabe models who'd flocked to the agency after all the media attention about the abduction . . . and the word of an opening on Katie Chatwin's roster. Now they stared in shock, or clutched their portfolios and cowered; one of them even raised hers as a shield after witnessing the heavily pierced young woman grabbing the gatekeeper. Another gangly girl in impossible heels decided to make a run for the elevator—this was Columbine High School country, after all—and promptly crashed to the carpet.

But Darcy's eyes never strayed from Jackson, who managed to say, "What did *we* do to her? More like what did *you* do to her?"

It was better by far that the frame lay broken on the desk because Darcy barely restrained a powerful urge to smash it over his wickedly handsome head.

"What's *that* supposed to mean: What did *I* do to her?" She wasn't so much in Jackson's face as crawling up his nose.

"You made her life hell," Jackson spit. "Everybody knows it. She said she wouldn't put *anything* past you."

Darcy stood there too stunned for speech: They suspected her. Of *this?*

But she's been abducted, Darcy wanted to scream. She's being held . . . *against her will.* That's horrible. That's the worst. When they take you away, anything can happen. Anything *does* happen. *I know.*

Dumbfounded enough to lose her sense of purpose, it took her several beats to find it again: "But *you* sent her off and *you* never checked where she was going."

"You're blowing smoke, and you know it."

"Fuck you, Jackson." Still shaken, and wanting to smack him *so* bad. *Smug son of a bitch.* "Where's your boss?"

"I'm right here."

Katie Chatwin towered over both of them. Six-one easily, and *then* you added the Jimmy Choos. A regal presence, even Darcy had to grant her that much. Every eye in the agency had turned to her: Could she tame the she-demon?

"You just calm down, young lady."

Darcy could have retched. "I'm not calming down, and I'm *not* a lady."

A set-up line if ever there were one, especially for Katie Chatwin, as handy with a riposte as she was with a rejection letter; but she let that one float away, perhaps because Darcy, despite her denial, had, in fact, released Jackson, who edged aside.

Katie glanced at him. "Cancel the morning. Reschedule everyone." Her imperious gaze returned to Darcy. "Please come back with me."

Darcy pointed to the broken frame on the desk and snapped at the young assistant closest to her, "I want that picture."

"She'll get it ready for you," Katie said, leading the way to her spacious corner office.

She immediately took up residence behind a glittering glass desk as she had on the other occasions when Darcy had been in there, back when her mother was still deluded enough to think her daughter might take up modeling. Like that was a *life?* Darcy claimed a dark leather sofa.

"Is he the FBI?" Darcy said when her eyes landed on a rotund man seated across from Katie. Someone from the Bureau had been leaving messages for her at work and at home.

Katie offered a smile that could have frosted molten rock. "Not unless they've started wearing Jhane Barnes."

Whatever *that* meant. She thought Katie might have been

referring to his shirt with all the stripes and swirls in fruity, tropical colors.

"This is Manser Hauer. He was the art director on the McFaddins ad. We were just discussing your mother's disappearance."

"She didn't *disappear;* you sent her to some shoot that didn't even exist."

"It could have happened to anyone in this business. The FBI told me that they're amazed it hasn't happened before. Models are flying off all the time," Katie waved her hand as if to shoo a fly, "and nobody ever checks."

"I don't give a shit what amazes you or the FBI. I want to know how the hell she flies to Bozeman, Montana, and gets in a white stretch limo and ends up with a bunch of loonies."

"I must say, given your history it's quite *touching* that you seem to care so much about your mother."

Darcy simply stared at her for a moment. The nerve of this woman, who excelled in a business that had no more conscience than a serial killer and treated models just as poorly, judging *her* devotion to her mother?

"She's my mom, you bitch. And they're holding her against her will."

Darcy was even more furious when she realized that tears were leaking from her eyes. *Where'd they come from?*

Katie picked up a remote, and a plasma screen TV came alive with CNN announcing an update of *Terror at Terra Firma.*

"Let's all take a breath," Katie said. "Maybe they've got something new."

Like I haven't seen a dozen stories already this morning, Darcy thought as she wiped her eyes again, feeling strangely self-conscious about tearing up.

A flashy female anchor cut immediately to the airport security video that the FBI had released in the stated hope that someone would come forward who'd gotten a good look at her mother's chauffeur, whose cap had been pulled down so low that the surveillance cameras, mounted above her, hadn't captured a single face shot. Two passengers had contacted the Bureau, but their physical descriptions of the driver had proved so spotty that agents still hadn't been able to cobble together a composite of the suspect.

They had traced the limousine to a Bozeman company, but it turned out that it had been rented to a woman with a phony credit card and driver's license. A Wal-Mart employee had found the vehicle by the store's dumpsters. Its engine had been wrecked by a sugary syrup that had been poured into the tank, and its windshield had been smashed. It had also been wiped clean of all prints except for her mother's, which had covered parts of every surface in the passenger compartment. Agents had speculated openly that she'd been desperate to get out.

The thought of her mother trying to force open the doors and windows still made Darcy wince. Her mom was no fighter. She was a wimp. A pushover. And no one knew this better than Darcy, who winced again, this time at how cruel she'd been to her mom for years. Her regrets—and the memory of the agonizing event that gave rise to them—haunted her now.

Like mother like daughter, but in a really horrible way, thought Darcy.

And now thirty-six hours had passed since the abduction without a single fruitful lead, other than a podcast of her mom, which had been untraceable and scrupulously edited to take out any identifying images.

It had appeared last night showing her mother and the male model from the McFaddins shoot; everyone else had been digitally disguised. Her mom had looked terrible—scared and *old.* No makeup, her hair a mess, fidgeting with it constantly the way she did whenever she was worried about how she looked, which was most of the time.

Off-camera, a woman whose voice had been altered electronically, was giving a speech that included several cutting comments about her mom's career. Despite herself, Darcy had nodded. In some ways, the woman was saying the same things that she'd said to her mother. Then there was a bunch of stuff about Gregory Bateson's double-bind theory, which Darcy had heard about, probably in an anthropology or psychology class.

So the people who'd abducted her had some interesting ideas but they were definitely not on planet earth, even if they were calling their hideaway "Terra Firma." More like "Terror Firma," if Darcy's own experience as a scared captive meant anything. And she seriously doubted they'd ever change her mom's mind.

Whoever they were, they'd nailed the publicity. All the big TV networks and cable news shows were running stories and re-airing the podcast, which CNN had up on the screen right now. And people were talking, that's for sure. This morning everyone at the local coffee shop was jabbering about it over their triple-shot lattes, using "double-bind" like it was part of their everyday conversation and wondering out loud what kind of place she'd been taken to.

"Shangri-la," one of the baristas said.

Two girls laughed when they heard her and said that they wished they'd been taken instead.

"That guy on the poster's hot," a friend chimed in.

Darcy doubted Terra Firma was any kind of paradise, not with the look on her mother's face. Most times she could put on a good front—she'd done it every day as a model—but she'd looked petrified.

CNN cut to a commercial break.

"I didn't hear anything new." Katie hit mute on the remote. "You?"

Darcy shook her head. The tutti-frutti shirt guy didn't respond. Katie nodded at him.

"Manser came here at my request. He found the guy in the McFaddins ad. In fact, the FBI's coming over here this morning to talk to him about that."

"When?" Darcy asked.

Katie looked at her diamond encrusted watch. "In about an hour. Don't worry." She looked at the art director. "Go ahead, tell her. She *is* the daughter . . . "

. . . *after all. Why don't you just say it, you bitch.*

Manser adjusted his blue-tinted metal frames and looked openly at every piercing on Darcy's face, his eyes like a pencil in a connect-the-dots game.

"I didn't find him through an agency. I couldn't find anyone who looked authentic enough. Even the models with tattoos looked too tame. I didn't want tame, I wanted feral. So I started going to body-art shops. They have portfolios too." Said as if this would be a bulletin to her, as if shots of her own piercings weren't already on display at Mechanical Designs a few blocks away.

"We ended up emailing every shop in the region. I offered a nice finder's fee to anyone who could come up with the right face and body. That's when Razor's Edge in Boise sent me his head shots."

"What's his name?" Darcy asked.

"For what it's worth, he said it was Buckminster Bateson."

"I don't get the Buckminster part."

"It's a little before your time," Katie chuckled mirthlessly. "Buckminster Fuller was a contemporary of Bateson's. He invented the geodesic dome. The bush hippies love them. The domes look like carbuncles in the woods."

"I hired him," Manser continued, "on a royalty-only basis—seventy-five percent of the poster sales."

"So where's the money going?" Darcy said.

"We know where it's going, but we don't know where it ends up. All the payments are wired to a bank in the Channel Islands. From there, we don't know. As soon as I saw that podcast, I tried reaching him through the Razor's Edge again, but it turns out that they'd contacted him through an intermediary who's also disappeared."

"So that's *it?* We get to see my mom on a podcast and that's it?"

"Not quite *it*," Katie said. "The FBI's working hard to find her, but they're wondering why you haven't returned their messages." Katie stared at her.

"So what'd you tell them?"

The stare never strayed. "I said you had 'authority issues,' and issues with men."

"Not all of them."

"Yes, your mother told me about Dakota."

"His name's Kodiak."

Katie shrugged. "Call the FBI, or wait here with us till they come over. If you really want to find your mother, they're your best hope."

"What are you doing, other than talking? Are you going to hire some private detectives, take out ads, get her face on a milk carton, do *something* for her? She's been here longer than anyone else and she's earned you a fortune."

"Those are good ideas. I'll think about them."

Right. This was the real Katie, the businesswoman who'd scrape dimes off a bloodstained street. "Don't think too hard."

Darcy had the urge to take out her gun, wave it around, squeeze at least one real emotion out of Ice Queen Katie, even if it were fear; but another display of wild anger would only spark their suspicions again, and she hoped she'd dampened them over the past half hour.

And you didn't get a gun to make empty threats, she reminded herself. *You got it because you had no choice.*

She rose and walked out the door. When Jackson spotted her coming, he dodged to the other side of his desk.

"You," she pointed to him, "put me through to her next time and I might not have to come down here."

Jackson's assistant nervously held out her mother's portrait. Darcy grabbed it, and on the way out noticed that another model's photograph had already been hung in its place.

*

Johnny Bracer slumped in the driver's seat of a Dodge Durango as white and dirty as the stumpy snow banks that lined both sides of the street. He could watch a place with his eyes barely open, resting on the borderline of sleep and surveillance. He'd been doing it for more than twenty years, and for the past hour he'd had his slits fixed on the red brick building.

He was listening to Weather Reports' *Black Market* when Darcy walked under the stained glass archway depicting Saint Michael slaying the dragon, and then passed beneath the dark gaze of a gargoyle perched on the corner of the building's second floor. She never noticed his eyes tracking her. Johnny Bracer had the good fortune of looking as anonymous as death. He was a bounty hunter, and as soon as he'd seen that podcast with Sonya Adams, he knew a reward would be in the offing.

It was like hearing the clatter of silver dollars when the one-armed bandit started spewing the cherries your way. He figured he was going to need a pretty big bucket for this one, because when people started crapping on the oil companies, the sky was the limit. Johnny's gut, which he trusted as much as blue steel, also told him that those hippies might have something else up their raggedy ass sleeves. What, he had no idea, but why would they go to all this trouble just to nab some minor league model? Publicity? It would only get them nailed. There had to be something else going down, and he figured the oil companies were wondering the same thing. So it was any price for damage control, especially when the damage might not be fully spelled out yet. And that would mean finding Sonya Adams, pronto. Then shutting them all up before they could spring any real big surprises.

*

Darcy tossed a parking ticket into the back of her old Toyota Corolla, cranked it, and pulled away.

"Call the FBI." That's what Katie had said, but Darcy didn't think she could do it. After the experience she'd had with cops eight years ago, she preferred the much more personal and immediate means of protection that she carried in her pocket.

She was fifteen when she went to see her father for the last time. Every summer she was supposed to spend three weeks with him in Los Angeles—go to the beach, Disneyland, Universal Studios, that sort of stuff—but they'd missed the previous year because he'd been "caught up with some pretty big deals."

Those deals must have gone south, because the summer of her fifteenth birthday he was still trying to make it as a screenwriter, heading down to a Starbucks on Sunset every day with his laptop and a head full of ideas that never came together in a single coherent story. Somehow he made a living, though never enough to help support her, a point her mother made whenever his name came up.

But he did have friends, and they had friends, and they all came by his apartment, where she slept on the couch and had to wait for them to leave before she could go to bed. One of those friends took an interest in her.

She'd been in full bloom. Every girl has a season when she's radiant as a summer flower, and Darcy had the misfortune of having experienced hers during that visit to Los Angeles. She felt her power as a woman for the first time, saw the way men noticed her, and the pushier ones tried to talk to her, make *suggestions*.

Keith had taken a smoother approach, just a "Hello" the first time he'd dropped in for a visit, barely a glance; and then each night he'd strung out the greeting until they were talking, laughing, relaxed. She could look back now and see that it was a practiced routine, and that he must have had plenty of opportunities to get every punch line down pat, but she'd been fifteen. She thought he was funny for *her*.

Her father said Keith was going to be a movie producer. He spoke of him with great regard, especially when he told her that

48

Keith had inherited some money and was pouring a lot of it into one of his ideas, a *Westworld* kind of film. It had been really big before she'd been born, and in Hollywood imitation was truly the best form of flattery.

But there was the other kind, too, and Keith began to say those words to her softly: *You're pretty, girl. You've got great eyes. They could light up a screen. Darcy, that name's a keeper, and so are you.*

In a vague way she knew he was seducing her, and in a vague way she didn't mind. But nothing stayed vague as it should have when you're fifteen and a guy says he's thirty-one (actually forty-two, but that was the least of his lies).

A week before she was to leave she awakened to find a note from her father saying he'd gone to meet a "script doctor."

She washed up, changed, and had just gagged on a mouthful of old, fizzy orange juice when Keith dropped by. All the other times he'd come over at night, and she still wondered if it had been planned, even in a *vague* way: I'll put more money into your screenplay if you'll let me date your daughter ("date" being the vague part that wouldn't stay vague).

"Mind if I come in?" he'd said at the door, smiling as she stepped aside with the news that her father had left earlier. But she wasn't worried. Men liked her. That's what happened when you got older. If you were lucky. Look at her mom. She got paid a lot of money for looking good.

Darcy didn't even worry when Keith finally kissed her. She'd seen it coming and let their tongues touch. But a kind seduction, weird as it would have been with one of her father's friends, wasn't what Keith had in mind. Kindness wasn't part of his kink. And Keith, the would-be producer, was a cop.

*

Darcy turned her battered Corolla into the frozen mud ruts of her driveway and parked in front of the single car garage. The peeling wood door hung on a single rusty hinge and didn't look like it had been opened in years. She wondered about the vermin living in there.

As she walked up to the house, Lotus, still in her kimono, opened the door.

"What'd they tell you?" she asked, pulling Darcy inside.

"Not much."

Darcy tossed her coat on a broken backed chair. "The FBI was coming over, so I didn't hang for long, but they told Katie they're amazed it hasn't happened before. I guess these agencies are always sending models off without checking. And they suspect *me*. That's the big news."

"You're shitting me."

"Not a bit."

"That's bullshit!" Lotus said, trailing her into the living room.

Darcy took the couch, which had been covered with a green brocade table cloth since a pit bull owned by one of Lotus' friends had used it as a chew toy. Kind of matched the sheets hanging over the window and the ancient asphalt siding falling off the front of the house, leaving great gaps that made it appear mostly toothless.

"And they got that guy in the poster through some tattoo place in Boise." The TV was on. More of the same. "Mind if I turn this off?"

"No, go ahead," Lotus said, perching on the armrest.

The fire in the wood stove had burned out, so Darcy gathered up the kindling and an old *Rocky Mountain News*, found matches next to the hash pipe and had the stove roasting split logs in minutes.

Lotus was a great friend and roommate, but hopeless with the stove. A beauty, too, with full red lips and long shanks of fine blond hair, stunning enough to have disappointed a legion of men: Lotus preferred women. Liked Darcy that way, too, but Darcy had always declined, figuring it was the reason they'd remained such good friends: The complications of the flesh were never a factor.

Darcy had just settled back on the scabby couch when the door buzzer scowled.

She patted her pocket for her pistol. You live at the intersection of Meth and Crack, you check. Then she lifted the window sheet aside. A well-dressed man and woman stood at the door.

"I think we've got the FBI out there," Darcy said nervously.

"Great." Lotus adjusted her kimono, but modesty was not what the roomie had in mind: The filmy fabric gaped open in critical places and actually revealed more than it concealed.

Darcy hesitated before opening the door. "You think you might want to put on some clothes?"

"Are you kidding?"

Darcy undid a series of locks, wondering how desperate a burglar would have to get before going to the trouble to steal from them. What would he find? Three beaded necklaces, a quarter ounce of herb, and a pipe?

As she opened the door, Lotus draped her arm around her shoulders.

"FBI." The guy held out his ID. "I'm Special Agent in Charge, Roy Alston. And this is Agent Jen Suskin. You're Darcy Adams, right?"

Before she could finish nodding, he said, "We'd like to talk to you. May we come in?"

Darcy and Lotus stepped aside. The guy looked thirty-five, maybe forty, but round-faced and boyish with wispy blond hair. The woman looked harder, younger, with a dark bob.

Darcy closed the door and shrugged off Lotus, who flounced over to the couch and flopped down as carelessly as possible. That's when Darcy caught Roy-boy looking up her roommate's legs.

"Have a seat," Darcy said as she settled beside Lotus, who appeared as carnal as casual allowed.

Roy Alston pulled up a rickety wooden chair; Agent Suskin, after looking around carefully, sat on the edge of a stuffed chair that had suffered the torments of the pit bull only briefly.

"You live here?" Alston said.

"Among other things," Darcy replied.

Lotus laughed and lay back along the length of the couch, resting her feet in Darcy's lap.

"It's your legal residence?"

She nodded, thinking he'd probably grown up in prep schools, gone to a good college. Eager to fight the war on terror, and here he was stuck in Denver talking to her. *Poor baby.*

"And you are?" He directed the question to her roommate.

"I'm Lotus Land."

"That's your legal name?"

"Yup."

Darcy casually draped a quilt over Lotus' legs and whispered, "Don't lie to them. That's how they got Martha Stewart."

"Whatever," Lotus said. "My real name's Sharon Krantz."

"With a 'K'?"

She spelled it.

"And you're . . . what? Her roommate?"

"Well, I applied for lover, but . . . " Lotus shrugged, "the position wasn't open. So to speak."

"You know about the Razor's Edge in Boise?" Darcy asked him, quick to change the subject.

"Yes. What do you know about it?"

She told him what she'd heard from the art director, Manser Hauer.

"We have agents over there talking to him right now. Is that everything you know about the Razor's Edge?"

"I'd never heard of it till this morning."

"I understand you shook them up over there." Alston smiled.

"Only Jackson, Katie Chatwin's assistant."

Alston kept smiling when he said, "Apparently he wants to press charges."

Oh shit. Not in the middle of this.

"Can you tell me how the investigation is going?" Darcy asked.

"All I can say right now is we're following every possible avenue of inquiry."

"Not so great then, huh?" said Lotus.

Alston ignored her. "What was your relationship like with your mother at the time of her abduction?"

"We haven't been getting along for a long time. But I thought things might be getting better. She put together dinner at her place for my birthday just before she was taken."

Alston sat forward. "Are you saying she was abducted on your birthday? The same day?"

"That's right."

"That's quite a coincidence."

"It is what it is," Darcy said, irritated by what he appeared to be implying.

"Did you drive her to the airport?"

"No. If you're going to find my mother you're going to want to know everything you can about her, so let me tell you that she'd sooner shop at a Salvation Army than get in a piece-of- crap car like mine. She probably drove herself the way she always does."

"She owns a Lexus, right? New?" Alston said.

"I think so. I really don't know my cars. It's nice."

"What did you do after you left your mother's house?"

"I went to work."

"This would be at Rio deGenerate?" Agent Suskin spoke for the first time.

"No, at the reception desk at the Brown Palace." Denver's most elegant hotel. "A joke," she added when Agent Suskin started writing this down.

Suskin's face reddened. Alston came to her rescue: "Sarcasm isn't going to help us find your mother."

"But maybe you don't want us to," Suskin added.

"Of course I want you to find her."

"Do you know him?" Roy-boy held out an eight-by-ten of the poster.

"No. And all I know about him is what that art director told me this morning."

"So you're sure you've never seen him before?" Alston said.

"Yes, I'm sure."

"But you have seen the podcast, right?" Alston again.

Darcy nodded.

"What did you make of your mother's condition?"

"She's pissed-off but I think she's all right. At least right now."

"Did your mother have any enemies?" Alston asked.

Darcy shook her head.

"What about your father? Were they still fighting?"

"That stopped a long time ago. They didn't talk at all. And besides, he's not the type."

"The type?" Alston.

"To abduct her. He's too self-centered to have anyone in his life, much less her. He ran away from us as soon as he could."

"You sound bitter," Suskin said.

"You're so quick, you must work for the FBI."

"Where's your father now? Do you know?" Alston leaned forward.

"L.A. Studio City, the last I heard."

"Do you have his address and phone number?" Alston.

"No. But I'm sure you can find it in my mother's stuff. Or you could call information."

Lotus laughed again. At least one person was enjoying this.

Alston asked several more questions before telling her that the Joint Task Force on Terrorism was investigating her mother's abduction.

"Really?" Even though she'd called the place "Terror Firma" to herself, she'd been thinking of it more as terror with a small "t." Not the World Trade Center.

"That's right. And Agent Suskin and I are part of the task force. We have reason to believe that they've also abducted others to their compound."

"Models? Wouldn't that be easy to check?"

"Models, women, children, young men, anyone they can recruit or abduct. We don't know how many people they've grabbed, but we doubt it's just your mother."

"That's not what they said on the podcast."

"Do you think they're going to announce that they've made a lot of other abductions?"

"But nobody else was on the poster." Darcy heard a perplexed, pleading tone in her voice.

"You're making the mistake of applying rational thinking to irrational people."

"They didn't sound irrational. Extreme, maybe, but—"

"Are you defending them?" Suskin demanded. "Do you actually agree with them?"

Darcy could feel herself ready to explode. "I'm not defending them. They kidnapped my mother, for Christ's sake. I'm just saying it doesn't make sense that they've got more than my mother wherever they are. Can't we just focus on her? Or figure out where they are?"

"We are," Alston said. "And we will. They can't hide forever."

"Or even for long," Suskin added.

A moment of silence passed, and Alston told Darcy not to leave the city without talking to him.

Sure-sure, Alston, you'll be the first to know. She stood and opened the door. Hint. *Hint.*

*

Johnny Bracer watched the suits walk out of Darcy Adams' dump and checked the time. Not even thirty minutes. *What's that tell you?* he said to himself. *That she's not big on home visits, and the Bureau even sent over a girl. So kill the idea of knocking on her door for now. It'll be better talking to her at the bar. She can't go anywhere when she's working.* He could sit there and watch her for as long as he wanted. Take the time he needed to work out his strategy.

*

Lotus gave Darcy two thumbs up. "You were awesome. *Awesome.* Nobody scares you."

"That's not true. They scared me plenty."

Darcy started for her bedroom, saying she wanted to see if another podcast had been posted. "From Terror Firma," she'd almost added, but this was no time for throwing around words like that. Or even "the compound." That's what Alston had called it right from the start.

"Wait up," Lotus said, bounding after her.

A new podcast had indeed been posted fifteen minutes ago. Darcy stared at the laptop, mesmerized by her mother's appearance. It was so weird seeing her walk in the snow with that guy from the poster, like the famous picture of the pair had come to life. Of course her mom wasn't in a pants suit now, but some kind of fur coat; and he wasn't kneeling at her feet; he had his arm on her like he wasn't letting her go.

Her mother looked furious. Darcy wondered if they could tell she was about to explode. Right then a woman's voice—it sounded like the camera operator's—asked her a question in an unaltered voice:

"We know you're upset, but is there anything you're starting to like about Terra Firma?"

"Are you kidding me? I'd like to leave, if that's what you mean."

"What don't you like then?" The woman sounded sympathetic. Her mother wasn't buying it.

"I *hate* the lack of fac-il-i-ties." Every breath an oath. "*You* people," she spat the word, "don't even have basic grooming down. How can you expect to build a new civilization if you can't even make a decent comb?"

"Good one, Mom," Darcy said aloud. But Sonya wasn't done. She was telling the interviewer about her dry skin.

"You could use our skin cream," the interviewer told her. "It's naturopathic and made from olive oil, chamomile, rosemary, thyme, and lavender. It works really—"

"If I want a salad dressing, I'll let you know."

55

A sudden silence on the screen as poster boy continued to escort her angry mother. All of her life Darcy had seen her mom smiling and stylish on TV, and in magazines and newspapers, catalogues and flyers, but never like this, on a grainy podcast looking totally grim.

The front door opened and Kodiak's footsteps sounded in the hallway. He wandered in the room and put his hand on Darcy's shoulder, kissed her head.

She smiled at him and looked back at the TV as the guy ushered her mother toward what appeared to be a digitized door. That's when her mom spoke up again:

"I just want my daughter and my friends to know I'm basically okay."

Lotus squeezed Darcy's shoulder as the unseen woman asked another question:

"Are you getting enough to eat?"

"Look, quit while you're ahead," Darcy's mom snapped. "I'm not giving you people a testimonial. You've kidnapped me, and until you let me go we don't have much to say to each other. But just so no one out there worries, Yes, I'm getting enough to eat."

"So how are *you* doing?" Kodiak asked Darcy.

She told him about the ice queen, Katie, and the FBI.

"They came by *here?*" he said. "Already?"

"You just missed them."

As she finished her summary of the morning, he took her hand. It had been easy to fall for Kody. Tall and lean with the gentlest touch. She hadn't bothered with a boyfriend for a year before Lotus introduced them.

"An old friend," her roomie had told her.

"Then how come you've never mentioned him?" Darcy had shot right back.

"We've all got our secrets," had been Lotus' reply.

"We were just watching my mom." Darcy looked at the laptop. Her mother was now sitting by herself in a room.

Darcy wished her mother hadn't flown off on her birthday, and not just because of this mess. She'd finally decided to talk to her openly, honestly. That was a hard place to get to with her mother, but that was the reason she'd called her at the last minute asking to come over. She'd been seeing a therapist, trying to work out all this awful . . . *shit,* and she'd realized that she had to talk to her mom. That nothing would ever be right between them until she told her why her life had turned so sour eight years ago.

But right after blowing out the candles on her cake, right after they'd known their softest moment together in years, right after saying she really needed to talk, her mother had started blabbing about having to leave, and it was the same old blah-blah-blah-blah-blah: "Got to catch a plane." How many times had she heard that line? Plenty, the summer she'd come back from L.A.

I just wanted you to slow down, and now look at you.

"She doesn't have much choice, does she?" Darcy said, finishing her thought aloud.

"What do you mean?" Lotus said.

"She was always running off to one modeling job or another. She never had any time to talk. And look at her now." Her mom was staring off into space. "It must be driving her crazy."

"Maybe she needs to be doing this," Kodiak said.

If anybody but Kodiak or Lotus had said that she really would have screamed, but it was the Buddhism talking. They believed karma dictated circumstances. Everybody thought that was such a cool idea but Darcy wasn't buying it, not after what she'd gone through when she was still pretty much a kid. All that shit was suppose to be her fault? No way.

Nothing good comes from being held against your will. Nothing.

The unseen woman broke the silence on the podcast by asking Darcy's mother what she thought of the double-bind theory: we crave the oil even though it's killing us.

"You've got me in a bind," she said icily, "so I'm not feeling real good about whatever philosophy you're following."

The podcast ended.

Kodiak lit the pipe and offered it to Lotus. She took a huge hit, holding it for almost thirty seconds before exhaling a thick cloud.

Darcy took a pass on the herb and replayed the podcast, wondering what her mother would do if *she'd* been the one taken.

She was still asking herself that question after crawling into bed. A night of bartending would begin in a few hours—listening to the lunacy of hard-core drinkers, breathing in their smoke till she smelled like an old ashtray—and she needed to brace herself for the shift. Darcy hated her job, but at least tonight it would get her away from the creeps in ties who'd started knocking on her door. She'd pretty much stopped drinking after she'd begun serving at deGenerate. Watching people get wasted was like looking in a mirror and seeing your own worst features. Which was basically how her mother had taught her to look at herself. *What a great example.*

She was always saying she was too fat or too thin, though she'd *never* been heavy. Or too big in the bust or too small. The same for her eyes, lips, chin, cheekbones. It was crazy. Darcy had grown up thinking a mirror was a means of discounting yourself, like a big plate glass showroom window announcing, "Values Slashed! 50% Off Everything!" That's what a mirror had become in their home, a means of selling yourself short. How come her mom could never see that?

She wondered what her mother thought when she looked at herself now without makeup, in *braids.* She never wore braids, not even to the beach. And she was always busy doing something. She must be bored to tears. Or frightened to death.

And then Darcy noticed that the bed sheet was damp and that she'd been crying.

She wiped her eyes and asked herself again what her mother would do if she'd been abducted instead.

*

A guy at the bar had been staring at her since he'd sat down a couple of hours ago. All he'd said since then was, "I'll have another," but he'd said it five times. *Hurricanes.* She wished *he'd* blow away.

His eyes sure did plenty of talking, scoping out her body like it was for sale. A lot of stuff changed hands in Rio deGenerate, but the bartender's body was not among them. She'd like to have "Eyeballs" bounced, but you can't have a guy bounced for staring at your butt, or the place would be empty.

She didn't want to have to stand near him, but he was sitting on the bar side of the sink and she had to catch up on glasses before they got super busy. Soon as she started washing them, she felt the air shift, like he'd breathed in too deeply or exhaled too hard. *He's going to say something.* She could read these guys better than they could read themselves, especially after they'd downed five tall red ones.

He cleared his throat. "Hey, Darcy, I can find your mother for you."

She threw him a cold look, thinking, *How the fuck do you know my name, or that it's my mother?* But she'd never give a barfly the satisfaction of seeing her surprise.

"Who the hell are you?" sufficed instead.

"What if I were to tell you that I'm a guy who finds people for a living, and that I've found a whole bunch of them?"

"I'd ask why you aren't working for the FBI?"

"Why, you love them?"

"Nope."

"Me neither. That's why."

She washed the last of the glasses as he droned on. So he was a bounty hunter. So he'd found all kinds of people. So what? She didn't like him, didn't trust him, and found his vibe genuinely repulsive. Like a reptile. Not that he was bad looking. If he hadn't made himself conspicuous by staring, she might not have noticed more than his money. He had the bulky body you'd expect of someone who hunted people for a living—about six feet tall, two-hundred twenty pounds—with black hair shiny as new vinyl and combed back like Johnny Cash in his break-out days. His face was shaved except for a crumb-catcher beard right below his moist lips. A standard-issue affectation until she spied the white streak growing right down the middle, like a baby skunk had crawled into his mouth. She'd never want to find herself alone with him; his dark eyes were still pawing her.

But what worried her right now was that if he'd found her, the reporters and TV crews couldn't be far behind. Her whole life would be splashed all over the place, every dirty little detail from way back when. And here she was, stuck behind this bar for another six hours like a goddamn duck in a shooting gallery.

A biker gone to belly caught her eye and raised a finger. She'd just slid another Coors into his massive hand when the bounty hunter ordered his sixth Hurricane.

As he did it, the answer to Darcy's earlier question hit her with stunning force: Her mother would do *anything* she could to find her. She'd tear down rock walls till her hands bled and her bones broke. That's what a mother does, even when her daughter screams that she hates her.

The memory of those words felt sharper than a piercing.

I'm out of here.

She bolted for the door of Rio deGenerate, leaving behind three drink orders, including that Hurricane for the bounty hunter.

But the man himself wasn't so easy to escape.

Chapter 6

Sonya clutched the blankets to her chin and eyed the room warily. The door hung open a few inches, but Desmond was assuredly not in there. A huge relief. Yesterday morning she'd awakened to find him sitting casually on the side of her bed.

In those first few fuzzy seconds of consciousness she'd actually thought she was back in Denver with Paul. But a nasty jolt to her adrenals came with the shocking realization that she was definitely not in her own bed; moreover, she'd broken up with her long-time boyfriend months ago.

She'd screamed at Desmond to get out and had shouted for Andromeda. That had made him smile.

"We're all alone, but she's okay with you and me. We're relaxed here." Then he'd leaned so close she could smell his sour morning breath. "Let's commit some 'crimes against nature' while you still can."

Was he mocking their elderly leader, Chandra, by quoting her from the other night? His last words—"while you still can"—left her far too shaken to think clearly. An instant later her fear spiked when he gripped her thigh so firmly that it felt like the quilt had dissolved in his hand.

"Stop it," she gasped. "That really hurts. Go away."

"I'll be watching you whenever and wherever I want. *Everything you do.*" He jerked the blankets from her hands, uncovering her to the waist.

"So you *do* wear them to bed." He fingered the collar of her long johns—she feared he'd tear them off. "I wondered if you slept naked."

She slapped his hand away. He responded by pinning her thin arms to the bed, terrifying her with his quickness and the way he leered at her body, like he could look right through the well-washed wool.

"We might as well get along," he whispered.

"Stop it!" she yelled, trying to push him off. But God he was strong, all big bones and hard muscle, and he didn't release her until he was ready. Then he backed out of the room *smiling,* leaving her with such a clear sense of violation that she'd immediately checked the bottom of her long johns to make sure he hadn't had them down while she was asleep.

This morning she mentally noted the date, and promised herself that she wouldn't lose the soft comforts of time, even if the Abolanders refused to use clocks or calendars. With fresh snow dusting the sill, it was hard to believe that winter wouldn't begin officially for several days. Harder still to believe that they'd ever let her leave.

They'd yet to pronounce her sentence or give her any idea when they would. Not another word had been spoken about it since the old woman had acted as judge and jury on Sonya's first night there; but after scaring her almost senseless with the dark threat about her "fate," the woman had finally ordered her fed.

Ravenous, Sonya had torn into the meat with both hands, even pawing the vegetables before noticing the rough wooden spoon next to the parsnips. She'd halted, imagining how she must look to the crowd. *Like an animal.* Right then she'd known she must never again let herself look less than human to them.

To make herself appear even more of a person in their eyes— and less easy to kill—she'd talked to anyone who would listen about herself, her daughter, parents, friends, anything personal that would make it difficult to objectify her. Those were tips she'd heard on *Oprah* just last month.

And though extraordinarily hard, she'd turned on her smile. She'd used it countless times to land modeling jobs. Maybe, just maybe, it would help land her freedom. She was already thinking about escaping, and if she could forge friendships the Abolanders might prove less vigilant. She'd even toned down her temper for the podcasts. So get them *all* smiling, she told herself.

And then get out.

She pulled on her deerskins so she could make the trip to the "kitty box," as she thought of the composting toilet they shared with two other houses. But she faltered as soon as she opened the door to the living area: Andromeda, Desmond, and Juno lay naked and entwined on a large fur on the floor. More of Aboland's "free expression in body and spirit" that she'd been hearing about, mostly from Desmond, who appeared the chief beneficiary at the moment. But it was Juno who spoke up now:

"Want to have some fun?" the dogsled driver asked in a voice one degree warmer than ice.

Sonya managed a shocked demurral and headed for the door.

"Think about it," Juno demanded.

But Sonya was already in her coat and on her way outside, where she immediately encountered Gwen, the young woman with the camera who shadowed her for the podcasts and kept her under constant scrutiny.

Sonya hurried past her toward the toilet, fussing with her hair for a moment before realizing how ridiculous it was to worry about her appearance anymore.

Worry about escaping.

She closed the toilet door and looked for the lock before remembering "There are no locks in Terra Firma." She couldn't recall who'd said that to her first, probably that creep Desmond, who made obvious use of an open-door policy.

After wrestling off her deerskins and long underwear, which clung to her oily skin like sap, she relieved herself. It didn't smell nearly as bad in the kitty box as she'd expected it would at first. She figured the cold weather helped.

What did smell, she suddenly realized, was her own rank self. She hadn't sponge-bathed in the bedroom because of the threat of Desmond bursting in. The Abolanders used the hot pools, but she didn't want to be seen naked by *any* of her captors. It wasn't nudity per se that bothered her. As a model she'd routinely disrobed around her co-workers. It was her fear of taking off her clothes around people crazy enough to kidnap her. It would be one more coercion in a whole series of them: eating on their schedule, sleeping on their schedule, appearing on their podcasts in *their* animal skins. No privacy in her own bed.

Where's it going to end?

If she didn't escape, probably in a hellish blaze of glory during some stand-off with law enforcement. And if she did escape, then what? They'd already destroyed her career. They'd turned everything she'd ever accomplished into a mockery with the podcasts.

You should be so lucky.

On her way back to the house she heard the chipping sounds of the flint knappers. As far as she could tell, they labored at the bottom of the food chain, along with the Abolanders assigned to smashing nutshells open with rocks (an approved tool, evidently, of the Pleistocene). The hunters, predictably enough, stood near the top of the chain. Somewhere in between lay the weavers and soap makers, smithy and hide tanners, and all the others who provided the essentials for living here.

The breakfast gong sounded as she reached the front door. She turned right around, glad to be spared the threesome.

At once Abolanders began to emerge from their homes and head to the community center. Sonya joined them, sitting at the table to which she'd been assigned. At every other meal, the missing Andromeda and Desmond had sandwiched her between them.

Gwen made her suffer the camera through every sip of tea and spoonful of oatmeal, which Sonya downed quickly, hoping to be spared the presence of her "roommates," a term Andromeda had actually used.

Various members stood and made announcements; but breakfast and lunch, as much as she could gather, were casual affairs compared to the pageantry of dinner.

As she headed back to the house with Calypso now guarding her—the burly driver had taken over so Gwen could eat breakfast—she realized that everything in the background of every single shot could be a clue to her whereabouts: the mountains, river, buildings, hot pools. *All of it.* With satellite reconnaissance, it shouldn't take investigators long to match these clearly identifying features to the podcasts.

So when Gwen's around keep it slow so she gets shots of you in front of all that stuff.

She stepped up to the door, freezing at the threshold when she heard Desmond hurrying up behind her, telling Calypso that he could watch her now.

She did *not* want to go inside with him. She stood unmoving, unsure. Too easy a target, he made her realize at once.

"When are you going to bathe?" he whispered, so close she felt his hot breath. "You smell worse than the goats."

"Then get away from me." Everything about him scared her, and she'd had to force herself to hold her ground.

Now she made herself turn around to confront him directly, spotting Andromeda walking up. He changed his tone at a glance:

"Being overly concerned about nudity is an outmoded concept derived from religious precepts that have no place in Terra Firma."

"In other words, you want to see me without my clothes on."

"I already have," he said unabashedly and without missing a beat.

"You're disgusting."

"What's going on?" Andromeda said.

"He wants to watch me take a bath."

"I want her to stop smelling like a goat. She's stinking up the place."

Andromeda massaged his shoulder. "It's not that bad. Just be patient."

Yes, hold your breath. Sonya meant it in every possible way.

Andromeda faced her. "We've just spoken to Chandra—" the old woman—"and you'll be taking a tour of Aboland this morning with Calypso and Gwen. It's about time you saw all the amazing things we're doing here."

"A *tour?*" Sonya's first impulse was to refuse to go along with their "education efforts," another absurd term Andromeda was fond of. But if she wanted to win them over, she'd have to cooperate; and if she wanted to escape, she'd surely have to get a good look at the place. *A break from him too*, she thought.

Desmond glared at her. "You're going, like it or not."

"Fine. When?"

"As soon as Gwen's done eating," Andromeda said. "Calypso's gone for her now."

"Here they are," Desmond said, looking past his partner.

Calypso led Sonya out of the circle of homes, saying "All of this is Aboland," as he gestured vaguely to the outlying land and forests.

After that he didn't say much at all, and she thought the taciturn driver was a peculiar choice for a tour guide, though his bulk gave him obvious qualifications as a guard, which was probably their highest priority.

Not that Sonya needed anyone to draw her attention to the raw, glacier-raked splendor of the surrounding mountains. Their snowy peaks glinted majestically in the bright sun, and she wondered if the grandeur was another reason they wanted her to take the tour. Were they deluded enough to believe that if they showed off the place on a beautiful day that she'd fall in love with it and offer them hosannas on their podcasts?

Never. A vow she'd taken several times since they'd dragged her here.

But the idea that they might care what she thought encouraged the hope that they wouldn't behead or otherwise brutalize her, and she had to concede that they'd found a stunning spot to build their illusions. Not just the towering mountains, but the tamer views too: When she came to the barn and corral, the sun-blanched whiteness of the snow contrasted so richly with the black, brown, and fawn horses that it seemed to saturate them with color, to raise reds and violets and pure hints of purple from their sleek winter coats.

A cow lowed, drawing her eyes to a goat herd, which shifted mysteriously, like a school of fish suddenly changing direction.

Beyond the corral, right before the settlement surrendered to wilderness, five archers were shooting at a deer-shaped target. Akiah turned and walked up to her. "How do you like the place?"

"You're kidding, right? I'm a *prisoner.* There's no *liking* the place."

"A lot of people want to come here. More every day."

"I'm not one of them. I hope they're cops coming to rescue me."

"Don't waste your time hoping for that. Cops, FBI, they don't have tattoos, piercings, not like us anyway. They're not part of the tribe. We've got our underground and lots of people helping us in any way they can. They're not going to send us cops."

He tugged off his fur hood, and she spotted the knife with the bone handle poking out of his balled-up dreads. Then he stretched his neck, and the cords on both sides stuck out, reminding her of the way his veins had protruded at the McFaddins shoot, like he'd been shrink-wrapped with tattoos.

"I guess you can always tell your people by the smell of pot." She'd noticed it a few times.

"Burning some bud isn't a big deal here. It's not like everybody's high all the time."

You're blowing it, she told herself. *Be nice. And smile.* She managed a quick one, and toned down her half of the exchange by nodding at the target and asking, "You good at that?" as if she really cared.

"Junior national champion. But then I gave it up for hunting. My mother was right: competing was pointless."

"Not if you're going to the Olympics."

"*Especially* if you're going to the Olympics. The very idea of a country is insane. You create borders and borders create wars. I wasn't going to honor that by going to the Olympics. We came here. It's better."

"'We?' You and your mother?"

He nodded.

"Who is she? Have I met—"

"Chandra."

"Really?"

"I was a surprise. She had me when she was forty-six."

"And your father, is he—"

"Never a factor."

Never true, but she was through challenging him.

"So when do you go hunting again?"

"Tomorrow. I found an elk herd just over that ridge."

He pointed to the mountains. He could have been pointing to Mars for all the help it gave her, but she immediately wondered what lay beyond those peaks and glaciers and high valley passes. More mountains? Or a town, a road? Cars? People? This was America, *Three-hundred million consumers.* How many times had she heard that number? *You're bound to bump into a few of them, even out here.*

As Akiah resumed his target practice, she asked herself how they'd hauled all these building materials up there. Stuff like the lumber. You can cut down trees until a forest looks like Gettysburg, but without a mill all you can build are inefficient log cabins; and there wasn't a log cabin anywhere in Terra Firma.

And what about the concrete for the floors, and the other heavy stuff like the sinks, the smithy's anvil, and all the wood stoves? Everything they'd have to truck in, most likely in summer. *They've got to have roads around here, and if there are roads there might be a way home right around a bend. You could ski out.* She'd seen Abolanders moving around on skis that looked like they'd been stolen from a museum, wood with leather bindings, ancient stuff; but those kinds of skis had been used for centuries in Norway, and she'd have been happy to abscond with a pair.

The same for the ice skates. Every day children glided on the frozen river. Adults too. Old skates, but they worked well enough.

"I wish I had a river to skate away on . . . "

Joni Mitchell played in her head again. You could sure tell she'd grown up in the north country. Sonya, too. Her early childhood in Colorado had been filled with ice-skating, skiing, and summertime camping. Her parents had embraced the outdoors with the fervor that some people reserved for religion or Mahjong, and they'd wanted Sonya to enjoy it too. But her teen rebellion had carried her far from nature's rough edges to the crisply presented world of fashion. Until now.

She walked on, scheming once again to escape, remembering how emphatic Juno had been when the dogsled driver had warned her that she'd die if she tried to flee Aboland, that the cold or the cougars would kill her. *Too emphatic.* Maybe the Abolanders were more worried about her survival than her death.

All those hours of driving and dog sledding could have been nothing but a big dodge to make her think she was in the middle of nowhere. And here she'd tried to be nice to her chief kidnapper.

But that's good, she reminded herself. *You're selling another fantasy, this time to a tribe of true believers. They want to believe you, they're the perfect buyers. Make them think you're settling in . . . and you might get out alive.*

These were the thoughts that occupied her as she skirted the copse that separated the barn and corral from the rest of Aboland, and quickly passed the kennels where the dogs yapped incessantly. She paused when Calypso opened the door of the blacksmith's so she could watch him forge square nails. Calypso also had her look in on the weavers, and the soap and candle makers. She played her part, but mostly she kept an eye out for the storage areas where skates and skis might be kept.

There are no locks in Aboland.

Before lunch he led her over to a snow hill where children were sliding down the slope on straw mats. Several boys and a girl were building a fort near the base, all of them watched over by their parents and a child care worker.

Three pregnant women were bundled up on a bench. The woman closest to her smiled. "I'm Ventura, and this is Crystal Heart and Merryweather." She lifted the blankets to include her, by far the friendliest gesture she'd received since arriving here. Neither Calypso nor Gwen objected when she sat beside them.

Why would they? You look like you're joining up.

Sonya glanced at her guards, "I come with some baggage."

"Oh, that's okay," Ventura said, waving at Calypso and the camerawoman. "We're going to be famous."

"Infamous," Crystal Heart laughed, her blond dreads barely contained in a huge blue knitted hat. "When they post pictures from the podcast, the FBI will call us, 'The three pregnant women on a bench.'" She surprised Sonya with how easily she joked about such a serious matter; but Sonya recalled how her own pregnancy often made other concerns seem trivial, some ludicrously so.

"That sounds like the name of a painting," said Merryweather, who quickly pulled off her mitten and stuck out her hand in greeting. "I'm the bowling ball about to give birth," which sparked another round of laughter.

Ventura, hands over her big belly, looked at Sonya closely and said, "How are you doing?" in a voice so earnest that Sonya almost choked up.

But that might be part of their strategy, too, right? Make her break down so they could put her back together again as *their* poster girl.

"Okay," she managed before changing the subject abruptly: "Do you have a little one out there?"

Ventura turned her placid gaze to the snow hill, saying, "I have a four-year-old, Willow. She adores this little park."

Sonya watched Ventura looking for her daughter among the dozen or so children milling like ants on the hill.

"Where *is* she?" Ventura tried to sound casual, but the undercurrent of worry was clear to Sonya.

"What's she wearing?"

"A red sheepskin coat."

Ventura pushed aside the blanket and struggled to her feet for a better look, calling out her child's name much more loudly.

"I don't see her either." Merryweather also stood.

Now Crystal Heart rose too, and the blankets tumbled to the snow.

"She's gone," Ventura said.

What's the worry? Sonya said to herself. *It's not like we're in—*

"Beet juice," Ventura said. "We dyed her coat with beet juice."

An odd fact, offered as they sometimes are by people who find their world rapidly filling with their worst fear, who try to rescind disaster with an everyday detail.

"I'll check over there." Calypso ran toward the child care worker, who was staring past the snow hill.

Sonya felt a palpable panic setting in.

"Cougars . . . " Ventura said to Sonya as she trudged toward a broad stand of trees to their left, ". . . took Starling last year."

"Ring the gong," the child care worker shouted.

Sonya offered Ventura her arm, the memory of losing Darcy at three years of age at LAX as alive now as it had been in those terrifying minutes. Her daughter had been within sight one second, and in the next she'd disappeared behind a rush of deplaning passengers. When they'd moved on, Darcy was missing.

Sonya had shrieked her daughter's name, raced into shops on the concourse pleading for help. People had stared at her like she was a freak. A half hour later, with the help of airport security and two LAPD officers, she'd spotted Darcy's little feet under a seat in a boarding area three gates away, where she'd hidden in fear of thousands of unfamiliar faces.

"You think she's in there?" Sonya pointed to the woods.

"I don't know," Ventura said, almost breathless from moving through the thick snow, "but I know it's the one place I don't want her."

"I'll run ahead and check."

Sonya rushed into the woods saying, "Willow, Willow," in as loud a voice as she could keep calm. She didn't want to frighten the girl, and assumed the four-year-old would have no way of recognizing her. She heard Calypso searching the forest about a hundred feet to her right.

As the shadows under the trees darkened, a flash of movement made her turn quickly to the left, where a mountain lion settled into a crouch no more than twenty feet away, its eerie blue eyes traveling from Willow to her.

Chapter 7

Sonya froze. The sight of the cougar left her as rigid as the little girl sitting in the snow. For eternal seconds the triangle of animal, child and woman remained unmoving. Then with no more thought than she'd give to breath itself, Sonya began to inch toward Willow, keeping her eyes on the huge lion, at least seven feet from its reddish nose to the tip of its twitching tail. Its teeth were bared, its ears pinned back.

My God, it's going to spring.

The girl started to sob.

"Willow, it's okay," Sonya said in a deliberately loud voice. "It's just a big old cat. Please don't cry, and I want you to stay really still. Do you know how to play freeze tag?" The whole time she talked, Sonya moved closer to her, saw the girl nodding her answer, and said, "Good. I want you to stay frozen right now. That's *really* important."

Four more steps and she could stand in front of her. As she eased forward, she slowly slipped off her bearskin coat, then raised it high above her head, making herself look as large as possible.

One more big step and she'd be standing between Willow and the cougar. But that's when her leg post-holed in the snow, all the way to her thigh. She almost toppled over, and felt a stabbing spasm in her lower back when she righted herself. To her horror, the lion's hind feet pumped, ready to leap.

She drove her leg up out of the snow, suppressing a gasp from another stabbing pain, desperate not to appear stricken to this predator, and watched its feet still. She had now placed herself between Willow and the animal.

The beast peered at her, its blue eyes no more feeling than an ice cap. The white muzzle remained drawn, the teeth bared, the face as frightening as ever.

In her struggle to stand, she'd dropped her coat. She retrieved it and slowly raised it over her head once more.

"Stay right where you are, Willow. Remember, this is like freeze tag. No moving."

With one hand she reached back blindly and patted the girl's hooded head. Even with this brief touch, she felt the child shaking terribly.

Sonya couldn't remember whether she should return the cougar's gaze, so she stared at the white fur on its chest. All she knew for certain was that the creature's eyes never left her. *Just stand your ground. Look big.* Those were the warnings that came back to her most clearly.

Several bleak seconds passed before an odd whizzing sound startled her, something like a cat's hiss; but it was an arrow, and it struck the animal's hip.

The cougar jerked forward snarling, as if to attack, then spun around and raced away in a wild scramble of blood and snow.

Sonya turned and saw Akiah with his bow, and a shorter man wielding a spear. Two big, dark dogs with pointy ears howled and sprinted past them. Gwen stood to the side with her camera. Calypso ran over to Akiah.

"Take her and go back," Akiah shouted to Sonya as he started after the animals.

She scooped up Willow, enduring another stab of pain in her back, and lunged toward the edge of the woods. She spotted Ventura bent over, barely holding on to a tree trunk, breathing heavily. Crystal Heart and Merryweather, appearing as exhausted, trailed a few feet behind.

"I tried to help you," Ventura cried to her daughter.

Willow reached for her mother from Sonya's arms, but Ventura was too weak to take her, offering only her wet face for the girl to hug.

The grilling pain in Sonya's back buckled her knees, and she sank to the snow still holding Willow. Ventura kneeled too, and wrapped herself around her girl. Crystal Heart and Merryweather settled beside them, reaching for Sonya, and the three women formed a snug circle around Willow and her mom.

Ventura rocked her daughter gently, weeping loudly. Crystal Heart, kneeling next to Sonya, whispered, "Thank you. You don't know what it's like to lose a daughter but we do."

Crystal Heart crumpled to the snow, and in that instant Sonya knew that it was her girl who had been killed by the cougar last year.

Sonya hugged her closely, tears streaming from her own eyes. She realized that as hard as it had been raising Darcy, her daughter was alive. And then she felt an outpouring of raw love for her that she hadn't known in years, since Darcy had come back full of fury from visiting her father, no doubt fuming over the exciting, glamorous life she could have had if her mother had remained married and stayed in L.A.

Merryweather led Ventura and Willow out of the forest, and Sonya held Crystal Heart's hand. No one spoke; only sobs of grief and gratitude filled the frigid air.

Sonya watched Ventura and Willow walking side by side, and winced when she remembered how she'd grabbed Darcy at LAX and spanked her, telling her never to wander off like that again. Remembered, too, the cop by her side saying, "It's the only way they learn."

But what had she learned? Sonya asked herself now, as she had so many times before.

She limped back toward the circle of homes with only Gwen to guard her. If they really were out in the middle of nowhere, what was the point in having Calypso around? she wondered.

"You should have one of your roommates work on your back before you start having serious problems," Gwen said from behind the viewfinder.

What are you, part of the grab and grope team? Sonya said to herself. To Gwen she proved almost as blunt: "There's no way I'd ever let them touch me."

Gwen lowered her camera. "What do you mean? They're massage therapists. That's what they do here."

"Believe me, they told me."

"They're really good. Here, let me help you." She offered her hand as they made their way over the trunk of a fallen tree.

Sonya looked closely at Gwen, paused, then plunged ahead. "To put it to you straight, Desmond scares the shit out of me. When I woke up yesterday he was in my room, and then he pinned me to the bed and said he'd watch me 'whenever and wherever' he wanted. He also said that we might as well 'get along.' I knew exactly what that meant. And this morning he told me that he's already seen me naked."

Gwen stared at her. "That's *wrong*. No one's allowed to do that stuff. I'll report him to the Council. Just because you were brought here doesn't mean you have to put up with *that*."

"I don't know if you should. He's scary."

"There won't be any repercussions. No way. What about Andromeda? Is she okay?"

"I wouldn't go that far but she's definitely not as bad."

Gwen, head shaking, took her arm again. "Come on, let's get you back there. Maybe she can do something."

Andromeda listened without expression as Gwen told her what had happened in the forest. She finished by glancing at Sonya and saying, "She hurt her back carrying Willow and needs *your* help," pointedly ignoring Desmond, who sat a few feet away.

Andromeda nodded, offering no hint of enthusiasm.

"But I want him out of here." Sonya spoke up with her eyes directly on Desmond. Gwen, still by her side, now stared at him too. Andromeda hesitated, then looked at her partner.

"Maybe you should go, just for now."

Desmond leaped from his chair in anger, his eyes sweeping over the three women before he stormed out the door.

Sonya managed a sponge bath before stepping slowly from the bedroom, fearful that Desmond had returned. But Andromeda waited alone for her, and had hung long curtains to form a private area around her massage table.

Gwen had been right in saying there would be nothing untoward in Andromeda's treatment, which relieved her pain considerably. She massaged Sonya in silence, breaking it only briefly.

"That was really brave, what you did."

Sonya thanked her, smiling without effort or artifice.

Andromeda had worked gently into the tender tissue deep in Sonya's lower back when wild cheering erupted throughout the community.

"They must have got that cougar," Andromeda said.

The cheering grew louder.

"Hold on a second." Andromeda stepped to the other side of the curtains. "I think they're headed here," she called to her. "You'd better get dressed."

By the time Sonya joined Andromeda, the small front window was already filled with Abolanders marching toward the house, beating drums and carrying blazing torches.

"I'm sure they're here for you." Andromeda opened the door.

The crowd included most of the settlement. Akiah and his

fellow hunter stood at the very front, their shoulders supporting a lodge-pole pine from which a dead cougar hung, its paws bound front and back.

As if on cue, the drumming stopped.

Sonya approached the door, seeing the animal clearly now. It looked huge and frightening, even in death, and she was frankly amazed that she'd faced it down. Five arrows protruded like quills from its tawny coat.

A strange silence greeted her, and then a drummer took up an African tribal rhythm. Quickly, a half dozen others joined in, the polyrhythmic beat unsettling as sudden ice.

In the red glare of the torches, the stark faces staring at her burned with an unearthly glow, and clouds of breath swirled in the cold air like smoke. Through this pall she saw Akiah looking directly into her eyes.

His mother, Chandra, walked up to her. The drumming stopped again. She peered closely at Sonya before speaking,

"We are honored by your courage."

Sonya started to disagree, believing a display of modesty would become her; but Chandra raised her hand for silence and drew Willow from the crowd to face her.

"And we are grateful."

The drums started back up and the procession moved on.

"Bye-bye." Willow turned to leave, then without any apparent prompting she threw her arms around Sonya's legs. Sonya crouched and held the girl, smelled her sweet, soapy skin, and heard her say, "Thank you."

But their gratitude had not been spent.

At dinner, Chandra asked Sonya to stand beside her. As she walked up she saw that the old woman's hair, though completely white, was still thick and full; and as she drew even closer she noticed her striking cheekbones, as pronounced by the draw-downs of age as they might once have been by the high bright tones of youth.

"Your courage surprised us," Chandra said, "and it has changed our thinking . . ."

They're letting me go. A hope stillborn:

"In sentencing you, the Council of Consensus has decided to look upon your rescue of Willow as a 'mitigating circumstance.'

Therefore, we have decided to hold you for only one year in Terra Firma, or Aboland as we call it among ourselves."

A year?

Sonya tried mightily to maintain her composure, to appear even grateful. *They could have murdered you. But a year in this place . . .*

"Show her the photo," Chandra said. "This could be you at the end of the year."

The screen came to life with a mock-up of a new poster, courtesy of Photoshop or some other means of visual manipulation. It showed Sonya shoulder to shoulder with Akiah, both of them in deerskins and fur coats, standing in the settlement with steam rising from hot pools in the background. She experienced a brief moment of relief when she saw that even in this cockamamie vision of the future she bore no visible tattoos, though only her face and hands were uncovered. Then she noticed her hair and couldn't suppress a grimace; dreadlocks, matted and curled and falling to her chest. She also had enlarged holes for the bone "earrings" she was wearing. *Animal or human?* she wondered, forcing the memory of the crawly blanket.

A large hunting knife in a leather sheath hung from her belt, and she saw that with a little face paint she could have looked like Darryl Hannah in *The Clan of the Cave Bear.* She might have found this risible if she hadn't been staring at an outlandish fantasy that these people were determined to make real.

"You could have this life, if you open yourself to Aboland."

Said—and she could *not* believe they could possibly be this nuts —as if the ridiculous image of herself up on that screen were remotely appealing. Dressed in these skins for a whole year? *With bones in my ears, for God's sakes.*

Never! Never! Never!

"We believe that you have the strength to live with a planetary consciousness. And when you also see this strength in yourself, we think you'll want to become a fully active citizen of Aboland."

A year! That's all she kept thinking. *On this godforsaken chunk of frozen real estate?* Panic roiled her stomach. And then an intriguing possibility took hold: No matter what the old chieftain just claimed, the one-year sentence had been their plan all along, the very reason she'd called it an "experiment" on Sonya's first night here: to see if a model, their hated symbol of "rampant consumption," could be led, wheedled—whatever—to accept Aboland's strange strictures and ideology, its coercions and conceits. To see if she'd become a mouthpiece for the ideas they considered so crucial.

The cougar was just a convenient excuse.

And they could presume another benefit from announcing the sentence now, she realized. After making that threat about her "fate," they probably thought she'd see the year as a gift, maybe even regard them as kind and generous, humane to their hostage.

Go along with them, her thoughts whispered to her. *If they're arrogant enough to try this experiment—or simply so beguiled by their own beliefs to think you'll join up—let on that you're buying into their world. It just means ramping up your campaign to win them over by making them believe they've won you over. But you've got to "buy in" in small steps.*

And then take a huge one right out of here.

"Our scouts bring us new members all the time. Our satellite communities are springing up in Europe, South America, Australia, and Southeast Asia. But I say to all of you now," Chandra's eyes swept over the assembled, "that we must recognize the special status of Sonya Adams. Unlike every one of you, she did not come here of her own accord. Now that she's shown her bravery, we trust that her mind will be as strong as her heart. But it may take her time to see that what we offer is as invaluable as sunlight, water, or virgin land. Even if it takes her months . . ."

Try never.

" . . . we must show her the same respect we show one another. If we're right, and we *are* right, she will begin to assume her duties as you have assumed yours, and all the world will see this."

The Abolanders clapped wildly. Sonya worked up a smile. *Not too much,* she warned herself. *This isn't a Crest shoot, more like Preparation H.*

"We have one more way to repay your courage, Sonya. We understand from Akiah and Koka that the opal earrings that were taken from you during your rescue . . ."

Rescue?

" . . . were a gift from your mother just before she passed away." Chandra held up the earrings. "We will return these to you now, for today you embodied the fire that lies in the hearts of these precious stones."

She tried to hand the earrings to Sonya, who shook her head.

"Thank you for your kindness, but I wasn't truthful when I said that my mother had given them to me. I bought them on sale at Zale's. They hold no special value to me, and would be a cheap exchange for the life of a child."

She didn't turn from Chandra, neither did she say that her freedom would constitute a more proper reward; she let the unspoken remain silent, and more obvious by its absence. She also sensed that nothing in these pressing seconds should cloud her contrition. It should be as clear to them as the lie at the heart of her words was to her. But her mother would understand. If she were watching, Sonya believed she'd say, *You do what you have to do to survive, and if that means denying my last gift to you, then deny it.*

Chandra studied her openly before saying, "What would you have us do with them?"

"Whatever you need to."

Applause began once again and rose to a crescendo, letting Sonya know that she'd sewn her fiction into the seam of the settlement least likely to tear: their robust belief in their own virtue. She also knew that those opals had been stolen once more, this time by the lie that gave them away.

She sat before the applause could ebb, claiming modesty after securing the moral high ground, knowing that it was the right move. She was playing by instinct before this crowd as she had played by instinct before the camera, selling the most important illusion of her life—her honesty—to a crowd of willing buyers. But even this victory, rooted in ruse, proved terrifyingly brief.

*

At daybreak she was jarred by a fist pounding on her bedroom door. Before she could blink herself fully awake, her roommates rushed in the room, Desmond shouting, "Get up *now*. And get your clothes on."

Sonya jerked herself up into a seated position as the gong at the community center sounded over and over.

"What's going on?" she asked, sleep-addled.

Akiah raced in. "You've got thirty seconds to throw on your skins."

In the background she began to hear *whup-whup-whup,* and it took several seconds while she groped for her buckskins before she recognized the sound of a helicopter.

Calypso hovered behind Akiah, Andromeda, and Desmond.

"Can I have some privacy at least?" Sonya snapped.

"Thirty seconds," Akiah snapped back, "and then we carry you out."

She swore as he slammed the door hard enough to rattle a native doll on a vaulted shelf above the bed.

When she stepped from the bedroom, Akiah draped her bearskin coat across her shoulders and slapped an oversized fur hat on her head. He grabbed her boots, ordering her to put them on quickly.

The sound of the helicopter grew louder as they started out the front door, and she was surprised to see the pathways packed with Abolanders moving every which way. Except for meal times, she'd never seen them out all at once.

She also found it odd that after all their applause last night no one greeted her. In fact, they looked right through her. The dogsled driver Edson, who'd been friendlier than most, passed with his eyes trolling the snow.

Akiah and Calypso guided her forcefully past the houses, kennels, and the copse that separated the barn from Terra Firma proper. As she glanced at the horses, they turned her onto a trail that led directly to a deciduous forest about a hundred feet away.

The chopper now sounded as if it might be directly overhead, so before passing under the trees she made a desperate attempt to rip her arms free to wave and shout; but her escorts held her so firmly that her sudden thrust sent a sharp pain into her tender back. She succeeded only in turning her head upward, spotting the chopper as it flew over the copse.

It had gold lettering on the cabin, most of which was too small for her to make out; but an *Au* was large enough that she could read it without her glasses.

And then she saw Desmond. Following them.

"Not *him,*" she shouted at Akiah, who turned around.

"Go back," he yelled at him. "You're not on this detail. You know that."

"I'm backing you up. Look at her."

Sonya was struggling.

"Just go back," Akiah repeated fiercely.

He and Calypso forced her beneath the naked, skeletal trees. Then, as the path grew narrower, Calypso fell behind and Akiah held her close, as a lover might, with one hand wrapped around her lower back and the other gripping her arm; but there was nothing tender in his intimacy.

Not a single leaf hung from the trees. The trunks and limbs looked destitute, branches twisting upward in wild tangles to block out most of the gray sky with their tortured shapes. The woods appeared, in a word, abandoned, like nature's homeless.

The climb steepened and Akiah breathed deeply as he drove her forward. A hummock rose to their left. She'd no sooner noticed its humped form then he forced her toward it.

Calypso fell farther back. Even so, when the *whup-whup-whup* of the helicopter faded, she could hear the scratchy sound of him sweeping away their footprints with branches.

Akiah herded her around the hummock. On the far side they came to a granite overhang shadowing the opening to what looked like a cave. She figured they'd force her in there like some animal, keep her under guard, a threat that was enough to make her want to scream; but their plans proved far more frightening.

Akiah continued to hold her tightly as he waited for Calypso, who followed moments later with the branches.

In yet another move that looked well-rehearsed, Calypso hurried to the mouth of the cave and swept a small covering of snow from the earth, revealing a thick wooden hatch. He strained against a heavy forged handle before the hatch gave way.

"I'm *not* going in there," Sonya shouted.

Akiah pushed her toward the opening until they were standing over it, watching Calypso climb down a wooden ladder into the pitch.

"Jesus," she swore.

Calypso lit a candle, and the hole revealed itself by degrees: dark earthen walls, a bench with a bunched-up fur, a simple wooden cabinet, planked floor.

"Get down there," Akiah said, "or we'll make you."

She turned from the hole to him. "You're a bastard. You think you're some goddamn noble savage, but you're a bastard."

"I am actually, and I'm proud of it. Now get . . . in . . . there.

Calypso."

The stocky man lunged for the ladder, and when she saw the infuriated look on his face she stepped forward.

Akiah held her while she found her footing. His touch was almost gentle.

Because you're doing what he wants.

She descended unsteadily into the shifting candlelight and dark shadows.

The hole could not have been more than six feet square, about eight feet high, with a ceiling at least three feet thick.

She immediately feared a cave-in, being smothered to death in darkness; and as she stepped down to the planks she asked in alarm, "Is this thing going to fall in on me?"

"It's reinforced," Akiah said. "That's not going to happen." He looked at her from the hatch opening. "You've got lots of candles down there, and some nuts and dried fruit."

Calypso opened the cabinet and pointed to the supplies. Without admitting it, she was grateful for the extra candles because she'd already begun to dread sitting in this hole in complete darkness.

Like a tomb.

"The books, too. Show her those."

"Right here." Calypso tapped a stack wrapped in oilcloth, presumably to keep the pages as dry as possible. The hole was extremely damp, and a drop of water struck her nose as she stood there. She swiped angrily at it.

"Watch out you don't run into these things." Calypso lifted the burning candle until the light fell on dozens of pale roots hanging like snakes from the naked earth above them.

A shiver shook her shoulders and arms.

"We won't keep you down there any longer than we have to," Akiah said as Calypso started up the ladder. "Don't waste your energy screaming. Someone could be standing right over you and they'd never hear you."

"Who are they?"

Akiah shook his head, then moved aside for Calypso.

"They're going to find this place when they search for me."

His face reappeared. "Nobody's ever going to find you here. But they're not even going to be trying. That's not why they're here."

"Then who the hell are they?"

Akiah closed the hatch. A moment later she heard the harsh truth of latches and locks, and the scratchy sound of branches sweeping away the last of her trail.

I thought I had them in my corner.

She was thinking of how she'd assumed she'd won their confidence last night, and how that might have helped her escape before winter descended in all its fury. And here she was locked in a hole.

She wrapped herself in the fur and sat studying every square inch of the room until she convinced herself that she was truly alone.

Just as she'd settled back, she heard a telltale squeak and her stomach tightened. She picked up the candle and saw a mouse staring at her from about three feet away. She *hated* mice, but at least it wasn't a rat. They scared her senseless.

"Shoo," she hissed, stomping her foot, which sent the mouse scurrying for the shadows.

Another ten minutes of intense alertness passed before she could settle back on the bench again.

Hunger prompted her to open the bag of nuts and dried fruit, pecans mixed with shriveled wild berries dark as bugs (but sweet). They hadn't left her water, but the roots and walls drooled constantly, and she noticed little pools on the planks. She wouldn't die from thirst down here.

She lit two more candles to spread the light, and then unwrapped the books, mostly novels, including Herman Hesse's *Siddhartha,* which seemed all too appropriate for this crew, and Ed Abbey's *The Monkey Wrench Gang.* In a wry voice she said to herself that they certainly let literature inform their lives.

She was reading the back cover of a book by Noam Chomsky when she remembered a bumper sticker on her father's old Ford Comet: *AuH2O in '64.* By the time she'd been old enough to read it, the letters and numbers had mostly faded. Her father had explained that he'd stuck it on during Barry Goldwater's presidential campaign. *Au* was the chemical symbol for gold. That's why Akiah said the helicopter hadn't come looking for her. It probably belonged to a gold-mining company.

What would a gold-mining company have to do with Terra Firma?

It was far easier to make sense of the Abolanders charging down the paths in every possible direction than to puzzle out a mining company's interest. They were diverting attention from the two men dragging a female captive away from the settlement.

With Desmond lurking behind, she reminded herself uneasily.

The Abolanders must have practiced handling moments like this endlessly to have pulled it off so smoothly. But they hadn't planned on that helicopter's arrival, clearly.

Why *would* a gold company fly in so suddenly? It was hard to picture the Abolanders welcoming them. A *mining* company? Tearing up the earth for treasure would symbolize everything they opposed.

Right?

But as she sat there listening to the *plink-plink-plink* of water dripping from the earth above her, she realized that she'd hardly begun to mine the secrets of Terra Firma.

A drop of the icy water struck the back of her neck, the bare skin between her braids.

She wiped it away, shivering again and looking up for the source of the insult. What she found herself staring at, though, was the hatch. And what she found herself thinking sent another vicious jolt of fear through her system:

Where's Desmond?

Chapter 8

Darcy hurried across the Rio deGenerate parking lot to her rusty Corolla, yanked open the dented door and cranked the ignition.

Johnny Bracer edged along the bar's brick wall, a spectral figure in the falling snow. When she began to back out of her space, he ducked into his Dodge Durango

Darcy turned on to the street and thrust a finger at deGenerate's large neon sign, a woman's pink bottom flossed by a blazing purple thong. She was never going back.

Calm down, she advised herself, *and go slow. It's slick.*

Slow was not what she wanted, but she focused her attention on the pinstriped streets all the way home, beaming when she saw the house lights burning. She needed Lotus and Kodiak, and hoped they weren't too high to hear her out.

Her roommates were lounging in front of the crackling woodstove, listening to Phish. Darcy turned down the sound, shaking her head when Kodiak offered her the pipe. The air was rank with the sweet scent, and her eyes burned. It hit her right then that this was no way to live—shitty, dog-chewed furniture; a run-down house in a drug-riddled 'hood; always scraping for rent, food, the basics. And high all the time, though she'd been backing off the bud even before her mother was abducted.

"I'm going to find my mom. I'm not waiting around for the FBI."

Lotus sat up. "What?"

"My mom wouldn't wait around for someone to find me, and I'm not going to either. I don't trust them," Darcy said as she scooted between Kodiak and Lotus on the ratty couch. "You heard that guy Alston. Did they sound like they had an agenda or what? 'Joint Task Force on Terrorism.' What's that about?"

"You know what that's about," Kodiak said.

"What's with your pack?" His backpack and a dark green duffel lay on the floor.

"I was going to talk to you about that." He pulled her close. "With the Feds coming around, I got to get away, let things settle."

"Hold on, I need you to help me." Months ago Kodiak had

alluded to having "worked" with the Animal Liberation Front. But he'd never said what that had entailed, and he'd been circumspect about much of his life before meeting her. "I need you to put me in touch with the ALF underground."

"I don't think I can do that."

"What do you mean you don't *think* you can do that? Isn't that why you're leaving, because of them?"

"All I can say is that I can't be having the Feds asking a bunch of questions about me. I'm getting out in the morning."

"With me."

"There's no way I can take you into the underground."

"But what if they know how to hook up with Terra Firma?" Darcy hated the beseeching sound of her voice.

"You really think so? Those Terra Firma people are hurting animals, skinning them, eating them—that's everything ALF hates."

"But they sure feel the same about the FBI," Darcy said. "And I've got to think they're totally down with what the Terra Firma podcasts are saying about oil and global warming."

"They don't let outsiders in, Darcy."

"I want to try."

"Think about it." Kodiak squeezed her knee gently. "The FBI's going to have their eyes on you. You could end up leading the Feds right to any ALF who help you. A bunch of them just got busted. They're going to be *real* jumpy."

"That's why I need you."

Kodiak took a deep breath but said nothing. His eyes settled back on the coals glowing in the wood stove.

The FBI wanted ALF for burning down meat-packing plants, fur farms, even a ski lodge in Vail. Darcy knew all about that stuff. But they'd kept a whole lot of animals from slaughter and never killed anyone. If they'd needed a safe house, she would have helped in a heartbeat. And then she stared at Kodiak—never a last name, "Just Kodiak" he'd told her when Lotus had introduced them—and wondered if she already had.

"What do you know about Terra Firma?" she asked him.

"Not a thing. I swear."

He wrapped his arm around Darcy's shoulder. So did Lotus. Darcy looked from one to the other.

"You're both on the run, aren't you?"

Lotus shook her head, but Kodiak avoided a direct answer by saying, "I will be now."

Lotus buried her face in her hands and began to cry so hard she shook.

Darcy pulled her close, rocking her as Kodiak leaned over and spoke softly to Lotus. "We knew this day was coming."

What's that suppose to mean? Darcy asked herself. Was this one of Lotus' "secrets?" They'd met five years ago in school, clicked right from the start, but then this kind of stuff would come up and she'd wonder if she really knew Lotus. Darcy stared at Kodiak. *And who's he?* The guy she'd been sleeping with for six months.

"I knew *you'd* be leaving, maybe," Lotus said to him, her face still in her hands. "But not both of you, not *now*." She looked up through the tears. "I can go too."

Kodiak shook his head. "We'll meet up later. Get ourselves another place when all this blows over."

"When's that going to be? Two years from now? And what do I do till then, wait around for you guys to call or text me?" She looked at Darcy. "I love you guys, and our house is splitting up. That's what happening right now. Don't you see it?"

"You go with me," Kodiak said, "and they could get you for harboring, aiding and abetting, plus whatever charges they trump up on you. You stay and you can play the innocent. You *are* innocent. Left all alone by your friends."

"They'll never buy *that*."

"They don't have to. Just buy time. A day. Two. Give me three days and I'll be so far underground they'll never find me. And they don't have anything on you, Lotus. Not a thing. *You know that*," he added in an odd voice.

"I promise I'll be in touch," Darcy said to Lotus. "I couldn't *not* be in touch." She turned to Kodiak, "You've got to help me get to the ALF. I just need that first contact."

He shook his head again. "No way."

Lotus reached across Darcy and held Kodiak's smooth face in her hands, stroking his cheeks with her thumbs. "It's her mom," she said. "You really do have to help her. After that, you can be on your own." Then whispering, though it was impossible for Darcy not to hear, she said, "It's payback time, Kody."

*

Passengers for an American Airlines flight from Chicago O'Hare to Miami crowded closer to a television screen tilted down toward the departure lounge.

A blue-suited gate attendant announced that boarding was about to begin. "Quiet!" snapped a tall man in a dark overcoat. He and the other passengers had their eyes trained on CNN, which was airing a Terra Firma podcast that did not feature Sonya Adams. Only a document stamped *Top Secret* filled the screen, though the altered voice of the woman remained the same.

"On Christmas day, Terra Firma will post this highly classified CIA report on the Web. It will be our gift to the world. But we are sorry to say that it is far more frightening than any act ever contemplated by any terrorist anywhere. 'Methane: Global Warming and Global Security' was authored by scientists with the highest security clearances in our government." The podcast showed a close-up of the title. "The report reveals that officials know that massive deposits of methane that had been frozen in the seabed of the Arctic Ocean for millions of years are releasing into the atmosphere in amounts far greater than has ever been recorded—or revealed—publicly."

"Oh, my God," a woman said.

"Methane," the altered voice on the podcast continued, "traps heat at more than twenty times the rate of carbon dioxide. For eons the frozen seabed, like the permafrost on land, has sealed billions of tons of methane under the Arctic Ocean. The methane was stabilized by cold temperatures and the pressure of the water above it. But temperatures have increased dangerously in the Arctic, and the methane is now releasing from the seabed over thousands of square miles in what scientists are calling 'methane chimneys.'

"Huge releases of methane in the past have been linked by renowned scientists to the hothouse conditions that gave rise to dinosaurs.

"We will give the government till Christmas, just ten days, to publish this report first and explain why it has hidden these terrifying developments from the world's people. We say to the government: break your ties to Big Oil, Big Coal, and big money."

"Dinosaurs?" A young man with an iPod pulled out an earbud. "Did she say 'dinosaurs?'"

*

The next morning Lotus drove Kodiak's beat-up blue Nissan pickup to a used car lot and sold it. On her next trip she unloaded the Corolla for four-hundred dollars, using the proceeds from both sales to buy a battered Suzuki that was about the size of an old combat jeep, though not nearly as rugged.

Lotus then drove to Denver's tiny Muslim district and bought a black *abaya*.

About the time Lotus left with the Corolla, Darcy darted past the garage and hurried down the ally behind her house until she came to a main thoroughfare, waiting until she spotted a city bus rumbling along.

For the next hour and a half she transferred randomly, eyes always behind her, before rendezvousing with Lotus in the restroom of the downtown Denny's. That's where she changed and that's how she slipped out of the city—as a devout Muslim on a Greyhound bus. If anyone had looked at her closely, they would have noticed the tiny specks where rings and studs once threaded her skin; but people avoided her. And the *abaya* was so far removed from her known style that she thought she could have walked right into The Chatwin Agency without being recognized immediately.

Kodiak had said they should meet up at the bus terminal in Salt Lake City at three on Monday afternoon. Not one word about where they'd go from there.

The trip included stops in almost every tiny town along the way, where she spotted newspaper boxes with headlines screaming "Dinosaurs!" also "Killer Methane," and "Terra Firma Claims Doomsday Scenario."

Now that the group was getting people really riled up, maybe they'd release her mom. *You've made your point, let her go.* But they probably wouldn't give up their big attention grabber until the report got posted on the Web. But why was Terra Firma waiting around? Darcy wondered. They could have posted it right away. Maybe they really were just a bunch of drama queens trying to squeeze her mother's kidnapping for every last drop of publicity.

New towns brought new passengers, many of whom threw her startled looks; but no one sat next to her, even when the bus grew crowded. Their reactions reminded her of a book she'd read in high school, *Black Like Me.* A white writer had dyed his skin and traveled the South "passing" as a black man to learn first-hand about racism. She glimpsed his descriptions of bigotry in the distasteful glances that greeted her, and heard it from two burr-headed Marines in dress uniform who laughed loudly about the "raghead."

Repulsive, but their reaction also reassured her that her disguise was working.

She also heard people talking about a "new dinosaur age," mostly parroting what they'd obviously heard on the podcast, or on much of the media coverage.

After sleeping fitfully, she returned to a global warming book that she'd enclosed inside the cover of a Koran, turning immediately to the pages devoted to methane. She read that paleontologists were now beginning to think that methane may have been responsible for the biggest extinction of life in the planet's history. Two-hundred forty-five million years ago, nine out of ten species became extinct. That's when the earth's atmosphere, heated by carbon dioxide released by huge volcanoes, triggered the discharge of massive amounts of methane from the ocean floor and tundra. The methane quickly raised the already warm temperatures, paving the way for "the dominance of the dinosaurs," in the words of the author, Tim Flannery, a distinguished Australian scientist. He also wrote that the release of so much methane from the seabed could lead to tsunamis.

Jesus freakin' Christ. Darcy looked at the arid canyon country of eastern Utah, wondering what could possibly be in the CIA report to top those dire outcomes.

She finally arrived in Salt Lake City in mid-afternoon on the second day. Not one for the tourist brochures. Gray with drizzle, though barely above freezing. The mountains that towered in the distance were hidden by clouds thick as woolens.

She wheeled her suitcase down the street, surprised by the lack of reaction in Mormonism's sacred city. But as she searched for the Motel 6 she'd seen listed on the bus station bulletin board, she heard snatches of foreign languages and figured the church's missionary zeal brought lots of unusual sights to the city. A Muslim woman? No big deal. A convert in all but the clothes. And the modesty would become her here.

After checking in she hit the TV remote to catch up on the coverage, and was so stunned that she had to sit down on the bed.

Terror at Terra Firma was still CNN's headline, but right

below it her own face stared back; they'd lifted the photograph from her driver's license. With her facial hardware she looked very different from the reflection she glimpsed in the motel room mirror, but definitely identifiable. All her caution had been warranted from the second she slipped out of her house to the pressing moments when she'd pulled on the *abaya*, which she'd kept low on her forehead, and a scarf, always high on her chin.

The female anchor announced that assault charges had been filed against her "for what federal agents are calling a 'vicious attack' on an employee of the Denver modeling agency where her mother worked."

Then Special Agent Roy Alston popped up saying she was also wanted as a material witness in the abduction of her mother. The implication was clear: She was still viewed as a major suspect in the kidnapping. Her disappearance had only ratcheted up the Feds' suspicions.

The anchor returned with news that a federal grand jury had been impaneled in Denver, which left Darcy holding herself.

She watched Agent Jen Suskin escort Lotus past a throng of TV crews. Her roommate smiled at the cameras flashing in her face and gave no appearance of being intimidated.

As Suskin steered her into the Denver Federal Building, Darcy realized she'd be missing Lotus for a long time. Her stomach felt hollow as a husk.

The anchor introduced a feisty looking correspondent with a globe of carefully sprayed hair. He stood in front of the courthouse reporting that after a brief appearance before the grand jury, Sharon Krantz, "aka *Lotus Land*," he added with emphasis, had been jailed for refusing to answer their questions.

Darcy wanted to hug Lotus right then, and thought it was amazing in the most wonderful way how a friend can become a hero in an instant.

CNN wasted no time in putting up the latest podcast, grainy like the others but not nearly as grim. Her mother's smile, more familiar to Darcy and far more practiced than her own, beamed from the TV as wholesomely as it had from hundreds of ads. Darcy thought she could have been selling toothpaste again for all the white she was flashing.

What is she selling now? Darcy wondered. There were times in her teens when she'd loathed that smile. She'd be upset and yelling, and her mom would switch it on like a flashlight, which would only enrage her more. Now it just looked phony.

"I'm getting along better now. The people here are treating me okay."

"No *way*," Darcy said, reading the obvious lie.

But doesn't that tell you something? she suddenly realized.

CNN took the podcast right off the air, leaving her daughter to assume that there were no "colorful" outbursts this time, no sarcastic cracks about salad-dressing skin cream.

But the network might also have been eager to show the President hurrying across the tarmac to Air Force One, pausing only long enough to deny the existence of any "top secret CIA report," and to say that it was clear that Sonya Adams was in "extreme danger," and that, "These homegrown terrorists are playing into the hands of those who would destroy this country."

"Despite the President's denial—" the anchor was back on screen—"a record number of Freedom of Information Act requests have been filed since Terra Firma announced that it had the CIA report." Video of a mob pressing against a counter appeared. "News organizations from around the world went shoulder to shoulder with environmental groups today to try to put in their requests first."

The *President's* talking about it? That's what dumbfounded Darcy. What the hell were the Terra Firmans saying now?

The same message they'd been repeating for days: "A damning indictment of what they call 'government inaction on climate chaos and its threat to all animal species,' which they blame on the 'trillion dollar influence of Big Oil and Big Coal,'" according to the anchor, who said the "terrorists" were now ending each podcast warning followers not to try to find them, urging them instead to build their own settlements.

"Today they began to issue guidelines on how to set up communities appropriate to their 'tribe.'" The studio anchor arched her eyebrows.

Guidelines?

Darcy pulled out her laptop for the first time in twenty-four hours and linked to the podcast. She watched her mother smiling, exuding all that good cheer, for no more than thirty seconds before scrolling ahead to the guidelines and scanning them quickly: "Fertile soil untainted by pesticides and herbicides; clean air," Darcy read aloud. "Pure water uncontaminated by pharmaceutical residues; abundant wildlife; a remote location; tribes people skilled in engineering, construction, hunting, farming . . ." The list went on.

Darcy turned back to the television when CNN showed demonstrators outside the White House demanding the release of the CIA report.

"Anybody who's been following this has known for months that scientists have been reporting that methane's literally bubbling up from the bottom of the Arctic Ocean and arctic lakes," a long-haired man in a cable knit sweater said, "so it's not hard to believe that there's even more dangerous news in that CIA report."

"Only yards away," the anchor said over video of furious-looking men in suits and ties, "counter demonstrators had to be held back by police." The men were shaking their fists and screaming "Death to terrorists, death to terrorists."

*

The next day at exactly quarter to three she started back to the bus station in her *abaya*, arriving only moments before Kodiak drove up in the Suzuki.

She dropped her suitcase in the back and looked around as casually as she could; but there was no telling if anyone was watching, not from that glance. As she opened the passenger door, two shiny Chevrolet Suburbans filled with kids passed. "Mormon assault vehicles," Lotus had once joked.

When she climbed in and looked at Kodiak she blurted, "You didn't!"

His beautiful blond hair. Cut off, leaving him with a strange resemblance to Special Agent Roy Alston.

Otherwise not a word passed between them; the nervousness in the Suzuki was enough to spark a pipeline.

*

Johnny Bracer had never lost sight of Darcy from the time she'd ducked out of the back of her house to the moment she left Denny's in one of those weird Muslim dresses, or whatever it was.

Johnny had to give her an "A" for the outfit. He'd chased down all kinds of scum, and every last one of them had thought they could get away by blending in. But sometimes you had to stand out, become such a sight that you were automatically dismissed by the "eyes" that wanted your ass the most.

That's how the Bureau had missed her. He'd bet a box of hollow points on that one. He didn't much care for the Feds, but he had to keep his in's with them. With all the Homeland Security changes in the past decade, his federal contacts had been bounced around more than bumper cars, but a few of them had survived. Guys who knew how to dance the bureaucratic two-step. Guys who knew you needed all kinds of help to get ahead, get your man. Or woman. Guys willing to keep Johnny Bracer buried deep in the Bureau's shadow budget, to give a call when they really needed help.

A day after the first podcast, one of his longest-standing contacts had told him about the reward for the "safe return" of Sonya Adams. A measly one-hundred k. Who were they kidding? With all the media she was bringing to Terra Firma, she ought to be worth a ton more. Wasn't the price on bin Laden's bean twenty-five mil, "Dead or alive?" They could sure pay an even mil for Adams. Thanks to her, those hippies were getting tens of millions of dollars' worth of free advertising, and the way he saw it, all of it was coming at the expense of the oil and coal companies. Someday—and he figured it was coming soon—Terra Firma could be costing certain people so much money that bin Laden and his boys might end up looking like pikers.

The crazies were already taking to the streets in D.C., New York, and San Francisco, demanding the release of the CIA report. *If it exists.* Johnny kind of thought it did. Right from the start he'd suspected that those hippies had something else in store. His feelings about the report had been bolstered this morning when his contact had called to say that the ante had been raised to $500,000. "A contribution from an anonymous donor. They want them found fast." Not that the donor could be truly anonymous. That's just how it would get pitched to the public, gullible as greed. Get their eyeballs in overdrive . . . for all the good it would do. You have to be practiced in the art of detection. He guessed the Bureau was already spreading the word to their informants in the radical environmental groups, if they had any left.

As for the reward money, it didn't take a genius to figure out where it was coming from—the Exxons of the world. They were making fifteen-hundred-dollars a *second.* Forty billion in the last year of earnings. More than most countries. He'd just heard about that on the drive up here. The Terra Firman loonies were trying to pin this methane rap on them, and from what Johnny had seen, Big Oil would do anything to make them go away.

Happy to oblige, he thought. As a contract player with the Bureau, he could take certain liberties when he questioned suspects, a privilege denied—at least on paper—to the agents themselves. Not that they didn't share in the fruits of his labors.

Johnny intended to deliver. He'd follow Darcy Adams to her mother, or come up with another way to find the model. And then he'd bring in the Bureau like he always did, but only after his own stake was secure. Initiative and enterprise have to be rewarded, and the reason he knew right from the get-go that darlin' Darcy was headed to the bus station in Salt Lake City was that he'd set up a laser eavesdropping device in her crappy garage and aimed it at a window on the side of her house. He'd heard everything, her destination, plans, even her long good-bye with her roommates.

And there was nothing better than being in the know.

*

"How far do we have to go?" Darcy had first noticed snow in the mountains just east of the Idaho border. About a foot of it now rose on both sides of the road. A scattering of flakes had been falling for the past half hour.

"All the way to the Sawtooths, north of Sun Valley."

"Oh, the rich and the famous."

"Yeah, well, we're heading to the not-so-rich and the infamous living off the grid."

"Is it someone with ALF?"

"It's a safe house network," Kodiak explained. "Some of them are Animal Liberation, and some are supporters. They help out when the Feds come knocking. They've been doing it for a long time and they're good at moving people around."

"How well do you know them?"

"I know just enough to get us in the network. After that, we'll just have to see what happens."

"Are these people . . . dangerous? They're wanted, right?"

"Not as dangerous as the ones you're running from."

Darcy gazed at the frozen world rushing by, no more comforted by Kodiak's words than she was by the car's tiny heater. She pulled out a bag of raw almonds. "Want some?"

"Sure." He offered his first smile since picking her up.

"You're tense, aren't you?" Darcy said.

"I guess I am. The Feds got lucky and made that big bust a few months ago that I told you about. They nailed all these people I used to know, and they're going after them with the terrorism laws. They're trying to put an old buddy of mine away for life on arson charges."

"For life? Did anybody die?"

"Nope, just property damage. And he saved a bunch of animals from dying."

"You think any of them will talk?"

"Some of them already are. The government threatens to put you in some gang-infested prison and starts telling you how the Black Gangster Disciples will punk your ass out and you'll be turning tricks for them twenty-four-seven, that's enough to scare a lot of people."

"Does the ALF know where you've been?"

"Nope. I've had zero contact with them."

"Are they going to want to see you?"

He glanced at her. "My contact will."

"A woman, right?"

Kodiak smiled, more easily this time, and she had her answer.

She wasn't jealous. It hadn't been that kind of relationship, and she'd known that within a few weeks of getting together with him.

"A temp in the office of love." That's what Lotus had called him after Darcy had confessed that she didn't see them making it in the long run.

Later, she'd wondered if Lotus had primed that line because she'd known enough of his hidden history to predict his romantic future. Those secrets again, whatever they were.

No matter who he was, or what he'd done in the underground, Darcy would miss him. *And who knows*, she thought, *maybe now that we're about to part, he'll give up his past.*

As they drove farther into Idaho, the sky darkened and snowflakes began to fall in great white sheets. At first they splattered the windshield and melted right away; but within twenty minutes of driving higher into the mountains the flakes grew firmer, and the flimsy wipers barely kept them from smothering their view.

The center line disappeared, and Kodiak had to keep his speed down around thirty-five.

"I'm telling you, it doesn't work," he said as Darcy reached for the radio. She tried it again anyway, desperate for an update. Same old static. The defroster was little better, sputtering a stream of tepid air that barely kept the windshield clear.

The snow thickened, forcing Kodiak to slow down even more. "At this rate, we're going to be driving all night."

"You want me to spell you?"

"No. But I'll take some of your ginseng."

Around two in the morning he still had to pull into a Husky truck stop for tea. A couple of hours later he turned into another one.

"Twenty minutes and I'll be fine." He bunched up a sweater for a pillow and closed his eyes.

The engine idled till it ran out of gas. They awoke at twenty after six almost frozen. Darcy wanted to go into the Husky to warm up, use the bathroom.

"No way. I'll get a gas can and get us going. We'll warm up that way."

A weak promise with that two-bit heater, but Darcy knew he was right. Ten minutes later they were on the road. He found a rest stop just before they came to the highway to Sun Valley. It might have been an anomaly or it might have been global warming, but after the near blizzard they'd faced during the night, there was surprisingly little snow as they headed toward the famous ski resort. Barely any at all atop Bald Mountain, which had squiggly white lines running down its face where the snow-making machines had whipped up carefully directed storms.

The Suzuki looked like a gnat among the armada of SUVs sailing past them. She spotted a shiny black Hummer with a BIGNTUFF vanity plate, and wanted to key it. She'd done it before. They were raping the planet, and every time they pulled up to a pump they raped it again. She wished she could shout to the whole country, "Slash their tires, smash their windshields. Scratch 'rapist' in their doors." Some jerk pays eighty grand for a car that makes the planet choke, he deserves it.

She told Kodiak what she'd been thinking. He surprised her by shaking his head.

"What do you expect people to drive? The government's been

handing out all kinds of tax breaks for buying and making them."

"I expect people to be less oblivious," Darcy said.

"Then you're expecting too much. Times are tight. I'll bet a lot of people would love to get rid of their gas hogs, but they can't afford to. They're barely getting by."

"Then give them tax breaks so they can get something smaller."

"Now you're talking." Kodiak gently squeezed her leg.

Darcy liked his touch and knew she'd miss it, but the sweet distraction didn't last long. "I think times are going to have to get a lot harder before people change."

"No, that won't do it. The harder it gets, the more people will buy simple answers. It's going to take a revolution."

"That scares me. The other side has all the money and guns."

"Money?" Kodiak laughed. "It's *our* money that's keeping *them* alive. Those banks made hundreds of billions off bogus investments, and now 'we the people' get to bail them out. It's socialism but they're too scared to say it. As for guns, they're not doing them much good these days, are they? They're losing everywhere they use them. I actually think what the people are doing at Terra Firma's a great idea."

As she swung around in her seat, mouth open in shock, he said, "Hold on. I know it's your mom, but look at the publicity they're getting. It's like they're birthing the post-petroleum world every minute of the day. The genie's out of the bottle."

"Yeah? And how much credibility do *they* have? They sound like a bunch of whackos, and you know it. They *are* a bunch of whackos."

"In an insane world, the sanest things sometime seem crazy. Everyone thought John Brown was insane at Harper's Ferry, but it was the country that was insane for allowing slavery. And these people at Terra Firma aren't blowing up the World Trade Center. They're using one woman—" he lifted his hand—"I know, I know, they kidnapped her—to bring a crucial message to the world, and they've become such a threat that the President's starting to go after them."

"Jesus, Kody, they're holding her against her will. Shit really happens when they've got you like that. We don't know what's really going on there. They're only showing us what they want us to see." Tears streamed down her face.

Kodiak pulled her close. "They're not hurting her. You know your mom, and you'd see it if they were. Why are you crying?"

She yanked away from him and leaned against the door, staring at the cafes and ski shops along the length of Ketchum's Dodge City façade, the smiling faces milling in the sun. Little kids in puffy snow suits and teenagers horsing around, like she'd done long ago, before she'd grown up so fast that for years she'd forgotten that she'd ever been a child. A world away from Keith the cop.

Darcy couldn't look at Kodiak when she started speaking again because he was right, her pain wasn't just about her mom; and soaking up this sparkling world, even though she didn't believe in their shiny cars and fur coats and constant consumption, made it easier to dredge up the dirt, like the gloss and glamour of this skin-deep culture could let her take all the ache she'd ever known and dump it on one of these shrewdly designed ski runs so she could watch it slide away.

"I need to tell you what happened to me when I was fifteen," she began.

She didn't pause until she'd described how Keith had shown up at her father's apartment and kissed her. That's where the story always died, choked to death by her throat's miserable muscle memory.

"There's more, isn't there?" Kodiak rested his hand on her leg again.

"Oh, Kody . . . " The goddamn tears. *When the fuck do they stop? When does all this goddamn fucking pain go away? Shit.*

Kodiak swung into a parking space and turned to her, taking both her hands in his. They were warm and felt so good, like they could melt the icy blades inside her.

"After we kissed I figured he'd go, 'Oops, big mistake. We shouldn't have done that.'" Her voice rose and she laughed shrilly, as she sometimes did when she tried not to cry. "The way, you know, kids kind of expect adults to set the limits. But he didn't. He said let's go for a ride. I told him no, but he grabbed me and kissed me again. This time I tried to stop him and he punched me in the stomach. It wasn't a hard punch but he got me right where it really hurts. Then he said his car was in the parking lot and he was taking me to it, that I'd better not try anything. Anything? I was too fucking freaked out to try anything. He got me in the car and told me not to move a muscle.

"My stomach still hurt and at the same time I felt completely empty inside, like the worst stuff was about to fill it. He drove all the way out to the desert, where he had his stupid little A-frame cabin. There was nothing else around. He pushed me into his bedroom and told me to take off my clothes. I told him no, and he shook his head and walked up to me and I screamed, 'I'll do it.' I knew he was going to punch me again and I didn't want him to. But what I wanted didn't matter. He started hitting me once I was down to my underwear, shouting, 'Take it off.' He was hitting me the whole time, sometimes slapping me and sometimes with his fist, but never as hard as he could have. It was like there was always that thing that it could get a lot worse. And it did. That's when the rapes started."

She burrowed her face into his shoulder. Kodiak held her tightly. Her whole body shook. Neither of them spoke. People walked by; some of them glanced at the young couple in the tiny old SUV and looked away as quickly. Grief had no place here.

She didn't lift her head when she spoke again. "He kept me locked up for five days. I heard him call my father, say we were out at his cabin having a 'good time,' and my fucking father never came." She sat up. "This goddamn cop's raping me and my father never comes. I was bleeding. I'd even started coughing up blood."

"Five days?"

"Five *fucking* days. And then he just drove me back. Like nothing happened. He dropped me off and my father says, 'How was it? You have a good time with Keith?' *I'm fifteen years old.*"

"What did you tell him?"

"I told him he'd raped me, and my father says, 'Rape?' And I'm thinking, *Finally, he gets it,* and he says, 'That's a strong word. You sure you want to say that?'

"I grabbed the phone and called 911, and he grabbed it right out of my hand and said Keith was a cop. Was I crazy? They'd never believe me. I said they'd believe me plenty when they looked, and he goes, 'Nobody's looking. What's done is done.' And you know what? He was sure right. What was done *was* done. I went home in pieces. My mother wasn't even there when I got back. She was off on some ad for Pendleton Mills. The only reason I remember was she came rushing in the door the next day saying I just had to see

these great pictures from the shoot. No, 'How are you? How was
L.A.?' Just pulling out a bunch of Polaroids, like I'd actually want to
see pictures of her standing around with a bunch of stupid phony
Indian blankets. I looked at her and started screaming, and I couldn't
stop for a long, long time."

Kodiak wiped away her tears as a meter maid slapped a ticket
on the windshield. They both froze, but the woman mouthed, "I'm
sorry," and moved on.

"I hated my mom, and you know why? Because she was
around. She was an easy target. And she wasn't perfect, that's for
sure, and that made it easier to put all the blame on her too. I didn't
start understanding any of this till a few months ago." Darcy looked
out the window. "At least she tried. My father didn't do shit." She
turned back to Kodiak. "We'd better get out of here."

He opened the door, grabbed the ticket and tossed it on the back
seat.

In moments they were passing hundreds of millions of dollars'
worth of private jets—Lears and Gulfstreams as common as
Beemers and Hummers on the other side of the airport's tall cyclone
fence.

"Doesn't Demi Moore live here?" Darcy said, trying to change
the subject as if she hadn't just confessed intimate details of a week
that had changed her life forever.

"That was when she was with Bruce Willis. I don't know
anymore."

"What I want to know is how do we know all this celebrity shit
but we don't know the important stuff?"

"We know it because it's everywhere. When everyone knows
your mom's name, then we'll be making progress."

"The weird thing," Darcy said as they began to leave Ketchum
and Bald Mountain behind, "is that all of this is incredibly beautiful
as long as you don't realize that it's part of a really bad dream."

"That's what they're saying at Terra Firma. They're not some
fucked-up cop. They're not raping your mom, and I think you know
it. They're making everyone look at how the world's getting raped."

"But if you're right about Terra Firma, and I'm not saying you
are, but *if* you are, why do you want to help me find them? Because
I'm going to get her out. I want to make all this crazy shit stop."

He took her hand as he drove. "Because she's your mom and

you're really worried. And because I think if you do find her and you can get her out of there, you won't burn them. And I'm really worried about what'll happen if the FBI finds them first. I can't believe they're not going to find them soon and . . . "

He stopped talking so suddenly that she swung sideways in her seat again to get a better look at him.

"What? Say it. Find them soon and what? What are you worried about?"

"Waco."

The same fear had gripped her too, but she'd refused to give it any air, frightened that even talking about it would make it real. What had she been, seven, eight years old, sitting in front of the TV when the "rescue" went all wrong? Like maybe it was never suppose to go right in the first place. All those "abused" kids the FBI rescued by burning them to death. Haunting, that's what those pictures were.

"I've been thinking about that too," she said, "and even if the people at Terra Firma are a bunch of whackos, they could easily be a much bigger threat to the government than the Branch Davidians ever were."

"Could be? Try definitely. That's why the government keeps pumping up the threat to your mother, so they can go storming in there when they find them and destroy everything. And if that methane report is real, and I'll bet it is, it's going to get really bad. But that doesn't mean *you* need to buy their bullshit about your mom being hurt or her being in danger."

"I hope you're right."

"I'm not saying I know them, but I know people like them. They're not threatening her. This isn't the SLA, and your mom isn't Patty Hearst. You even agree with most of what they're saying, except the meat part."

"That's a big part, Kody."

"Okay, it is for me too, but the most important part is the oil. We can fight over the scraps *after* we make sure the planet's got a future. Without that, we're all toast. Literally."

"Would your friends in the ALF agree?"

"Probably not."

"So I actually found a moderate bone in your body?"

"Never." He laughed.

They drove into Stanley, a mountain town where it looked like almost every home had been built out of Lincoln Logs, and headed northwest till they arrived at a turnoff for Payton, about fifteen miles away.

Less than halfway there Kodiak put the Suzuki in four-wheel drive and turned onto a narrow ridge road. Within minutes Darcy saw steep cliffs spilling away from both sides of the car, and she wondered what they'd do if they met oncoming traffic. It was like driving on a towering, single lane bridge without guard rails. She kept her eyes pinned straight ahead, too fearful to look into the void looming left and right.

The tight, terrifying passage ended at a broad, snow-covered expanse where a mile of poorly plowed road led to a rutted driveway.

Kodiak eased the Suzuki over snow humps big as tires until they pulled up to a board and batten house that faced south toward a winter stilled meadow. Tall, undraped windows rose from the floor to the ceiling. Large rectangular solar panels rested on the roof. A snow-crusted tractor sat in the side yard, a plow attached to the back. A rusty Toyota truck slouched nearby.

As they climbed out, a Great Pyrenees dog, white as the snow and larger than most drifts, bellowed and bounded straight toward them.

Darcy backed up, looked around frantically, and caught the face of a woman in the window. *Do something,* she thought as the dog pulled up about ten feet shy of them, its tail oddly swishing the powder while it continued to bark. A second later the woman threw open the door and faced them down the barrel of a rifle.

"Je-sus," Darcy stammered. "What the hell is this, Kodiak?"

But he wasn't looking at her. He had his hands out to the dog, "Easy boy, easy," and his eyes on the woman.

She peered at him closely down that barrel, then lowered it no more than an inch and said, "Wendell?"

Wendell?

*

Johnny Bracer took a pass on the driveway. Way too soon for up-close and personal. He'd been tailing them all goddamn day, and this last stretch had been a pain in the ass. He'd had to stop a whole bunch of times and wait for them to move on. You show up in some guy's rear view out here, he's going to notice.

So it had been stay back, *way* back, and creep along in the Durango.

When they'd started down the driveway, he'd spotted a gray stream of smoke coming up from behind some trees. Got to be a house hiding back there, but this far out in the boonies it's going to be off the grid. And if it's off the grid, there's no telling what you're going to be walking in on. Johnny didn't like surprises.

Soon as that little jeep turned out of view, he drove on. He had no idea where this frozen road would take him, except for past here, and for now that would do just fine. But he figured it was a sure bet that he'd end up having to pull out his topo maps and GPS and do some bushwhacking. Set up some surveillance and see what darlin' Darcy's up to with these folks.

You get your answers in all kinds of ways in this business, he thought. Sometimes you get them fast, and sometimes it's slow. Sometimes they're all Yes, and sometimes they actually try to say, No. But when it came to negativity, Johnny Bracer had his ways. That's why the Bureau loved him. He'd never take No for an answer. Didn't have to, because he knew how to use the toughest tools of his trade.

Chapter 9

Sonya lay in the freezing near-darkness, wrapped in her bearskin coat and the fur blanket. A half hour, maybe an hour had passed since Akiah and Calypso had closed the hatch and locked her in the hole. Without her watch, it was hard to tell. Time enough that she'd begun to worry about how long she could endure the frigid temperature. And plenty of time to worry about that creep, Desmond, sneaking here to visit her alone.

The mouse—*thank God*—hadn't reappeared. She told herself that it had probably scampered back to its nest; and then she did her utmost to put aside thoughts of the snakes that prey upon them, not an easy task with all those pale roots spiraling down from the dirt ceiling.

She'd tried reading the Noam Chomsky book, mostly to appease Darcy, imagining how she'd tell her that she had read him while stuck in this burrow. But she'd had to put it aside after a few pages. Much too dense and depressing for these circumstances, although it prompted her to wonder how she, of all people, had ended up raising a daughter who cared so much about issues, politics, social conditions—whatever you want to call it.

Years ago she'd given up even trying to make sense of all the craziness in the world, though as she looked around she couldn't avoid asking herself if a little more knowledge might explain how people could be so driven by a single idea that they'd lock her in a hole in the ground. She found some immediate solace in poetry, which she'd first taken seriously as a lit major, murmuring two of Yeats' most well-known lines from *The Second Coming*: "The best lack all conviction, while the worst/Are full of passionate intensity."

"Or the worst throw you down here," she continued aloud, her eyes quickly surveilling her cell.

The pit reminded her of the spider hole where they'd found that tyrant, Saddam Hussein, although she should be so fortunate as to see her hatch opened by the U.S. armed forces.

I've got to get out of here.

And by "here" she meant not only the hole, but all of Terra Firma.

Though loathe to expose herself to the cold, she knew she had to climb the ladder on the off-chance that the hatch would open. It would be a bitter realization, indeed, to find out later that she could have climbed right out of here for a quick flight to freedom.

But you heard the locks.

Doesn't matter, you still try the door that locks you in, she scolded herself. People make mistakes, fail to throw a latch. You don't sit around like a lump waiting for a miracle.

She shed the blanket and looked around. The candle on the cabinet flickered, stilled, and flickered again. When she stood, she had to dodge one of the low-hanging roots. They made her shiver, as if they were real snakes; and she glanced around to make sure that a rattler hadn't slithered into the hole.

More flickering from the candle on the cabinet. Every little movement set this place astir, as if the walls were twitchy with exposed nerves.

She gripped the ladder, feeling the chilly dampness on her bare hands. Three steps were all she needed to reach the hatch. No handles from this side, just thick heavy boards that had been hammered together.

She placed the flat of her hand up against them and pushed to no avail. Pounding yielded nothing, either.

As she stepped back down, she saw the cabinet candle flicker faster than before. She glanced at the one on the bench expecting to see its flame dancing as well, but its wick burned straight as a candle in a Georges de la Tour painting.

Air's coming from somewhere.

She moved over to the cabinet, placing her hand, still moist from the damp ladder, around the candle. That's when she felt a slight stream of air, and swiftly traced its path to a half inch gap separating the cabinet from the dirt wall. Leaning her face close to the opening, she heard a soft soughing, as if issuing from a distant world.

Without pause, she pulled the cabinet forward, scraping the legs loudly on the rough planks. Then she plucked the cabinet candle from its waxy base and reached over the top, shocked to find a two foot square of plywood set into the wall.

Still bending forward, she moved the candle along the top edge of the board, watching the flame flicker from one end to the other.

With her free hand, she tested the wood to see if it would budge. It wouldn't. She pulled a little harder, then stopped and asked herself the obvious question: Why open it? She'd been so fearful that this dank hole wasn't secure and that a snake or some other awful creature would slide in, and now she was trying to open it herself? What if a snake were back there? Or hundreds hibernating in one of their hideous nests?

But if she could work the board loose she might find a way out of this prison. Maybe it would lead her up to the cave she'd seen by the hatch entrance. *There must be a reason they're hiding this thing.* She might reach the very people who could fly her away from Terra Firma and the crazies who'd locked her in this hellhole (never had the term seemed more appropriate).

If you wait around much longer, it's not going to matter, she told herself. *They'll be back.* A moment later she set the candle back on the cabinet and worked her way around the corners with the idea of really trying to pull the plywood loose. If it proved as unyielding as the hatch, then the decision would be made for her. If it did come loose, she could peek at what it covered up and, if threatening, jam it back in place.

She dug her fingers between the moist earth and the upper edge of the wood, and pulled. It didn't give. She forced herself to try again, this time by digging her fingertips in a little farther until they poked through the damp earth to an opening, gasping the instant she felt them dangling in the dark world on the other side of the board, like bait waiting for the bite.

In a sudden panic, she yanked as hard as she could, as much to get her fingers out of there as to make an honest attempt to get *all* of herself out of *here*.

The top of the plywood snapped off, sending decayed chunks flying to the floor and leaving a five-inch opening between its rotten remains and the earth into which it had been set.

"Oh, shit."

Here she'd been worried about a creature getting into her cell, and now she'd as much as rolled out a carpet for it, or *them*.

She grabbed the candle and held it fearfully to the dark opening. The light still flickered, this time mostly from her shaky hand. It lit up an area extending no more than a few feet into what appeared to be a tunnel roughly the same shape and size as the plywood cover.

As she stood there staring into the blackness, rigid with the cold and the worst fears of what might lie within, she realized that the soughing she'd heard moments ago now sounded far more formidable, as if deep in the tunnel a giant beast were breathing, making the candle in her frozen hand flicker, throwing shadows across her tense face as it lit up her fears.

A bear's den.

Did you just break into a bear's den? Seconds passed before she recognized that of all her fears this morning, this one reigned as the most improbable. But she'd learned long ago that fears rarely have triple-digit IQs.

She studied the broken opening, confronted by the very real decision of whether to soldier on or to push the cabinet back against the wall, hiding the damage and closing up the tunnel, or whatever it was, as best she could.

But as she stared into the darkness, she thought of the caged bird whose door is suddenly opened. As the fable has it, the bird's enslavement is so complete that it never flies away.

In two quick efforts she tore off the rest of the plywood cover.

Crouching, wiping her hands on her bearskin coat, she reached into the tunnel with the candle, lighting the darkness only to discover an even deeper blackness several feet away. She also heard the soughing more clearly now. It sounded neither of man nor beast, and grew more chilling for its mystery.

She lit a fresh candle and left the one she'd been holding burning on the cabinet in a cooling circle of wax. To save it for later, she blew out the one on the bench. Then she thought to stuff a spare and the matches into her buckskin top where she could reach them if the one in her hand failed. Or burned out? Could she possibly bring herself to stay in there that long? Would she have to?

Forcing aside these uncomfortable questions, she began to crawl into the tunnel, moving only far enough to light up the deeper blackness she'd spied from the opening. Her feet were still hanging outside by the cabinet.

The tunnel appeared unchanged up ahead. Only a root violated its absolute emptiness, a slender length as pale and hairy and snake-like as all the others.

She crawled forward on her elbows, always careful to protect the candle so she wouldn't snuff it out. It now flickered as much from her exertions as it did from the streaming air. As Sonya began to perspire, she felt the current on her face.

The root, its fine hair dripping moisture, brushed against her cheek and then slid along her bare neck, making her shudder.

But oddly, as she moved forward her fears lessened. Motion, she reasoned, was distracting, though she had no sense of whether she was crawling up or down or across a comparatively flat plane.

And then the tunnel tightened, though not sharply at first. She had to duck a number of times, but it wasn't until she was forced to turn her face to the side to slide it under a protruding rock that she had to take full note of the walls and ceiling closing in.

Carefully, she worked her way forward until she felt the pressure increasing on both sides of her face and head. Her arms still had space, though not much; the wall she faced to the left provided no more than four inches of play.

The candle burned before her eyes, and for a few seconds she found the smell of warm wax comforting. Inching the flame forward, she saw that about fifteen feet away the tunnel began to twist, as if the floor were determined to become a wall, and that the tightening continued for a few more feet before the sides and ceiling disappeared into a blind curve.

She attempted to flatten her face even more, but the bulky fur coat stopped her; and even though her ears and the sides of her head were grinding into the gritty dirt so hard they ached, she could not move another inch forward because the coat was crammed up against the rock that was poking down. She'd have to retreat and take it off if she were to pass beyond this point. But when she tried to push herself backward, she was shocked to find she was stuck; and this made her cry out, for she had the startling vision of herself trapped in the hollows of the earth. Permanently.

Calm down, she whispered to herself in the quavery light. *You got in, you'll get out.*

She pointed her toes as much as she could in her boots, and tried to drag herself backward while pushing furiously with her hands. She didn't move a millimeter, and the candle went out, leaving her in the blackest darkness she'd ever known. It took her a moment to realize that she'd dropped the damn thing, and another piercing second to understand that she couldn't relight it because she was pinned between the ceiling and floor.

To this point, she hadn't panicked fully; but fear now erupted, in her belly first, then everywhere, terror as dark as the air that enclosed her and as greedy as the earth that held her tight. For about a minute she avoided fully facing her horror by wiggling, fighting these harsh physical restraints with subtle movements, scouting for space. But then panic, real and overpowering, made her shake insanely. Screaming, then shrieking, she rocked and pushed and shoved . . . and felt the fur give. Not much, but any movement in this vise heartened her.

Grunting loudly, she pushed with her hands and clawed with the toes of her boots, scraping her chest against the rough floor. She gained an inch of retreat, then another, as the coat gathered up around her neck. The inches turned into a foot, and the coat crept up over her head, a suffocating presence. By the time she forced her way back to the entrance, even her arms were bound by the bunched-up bearskin.

She yanked herself out of the tunnel and crashed blindly into the cabinet. She tried to stand while tearing the coat off inside out, stumbled, and landed against the wall. She finally wrenched her arms and head free and tossed the coat to the floor. A powerful urge to stomp it almost overcame her, but she had trouble catching her breath and realized she was on the verge of hyperventilating from fright. Shaking horribly, she sat on the cabinet hugging herself. She didn't let go of her arms till she gained a measure of composure. Only then did she relax enough to let her hands droop to her sides, knocking over the cabinet candle and snuffing it instantly. Leaving her in darkness once again.

She jumped up and reached inside her top where she'd stuffed the spare candle and matches, but they were missing; and with a thudding sense of dread she saw how they must have worked themselves loose as she dragged herself backward.

Don't panic.

She felt her way around the cabinet and opened it up, searching by feel for more matches. She found the stash of candles but— *Goddamn it to hell* —no matches.

She swore loudly now and stomped her foot. *How could I let this happen?* Ending up in the dark had been one of her biggest fears when they'd put her down here.

You don't have a choice.

She said this to herself even before looking in the direction of the tunnel. Those matches were in there, and if she could bring herself to climb back inside she'd undoubtedly crawl right up to them.

But seeing herself crawling in the darkness made her fear everything else that squirms through the earth, from skinny worms that feast on rotting flesh to huge thick snakes with hungry, hooded eyes, all the predators that dig their dismal burrows far from the sun and hunt the unwary. That might, in fact, be inching toward her at this very moment.

Cold, shaky, scared, she wrapped herself in the fur blanket and sat on the bench. She could see nothing but blackness, and could think of nothing but the slithery animals that might be staring back at her. More of Yeats' poem came to her, but this time his words offered no comfort. She confined them to her silence for fear of letting loose their harrowing threat: *And what rough beast, its hour come round at last/Slouches towards Bethlehem to be born?*

Still shaking, she felt around for the candle on the bench and grabbed it to replace the spare she'd lost, then edged back around the cabinet, tripping on the coat. She kicked it away, finally satisfying her fury. She wasn't about to put that back on. She wanted to move quickly and fewer layers would help. To that end, she considered the buckskins. The skirt was clearly unnecessary, so she took it off right away. Then she thought about how she'd been stuck and that she might encounter more tight spots (the first suggestion, even to herself, that she hadn't given up on escape).

"You don't need them," she said aloud, pulling off her boots and pants and shirt before slipping the extra candle into the top of her long underwear.

She ran her hands over this sleeker version of herself, seeking assurance that she'd make it past the point that had snagged her.

And if you do, then what?

Then I'm going to get out of here, that's what. I've had it.

And what if you get really *stuck?*

I'm not going to get really stuck.

But the dialogue, scanty with grace or the forgiveness of fears, forced more of itself on her.

No, you really could get stuck.

So they'll find me crammed up inside the tunnel. They're not going to leave me there. I'm way too valuable to them. Better than sitting around like that bird in the cage waiting for some claws to drag me out of here. And if I can't get past that tight spot, I'll come back here with the matches and light this place up like Times Square. Then I'll wait around for them, eat some nuts and berries and start another book, maybe Siddhartha. And now that I've seen this hellhole and know what they really have in store for me, I'll get out of Terra Firmaville as fast as I can. Starting now, if I'm lucky, and that helicopter's still here.

She felt around for the opening and climbed back in, moving much more quickly this time. Only the cold felt more daunting, and she was grateful for even the thin layer of long underwear and socks.

Right at the spot where the tunnel tightened she found the matches and lost candle, vindicating her decision to go after them; but she had to retreat several feet before she had enough room to use both hands.

When the match sparked, she lit the candle and smiled for the first time since awakening to the pounding on the bedroom door, beaming almost as brightly as the burning wick before sliding the matches back into her top. Then she moved with a greater sense of assurance than she might have known had she never lost the light.

At the tight spot, she paused to size up the passage.

Maybe she shouldn't have. The candle lit up a ceiling hovering no more than six, *maybe* eight inches from the tunnel floor. Then she noticed anew that about fifteen feet past the low point the tunnel began to twist strangely, with the floor canting up to the left, reminding her that she'd have to work her way into that blind curve at an awkward angle.

First things first, she told herself, staring at the rock coming down from the ceiling right in front of her. Her stomach churned, and she had to assure herself that she'd almost cleared it with a lot more clothing.

Clutching the candle in her left hand, she turned her head sideways and forced herself forward, soon realizing that she'd overestimated the gain from shedding her coat and buckskins. Dirt and rocks scraped both sides of her head, and a sharp stone cut her right ear.

Stop.

Her heart was thumping so loudly she could hear it.

Catch your breath.

The pressure was now bearing down on her head and upper back, and she implored the heavens to open up the tunnel soon. Becoming trapped down here suddenly loomed as a very real danger, one that she could no longer dismiss as easily as she had back in the hole.

But you're not stuck.

She slid her head forward, feeling unnerving resistance from the rock. Still, by working her shoulders, hips, and arms she managed a precious few inches, farther than she'd traveled on her first attempt. In another minute she'd wiggled past the protrusion.

Quickly, she crawled to where the floor began to tilt up to the left, like the sharply slanted rails of a roller-coaster that make riders feel as if they're defeating gravity.

To move at this odd angle, she had to shift on to her right hip and claw at the wall while keeping the candle alive, an ordeal that looked like it would become much more trying when the blind curve forced her upper body to bend.

Despite this, she made quick progress here, gaining a couple of feet in less than a minute. But it was almost as if she'd been lured into moving on, because when she tried to continue her hips jammed against the same narrow spot that only moments ago had allowed for the passage of her shoulders.

She could *not* move, and the tunnel had left her in a near-fetal position. She felt like she was in a full body cast. It was a crushing sense of confinement. Utterly nightmarish.

To add frustration to horror, she could see that less than three feet away the entire tunnel widened by several inches.

Her hips felt strangled, and she had to remind herself that she'd managed to wriggle her shoulders through there without much difficulty. What frightened her more, however, came seconds later when she noticed that most of this narrow, twisting section had been carved entirely from rock, which made sense: Rock is a lot harder to remove than dirt, so whoever had dug the tunnel had taken out no more than necessary. But seeing that it was rock absolutely terrified her because if she really were stuck here, how could she ever get out? It's not like Akiah could take a pick and shovel and dig her out. That she'd even thought of him as her savior spoke volumes about her situation.

You're getting way ahead of yourself here. Slow down.

She steadied her breathing, and labored even harder not to see herself entombed down here forever. Then she forced herself to relax her muscles. While trying to keep them unflexed, she pulled on her right hip and then her left, and sensed the slightest release, although she wasn't certain at first that she'd actually moved forward. It wasn't until she'd spent long minutes keeping her muscles as calm as possible while she shifted side to side that she saw that she'd gained about two inches.

Encouraged, she continued this delicate dance, and with a surge of relief felt her hips pull away from the claws of the earth. A minute later she crawled to where the tunnel widened and appeared to level off, no longer forcing her to move along at such a peculiar angle.

But as soon as she thought about having to back out of that tight, twisting passage she realized that she'd been so focused on getting through it that she hadn't thought about the possibility that she was locking herself in the tunnel for good.

You won't have to back out. You're getting out of here.

But maybe if I do, arguing softly with herself, *I'll be able to turn around first.*

Hard as she tried, she couldn't bring herself to believe she'd ever find a place wide enough for that, not down here. It was like crawling through a coffin. She barely had enough space to drag herself forward on her elbows. It made her flinch just to imagine her body all balled-up from trying to turn around, stuck forever in some awkward position with her chin pressed to her chest and her back wedged against the ceiling and wall.

No, just go on, she told herself. *Don't even think about that stuff.*

She'd traveled about thirty feet when the air current streamed directly down on her head. It felt like the cold hard breath of earth itself. She looked up and saw a dark opening the size of a grapefruit, and though greatly alarmed by what she might find in there, or what might reach down for her, she held up the candle, revealing what looked like a tiny tunnel rising up into the earth. The current almost blew out the flame, and she had to cup it protectively.

So that's where it's coming from.

But it wasn't the source of all she was hearing. An eerie noise still emanated from deeper in the tunnel. She listened as the air current moved over her body, damp with fear despite the cold temperature.

It wasn't until she'd rounded a sharp corner a few minutes later that she recognized the sound of rushing water. It rose to her ears so fast that she feared she'd drown in the next few seconds, forcing the memory of a frightening movie in which a tunnel filled with a churning wall of water.

She gripped the moist ground, bracing herself for the flood. But it was only the *sound* of water. A lot of water.

She held the candle over the earth right in front of her, expecting to see small pools or rivulets offering evidence of much more water nearby. But she saw nothing of the sort. She did spot a strand of spittle hanging forward from her lip, almost touching her nose and forcing her to realize that she'd been crawling down into the earth, not up toward the cave. The upset of expectations was so swift it was like the time she'd taken a big tumble while skiing deep powder, and found herself having to drool in a snowdrift to tell which way was up.

She took a moment to get settled and assure herself that the tunnel could start climbing at any time. But she also cautioned herself to be careful. The thought of spilling down into the rushing water was terrifying.

But you're not even sliding, she told herself. *You're still having to work like a dog to move along, so keep going.*

As she crawled around a second, even sharper corner, the sound of the water grew to a raging bellow. She thrust the candle as far as she could, dragging herself on one raw elbow until she spotted a strange shiny surface rising up twelve feet in front of her, reflecting the candlelight so suddenly that she startled.

A fresh current of air, whipped aloft by the flow, moved across her damp face and made the candle flicker wildly.

She had come to a "T" intersection where the tunnel stopped at the loud rushing water, whose surface looked swollen and curved. *Like the side of an eel*, thought Sonya, an endless, sinuous body racing through the earth.

The furious fat stream appeared as fast and powerful as a jet fired from a water cannon, and many, many times as thick. *An underground river*, she thought. She was so taken with its strange appearance and raw power that at first it didn't occur to her that she'd come to a dead end. And she couldn't understand why it didn't burst into the tunnel and drown her

A moment later she got her answer.

She crawled forward for a better look and started to fall. She screamed and jammed the heels of her hands into the slick rock, dropping the candle and putting it out instantly; but still she slid, gaining speed, on the verge of toppling. The ground vibrated with the furious flow, and the roar of its fierce passage exploded in the plunging darkness.

Cold mist coated Sonya's face, and she sickened with the vision of herself swept like a seed into the blank bottomless bowels of the earth.

In her final frenzied panic, she reared up on her hands and knees, driving her back into the low ceiling and arresting her slide only inches from the water, though she could not see this. She could only sense the flow's imminent presence in the waves of mist now pulsing madly against her face. They felt like the cool velvet hands of death itself.

Breathing so hard she could hear only the sound of her fear, she backed up, terrified of slipping even slightly, knowing that the flow moved so fast that it need catch only a hand or a limb to claim all of her.

Another step back, and another, her head pounding with blood's angriest rhythms.

After a frantic, sixty second retreat that felt more treacherous than a cliff walk, she collapsed to her belly on safer ground, crying and hugging the dirt. Many more seconds of relief passed before she reached in her top for the spare candle and matches. She fumbled with them but struck the match on the fourth try and lit the spare, then looked down the slope and saw that the candle she'd dropped must have been carried away by the water.

This is it, she admitted to herself, *there's no way out.*

Backing up proved awkward and time-consuming, and she guessed that it took about twenty minutes to retreat to the tight, twisting passage.

Before working her way in, she checked her candle. It had burned down almost to her hand. Maybe she'd get another five minutes of light, but certainly no more. It was such a tight section, she wasn't sure she'd be able to keep it lit anyway.

She snaked her legs into the constricted space, easing them past the rock walls until she had to navigate an even narrower point that did not feel at all familiar.

Of course not, you're going backwards. Look, you got in, you'll get out.

But she didn't feel as sanguine as those thoughts would indicate, and in the next few seconds she held the disturbing view of herself as a cork bulging from a bottle.

She exerted herself much harder, felt her long underwear tearing and her skin scraping viciously against the rock. But she gained nothing.

She twisted more to the side, remembering how she'd emerged from this nightmare at an angle last time; and this did, indeed, move her inches along until she found herself in the bent over, near-fetal position from which she'd freed herself earlier. But this was also the point where she'd felt most confined, as if in a body cast with the wall mere inches from her eyes. She couldn't even see the candle any longer, which she had to hold to her side.

It felt much harder to push back through the narrowing than it had been to work her way past its numerous small, jutting obstacles. One of them still pressed its nasty edge into her thigh, and this more than anything made her realize that she'd stopped moving, that she was locked down around her hips, which seemed patently unfair: She'd always been fairly proportioned, so why the hell couldn't she get past here?

As she swallowed to try to contain her mounting fright, the candle burned down to her hand, scorching her thumb and index finger. She cried out, dropping it. Darkness descended immediately. She pressed her singed skin against the cold rock and held it there.

But even the burn, which began to blister, couldn't compete with her born-again panic.

Come on, I got in, she pleaded to herself, *I* can *get out.*

But she couldn't. Not even relaxing her muscles could move her back through this torturous passage.

Her stomach boiled with anxiety, a siege of raw, wretched terror that left her twisting violently—brief, brutal movements that bruised and bloodied her, but gained not a hint of retreat.

She began to weep loudly, and this was the first sign that a peculiar madness had set in, that the rigid shackles of earth that had claimed her body were now claiming her mind. Horrid, tumultuous sensations forced themselves upon her until all she could feel was the massive, malevolent pressure trapping her in the cold hard ground. Her eyes offered no salvation, only a blinding loss of light. Open or closed, she knew but a blank universe of compressing darkness, the grotesque horrors of the living grave.

As the madness marginalized the last of her sanity, and her thoughts careened with the wildest fears she'd ever known, the frigid dampness seeped into her core and became a cruel, kindred assault. She shivered uncontrollably.

A noise rose near her feet. In the same instant she realized a sock had slipped off in her struggles, and she felt her foot's naked vulnerability.

The sound petrified her. It did not come in kindness. Or in rescue. Not to a mind maddened by the worst the earth could offer. No, to Sonya Adams deep in this dark stranglehold, the predator had come finally to strike.

Chapter 10

"It *is* you, Wendell."

The woman rested her rifle against the house and raced toward them. She was tall, tan, and strikingly attractive, laughing joyously as she threw her arms around Kodiak, or *Wendell,* kissed him on the lips, and hugged him hard enough to lift his feet off the ground.

"It's your hair. I almost didn't recognize you." She rubbed his head. "Why'd you do it?"

"I'm on the run."

"Ah." Her eyes hardened a little under her straight black hair and brightly beaded headband. "Who's your friend?"

Kodiak introduced Darcy, and despite her moment of hesitation Poughkeepsie gave her a warm, welcoming hug. Her thin arms felt hard as vine maples, even under her bulky red sweater. Darcy thought she might be Native American.

"You too? On the run?"

Before Darcy could answer, Poughkeepsie said, "You *are.* I recognize you now. You're wanted, woman. You're *really* wanted." She noticed the *abaya.* "Muslim drag, nice getup. Tell me what's going on. No, come in first. If I'm going to get busted for helping you guys, I might as well do it right. Oh, and this is Chaska," nodding at the Great Pyrenees. "I got him right after you left."

When they entered Poughkeepsie's house, the warmth felt so good that Darcy shed her Goodwill parka and recycled boots and settled on a futon couch by an old wood stove.

Poughkeepsie poured them green tea from a kettle simmering on the cook plate, and asked if they were hungry.

"Of course you are," she said right away. "We're always hungry when we're on the run. I'm vegan. Is that okay with you?" She directed her question to Darcy.

"I am too. That would be great."

Poughkeepsie served them rice noodles with carrots, roasted beech nuts, and ginger-marinated tofu. Not raw food, but as a guest Darcy would eat anything short of meat.

When Kodiak started filling in Poughkeepsie about Darcy and her mother (and his latest *nom de guerre*), their host pointed to a closed laptop and said she'd been following the story closely, "But I never thought it would show up on my doorstep."

"Well, here we are," Kodiak said. "And she wants to go there, contact someone who could get her inside."

"You're not the only ones trying to find the Abolanders. They're going to be real skittish. I hear they've been very secretive for the last few years. When this broke, I figured it was probably because they'd been planning some kind of action for a long time."

"So do you know where they are?" Darcy said.

Poughkeepsie shook her head. "*I* don't."

"But you know someone who does," Darcy pressed.

"I know someone who *did,* who spent time with them in the late nineties, but I can't turn you on to him. They're an incredibly close-knit group, even the ones who've left."

"But maybe you could let him know who I am."

She turned from Darcy without responding and said to Kodiak, "I haven't seen you since Oregon. You've got to tell me what you've been doing, where you've been, and . . . " she glanced at Darcy, "who you've been hanging with."

Chaska scratched the door, and Darcy said she'd let him in.

"Use the rags on his feet, okay? They're right there by the kindling." Poughkeepsie pointed to a pair of old hand towels hanging above a wooden box.

The huge dog dutifully lifted each leg for the paw drying. Then he settled next to Darcy, yawning as Kodiak finished a breezy run-down of his past two years.

"So you haven't taken any actions during that time?"

"None. I've been lying real low."

"But now because of her, you're thinking they'll want to know more about you."

"I'm hoping that's all it is, and I'm hoping that by splitting I can put a stop to any real digging."

"I doubt that."

"You're probably right, but it's not like I could hang around and find out."

"Your friend, this Lotus Land, she's not going to talk?"

"I told her to give us three days, but she'll never talk. She's tougher than I am."

"Still, it doesn't make me very comfortable," Poughkeepsie

added.

"She refused to talk to a grand jury in Denver. I saw it on the news," Darcy said.

"Maybe for now," Poughkeepsie said. "But after they hold her for contempt, she might change her mind."

"It doesn't matter," Kodiak said. "At this point, she has no idea where we are."

"But she knows we're off trying to find Terra Firma," Darcy said, suddenly and strangely panicked.

Kodiak must have sensed this because he turned to her and took her hands. "Lotus loves you. She told me the first time she met you she knew you guys would be friends forever. Look, you two," his eyes moved to Poughkeepsie, "she was born in the underground. Okay? Her parents have been on the run since 1973. A midwife delivered her in a commune in Vermont and three days later she was on the run for the first time. The underground's been her whole life. Being an outlaw's in her blood. She'd never burn anyone."

"Does she have good paper?"

"She's got *real* paper. Birth certificate, social security, passport, you name it. It's all real, and none of it's connected to her parents."

"You've given us enough to get a pretty good fix on her."

He shook his head. "No, I haven't. And you really are going to have to trust me on that."

Lotus, an outlaw all her life? Darcy knew it was true the moment Kodiak said it. She was the most flamboyant, outrageous person she'd ever met.

"I know you probably hate what the Terra Firmans are doing with animals, but—"

"Hate it?" Poughkeepsie interrupted her. "It's horrifying what they're doing, but even though they've got your mother I'd be lying if I didn't admit that part of me is really cheering them on. I know it's a drag for your mom, but it's truly inspired. All that stuff about methane's got reporters interviewing scientists all over the world. I follow this kind of news, and even I didn't know how bad it was getting. They're finding methane concentrations off the coast of Siberia a hundred times higher than normal. There's intense interest now. There were so many hits on one of the big science blogs that the server crashed."

"Have they released the report?" Darcy asked.

"Nope, Christmas day, that's what they're still saying."

"Happy holidays," Kodiak crooned.

Poughkeepsie laughed and opened an old roll top desk, revealing a Sony TV with a three-inch screen. "You two seen any of the coverage in the last twenty-four hours?"

"No, the radio in our car was a piece of junk," Kodiak said.

"Wait till you see this. It's getting really wild in Terra Firma, too."

She switched on FOX, which was in the middle of re-running a podcast that drew Darcy closer to the tiny screen. It showed her mother facing a cougar in a snowy forest. Then the video switched to a little girl, whose face had been digitally mixed, huddling a few feet away from her.

"Holy shit. Is my mom okay? Tell me now."

"Yes," Poughkeepsie said. "Both of them are a lot better off than that poor mountain lion."

Darcy stood transfixed as her mother moved slowly in front of the girl, raising and then dropping her coat before sinking deeply into the snow.

The cougar's hind legs pumped, and Darcy shouted, "No."

"She's okay, I swear," Poughkeepsie said. "Your mother and the girl, they're both fine." She sounded impatient, even angry for the first time; and within moments Darcy saw why: The cougar was struck by an arrow, and even on the miniscule screen she could see blood on the snow as the animal raced away.

The podcast cut to video of her mom, and Darcy watched her carry the little girl to a pregnant woman whose face had also been digitally mixed.

"They killed the cougar." Poughkeepsie shook her head as the FOX anchor reported that the latest podcast had brought a series of strong reactions from officials in Washington.

He threw the story to a stately looking correspondent sitting alongside him in the studio, who quickly quoted a Department of Homeland Security spokesman as saying the video showed the "profound dangers" to which Sonya Adams was now subject, and underlined the need for an urgent rescue.

"But the problem," the correspondent continued, "is tracing the podcast. Here's the FBI's Special Agent in Charge, Roy Alston:"

"Every one of these podcasts," Alston said from behind a desk, "has been scrupulously doctored to remove any identifying features that could lead us to Terra Firma."

Alston lifted large, still photos and pointed to the area behind Sonya's head. "When she's clearly outside and we could expect to see identifying features, the background has been digitally altered."

"So while Terra Firma criticizes technology," the reporter came back on camera, "they're using sophisticated means to release only the pictures they want us to see. But did Sonya Adams really save a child's life? Homeland Security officials point out that this podcast was heavily edited. It took time to produce, and it does not show Sonya Adams in a stream of uninterrupted video, as we've seen her in earlier podcasts. Officials say that it's far more likely that Terra Firma set up what you just saw, and placed Sonya Adams in great danger for propaganda purposes, just like the group's threat to release that so-called 'Top Secret CIA Report' on methane. The CIA issued a 'No comment' on the report but Homeland Security officials insist that the report is a fake. They remind us that Terra Firma's stated goal is to convert Sonya Adams to their beliefs, and by extension the group also wants to convert the American people. This highly edited podcast makes it look like Adams is already becoming one of them."

The reporter signed off, and the FOX anchor, frowning at the camera, said "Shockingly, more than a thousand protestors showed up outside the White House today to demand that the President release the fake report." The newscast cut to video of protestors chanting "Release, release, release it now!" before returning to the anchor, who said that they had a live interview with one of the demonstrators, Wilma Harris.

"Why do you think the report is real?" the anchor asked. "Homeland Security says it's a fake, and all we've seen of it from Terra Firma is a cover that could be produced on any home computer." The anchor chuckled, "Not that they're likely to have one of those."

Wilma Harris, middle-aged with braided gray hair, took a breath. "As you might have noticed, they're podcasting, so clearly they have access to computers. But the reason we find the report credible is that the threat from methane is very real. Large scale—"

"You claim it's real, but who are you?" The anchor shook her head. "Do you have a PhD. in geology?"

"I'm an interested citizen who's read a lot about the methane releases, and they could be much more dangerous—"

"Dangerous? Are you actually buying the terrorist spin hook, line, and sinker?"

"It's what credible scientists have been saying for months now. Methane can be much more dangerous—"

"You just said that. What I want to know is, what's the big deal? Methane's as natural as air. Aren't *you* just heating up the controversy?"

"Please let me finish a sentence. Big releases of methane will heat up the planet very quickly." Wilma Harris was speaking rapidly now. "And then when methane oxidizes, it turns into carbon dioxide, so we'll be getting a one-two punch. But news about methane has been grossly underreported by the mainstream media for—"

"A lot of 'blaming the messenger' is going on," the anchor said, cutting off Harris. She turned to a correspondent, who'd joined her at the news desk. "You have some real news to tell us about, don't you?"

"Yes, Shawna, real news about the very real obstacles facing investigators." Here's Assistant FBI Director Brook Lanly, from an interview I did just a few minutes ago on the firewalls used by Terra Firma podcasts."

A middle-aged African-American man appeared in close-up: "It's like trying to locate Islamic militants through their websites. It's a huge part of the battle, and these terrorists have extremely refined and multifaceted systems to avoid being traced."

Darcy shook her head. "Is this on all the time now?" she asked Poughkeepsie.

"Twenty-four-seven ever since they released the cougar podcast yesterday afternoon. Methane? That's getting people thinking. But fighting off a cougar? That's reptilian brain all the way. It's one of the most downloaded podcasts in history."

"Can we go to it?"

"Don't have to. I downloaded it too." Poughkeepsie shut off the TV and opened the laptop. "As far as spin goes, Terra Firma's incredible. If we'd have thought of something like this, we'd have done it too. But everything came together once your mom did that poster. That one image really clicked with people. Nothing like seeing a rich, arrogant white woman lording it all over the natural world."

Darcy wanted to scream. Sure, her mom was kind of clueless and pampered—and they'd had terrible fights set off by Darcy's rage over the rape, a trauma that she herself was only beginning to understand—but to celebrate her mother's abduction? Before she could object, Poughkeepsie caught herself.

"I can't believe I said that. She's your mother. I'm *so* sorry. They seem to be treating her well," she added in a rush of words.

"Let's hope," Darcy said.

Poughkeepsie brought up the podcast, and they watched a longer version of the cougar incident. Then she played a podcast from this morning that showed Darcy's mom in a close-up at dinner. The faces in the background had been blanked-out once again.

But Darcy thought the altered voice sounded like the same woman who'd been giving a speech on the original podcast. The woman announced that because of her mother's courage in facing down the cougar, she would be given "only" a one-year sentence to Terra Firma.

"A year," Darcy shouted.

Poughkeepsie nodded.

"That's insane." Darcy turned back to the screen as the woman said that the group wanted to repay Sonya's bravery by returning her opal earrings to her, acknowledging that Sonya had received them just before her mother had died. Darcy hadn't known they'd taken the earrings, but thought their return indicated that the Terra Firmans might be treating her mother reasonably. Then her mom shocked her by saying she'd really bought them at Zale's, and that the group should do whatever they wanted with them.

"No, that's not true. Gram *did* give them to her. I know because when she was dying she said someday Mom would pass them on to me."

"That's strange," Poughkeepsie said.

"She's trying to win their confidence." Kodiak tapped the desk. "I'll bet anything that's what it is. Give them lots of strokes, make them think you're buying the whole package, and then try to get the hell out of there. Winter's about to really kick in, and if she's thinking about escaping she doesn't have much time."

"But you'd think they'd be smart enough to know they're getting stroked," Darcy said.

"Maybe, but everybody likes to think they're getting converts. That's how we fucked up with ALF informants. They were so into kicking ass that we didn't ask enough questions."

"A lot of people are going to be doing a lot of time." Poughkeepsie looked away.

"I got a friend who's going to be doing *life,*" Kodiak said.

Poughkeepsie clicked off the podcast, saying it was over, before turning back to Darcy. "So what can you do for us?"

"What do you mean?" she asked.

"ALF. If we hook you up with a contact, what are you going to do for us?"

"I'm not sure there's anything I *can* do for you."

Poughkeepsie laughed again, but warmly. "There's plenty you can do. You're vegan, right? And you're going to get a lot of publicity when you show up there. You'll be on their podcasts right away."

"And I'm going to get arrested on assault charges if I ever get my mother out of there."

Poughkeepsie waved her hand dismissively. "They don't want you for that. They just don't want you beating them to the punch. You think if you get her out of there the FBI would dare to have you prosecuted? Hell no, they'll give you a medal for shutting up Terra Firma."

"So you want me to thank ALF publicly, because I don't mind doing—"

"No. Don't *ever* mention anything about us. We've got enough charges pending. But you could use your fifteen minutes to come down hard on animal testing, slaughtering, hunting, trapping, wearing furs, the whole agenda."

"No problem. I'm totally with you on that stuff."

"I didn't think it would be much of a stretch."

*

Poughkeepsie woke Darcy a little after seven the next morning. She'd slept blissfully on the futon couch. No bad dreams. And no idea where Kodiak had spent the night. She tried not to care, but it was hard. He was sitting at a small table sipping tea, smiling at her.

"You've got a long drive ahead of you," Poughkeepsie said.

Darcy sat up straight away. "Really?" Chaska ambled over, nudged her hand with his snout. She rubbed his huge head. *What a sweetie.*

"You have to head north to a border town near Coeur d'Alene. Lose the *burqa*. That's no area to go around dressed like that."

"Am I going to meet someone from Terra Firma?"

"You'll be meeting a contact. They're only willing to meet with you, so this is the end of the line for Kodiak. They emailed me this morning."

"Are you encrypted?"

"Are you kidding? The guy you're going to meet is part of our network. I'd trust him with my life. Now he's trusting me with his. So don't ever burn him. But if they torture you and you have to give him up, buy him as much time as you can."

"They're not going to torture me."

"Right. I forgot. Americans don't torture prisoners."

"But I'm not even—"

"Don't kid yourself." Poughkeepsie sat beside her. "They're putting the torch to other Americans, so don't think they won't do it to you. All I'm saying is if you ever have to give him up, you buy him time. You always buy your people time to get away. Even if it hurts real bad."

*

Johnny Bracer had kept his monocular trained on the glass panels of that cabin since yesterday afternoon. He'd had to snowshoe through three miles of drifts just to get set up. A real pain in the ass. Then this morning it was wait, wait, wait for the clouds to lift.

That's when he saw that the shitty little Suzuki was gone, and that there was no sign of Darcy, only that fine looking woman and her dog. He had no idea who she was but he figured she'd be good for darlin' Darcy's next step and maybe the one after that too.

But he faced a true dilemma: go right in there and find out where she'd gone, and if lover boy went with her, or wait to see if by some chance Darcy was still there. Lover boy could have left on his own in the car.

He gave it a moment before conceding that he couldn't make any kind of move until he knew for certain who was in that house, but it was hard to see with all the glare on the glass. If he went in and found Darcy, the gig was over, unless he could persuade her to let him come along while she made her way to hippie heaven. That *could* be done, but his experience told him that every day from now on he'd be stuck having to persuade her all over again, and that gets plain messy. Better to let her lead and he'd follow.

On the other hand, if she and lover boy had taken the Suzuki, then all he'd have to do is persuade the attractive miss over there to tell him where they were headed. Simple one-stop shopping.

*

Slippery roads all the way north, but Darcy had grown up driving in Colorado and knew better than to hit the brakes hard or make any other sudden moves. In this cautious manner, she drove 179 miles before pulling into the cheap-looking motel where she'd been told to wait, "for days, if necessary."

She kept her knit hat pulled down to her eyebrows and her scarf up to her nose. Not that it mattered. The owner barely glanced at her. He looked older than stone, and no friendlier than ice.

"Pets?"

"No, none."

"Good."

That was the sum and total of their conversation, though why he would object to pets was a question with no obvious answer. They couldn't have smelled worse than the room, which rivaled Rio deGenerate for the stench of cigarettes.

After flipping on the lights, she immediately locked up. Checked the shower too. She couldn't help herself. It felt like Norman Bates country.

She made a brief meal out of sunflower seeds and an organic Clif bar, her lone concession to processed food. Not much else had been available in the truck stops, and she'd known better than to walk into a restaurant where she'd have had to take off her scarf.

The TV looked like a sad, dead rabbit with its old antenna drooping to the sides. Nothing but fuzzy figures till she moved the bent ears around.

A late night newscast on the CBS affiliate led with a three-car pile-up in Coeur d'Alene before cutting to her mother's story. More podcast of the cougar. She turned it off when they went to a car commercial.

Exhausted, she brushed her teeth, catching her foamy reflection in the mirror and remembering how often she'd shared this bedtime routine with Kodiak.

In six months she'd shared a lot with him—memories, beliefs, ambitions—and yesterday in Sun Valley she'd finally shared her most sorrowful secrets.

The irony now had her gripping the sink. Before they'd parted she'd wanted to know about *his* past, but instead she'd ended up revealing the harrowing details of her rape.

He'd comforted her and, as always, he'd listened closely. But that's all Kodiak had ever done: listen.

As she crawled into bed, she realized that she still knew nothing of his hidden history.

Who is he?

*

The dog was big, but Johnny Bracer didn't take it for a killer. How many big white fluffy dogs are killers? Answer? None that he'd ever seen.

Now lover boy with his new haircut might be a different story. Guys could get funny with girls around. Johnny had just spotted him sticking his head out the door to call Fido. Thank you very much, sir. You've just made my job so much easier.

But there was still the problem of getting in there with that dog. He didn't want to shoot it — too noisy — but if it started barking he'd never get the jump on them.

Goddamn dogs. And the day was running short. *Just make your move.*

He pulled up in his Durango—white 'cause it looked government-issue when he slapped a red light on top—and the dog went off even faster and louder than he'd thought it would. In one of the tall windows he spotted real fear on the woman's face. It looked great, but he wanted both of them scared.

She didn't open the door, so he climbed out of the Durango with authority, feeling the bracing presence of his shoulder holster and the tiny Beretta he kept strapped to his ankle.

He started right toward the house. The dog came at him like a hundred-fifty pounds of pure fluff, stood there like it didn't know whether to bark some more or wag its tail. Didn't matter, Johnny wasn't worried about him. He was worried about *them*. They weren't playing to plan.

As he drew within twenty feet of the door, it flew open and she came out aiming a rifle.

Johnny wasn't unprepared for this eventuality.

"FBI. Let me show you my ID *before* you shoot."

She nodded without lifting her eyes from the rifle sight. Gingerly, he reached into his jacket and pulled out his private investigator's license. Far enough away, she couldn't tell.

"FBI. Boise. Frank Mathers. Now put that damn thing down and I won't have to arrest you for intimidating a federal officer."

"I can't read your ID from here."

He saw her talking out of the side of her mouth.

"I'm sending someone out to look at it. You show him."

"Fair enough."

He'd seen this movie before. Goddamn, he knew the ending too.

Lover boy stepped from behind her and walked toward him. Inevitably, he'd come between them, unless he was super-savvy.

Bracer placed the ID in his left hand, seemingly to give it to him.

Here you go...

The instant he blocked her aim, Bracer pulled out his Smith and Wesson with his right hand and grabbed the kid's throat with his left. He jammed the gun into his gut and forced him to turn around. The ID fell to the snow.

"Don't give me any shit," Bracer said in his ear. He had lover boy's neck in the crook of his arm and was using the full length of him as a shield.

He looked up at the woman, her rifle still raised.

"I don't care about him," she said in a gritty voice. "Take him with you."

Her eyes strayed to the dog, which was still staring at Bracer.

"You don't care about him?" He shook lover boy for effect. "Fine. Let's see."

He started forcing him forward, the gun grinding into his back. "I get to the door with him and you still have that rifle pointed my way, I'm going to make sure these charges stick."

"He's not a fed," the guy yelled.

So he'd read the goddamn ID on the snow. Bracer didn't think he could with his head locked up in his arm. Didn't think he could even talk. Wrong again.

She backed into the house, and he moved right in after her, still holding lover boy in front of him. The dog moved alongside them like it was another day at the fair. Once he was in the room with the huge windows he risked a quick look around. His eyes snagged on a print out from PETA, People for the Ethical Treatment of Animals.

He kicked the door closed to keep the dog inside. She was backed up against a wall about eight feet away, rifle still in damage mode.

"Who are you?" she demanded.

"Someone who's had it with your fucking games. You put that goddamn thing down or I'm shooting that dog of yours right in the spine."

It helps to know when you've moved beyond threats to action, and shooting a dog did not take a whole lot of gumption for Johnny Bracer.

She laid the rifle on the floor.

"Now get on the couch. You too, asshole." He shoved the guy toward her and swept the rifle aside with his boot.

Less than sixty seconds later he had them in Flex Cuffs.

"Where is she?"

"Where's who?" The woman said.

Johnny Bracer smiled, picked up the PETA print-out.

"What's your dog's name?"

No answer. No big deal.

"Here boy."

The dog came right over. *Finally, I get a wag.* He stroked his head before stepping over to a laptop computer on her desk. She was online, so he checked her list of favorites and had her pegged for sure.

He took out another plastic handcuff, rubbed the dog's ruff till his tail wagged again, then cinched the cuff tightly around his muzzle.

The dog clawed it, flopped to the floor, and clawed it some more.

"Sorry, buddy, but it ain't coming off." He eyed the tree huggers on the couch, then strolled over to the door where a hand axe rested against a box of kindling. He thumbed the blade. "You think he needs *all* of them?"

"What?" She sounded just this side of hysterical.

"They can still get around on three legs, but it's not particularly easy on 'em."

He kneeled heavily on the dog and grabbed his front paw, pinning it to the wood floor. He raised the axe. The dog growled.

"Sometimes I do this sort of thing even if you do answer me. Depends on how much you fuck around with my head first."

"Don't," she cried.

The guy whispered fiercely to her.

"I hear something about 'time?' Giving her time? You feel the same way if it was *your* foot, lover boy?"

He couldn't tell for sure but he might have spotted a flash of relief on her face. Not for long: Her eyes went wide as hubcaps when he yanked off lover boy's boot.

"Man, I'm taking off the toes first, and then I'm working my way up."

Lover boy started trying to kick, and Johnny knew he'd be a lot tougher to chop than the dog. Plus, she looked worried, maybe even sick; but he didn't sense the wild panic he'd heard a few moments ago over Fido, so he pushed the asswipe's foot away and went back over to the big stupid beast, once more pinning the dog's paw to the floor and raising the axe.

"I'll tell you," she shrieked.

"No," the guy yelled at her.

Bracer looked up, catching his own reflection on one of the glass panels. He looked scary, even to himself; but in a good way, like he'd already crossed the dark waters that separate a mind that's calm from a mind that's crazed. Deep water. Cold water. Water that runs all through you, numbs the weak spots and chills all restraint.

"Tell. Me. What?"

Her mouth didn't move and there was horror in her eyes, but she still needed convincing.

And that's when another thought wended its way into his mind: the woodstove. Hot enough to keep that kettle glowing. Hot enough for him.

He dragged the beast over to it, and even though she was screaming about some motel up in Coeur d'Alene, he was committed to a course of action and could no more turn back than he could turn that crackling fire to ice.

The dog growled viciously, jumped and bucked like he knew what was coming. She stood up, still screaming.

But it's too fucking late, isn't it?

He jammed the dog's paw right down on top of the stove, right next to the kettle, and held it there with all his might. The pad sizzled like fried meat and the animal quaked with a suppressed howl. The room filled with the stink of burning flesh and fur; and blood bubbled up from the sides, browned by the heat.

She came kicking at him. He pulled the dog up, tearing the paw from the stove, leaving the pad stuck to the surface, edges curling up, cooking. Then he grabbed her and shoved the animal's bloody foot right into her face, branding her from the corner of her mouth all the way to her temple, one big bloody paw print.

She screamed, and he pushed her away. The whole time lover boy sat there like he was watching *Nightmare on Elm Street.*

"You fucking . . . " her words spattered like the droplets of blood still bubbling on the stove. She staggered about the room holding her cheek with her cuffed hands.

"I'm asking you one more time, and then I'm gonna roast his legs one at a time."

She collapsed to her knees and started babbling.

Not good enough.

He lowered his voice, but not so she couldn't hear him. "I can't understand you. Slow down or I'm cooking him alive."

She was breathing so hard she could hardly speak, still holding her hands to her cheek like they could suck away the burning pain. But she *was* talking, giving him the name of the motel. Begging too: "Please don't burn him. Please don't . . . "

Before leaving he cuffed her wrists around lover boy's arm, then cuffed his wrists around a leg of the stove. That sure brought him back to life, jerking on those plastic ties like he was lashed to a cobra.

Johnny searched her wood pile for the heaviest, slowest burning logs, and stuffed them into every square inch of the stove. It would burn for hours. When the cuffs got hot enough, maybe they would melt. Maybe before he did.

Johnny smashed her laptop against the side of stove, spraying them with plastic chunks. Then he crushed the tiny TV with his boot and tore the house apart looking for cell phones. Didn't find any. They like the simple life, they sure got it.

The whole time the dog whimpered and held up his bleeding paw like he didn't know what the fuck it was. Johnny called him over, watched him hop on three legs, and cut off his cuff. He petted him just to see. *Yup, man's best friend.* His tail was still wagging, and he was still whimpering, when Bracer walked out the door.

He slashed all four tires on the old Toyota, opened the hood and slashed the wires too.

*

A knock woke Darcy to the early morning darkness. She stared at the door before checking the cheap bedside clock: 4:35. Would they be coming so soon? *Now?*

She crept to the window and cracked the curtain. The light by the door cast a yellowish glow on a man standing with his back to her. A big guy in a dark skull cap.

No car. Where'd he park?

You've come this far, do it.

She threw the lock and opened the door.

Chapter 11

A hand clamped down on Sonya's bare ankle so hard and fast it could have been a steel manacle snapping shut, sparking such a shock that she jerked her leg into the tunnel wall, bloodying her knee.

"You're not going anywhere."

Desmond's voice snaked through a one-inch opening by her pelvis that had done nothing to ease the tunnel's grip. Then he yanked on her leg hard enough to trigger a sharp pain in her knee.

"Stop it," she screamed in the blank darkness. "I'm stuck. I *can't* go anywhere."

"That's not true, Sonya. You got in there, and you're coming out."

He grabbed her thigh and tried to twist it. "Turn your goddamn body. *Get out of there.*"

She screamed again and tried shaking him off her leg, but he reached up to her mid-thigh and tightened his grip.

"I knew right from the start that you'd try something like this."

"Get your hands off of me." She wanted to swear at him, impugn his manhood, say anything that might stop him; but she was *alone* with him. Trapped in a dark tunnel. He had his hands. She had nothing. "I'm *trying* to get out." Fear restraining fury.

"I'll make sure you do."

He started twisting her leg again so hard she thought he'd wrenched her kneecap loose.

"Stop. Jesus, you're *hurting* me," she shrieked. "Please stop."

He might have laughed. But at least he'd stopped twisting her leg. She had only a moment of relief before he inched his hand farther up her thigh. Now she did lose all restraint:

"Get your hands *off* me," squeezing her legs together.

"I'm not letting go."

"I . . . can't go . . . anywhere." Clenching her teeth as she spoke. Still forcing his hand between her legs. Still feeling him *so* close.

"Let her go."

Akiah sounded like he was at the tunnel opening. Desmond's

hand snapped away from her. In surprise, she was sure. But his voice was smooth.

"I caught her trying to escape."

"She's stuck, right?"

"She *says.*"

"Sonya, are you really stuck?" Akiah asked. "Because you can't escape through there."

"I know that. I got stuck trying to back up. I just want to get out of here without being groped by him."

"I was trying to get her out," Desmond said.

"I want you out of there," Akiah said to him.

He retreated. Akiah told him to find Calypso and have him bring them a bucket of bear grease.

Sonya was shivering so viciously that her body shook against the rock walls and her teeth chattered like stones.

"You all right?" Akiah had crawled into the tunnel.

"Freezing. There's really cold air coming from another tunnel up in here."

"That's not a tunnel. That's a natural air vent. It's from a long way off. How far did you get anyway?"

"Something that looked like an underground river."

"Yeah, that's what it is. You're lucky you didn't fall in."

She thought he sounded friendly enough for having found her trying to escape. But she'd failed miserably, and she knew there was nothing like a humiliating defeat to keep you in your place. Aboland, in this case.

"I almost did fall in." She wanted to keep talking; it provided some distraction from the biting cold, the bitter darkness. "Has that ever happened?"

"Not to us, but it killed a few miners about a hundred years ago. The cavern that river goes through gets all filled up with spring run-off. No one stands a chance then. They say another guy got caught but it was in the fall and he was able to grab a few breaths along the way. It goes right out the side of a mountain."

"Is that what the gold company wants? To do some mining around here?"

"I wondered if you saw that."

"Well, is that it?" The cold was so bad she thought she'd start crying any second.

"No, there was never a whole lot of mining around here and it ended a long time ago."

"What then?"

"I can't tell you that."

"They're going to figure out you've got me. All they've got to do is look at the podcasts."

"You don't know what we're showing. We're blanking out everything in the background. And do you have an idea how many places there are like this? There's a ton of them, and it's all going on below the radar screen of most people. They can fly in whenever they want. They don't think anything's going on. Here's Calypso."

When Akiah returned, he reached up and smeared the bear grease all around her hips.

"What's that minty smell?" she asked.

"Wild peppermint. We put a lot of it in the grease or it would smell really rancid. I'm going to try to push you forward so I can lube more of the rock that's got you hung up."

While he put his shoulder to her feet, Sonya clawed the wall. Several grinding seconds later she felt herself break free. Not toward the entrance, but it gave Akiah the space he needed to grease the tight passage.

"Let's try again," he said.

In less than a minute she slipped past the rock's grip as easily as a snug ring that's been soaped.

The relief she felt at finally moving carried her quickly to the entrance. She dug out the matches that she'd buried in her long underwear and handed them to Akiah. Then she threw on her bearskin coat and shoved her feet into her boots, as driven now to climb out of the claustrophobic cell as she'd been to crawl out of the tunnel.

Calypso opened the hatch to a snow shower falling from a radiantly blue sky.

She scaled the ladder, and in seconds stood with the cold white flakes melting on her face, breathing deeply, grateful for the brilliant shafts of sunlight slicing through the skeletal forest. Her shivering finally subsided.

"How'd you find that tunnel?" Calypso asked as Akiah stepped up beside her.

"The candle wouldn't stop moving from the air that was

escaping it. So you better make a better seal before you put someone else down there."

"We don't make a habit of putting anyone down there," Akiah said.

He turned around and closed the hatch, and Calypso swept snow back over it.

"Don't put me down there again," she said to Akiah.

"You made the worst of it."

"Don't."

He shook his head. "No promises."

Jesus.

"I'm guessing you're cold and hungry, and you're definitely dirty. You better get some help with those cuts too. You want to clean up first?"

She nodded, still furious about his "no promises."

"We'll walk you back to the settlement."

Guard me, you mean.

He started leading her down the path through the leafless woods. "But first you should stop by the laundry and get some clean long johns."

"My buckskins," she said, alarmed at the thought of having to go back to the hole.

"I've got 'em." Calypso held them up. "I'll brush them out and drop them at your house."

They surprised Sonya by leaving her on her own at a narrow building with large, steamy windows. Half a dozen men and women were working with wooden tubs and washboards.

A cheerful girl of about sixteen handed her a pair of fresh underclothes, then waved at someone behind her. Sonya turned to find Gwen with her eye pressed to the viewfinder.

On your own? Don't kid yourself. Their movements are tight as a drill team's. Gwen lowered the camera and smiled, saying "Where have you been? I've been looking all over for you."

"I can see they're not keeping you in the loop."

"What do you mean? Hey, is this blood?" She pointed to a smear on Sonya's face.

"Long story. I'm going to the hot pools."

"You are?" Spoken by the young woman as if a great moral victory had been won by Terra Firma.

"I need a real bath. I'm filthy and I can't take it any more. But I'd like you to shut that thing off when I go. Will you?"

"Sure."

"And then why don't you join me?" She had her reasons for extending the invitation, and they weren't all friendly.

Gwen brightened. "All right, I will. Let me go put the camera away."

Sonya turned back to the laundry girl and asked for a towel and soap, then hurried to the rock-lined pools, picking the one closest to the river. She settled on a pine bench to take off her clothes, barely noticing the chill, which was considerable, so consumed was she with undressing in front of her abductors.

And God knows where Desmond is.

The hot water stung her cuts and scrapes when she first got in, but after soaping and soaking she felt almost comfortable, still marveling over the huge blue sky after enduring such tight, dark confines.

Gwen came bounding up naked, and Sonya noticed an orange sun tattoo radiating red rays from around her belly button. It made her wonder if Darcy had ever gotten "inked," the snake in the Garden of Eden that she'd planned to have needled into her neck.

I don't care, I just want to see her again.

"So where'd you get all scratched up and dirty?" Gwen asked.

"In a hole. When the helicopter came they put me in some underground prison cell that used to be part of a gold mine."

"It must have been pretty bad down there."

"It was, but that's not where I picked up these scrapes." She explained about the tunnel.

"God, that sounds like a nightmare. I couldn't have done it."

"You ever been kidnapped? You ever been forced to live with a creep who holds you down on a bed and threatens you? You ever been pushed down into a hole? You ever seen a helicopter fly by that could have you on it? You ever realize you could end up spending all your time in the Saddam Hussein Hotel if the people who kidnapped you start getting really nervous? I'm guessing the answer is 'No' to all of that, so until the answer is 'Yes,' believe me, you don't know what you're capable of. I sure didn't."

Gwen didn't reply.

"Look, I've got to ask you something that's been on my mind."

"Go ahead."

"Why are you doing this? Don't you realize that if you keep doing this you'll end up in prison for a long time when it's all over?"

"It's worth it."

"Worth it? What are you talking about? You're a young woman. You're smart and pretty and you've got your whole life ahead of you. Do you want to spend it in jail?"

"And do you want your daughter and grandchildren to live on a planet that's burning up, where hurricanes are ripping apart cities all the way up to Canada? Those storms are going to make New Orleans look like a great day at the beach. The heat's going to set off a whole bunch of infectious diseases—we're going to have huge epidemics. Sonya, the polar ice caps are melting, and they're going to end up drowning the biggest cities in the world. We're going to have hundreds of millions of climate refugees. And it could happen a lot sooner than people think because methane's coming up from under the Arctic Ocean right *now*. It's been going crazy up there the last two years. And there's more methane under the Arctic than all the carbon in the world's coal reserves."

"It's not that bad."

"Not that bad? You heard what Chandra said the other night. The computer studies have grossly underestimated the damage. Just look at the positive feedback loops that are kicking in."

"Look, if this is a lecture, I'm not in the—"

"It's not a lecture. But if you really want to know why I'm doing this, why *all* of us are doing this, then just listen to me. Those positive feedback loops are really scary. That's when the damage from climate chaos causes more damage, like when the ice caps melt. Then there's less ice to reflect the sun and more dark water to absorb it, and that raises the temperature of the water, which melts more ice and permafrost. And the warm water also releases more methane from the bottom of the ocean, which heats up the air even more. It's already happening. Temperatures are up four degrees Celsius in the Arctic. That's *huge*. Pretty soon we're not going to have an Arctic ice cap. But in America it's like, 'La-di-dah, no big deal.' Pay more at the pump. Have a rock concert with Cameron Diaz telling you to shut off the shower while you shave your legs. *But the earth is dying.* People are too. From horrible heat waves and droughts. And it's going to get worse. Soon. A lot worse. What do people need to wake up?" Gwen's eyes were brimming.

"And you guys thought the answer was kidnapping me to get attention?" Sonya took her hand. "There are other ways to do this."

"What?" Gwen said fiercely, pulling away. "Name a few. Lobby Congress? Oh, come on. It's talk, talk, talk, but nothing ever gets done. We have the best Congress the oil companies can buy, and everybody knows it. It's exhausting to even say it anymore. Write a letter to the editor? Been there, done that a thousand times. Block logging trucks? Get arrested? Done that too." Her tears flowed freely now. "Don't you see? All of us here, we tried everything we could to stop what they're doing to the planet. We even came up here to build a whole different life, but even here we can't escape it. It's right . . . "

"Escape what?"

"Climate chaos," she said quickly.

"No, you were going to say something else."

"Just that it's everywhere. If we don't do something our children and our children's children are going to look at us and say, 'What did you do to stop it?' And I want to be able to look them in the eye and say, 'Everything.'"

Her voice broke on that word, a vow really, and Sonya was shocked to feel her own throat thickening in sympathy.

"Does everyone here feel the same way?"

Gwen nodded, wiping away her tears. "We know what the authorities can do to us. We know that if they catch us they'll tear apart our families, put the kids in foster homes and send their parents to prison. They're the real heroes here, the parents. They're taking incredible risks."

"You *all* are."

"We know that. But we all agreed because we also knew that if we played this right, we'd reach millions of people. And you know what? Because of you, we're reaching *hundreds* of millions of people all over the world."

"I seriously doubt that."

"It's true. *Hundreds of millions.* And we're going to be telling them plenty. These podcasts have gone much bigger than we thought they would. People *are* waking up. You see, a big part of the answer *was* you. So if I go to prison, I go to prison."

"You may be risking more than prison, Gwen. You could be risking your *life*. The government is going to find this place. There have got to be people out there who know about it, and people talk. What if the police come running in with guns and tear gas and everything gets out of hand? You've got those children you were just talking about and—"

"We've got plans for that."

"So you think that could happen?"

"No, we think it's going to take the authorities a long time to find us, and when they do they're going to want to negotiate your release."

Sonya took Gwen's hand again. This time she didn't pull away. "You don't think you've been brainwashed?"

"I think that's the pot calling the kettle black, as my grandmother used to say."

"So how do you know you've got hundreds of millions of people watching?"

"I work on the podcasts with Akiah. I see all the news stories. You can't even imagine how big this is now. Web traffic, donations to environmental groups, demonstrations, petitions—everything's going viral. Even Akiah's amazed."

"And it was his idea?"

"Yup, he came up with it," Gwen said proudly.

Sonya sensed the infatuation immediately.

"Do you just work with him, or are you two an item?"

"An item? No."

"But you wouldn't mind, would you?"

Gwen laughed. "Is it that obvious?"

"Are you kidding? Does he have a girlfriend?"

Gwen shook her head.

"So do you think you two will get together?"

"That would be nice. Was he cool getting you out of the tunnel?"

"He was fine. Better than Desmond."

"Desmond was there?"

"He came after me alone and tried to drag me out by force. He hurt me."

"I reported him to the Council, just so you know."

"Thanks. I hope they do something. He had his hand up my leg.

I was so glad Akiah showed up." Which, she realized with a start, was an extraordinary statement to make about the man who'd abducted her, and who still used a lethal-looking knife as a hair stay.

Gwen smiled, and Sonya saw that the irony had registered with her too.

That's good, Sonya thought as she continued to chat with her. *Make yourself a person in her eyes.* Maybe she'd even planted the seed of helping her escape by mentioning those serious criminal charges Gwen would end up facing, although her responses had revealed a level of commitment that had been surprising to Sonya, who had never felt passionate about a cause. But if she could make Gwen a good friend, it might prove useful.

"I'm supposed to tell you that Chandra wants to see you after you're all fixed up," the camerawoman said.

"I'm sure I know what that's about. What was that gold company helicopter doing here?"

"That was something, wasn't it?"

"Gwen," Sonya made no attempt to hide her impatience, "can't you tell me anything about it?"

"Not really. They're not talking to me. When they come, they always go to Chandra's house and talk to her. They left with something in a plastic bag. I can tell you that much."

"A plastic bag?" That struck Sonya as a sacrilege in Terra Firma.

"I know. That was kind of strange."

"Like a grocery store bag?"

"No, bigger."

"Do you have any idea what was in it?"

Gwen shrugged. "Who knows?"

"Somebody does. Don't you people have any right to ask what's going on when a mining company plops a helicopter down on your property?"

"Oh, sure. The Council of Consensus gets briefed on everything, and anything that's important to the 'health and well-being of the members,' those are the exact words, is dealt with openly. But not the day-to-day stuff, because we tried that and it turned our meetings into marathon sessions."

"Do you think the Council will be talking about the helicopter and whatever was in that bag?"

"Oh, yeah, you'd think."

"Gwen, *please,* have they talked about it in the past?"

"You'd better ask Chandra."

Gwen looked away, and when Sonya caught her eye again the warmth was gone.

The mood remained awkward as they dried off and dressed. Gwen took off to retrieve the camera, leaving Sonya unguarded for the first time, her giddiness curbed by the vastness of her surroundings.

Gwen caught up with her again at the entrance to the clinic, a building about twice the size of the cute, cubbyhole homes.

The floors, walls, and cabinets looked immaculate in the sunlight streaming in from a row of narrow rectangular windows. So did the white sheets and comforters on the three beds lined up to her right. Each one held a young, droopy-eyed child.

A tall, dark-skinned woman in a white turban and white muslin pants and top walked out from behind a long curtain with a bowl of steaming broth. She smiled at Sonya and said she'd be with her in a moment, then placed the broth on a small table next to the girl in the middle bed. The girl ignored it, pulling listlessly on her thick braid instead.

The woman eyed the sleepy looking boys in the other two beds before turning to Sonya, saying that they had ground dogwood bark and arnica salve for her.

Sonya didn't know about either of these naturopathic remedies and would gladly have traded a big bag of nuts and berries for two Tylenol Extra-Strength capsules and a tube of Neosporin. The nurse, who introduced herself as Devaki, explained that the bark was a natural analgesic, and that the arnica would promote the healing of her cuts.

After rubbing the salve into her raw skin, and swallowing the ground dogwood bark with water, Sonya asked Devaki what was wrong with the children.

"This is nothing," she chirped in a strong Indian accent. "A little bug is going around, that is all. It happens. They will get better. You will see. So will you." She pointed to a shelf by the door where a pyramid of shiny green apples sat in a pretty indigo bowl. "Everyone takes an apple from our very own orchard. You, too, camera girl. Remember, an apple a day keeps the good doctor away."

Devaki sounded so much like a character in a Bollywood film that Sonya barely managed to stave off a silly grin till she walked out of the clinic, Granny Smith in hand.

But amused as she was, she remembered that Gwen had turned off her camera as soon as she'd seen the sick children.

She started shooting again as they walked to Desmond and Andromeda's place. The living room was curtained off for a massage client, so Sonya quietly asked Gwen to wait outside.

"But don't go away," she whispered, worried about finding herself alone with Desmond.

Gwen nodded and smiled, her warm self again.

Sonya slipped into the bedroom, finding her surroundings at once so familiar and yet so foreign that days could have passed, rather than hours, since her roommates had burst in here with Akiah to hustle her off to the hole.

Even the buckskins, freshly brushed and laid out on the quilt, spoke of a placid interlude so removed from what they had known. *The deceptions of small appearances*, thought Sonya.

She dressed and eased the door open, her attention snagged by a woman behind the curtain referring to the helicopter. Sonya paused, listening intently.

Andromeda—*thank God*—murmured a few words she couldn't make out before the woman insisted, "It *was* the blanket. You know the one."

She thought Andromeda assented, but it was so hard to tell. She sounded distracted by her work, and then her client said, "But why give it to them? It belongs to all of us."

A blanket? To a gold company? Why? Sonya leaned into the living room, missed Andromeda's response again, but heard the woman clearly:

"Yes, you do. It's the one we all donated some hair to. *That* one."

The one they threw on me during the abduction, Sonya remembered, bristling. The human hair blanket. Creepy as Desmond, and as sinister as the tunnel that had left her in his hands.

Chapter 12

"We're being followed. He thinks he's cute but I've had my eye on him since we took off."

Darcy had opened the motel-room door to a man with a crescent-shaped scar on his cheek and the thickest spectacles she'd ever seen. They made his eyes look miles away, or maybe they'd always seemed small and distant.

As they'd walked from her room, he said his name was Jangles, "Like in Bo, but just Jangles."

Jangles had parked his semi truck out by the highway. As getaway vehicles went, Darcy considered his a poor choice. Old and slower than sludge, it seemed to take ten minutes before he worked it up to sixty.

The truck wasn't a cover story. Jangles had been running forty-thousand pounds of skin magazines from a printing plant in Wisconsin to a warehouse in Seattle when he said he got a coded call on his CB. Wouldn't say from whom. Wouldn't say where they were going. Wouldn't say if he was part of the safe house network. Wouldn't say much at all until now.

"I should have known," he muttered. "Mercury's in retrograde."

"What's that supposed to mean?"

He pointed to a zodiac magnet stuck to the dash. "Everything's going to shit."

Darcy didn't know which was more disturbing: that they were being followed and couldn't outrun a motor scooter in this lumbering beast, or that the driver found their predicament predictable based on a poor alignment of the stars? Worse, she had just enough faith in astrology to make his concerns marginally her own.

She looked out at the tall side-view mirror. "The white thing?"

"Dodge Durango SUV, 2007. Passed us while we were getting going. No big deal, right? Four-thirty in the a.m. and a car passes. But we weren't on the road five minutes when I saw him two cars back. Cute, but not that cute," he added with a hint of anger, which made Darcy uneasy. Jangles had turned out to be even bigger than he'd looked from the motel room window. Had to be six-four, six-five. Taller than her father. Wider too.

"You always notice every car on the road?"

"I do when I'm running a felony three-to-five in the seat next to me."

"Three to five?"

"You're wanted. I'm fucked if I'm caught. But if that does happen, I don't know you for shit. You're a hitchhiker. That's my story." He nodded in a way that made her nod right back.

"Are you worried?" she asked.

"About him?"

"It's a him?"

Jangles pulled out a pipe and chewed on it. The black stem had more pits than a patch of bad skin. "Lone driver, thirty-five to forty. Dark hair. Could be government. Can't tell. Yeah, it's a him. And yeah, I'm worried."

"What do we do if he stops us?"

"He won't be stopping us. He'll have the cops do it. That's how they work."

"You been stopped a lot?"

"You could say that. Did a few years in the pen."

"For?"

He smiled at her for the first time, and it freaked her out to see his missing front tooth and that crescent-shaped scar that crinkled from a wicked-looking laugh line. But as uneasy as his appearance made her feel, his next words proved far more unsettling:

"You don't *want* to know."

*

The plastic cuffs never melted, only the skin on Kodiak's left arm. With his wrists bound around a leg of the wood stove, he'd made tortured attempts to shift the pain between his arms, but he'd been able to spare only the one he used the most. The left arm had slow roasted till it bubbled with blisters. The largest, big as a hen's egg, had boiled open a few minutes ago, drooling blood and a pale pink liquid down on his scalded hand. Poughkeepsie, still cuffed to him, watched and wept.

He'd given up talking. Given up screaming. Cried, that's all. And every few seconds he wrenched the cuffs. At one point last night he'd involved her in a mighty effort to try to upend the entire stove, but it was heavy, and fixed to the brick base and a metal chimney pipe.

Poughkeepsie, feeling him shake, thought of the brute who'd tortured her dog and left them like this. *That son of a bitch . . .*

" . . . is not alone," she finished aloud when two hulking black SUVs with smoked glass churned through the snow right up to the front of her cabin, filling those tall windows with the specter of six heavily armed men exploding out from behind the doors.

"Kodiak," she poked him, "someone's here. With guns."

He was kneeling, still jerking his arms helplessly.

"I don't care," he howled. "Get me loose, get me loose, get me . . ."

He'd suffered the most gruesome pain she'd ever witnessed, even worse than watching that monster grill her dog's paw on the stove. That had been absolutely horrific, but quick. Kodiak's arm had cooked slowly, the pain driving him insane for endless shrieking minutes. The sweet smell of his flesh turning to meat had left her nauseated.

The men, dressed in camo, boots, helmets, eye gear, burst in the door, weapons drawn. Their commander ordered four of them to search the cabin. He was large, square shouldered, with legs so thick they threatened to tear apart his pants like the bole of an oak bursting its bark. He studied Poughkeepsie and Kodiak, and announced his name—"McCarthy"—as if those three scarred American syllables were an irrefutable injunction.

"I'm burning," Kodiak yelled. "Help me."

McCarthy made no move to release Kodiak, whose shouts quickly escalated to shrieks again.

"Clear," a voice blared from Poughkeepsie's bedroom.

McCarthy eased off his helmet and goggles. He had short black hair, a tanned face, and calm gray eyes.

"Where is she?" he demanded.

"Where's who?" Poughkeepsie said.

McCarthy pointed to Kodiak, who writhed, cried, and pulled viciously on his cuffs.

"I'm asking *you,* Mr. Rotisserie. Where is she?"

"Motel," he gasped.

"Don't," Poughkeepsie said.

"Outside Kalispell."

"A warning," McCarthy said. "We're not playing charades here.

The faster you talk, the faster you're free, and outside Kalispell's the whole goddamn state of Montana."

"Pine Forest Motel. That's the name. Cut me loose," Kodiak screamed.

Another blister broke on his arm, and more of that pale pink liquid and blood drooled on to his cooked, swollen hand. He jerked wildly on the cuffs, spraying drops of his fluids on to the front of the stove. They sizzled and sent tendrils of smoke to the ceiling.

"When?" McCarthy asked patiently.

"Seven-thirty. Fuck," Kodiak screamed. "Help me, *please.*"

"Seven-thirty today? Is that right?" McCarthy directed his question to Poughkeepsie.

She didn't respond.

"Yesterday," Kodiak yelled.

"I'm looking for corroboration," said McCarthy, as if he had all the time in the world.

"You want collaboration. Go fuck yourself," Poughkeepsie shouted.

"What's she driving?"

"Suzuki." Kodiak sucked in a big breath. "'97."

"Color?"

"Dark blue."

"License plate?"

"Shit, I don't know."

"How about you?" he said to Poughkeepsie. "You want to help your friend here?"

"I don't know either," she said.

"What's she wearing?"

"Hat. Blue hat. Scarf. Jacket. What color?" Kodiak pleaded to Poughkeepsie.

"Brown," she said.

"She got on her studs and rings?"

"No," Kodiak shouted.

"She alone?"

"Yes. Cut me loose. Oh, God, my arm." Kodiak's head snapped side to side, like he was about to have a seizure.

"Hold on." McCarthy crouched near him and made a show of looking at his burns.

"Please," Kodiak wept, "let me go. The pain's so bad . . . " He shuddered so violently he couldn't go on.

A smile spread across the commander's face like an infection. "Sure, we can do that. Be *easy.* But long as you're talking and all, who's Lotus Land?"

*

The sun rose in the side view mirrors as Darcy and Jangles wheeled down the mountains into the wheat lands of eastern Washington. No snow or ice, only a dry road with dusty, plowed fields on both sides of them.

He'd just turned the radio back on when CBS News started playing an excerpt from a podcast Terra Firma had released late last night. In seconds, Darcy found herself stunned by the latest announcement from those nameless, faceless crazies. They'd launched what they were calling an *"American Idol-*style contest" to determine the most important documentary on global warming, oil, and "state-sponsored terrorism." Here she thought they'd be saying more about methane, but instead they'd lightened the mood and were billing the contest as "The First Annual Double-bind Documentary Film Festival."

CBS quoted Terra Firma as saying ten documentaries were eligible, including *An Inconvenient Truth,* Al Gore's Oscar-winning report on global warming; *The Oil Factor,* a look at the links between oil and the war in Iraq; *Crude Impact,* on the dire ramifications of human dependence on oil; and Michael Moore's latest documentary on the war on terror.

Terra Firma had made all ten documentaries available for free download, and had established a "voting center" on the Web where more than 1.3 million ballots had already been cast since it opened at midnight.

Moore, reached by CBS in Los Angeles, called Terra Firma's action, "A wonderful and outrageous act of piracy," saying further that he would not bring any legal action to try to stop the downloads, "even if I could."

Gore responded by demanding Sonya Adams' immediate release, but said he had no plans to try to stop the pirating of his film at this time. "I don't want to do anything that would inflame the situation or risk Sonya's safe return home."

Darcy had seen all of Moore's films, of course, and Gore's. And if she hadn't been caught in the middle of this crisis, she probably would have been downloading the docs that she hadn't seen.

Jangles was listening too, nodding his head, which put her at ease . . . a little. Hard to figure him. Blue collar to the bone, the kind of guy coastal eggheads dismissed as a rube, but down with the plan, from everything she could gather. That's when she realized that her feelings about Terra Firma had shifted from outright skepticism to . . . support?

No, no, she said to herself. They'd kidnapped her mother, but— and this one of those mega "buts" in her life—she was beginning to see why Kodiak and Poughkeepsie found their actions so appealing. Yeah, taking her mother was wrong, wrong as wrong could be, but everything else they were doing was . . . pretty damn cool? She sat there questioning this, but there was no other way to put it. It was like they'd pierced the veil of Maya, the world of illusion, as the Buddhists put it, to bring real light to some really dark stuff. The way they lived was walking the walk, and they were forcing global warming right into the face of the American people.

And then it hit her: *If they're winning me over, and they took my mom, they must be getting to millions of other people too.*

They were, but not all of them approved. The White House press secretary sounded an angry note when he spoke to reporters that morning:

"It's very clear that these terrorists are attempting to abduct the minds of millions of Americans the same way they abducted Sonya Adams. And it's also clear that by broadcasting their messages, you in the news media have become handmaidens to domestic terrorism."

Before breaking for commercials, the announcer reported that the latest CBS/New York Times poll showed growing support for Terra Firma's message, but not for its kidnapping of Sonya Adams. Thirty-seven percent of those polled thought Terra Firma had something important to say about global warming, methane, and the "oil crisis," and twenty-four percent now knew the meaning of "double-bind." But a scant three percent supported their kidnapping of Sonya Adams, and seventy-six percent thought the government should do all it could to prosecute those responsible for her abduction.

"That's up twelve percent in just a few days," Jangles said, "the ones supporting what they're saying. That happens again, about half the American peoples' be backing them."

Just so long as my mother doesn't get hurt, thought Darcy. Before the sun had come up, she'd had a horrifying image of her mother lying in a frozen forest, her face caked with blood, eyes open and unseeing. It had scared the shit out of her and made her desperate to come clean with her mom about all the crap that had kept them apart . . . *before* it was too late.

But the worst part of envisioning her mother cold and dead and alone was the eerie sense that it was a premonition, ruthlessly real and imminent.

Jangles glanced in his side view mirror.

"Can you still see him?" she asked. "Cause I can't." The sun blinded her every time she looked out.

"Nope, but he's back there."

"How can you tell?"

"Man doesn't follow you a hundred miles to drop a tail."

"You know who I really am, don't you? Not just that I'm wanted."

"I don't know shit, and I'm knowing less by the moment. All I know for sure is that somebody's back there watching us and they're probably doing it for somebody else 'cause that's the way the world works."

"So we're screwed?"

"I wouldn't go that far. The people waiting for you probably figured we'd be followed because whoever's tailing us wants to see where we're going. But where we're going is just a big honkin' truck stop this side of Spokane, and I'd better be hearing something from somebody on the CB before we get there or I don't know what we're going to be doing."

"Do you know how we're supposed to shake him?"

"All I know is I got forty-thousand pounds of porn back there and a sweet little hitchhiker up here."

That smile again with its missing tooth and crumpled scar.

"Don't get any ideas." She'd opened that motel room door without her gun, which could have been a mondo mistake; but it was in easy reach now and she wasn't taking shit from Jangles, or anyone else for that matter.

"Don't you worry none. I don't have any designs on you. But let's just say, hypothetically speaking, if I did know who you were,

I'd be in your corner getting you ready as ready can be for the big fight. But seeing as how I don't know who you are, you're just a sweet little hitchhiker to this good ol' boy with his stash of porn."

"You ever look at that stuff?"

"Not anymore. Why?"

"Just wondering."

"Make you feel better knowing that?"

"Yeah, it does."

"I used to, but I lost interest when they started shaving off their pubic hair. I used to be a logger too, but I couldn't do that no more either."

"Why's that?"

"You know the Olympic Peninsula?"

"Heard of it."

"It's up on the ocean on the other side of the state. Most beautiful place on earth when I was a kid. And we cut it to shit. I grew up cutting down trees like my daddy and everybody else's daddy, and one day I was walking down the main street in town and all I could see were stumps. We'd cut them right down to town till there was nothing left to cut. They shouldn't have let us do that."

"So now you drive a truck?"

"And all those trees have been turned into pictures of naked women with no hair on their privates. Go figure. Everything's getting cut. Just so long as you don't," he eyed her. "Deal is I get you there safe."

"What about 'Mercury in retrograde?'"

"Yeah, that's the scary part."

*

Commander McCarthy watched the prisoner whip his head between his burned arm and the hot stove in a savage attempt to tear off his cuffs with his teeth. The glowing metal broiled his scalp till it smoked and bled and drove him screaming back into a pathetic crouch.

Johnny Bracer had done a commendable job of softening him up, which did not surprise McCarthy. Bracer had served under him in Gulf War I, and they'd stayed in touch—you always kept a good man in your mental Rolodex—and McCarthy had followed his successes with the Bureau with interest.

Bracer had earned another commendation today by getting the

prisoner ready for a serious interrogation.

"Cut him loose," McCarthy ordered the goggle-eyed soldier standing directly beside him.

Goggle eyes drew a long blade from his heavy black service belt and leaned over the tortured man, who shook continually. Carefully, he sliced the plastic.

The prisoner rolled away from the stove, weeping and dragging the woman with him until she could slide her cuffed hands off his wrists.

"Get a doctor," she yelled at Commander McCarthy.

He nodded. "Soon enough, ma'am. You're not going to die. But don't think for a second that we're going to pay to get that all fixed up." He pointed to her ruined cheek. "Where you're going, the ladies like that. You'll see."

"You're insane if you think you're going to get away with this."

"We didn't do anything. Our hands are clean. But this guy," his gaze steadied on the well-done one curled on his side, "He's dirty. I'll bet you don't even know his real name. Your 'Kodiak' is Paul Raschman. Listen up, Paul, I'm talking about you now."

Kodiak didn't stir from his fetal position. McCarthy kept his eyes on him as he went on.

"We let him go in Portland and he fucked us. He promised to work with us, and he did." The commander smiled at the woman. "He gave up six of your best friends in the asshole liberation front. We watched them for almost two years. And guess what? You already know the answer, don't you? They led us to half a dozen other assholes, and then we rounded them all up. But you did a disappearing act on us, Paul." He nudged Kodiak's back with his boot. "You *burned* us. Look at me, boy." McCarthy's tone changed from angry to ugly, and Kodiak eyed him with the frozen fear of fallen prey. "And listen real closely because I'm losing patience here. I'm only asking you one more time: Who is Lotus Land?"

*

The CB came alive with constant chatter as Jangles and Darcy neared Spokane. Lots of talk about "smokeys" and speed traps in the western drawl that so many truckers affected when they got on a CB. The women too. Several of them jabbered about road conditions, but one of them sounded like a hooker. And this one, droning on about . . . *astrology?*

Jangles leaned toward the radio. When the woman's voice suddenly slowed for "Uranus in opposition," he turned down the sound and sat back, as if to steady himself.

"We get there, I'm pulling this rig into a long line of trucks and I'm keeping it running, just like we always do. I'm going to get out. This is going to be a huge place, there might be fifty, sixty trucks in the lot. Our tail'll pull in too—that's what the smart money's saying —and when he does, I'm going over to him and I'm going to start banging on his window, playing the outraged trucker. I'll be yelling about him cutting me off, 'You stupid son of a bitch,' crap like that. Anybody's ever worked in a truck stop, they've seen it before.

"Soon as I start over there, you got to get out your side, which'll be away from where I figure he'll be pulling in, which'll probably be the pumps and the restaurant. You start walking down past the trucks. If no one comes up to you and says your name, you go straight to the ladies and get in the last stall on your right. That's the plan. If it's full, you keep your head down and wash your hands, dig in your pack, whatever you got to do till it empties. Then you get in there and close the door and wait. Somebody's comin' to get you."

"Bang on his window? That sounds dangerous as hell. Are they paying you enough to do that?"

"Not a cent. I got some karmic debt and I'm cutting a check today."

Jangles took them onto the exit ramp, scanning the truck stop as he pulled in, parked, and hopped out.

When Darcy saw him heading toward the white SUV, she climbed down and walked past the rigs hoping to make it to the bathroom; but a short woman in a black ski cap strode up and said, "This way, Darcy. And don't look surprised and keep on moving, whatever you do."

"I've got to pee really bad."

"Hold it or pee in your pants. I'm not kidding. Come on."

Darcy walked beside her to a blue BMW motorcycle parked next to an old Econoline van with a bright mural of a snowboarder catching air. Three guys climbed out and eyed them. Ignored, they moved on toward the restaurant.

A couple of black helmets were strapped to the motorcycle seat.

"Put this on. And when you get on the bike look like you've done it before."

The helmet came equipped with a headset. The woman said her name was Eve as they rode out of the lot.

They never heard the gunshot.

*

"What do you want to be called, Paul or Kodiak? It makes no difference to me." Commander McCarthy sat across from his prisoner in the spare interrogation room: bare white walls, table, two chairs. And two of his men standing nearby.

"Kodiak." He hunched protectively over his bandaged arm. A medic had treated him.

"Okay, Kodiak. How's the arm feel now?" McCarthy laid only the weight of his thick fingers on the white gauze, but it was enough to make his prisoner gasp and beg for the painkillers in the commander's other hand.

"You mean these?" McCarthy held a prescription bottle just out of reach, shook them. "You want more than basic care, you've got to give us more than basic information. Otherwise, we're going to have to put you in a special cell. You don't want that. So let's get started. Who's Lotus Land really?"

When Kodiak looked away, McCarthy signaled his men. They seized the prisoner's arms and dragged him to his feet.

McCarthy spoke as if he couldn't hear the shrieks. "You won't last long in this cell, Kodiak. I know prisons, and I know men. You're not the kind who's going to make it."

They forced him through a gray metal door into what appeared to be an empty cellblock with dark, disturbing stains on the walls and floor, escorting him forcefully down a steel mesh catwalk to the last cell. The shirtless guy looming behind the bars could have been a linebacker for the Denver Broncos.

McCarthy saw Kodiak's horror when he spotted the swastika on the man's chest.

"This him?" the guy yelled.

McCarthy nodded. "Yeah, he's Paul Raschman, the terrorist we were telling you about. Kodiak, meet the Turbanator."

McCarthy unlocked the cell. "Right now, Kodiak, you could be called the fruits of war. Give me a shout if you change your mind."

As the Turbanator grabbed him, Kodiak yelled. "Lotus Land is the daughter of Drake and Nancy Cohenson."

"Let him go," McCarthy ordered. He led Kodiak back to the

interrogation room, where the young man told them that Lotus Land was born in a commune in Vermont.

He went on to describe how she rendezvoused with her mother and father every two months. Details like the pay phones they used and the drop spots. Everything they'd need to nail Lotus Land for aiding and abetting his prisoner, *and* to arrest her parents for breaking into a bomb-making plant in Texas thirty-eight years ago, where they splashed chicken blood on huge containers of napalm and wrote "Peace Now" and other obscenities in chilling red letters.

"You did well, Kodiak. But we can't let you go this time."

His prisoner appeared resigned to this, though he did ask for the pills again.

"After you're locked up." McCarthy always held onto what they wanted till he got what he needed.

He and his men led Kodiak back past the empty cells, drawing closer with every step to the Turbanator. When he stopped there, Kodiak shouted, "What's going on? I told you everything."

McCarthy shook his head. "Kalispell? You lie, you fry."

"You fucking snitch." The Turbanator crammed his thick arms through the bars trying to grab Kodiak, then seized the door in a sudden rage, shaking it so hard it sounded like the entire cellblock had come alive. McCarthy spied a vein throbbing in Kodiak's temple.

Softened up.

"Now tell me, Kodiak, where's Darcy going?"

"Pine Ridge Motel outside Coeur d'Alene."

"That's good. Now tell me why she's doing that."

"She's trying to find her mother."

"And she's getting help?"

Kodiak nodded. McCarthy opened the next cell down and watched his prisoner scurry inside.

"Don't ever fuck with me again. I'll feed you to worse than him."

McCarthy flipped a pill through the bars. Kodiak bobbled it with his good hand, and it rolled toward an open drain in the middle of the floor. He dived for it, crying out when his burned arm struck the concrete. But he saved the pill and chewed it fiercely, as though indifferent to the bitter taste.

*

The motorcycle with Eve and Darcy ripped down the interstate at more than ninety miles an hour. No concerns about the highway patrol: Every cop car had its red lights flashing and its sirens firing as it sped in the opposite lanes toward the truck stop.

As they neared Spokane, Eve veered onto an exit ramp and darted down surface streets nimble as a dragonfly, before taking the major route north, a congested commercial strip packed with big-box stores, Starbucks, and every other chain merchant imaginable.

They quickly hit a traffic standstill.

"We're lucking out," she said.

She instantly shot between two lanes of cars jammed behind a jackknifed semi, then slowed for a narrow section of shoulder around the rear of the tilted trailer.

The road opened before them and they left the crowded shopping district for the dull, depressed rural region immediately north of the city. All Darcy could see were broken fences and boarded-up houses. Broken dreams.

They whizzed by businesses still operating in buildings blackened by fires and never repaired; homes that hadn't been painted in decades, with American flag curtains hanging in cracked windows; and cars and bikes rusting in front yards where the *For Sale* signs looked older and more faded than the wan faces peeking out at the sleek motorcycle.

"Pretty sad, huh?" Eve said.

"I can't believe it."

"You spend much time in rural America lately?"

"No."

"Well, this is what it looks like. And Wal-Mart."

They passed *Vacation Land*, a creek side warren of battered trailers and grimy, vacant-eyed children hovering dangerously close to the road. They waved slowly at Darcy and Eve, as if their hands were underwater, submerged in the lake of another life.

Eve turned on to a street lined with leafless trees and muddy, garbage-strewn ditches. She slowed to navigate around pot holes, hanging rights till she came within sight of the two-lane again, then stopped.

"I'm trying to figure out if we're being followed."

"Are we?"

"I don't think so."

"Where you taking me? Can you tell me that?"

"Sure. A safe house about an hour and a half from here. You're going to be staying with me and my partner."

"For how long?"

"I'm not sure. You hear that?"

"What?"

Eve pointed above the trees. In the distance a big helicopter moved across the clear blue sky.

"That's a Black Hawk, like in *Black Hawk Down.*"

"You think they're after us?"

"No, I think it's for the Air Force Survival School. It's about thirty miles from here."

"They've got an Air Force Survival School up here?"

"They got them all over the world, are you kidding?"

Darcy hurried behind a tree and finally relieved herself. Fifteen minutes later they were back on the two-lane, speeding by a future that had yet to grieve the past.

*

Johnny Bracer had watched the big ugly trucker storm toward the Durango. He'd run down all the particulars on the rig and its owner hours ago: The driver had done nine years for the manslaughter of a New Jersey cop. It's helpful knowing a guy like that has two strikes against him already when he marches up to your window like he owns the day. Strike three was the trucker's temper —Johnny saw that right away—so he drew his gun, lowered his window, and before the idiot could scream two words that made any sense, Johnny spit right in his fucking face. The guy reached for him, and that's when Johnny let him have it.

As soon as the detectives arrived, Johnny gave them his specially embossed card with the phone number of his contact at FBI headquarters in Washington. Half an hour later the local yokels were giving him back the card *and* his guns.

It wasn't just the Bureau flexing. The detectives also had spoken to two witnesses who'd seen the convicted cop killer Jangles McDermott try to grab one John Bracer. Add that to McDermott's rap sheet, and it was game, set, and match. The senior detective even shook Johnny's hand and offered to drive him back to the truck stop. They hadn't even had time to impound the Durango.

Back in his SUV, Johnny called the Bureau for a rundown.

"You're out, right?" his contact said. No name. No need. Only one guy ever picked up when Johnny called.

Obviously, thought Johnny. "What gives?"

More than Johnny might have guessed. The President had raised the terror alert, activated the military wing of the Joint Task Force on Terrorism, and jacked up the reward for Sonya Adams to five million dollars, announcing that Homeland Security had obtained information indicating that Terra Firma was planning a deadly attack on civilians in the United States.

All good news, as far as Johnny was concerned, because the reward money was finally getting serious. But he wasn't the only one on the trail now: His old commanding officer from the first Gulf War, Justin McCarthy, had joined him in the field, running the military's side of the operation. Much as Johnny admired McCarthy, he didn't want to lose the reward. And McCarthy was getting close: The Air Force had already spotted Darcy Adams and another woman heading north on a motorcycle, thanks to a tip from some snowboarders who'd seen them leaving the parking lot.

"Don't worry," his contact assured him. "Your stake is good. We need you, and five mil goes a long way."

But the best news—and it was sweet as a custom gun grip—was that as soon as the girls reached their destination, Johnny's guy would call with the 10-20. The Feds wanted Johnny at the location "just in case." In case anyone required softening up, no doubt; and no doubt someone would.

As for the death of Jangles McDermott, no one at the Bureau minded a cop killer's demise. And evidently, McDermott was so far down the Terra Firma food chain that he might as well have been plankton.

But the big fish still need to be speared, a thought that made Johnny smile. His special skills, he was pleased to see, remained in full favor at the Bureau. And no price, not even death, was too high for them now.

Chapter 13

Sonya's appointment with Chandra had been postponed for four days running, which had been intriguing enough; but Aboland's elderly leader also hadn't shown up for any of the meals, which had led Sonya to ask Andromeda about her health as they walked back from dinner last night.

"She's fine."

"Then where's she been?"

"She's here. She's busy."

But why is she busy, Sonya asked herself. *Is it because of me? Have they already started negotiating for my release? Am I about to be rescued?*

Chandra's sudden disappearance was of particular interest because it came right after the arrival of the gold company helicopter and its departure with the human hair blanket, making Sonya wonder if Chandra had also taken off on the chopper.

Then there was the added mystery of Desmond. For the past three nights Andromeda had slept alone. Not that Sonya missed him around the house.

To add to all this, Gwen was not waiting with her camera when she stepped into the sunshine this morning and headed to the community center for breakfast. Unguarded for the second time. Not even walking by her lonesome to Chandra's house drew any notice from the Abolanders, which made her think that the tour with Gwen and Calypso might have been part of their effort to convince her of Aboland's isolation. She wondered, as she had several times, if they were protesting *too* much. And she assured herself that it couldn't be *that* remote. *You got in. You can get out.*

She approached Chandra's fully expecting another postponement. But the old woman greeted her cheerfully at the door of her attached house, which stood closest to the hot pools. Her white hair was wet and her skin glowed pink, as if she'd just come in from a satisfying soak. She did not look ill or bear the haggard expression of someone who'd been harried by long negotiations over the release of her prisoner.

In a spirited voice, she shepherded Sonya inside and let on that

Akiah had told her about the tunnel incident.

"Right." Sonya shed her coat and stole a glance at Chandra's face for the family resemblance; other than the striking blue eyes, she wouldn't have pegged her for Akiah's mother. "Putting me in that hole was a disgrace."

Chandra surprised her by laughing gaily. "Come sit." She gestured to a small wooden table with inlaid tiles that formed a vivid red mandala. "And if we hadn't, would you have kept quiet and not tried to get away in the helicopter? Come now, we're not fools here. We had to put you somewhere, and then you put yourself somewhere far worse. We left you food and blankets, and you got yourself stuck in that tunnel." Another chuckle escaped her.

"I don't think it's funny. I'll probably be down there all the time when they start closing in on you."

"They're not going to be 'closing in' on us."

But Chandra hadn't denied Sonya's core assertion, which she found as alarming as Akiah's refusal to promise that she wouldn't be locked in that hole again.

The old woman dropped tea leaves into a kettle, then jolted Sonya by speaking to someone in the shadowy living area: "You may go. We'll be fine."

Calypso stepped around a corner, throwing a stern glance at Sonya before closing the door behind him.

Chandra turned from the wood stove. "I trust you're not offended."

"You had him here to protect you? From *me*?"

"I like to gauge a mood."

"You have to do that often?

Chandra smiled. "No."

"How about giving away human-hair blankets? Is that an Aboland custom?"

"My-oh-my, the walls really do have ears. It was a gift from us to them."

"You can't possibly expect me to believe that."

"I certainly can."

"A human-hair blanket? Who'd want it?"

"They accepted it with kindness and gratitude as a symbol of our community. They're good neighbors. But don't go taking 'neighbors' too literally," she added quickly. "They're not anywhere nearby. That's why they fly in. You'd die long before you ever walked there . . . "

I'm not walking when I leave.

" . . . so save yourself a lot of grief and don't even think about it."

Another one of those dark warnings, first from Juno and Akiah and now from Chandra. Well, that iron cook stove and sink didn't trot in here on their own. They had to be hauled in, probably on roads that couldn't be too far away.

"Winter's almost here," Chandra said, putting out two blue ceramic mugs, "and no one survives for long in this wilderness without a shelter. We don't want you getting hurt."

"I'm too valuable to you."

Chandra retrieved the boiling kettle. "That's right, you are. There's no harm in your knowing that you're very valuable to our message for the world."

"Hundreds of millions of people are watching the podcasts?"

"Yes, everybody knows about you now. When this is over you'll be set for life. You'll probably become the face for a line of 'all natural' cosmetics. They might even call it 'Terra Firma foundation' or 'Aboland eyeliner.'" She dabbed the quote marks in the air with her free hand, clearly amused. "You're more famous than the President right now. Do you realize that?"

Chandra didn't wait for a reply. "But it's not about you or us. It's about the end of the world as we know it. It's about civilization collapsing. About millions dying of starvation or disease or natural disasters so horrifying that we can't even picture them. It's about wars killing millions more to claim the last drops of oil. It's about the government hiding the horrors of methane from people, which could absolutely seal our fate. And it's about our children and their children, and trying to save them from living in a violent, primitive, global cesspool. If we weren't focused on those critical issues, none of this would have resonated on such a planetary scale."

"But the reaction to my kidnapping is bigger than you thought it would be, isn't it?"

Chandra filled the mugs. "Not entirely. But it is intimidating."

"Excuse me?"

"Well, it's one thing to kidnap an attractive fashion model to make a point about climate chaos but it's quite another to suddenly put hundreds of billions of dollars in oil profits up for grabs because people are listening—I mean *really* listening—to what you're saying.

"Hundreds of billions? Come on. It's not like you're a bunch of terrorists blowing up pipelines. Or are you?"

Chandra paused as she sat. "Of course not. But from their standpoint what we're doing is far worse. We're changing the way people think." She laid a document in front of Sonya. "In one of our first podcasts we announced that we would release this top secret CIA report on Christmas day."

Sonya scanned the title. "Methane?" Gwen had mentioned it.

"It's a greenhouse gas, and there's a lot of it coming up from the seabed in the Arctic Ocean. The amounts that could be released worldwide are impossible to wrap your head around. Try 42,000 trillion cubic meters, and you don't need nearly that much to bake the planet. Scientists think that the last time methane heated up the earth, dinosaurs started thriving. Believe me, when people start thinking about T Rex stomping down their street, they pay attention."

"That's absurd. Dinosaurs aren't going to start tearing up their streets."

"That's true, people will all be dead by then; but dinosaurs are a great way to get them listening, and people will die if those methane releases keep coming. And their deaths will happen sooner rather than later because huge methane releases will cause quick increases in heat, so people are following everything we're saying very carefully. So is Big Oil."

"Why? You'd think they'd be happy. More dinosaurs mean more oil . . . eventually."

"I wouldn't be so flip. When Big Oil feels attacked, they can be brutal. You could write the whole of human history with the blood they've spilt."

"But this isn't about oil." Sonya glanced again at the document.

"We think it is. Methane's fuel. We don't believe for one second that the big energy companies don't have designs on it."

"What's it say in there?" Sonya reached for the document, but Chandra slipped it on to her lap.

"The first rule of public relations is that you get their attention, and the second rule is that you build interest by building anticipation. Then you can change how people think." She blew on her tea, sipped it. "How about you? Are we changing—"

"Wait a minute. Are you saying that you kidnapped me to get their attention, with the whole idea that once you had people watching your podcasts you'd tell them about that report?"

"That's right, but we also wanted to tell them about a carbon-neutral life with—"

"A symbol of rampant consumption living it."

"In a word, yes."

"How'd you ever get a CIA report?"

"You don't really think I'm going to tell you that, do you?"

Sonya shrugged. "Couldn't you have just slipped it to NBC News, instead of kidnapping me?"

Chandra laughed. "It would have drowned in a sea of trivia. It is not, most assuredly, getting drowned in a sea of trivia now. It's making people demand the release of the report from the government, which is exactly what we wanted to happen. We want people to take responsibility for the survival of the planet, and they haven't been doing that, not hundreds of millions of them, which is what it's going to take. But I'm curious about you: Are we changing the way you think?"

Sonya readied a sharp response, but checked it, knowing that any escape plans would be served better by suggesting that her thinking was changing. But she just couldn't resist the retort: "You mean, am I ready to sign on to the good ship Lollipop?"

Chandra laughed again. "Precisely."

"No, and I never will be, not while I'm a prisoner."

"As prisons go, this isn't so bad, is it?"

"How much time have you spent in that hole?"

Chandra waved off the gibe. "I expect there'll be plenty of time for you to change your mind. Speaking of which, what do you think of the change in your living arrangements?"

"Did you move Desmond out because of what he did to me?"

"We don't really know what Desmond did, now do we? But you're clearly upset by being around him, and we don't want to make you uncomfortable. Desmond himself agreed."

"He did?"

"Yes, right away. We're looking at having you here for a year. We don't want you tense and worried. We also can't have you twiddling your thumbs. I've been thinking about the way you protected Willow, and I'd like you to work with Sorrel over at the school. You saw her, she's the young woman who sounded the alert when Willow went missing. The children are still talking about you. You're a hero to them."

Sonya stymied an impulse to say that she had no interest in helping them; but she couldn't afford to indulge herself, not if she intended to gain more of their trust so she could steal everything she'd need to escape. So she tried to appear unperturbed, which wasn't easy. She'd rather do just about anything, even cook and clean, than chase after children.

"You're so quiet. Did I say something wrong?" Chandra wrapped her hands around the mug, tensing the tattoos that ran all the way to her nails.

"I don't have much of a maternal instinct."

Chandra raised the tea to her lips, eyes smiling through the steam. "What you did in saving that child tells me that you're more maternal than you're giving yourself credit for."

"Ask my daughter about that. You'll find out how maternal I am." But here, far from her old life, Sonya did feel such intense, instant longing for Darcy that it shocked her. She almost groaned aloud remembering the miserable summer when her fifteen-year-old girl returned from L.A. a furious young woman. How could she, a single mom, ever have competed with the novelty of the estranged father and the excitement of Hollywood? Screenwriters and film producers? Even the lesser lights of her ex's social circle must have seemed like silver-screen fantasies compared to life back in Denver. Darcy had resented her fiercely upon her return.

"Your daughter, really? What's she like?"

Sonya was so lost in her poignant memory that the question startled her. "The absolute opposite of me."

"Oh, I'd be surprised if that were true. Our children can be contrary, but they're rarely any more or less than apples falling from the same tree."

"Then this one rolled quite a ways."

Chandra lowered her mug. "Sorrel's doing face painting this afternoon. I'll bet you're good at that."

"Is that a dig at my work for the cosmetics industry?"

"No, it's just that I'm sure you understand how the face can be adorned. I'm never sarcastic, Sonya. It's a horrid quality for astringent souls. You, I've noticed, have a weakness for it; but you're better than that, and it has no place here. As for the cosmetics industry, I might as well tell you before someone else does that I was a model many, many years ago."

"You were?" Sonya caught herself before saying more.

"Before I got old and wrinkled, you mean?" Chandra smiled. "As I said, it was many years ago. I worked the runways of Milan and Paris and New York for two full seasons. I also had to go to agency parties but they told me to make sure I didn't say anything that anyone would ever remember. I was supposed to be as 'quiet as the flowers on the table.' I couldn't do that, so I returned to school and eventually got my doctorate in physics. So I understand the modeling world better than you might suppose. It hasn't changed much."

No, it hasn't. How many times had an art director leafed through her portfolio and said, "You were so beautiful?" As if beauty were the immortal province of only the young. "What did you do with your degree?"

"Well, if you must know, I worked for the old Atomic Energy Commission back in the late fifties, and then I did research on nuclear bombs. Isn't that—"

"That's how you did it."

"Did what?" Chandra sounded genuinely puzzled.

"Got the secret report. Someone you knew back then gave it to you."

"I'm not going to play *Twenty Questions* with you. I was about to say that I still find it appalling that I ever did that kind of research. And if I were at all religious, I'd have to do penance for several lifetimes."

"Penance? That sounds odd, coming from the mouth of an ex-model and nuclear physicist. Aren't those the words of a believer?"

"That just goes to show how much religion has infected our language. But everything has. And no, I'm not religious in any traditional sense." She leaned closer to Sonya, as if to confide, "Do you want to know what God is? What it really is?"

"I've been waiting all my life for this."

Chandra sat back, shook her head. "Sarcasm."

"I'm sorry. I'd love to hear it." Sonya was amazed at how

Chandra could leave her feeling chastened.

"It's very simple. The species needed to have a belief in God to create the religious laws that would allow it to survive. So in the same way that it had creatures crawl from the sea so they could eventually stand on two legs and build civilizations, it created a belief in God. *Don't eat pork,* which really could have killed you before the age of electricity. *No sex outside of marriage,* which was a very good idea before Sir Alexander Fleming came along and discovered penicillin. With every scientific discovery, the heebie-jeebies realm of religion was forced to shrink. The earth was the center of the universe . . . until Copernicus, and then the Vatican had to make some major theological adjustments. Humankind started in the Garden of Eden with Adam and Eve . . . until Darwin went to the Galapagos.

"Religion's purview is shrinking so fast that all it can offer is faith. God's become the Santa Claus of the creation myth. But now we've reached a point where religion has become such a threat to the survival of the world itself that—*Voila!*—the species is becoming irreligious. It's no longer helping the species to believe in God, so faith in God is dying. That's not a coincidence. The species has a meta-wisdom that's determined to let it survive."

"The fundamentalists seem to be flourishing." Sonya was thinking of the fanatics down in Colorado Springs who'd organized a massive letter-writing campaign and boycott to protest an ad showing her kissing a likeness of Darwin for a "fully evolved" energy bar.

"Of all stripes, I agree. But in most developed countries religion is dying the death it deserves. Most of Europe and Canada have already passed beyond this infantilizing state. The days of religion are simply numbered. It offers only fear and the delusion of comfort. You can't sustain true spirituality with either one of those."

"Then with what?"

"Hope. And hope doesn't need a God."

"Faith, in other words."

"No, faith is the last resort of the hopeless. But hope is based on an empirical understanding of the factors that allow us to survive and flourish, to use your word."

"Terra Firma?"

"One manifestation of hope, yes."

"But not God?"

"Belief in God is killing us, so the species is killing God. But—and this may surprise you—I do believe in the value of meditation."

"'A foolish consistency is the hobgoblin of small minds,' I take it." Sonya had always thought the Emerson quote had been worked half to death, and here she was flogging it herself.

"Not really. Whenever I'm faced with a major decision, I'll often draw the curtains and meditate."

"Is that what you've been doing?"

Chandra smiled, but offered no other response.

"I'm guessing you won't be putting your 'God is dead, let's celebrate,' message on your podcasts. I don't see that as a big selling point."

Chandra laughed heartily. "Believe me, I know enough about successful marketing to never put my thoughts on God into one of those."

Sonya smiled too, not over Chandra's views of God and religion, which she hadn't found at all convincing, but over the woman's essential good cheer in the face of almost certain defeat. Or worse.

*

Gordon Basch hurried down a walkway by the Potomac River, the Washington Monument rising in the distance. The gangly investigative reporter for *The New Yorker* had been breaking stories that altered American history since 1969, when he revealed that U.S. Army troops massacred scores of men, women, and children in and around *My Lai,* a hamlet in South Vietnam.

In the 1970s, Basch exposed massive illegal spying on Americans by the CIA. In the decades that followed, Basch continued to report on the most egregious abuses of the U.S. intelligence community. He broke the Abu Ghraib story, forcing CBS News, which had been appeasing the Pentagon by sitting on actual photos of the torture, to finally go to air.

Now Gordon had his sights set on another story, perhaps the biggest one yet. The sun beat on his shoulders, as if to remind him of the subject. Suit jacket weather, and it was December. The cherry blossoms were blooming earlier each year. They looked like they might go off any day now.

He spotted Claire in a powder-blue jogging suit, her golden

retriever, Blarney, by her side. The dog's sleek coat looked brilliant in the sunshine, the kind of canine you'd expect to see by a white picket fence in a RE/MAX ad. Except Blarney would tear off your arm with a flick of Claire's finger. Appearances were always deceptive in the intelligence community. Except when they weren't.

"Oh, hi, Gordon." Claire ran in place for a few seconds as she smiled at Basch, who nodded, giving her a full two seconds before he got to the point of their rendezvous.

"Just tell me, are those hippies hallucinating? Does the fucking report exist?"

Claire, pony-tailed for her run, a youthful mid-fifties, wasn't phased by his abrasiveness. They went way back. She'd trusted him before, but the stakes this time were larger. Huge.

Still smiling, stretching her quads as if their *tête-à-tête* were as unplanned as a sneeze, Claire said "What do you think?"

"I think it's real, and I think the only reason the hippies are holding it back is they don't have the whole goddamn thing."

"That would be a theory." Claire worked her calves. Blarney never took his chocolate eyes off Gordon. "You've done that, haven't you? Faked them with a partial." Partial report, she meant.

"Yeah, and *you* could cite chapter and verse on where and when. Act like you've got a royal flush and hope the government folds."

"They're not going to fold. They're going to squish them like a pile of ants." Claire's smile never failed her. She could have been talking about Blarney's crush on a chow.

"Then it's real. They wouldn't—"

"I didn't say that." Almost girlish in her demurral.

Basch took her arm. Blarney growled.

"It's okay, boy."

Gordon let her go. "There's no time. They'll kill them. Look, we know the goddamn methane's going off, that's no secret; but if it's as bad as they say it is, we have a fucking right to know. We get that report—and it's all there—we'll put it on the website right away, just like with Abu Ghraib. We'll fill the next issue with it."

Claire looked over Gordon's shoulder, as if she'd spotted someone. He glanced behind him, wondering who was coming up on them. Saw only the tall, pointy monument.

"You ever get the feeling that they're watching you?" she

asked.

"All the time," Gordon said. "Why else do we meet like this?"

"No, I mean Washington, Lincoln, Jefferson. All the reasons we do what we do."

"Come on, answer the fucking question, Claire. Is it real?"

"I think they are," she said, ignoring his demand. "And I think they'd be disgusted. Even a good president never gives up power arrogated by a bad one." She looked down, and her smile dipped for the first time. She spoke a single word—"Rendition"—so softly that Gordon barely heard her.

"Then you do it, Claire. You give back the power."

"Good seeing you," she declared, running in place again, jiggling her arms like a fighter coming out of his corner. "Enjoy the holidays."

Only Blarney looked back.

*

Gwen sat at a digital editing console in an underground cavern about twice the size of the cell in which Sonya had been held. But the floor down here was concrete and heated by the same thermal spring that fed all the buildings in Terra Firma, and the walls and ceiling were paneled with fir boards. Electricity for the editing gear and computer flowed from solar collectors in a meadow a few hundred feet away.

Akiah, pacing throughout most of the podcast production, settled beside her while she checked the online voting center.

"We've got another million since this morning," Gwen noted.

Bringing the total to 22.8 million ballots for the best independent documentary on global warming and the double-bind. Al Gore's *An Inconvenient Truth* was leading the other nine films with a hefty 42.3% of the vote.

"That kind of surprises me," Akiah said. "I thought the tribes would be piling it on for *The Oil Factor* or *Crude Impact.*"

"It looks like a lot more than the tribes are voting."

They also found a big jump in the number of documentaries that had been downloaded. Again, Gore's *An Inconvenient Truth* had been pirated far more than the others, almost 800,000 times.

"This is great, Akiah."

"Yeah, well, it would be better if the poll numbers were changing too."

"They are."

"I mean more. We're going to need a lot bigger numbers if we're going to get out of this thing alive."

He stared at the screen, appeared lost in thought.

"Maybe we should get back to work," Gwen said.

She rolled video of Sonya approaching the clinic for another treatment for her cuts.

"There," Akiah pointed, "that's where we need to get out. Before—"

"Don't worry." Gwen's fingers danced over the keyboard. "As long as we've got sick kids in there, I'm not shooting inside."

Akiah nodded and clicked a mouse at a desktop computer, bringing up a four-way screen. He'd been periodically checking IWT, Independent World Television; CNN; FOX; and the BBC for the Terra Firma story.

He turned back to Gwen as CNN began to run aerial footage of a man whose head lay in a puddle of blood at a truck stop near Spokane, Washington.

"Is that . . . " Gwen's fingers stopped moving.

Akiah glanced back at the computer screen, then rose from his chair, voice charging with emotion. "They killed Jangles."

"Oh, God. Did you know him?" She knew of the trucker and had seen a digital photo of him just a few days ago.

"I met him once. He was a great guy."

Right then FOX began broadcasting the same footage. Akiah turned up the sound.

"Jangles McDermott," the anchor said gravely, "was a convicted cop killer from New Jersey."

"Oh, fuck off."

Gwen had never seen Akiah lose his temper. "Why's he calling him a cop killer?"

Akiah glared at the TV. "He did kill a cop, but it's not that simple."

Eleven years ago, he explained, Jangles had pulled into a truck stop in New Jersey and heard people banging from inside a trailer.

"It was really hot, like in the nineties. They needed help."

He said Jangles went to his truck to get bolt cutters for the padlock. "But by the time he got back the driver and a cop had walked up. The cop told him not to worry, it was none of his business. Go on, forget it. They're fine. Jangles had been around. He knew the driver was hauling illegal aliens, and had probably paid off the cop. The pounding was getting fainter."

Akiah shook his head. "People were dying in there, and they must have heard Jangles and the cop arguing because they started yelling for help in Spanish, so he went to open it anyway. Soon as he did, the cop went for his gun." Akiah shrugged. "Jangles whipped the bolt cutter around so fast the cop never even got it out. Jangles is a big guy. *Was,* I mean. Killed the cop with one hit to the head."

Jangles, he went on, had found forty-eight people packed inside the trailer. Three of them were already dead, including a six-month-old Mexican girl.

"The ones who survived went straight to the hospital. Jangles did nine years for manslaughter."

"Did he know anything about us?" She felt bad for even asking.

"Not really. He didn't even know who he was bringing Darcy Adams to."

Akiah sat down heavily. Gwen let a minute pass before going back to work. They were editing a final scene of Sonya into the podcast when CNN aired video of a man and a woman who looked like they'd just stepped out of an emergency room.

"Turn that up," she said to Akiah.

The network identified them as fugitive members of the Animal Liberation Front arrested by federal agents investigating the abduction of Sonya Adams.

"Are they with us?"

"Yes," he said sharply. "I mean they helped."

"They're rolling them all up."

The right side of the woman's face was heavily bandaged. So was the man's scalp, and his left arm was in a sling. CNN said FBI agents were taking them into federal court in Boise, Idaho for arraignment on a long list of terrorism charges.

"How high up the ladder are they?" she asked.

"Just Jangles. That's all they knew about."

"So the Feds can't get them to say anything?"

"No, but it looks like they tried."

"Is it worth it, Ki?" The diminutive was her own endearment for him, but she wasn't sure he even noticed.

"People taking the end of life as we know it seriously? Yeah, it's worth it."

"No, I mean all this grief to get the daughter here. She could be nothing but trouble, and it looks like they're following her."

"They are, and she's heading to safe house a long ways from here. We figure that they'll wait for her to lead them here."

"So once she's in the safe house, she's not going anywhere?"

"No, we're still going to want to get her here."

"But why? That'll be incredibly risky for us. And it's already been horrible for the people helping her."

"They knew the risks, and *she's the daughter.* She's Sonya's only family. We get her with her mom, and the story gets even bigger. These things have to build all the time to hold the public's attention."

"But they could scoop her up a mile from here. We'd be totally hooped."

"They won't be able to, and then she's going to be one more person the Feds will have to be careful about if they want to come crashing in here. And we're pretty sure she could end up supporting us. She's a hardcore vegan. She's political and might even help convince her mother that what we're doing is right. We do know that she's not freaking out about us taking Sonya."

"That's hard to believe. She's trying to find her."

"Right, but now she's a fugitive too. And Jangles was going to send a signal if she acted like a loose cannon. He never did."

"But how are we going to get her out of that safe house if they're watching her?"

He gazed in her eyes, but Gwen couldn't tell if he were looking *at* her with longing or *through* her to the wall, the earth, to life in the unending underground. She chanced resting her hand on his sleeve and squeezing his arm gently, hoping to spark their first intimate moment, feeling it blossom readily in her own belly.

But all she received in response was a crisp rundown of what he called "Plan B." Its shocking details forced her hand from him and rid Gwen of any urge for intimacy or endearments, too frightened now for the sweet imperatives of touch.

Chapter 14

Darcy kept her arms snug around Eve's waist as she turned the BMW motorcycle onto a stone-scribbled two-track that wound up a wooded hillside at a daunting, thirty-degree angle, an obstacle course the refined street bike had never been designed to surmount.

"We're going to get bounced around," Eve said over the headset, "so if I'm leaning one way or the other, lean with me."

Though it felt fearfully at odds with reason, Darcy took her cues from Eve while pressed against the back of her black leather jacket.

Twice the rear tire spit out rocks before gaining traction, and each time Darcy stiffened. But Eve didn't spill the bike or seem the least bit ruffled, and after ten minutes of twisting up the rugged byway they rode out of the trees toward a wide, flat clearing with a ranch house.

A single cow stared at them from a pasture to the right. She stood only paces from a shed that pitched precipitously forward, its roof top heavy with moss.

The pale blue house looked sturdy enough, though, and it had a carport for a Kawasaki dirt bike and a black Jeep Wrangler, along with a wooden ramp that ran from the driveway to the front door.

Eve braked beside the mud-splattered Kawasaki, and kicked out the stand. Darcy hopped off, thighs and groin achy from hanging on too tightly; she'd been tensed-up the entire trip.

"I'll show you around later. Let's go in and I'll introduce you to my partner. His name's Avery."

They walked up the ramp as a handsome, short-haired man in a wheelchair opened the front door, greeting them warmly.

He held the door till Eve could get it, then backed into the dim living room, gray from the low-lying clouds. Eve flicked a set of light switches before giving him a kiss. Darcy noticed family photos on the wall to her left.

"You see anything unusual?" Eve asked him, which drew Darcy's attention to a compact telescope on a tripod by the front window.

"I don't know if we should make anything of it but I saw two twin-engine planes coming down through the clouds about five minutes apart. That was about a half hour ago."

An hour after the Black Hawk, thought Darcy.

Eve made the introductions, and he shook Darcy's hand. *Firm grip*, she noted, no doubt from rolling his wheelchair. Avery caught her noticing and answered the unspoken question by nodding at a wall full of motocross trophies. "The big race down in Washougal. I crashed and was trying to crawl off the track when a guy hit me between six and seven," referring to his vertebrae like they were old friends.

"You go to those races, you see lots of guys in chairs or getting around on crutches." Eve shook her head.

"You used to race too," he said.

"I quit while I was ahead. You hungry?" she asked Darcy.

Darcy realized at once that she was starving, and helped her hosts toss together a huge green salad with feta cheese. Darcy offered no objections; her personal credo now held that if people risked their freedom for you, you didn't turn down their food, no matter how it was cooked or processed. Except for meat: she still couldn't go there.

"We've got a big garden out back." Eve passed her a slice of home-baked baguette. "All in raised beds so Avery can work it. That's his great passion."

"These days," he said.

After they ate he cleared the table, and Darcy asked if they had any TV reception.

"Sure do," Avery said over his shoulder. "Satellite."

Eve worked the remote, clicking to CNN as a correspondent wrapped up a report on the President's latest fundraising trip.

The familiar logo, "Terror at Terra Firma" appeared over the anchor's shoulder before the screen filled with video of Lotus being led by two federal agents past a cluster of camera crews only hours ago. Her hands were cuffed, yet she was smiling and held her head high. *She looks amazing,* thought Darcy, the more so when she heard that Lotus would be facing seventeen terrorism charges, including the harboring of her fugitive parents, Drake and Nancy Cohenson, who'd been living under assumed names in Austin, Texas.

The screen split to show the middle-aged couple, gray and frightened, next to their defiant daughter. They were also cuffed, charged with sabotaging a bomb-making plant thirty-eight years ago.

Seventeen terrorism charges. Darcy sat on the couch thinking Lotus would be in prison the rest of her life, if they didn't torture her to death first. And her poor parents. She wondered if Lotus had been forced to give them up, then knew better: She'd never do that.

Eve handed her a tissue. Only then did Darcy realize she was crying.

"I'd like to let you talk it out but we can't be hearing any more than we have to. You want to get away from this? Go work in the garden with me?"

They walked out back where the raised beds had the picked-over appearance of late autumn. Only a long row of mustard greens remained.

"You need to get them out?" she asked Eve.

"No, they're even sweeter after they freeze."

"You've got a nice thing going here. Why are you taking such a huge risk to help me?"

"The less we say the better, right? If you do this life well, you never tell. We help out where we can. Let's leave it at that, except you're the first person I've ever been asked to pick up on a motorcycle. I'm very suspicious about that jackknifed truck in Spokane."

"Seriously? You think that was a set-up?"

"You do the math."

Eve grabbed the wooden handles of a rusty wheelbarrow and rolled it over to a stack of baled straw.

"Avery can't move these things. I thought we could spread it on the beds." She reached in her back pocket and flipped a pair of leather work gloves to Darcy.

They spent the next hour moving several bales to the garden, spreading the moist straw on the soil, talking little. Darcy enjoyed the work. *Chop wood, carry water.* That's what it's all about, she said to herself: mindfulness.

But an eerie feeling began to infect her. She started looking around every minute or so, expecting to catch an errant eye peering at them from the forest. It felt like she was back at deGenerate with a bar full of guys scoping out her bottom. Only worse. A lot worse.

To try to shake it off, she asked how Avery had adjusted to his injury.

"In some ways, really well." Eve straightened up, "But he's still thinking he'll walk again, and the docs say that's not going to happen. But he's so sure of it he won't let me sell his Kawasaki. I don't know, maybe it's good we have that bike right now."

Darcy saw her looking around too.

"What do you mean?"

Eve shrugged. "We've got a lot of trails around here, and they're a way out if we need them."

Darcy spotted a number of them. "Where do they go?"

"Pretty much in every direction. It's a complete maze in there."

"But you know them?"

She nodded. "I've been mountain biking and dirt biking in there for fifteen years. You can disappear for fifty miles back there. Maybe that's why you're here, in case we need them."

"You think we're being watched?"

"Maybe I'm paranoid, but I've had that feeling the whole time we've been out here."

"I started feeling that way a few minutes ago."

They both looked around. Darcy remembered one of Jangles' first comments, and wondered if Mercury were still in retrograde.

*

Johnny Bracer loved this part of the hunt, when the prey was all hunkered down, far from home, maybe thinking they got it made, or like darlin' Darcy, looking up every minute or two, shaky as shit. Animals sense the hunter, why not people?

He stayed in place, reluctantly. The Bureau said it was eyes-only time; and they had their boys right on his back, not a mile away, text-messaging like mad, telling him they were getting tons of info from other sources. What exactly, they wouldn't say. *Just keep your eyes on the prize, Johnny boy.*

Of course they didn't say Johnny boy, not to his face. But that's how they treated him. Nothing to get worked up about. He knew that if Darcy took off with her newest buddy, his job would be talking to wheelchair Wally, asking some very pointed questions while the Bureau handled the chase.

In fact, Johnny was preparing his questions right now, including a few that didn't have any answers. That *couldn't.* You can't hear the truth if you don't make them lie, and you can't make them lie if you don't make the truth the biggest prize of all.

*

Darcy was glad they were heading for the house. The sky was darkening and a chill had crept under her jacket. She couldn't tell if it was from fear or the cold damp weather, but it stalked her skin and made her shiver.

Eve touched her arm, startling her. "I'm sorry. I was just going to ask if you'd mind helping me grab some logs?"

Darcy forced herself to nod. Eve was already moving the wheelbarrow to the back of the house where split pine had been stacked five feet high for the length of the carport.

Darcy started loading it right away. Eve pitched in, then pushed the wheelbarrow just past the back door. Darcy grabbed an armful of the sweet-smelling wood, eager to haul it in the house and get away from the chill, the deepening darkness, the eyes that might be staring at them; but Eve stopped her, pointing to a horizontal door a foot above the foundation.

"What?" *I just want to go inside.*

"It's a wood box," she explained, unlatching the door. "You shove your logs in here and the inside door's right near the stove. You don't have to carry them all through the house."

*

Johnny liked wood boxes. Never seen one yet with a lock. You crawl in from the outside, and then you crawl right into the house.

Only bad part were the spiders, black widows and hoboes. More people knew about the widows, but the hoboes would leave you looking like a leper. Nasty fuckers, and aggressive as hell. But Johnny didn't have any big fear of them, just a healthy respect, and he knew they could help you out in a pinch.

*

As soon as Eve and Darcy stepped in the house, Avery wheeled out of his office with a slip of paper for Eve.

She read it and tossed it in the wood stove before asking Darcy if she wanted to catch any more news while they got dinner together.

"I can help."

"No, sit and warm up. You look cold. Here's a throw. I'm going to put on some news. It's northwest stuff and weather. We usually catch it while we're cooking. Is that cool?"

"Sure." *Be a break from Terror Firma,* she said to herself as she wrapped the wool throw around her shoulders.

But the first headline brought Darcy right back to her most immediate fears:

Terror suspects arrested in Idaho, blazed across the screen as she watched Kodiak and Poughkeepsie hustled to police cars.

What did they do to them?

Kodiak's head was bandaged, and his arm was in a sling. And Poughkeepsie's pretty face was wrapped in gauze.

The news channel reported that they were longtime fugitives wanted in a series of fire bombings in Oregon and Washington, and had been taken into custody this morning.

Then, without linking the cases, they aired the gruesome video of Jangles McDermott lying dead at the truck stop. Darcy cried out before catching herself and covering her mouth. A reporter identified him as a "convicted cop killer gunned down during a robbery attempt."

She saw that Eve and Avery had moved into the living room. "He wasn't robbing anyone. He's the guy who drove me to the truck stop. He was going to distract a guy who'd been following us so I could get away. With you. I can't believe they killed him."

But even then Darcy knew her grief wasn't just about Jangles, or even the savage reprisals against Kodiak and Poughkeepsie. It was also her fear that the men who had attacked them were drawing ever closer to her. Then her eyes drifted to Eve and Avery and she worried about them too.

"You guys are going to have to be real careful."

Eve nodded and looked away. Neither of them asked questions about Jangles, and Darcy wished she hadn't said anything at all. Information was implication. *Keep your mouth shut.* The urgent unspoken language of the underground was scary enough without telling them things they didn't need to know.

A commercial break ended and the newscast showed Al Gore trying to leave the University of Washington after giving a speech on global warming. A mob of reporters was demanding his reaction to all the votes his documentary was getting in the Terra Firma contest.

Gore looked exasperated. "I have no interest in having my film in any contest run by a bunch of kidnappers."

"Would you be a mediator if this crisis ever called for it?" asked a tall woman with a glacial stare.

Gore gave up trying to escape the gaggle. "I'll do whatever legitimate law enforcement authorities think I should do, and talking to those kidnappers has not even been—"

The rest of his words were drowned out by the loudest, most frightening explosion Darcy had ever heard. The house shook violently, rattling chairs, tables, the refrigerator. Books bounced off shelves, and cabinet doors flew open. Plates, bowls, and glasses crashed to the floor, scattering shards that drummed insanely on the tile.

She was certain she was caught in an earthquake, making no sense of the sound at all. Eve rushed toward her, shoving her pack in her hands and shouting, "Move! Move!"

*

Johnny Bracer saw a fireball that looked a hundred stories high, and so bright it made the twilight look black by comparison. Two, three miles to the south. He stood and stared at it openly, breaking cover and not giving a good shit.

He pulled out his cell as certain of a message as he was of the night ahead. Simple words appeared on the tiny screen: "Question subject(s)."

Another message came right up: "Refinery Wayside + pipeline." No need to explain, not with a sunrise at sunset.

That's when Johnny heard the Kawasaki whining like a million mosquitoes as it disappeared into the trees. Running without lights. A glimpse and it was gone.

He grabbed his monocular and tried to pick it up in the woods, but it was shadowy and the damn evergreens were thicker than pigs in Arkansas.

He doubted the Bureau had anyone left to follow the bike. All of the Task Force must be scrambling, closing off roads and stopping everything that moved.

There she goes. Say bye-bye.

He turned to the chore at hand, making his way along the periphery of the woods till he thought he could dart unseen to the woodpile by the rear of the carport. He was looking around when a chopper surprised him, flying so low he could make out the struts. Suddenly, a powerful spotlight swept over the garden and tracked swiftly to the trees. Long columns of light lit up the woods with the intensity of white phosphorous. Johnny watched to see if he could pick out the bike but too many trees still stood in the way. *If that's McCarthy, he'll run them down, and then he'll make them wish they'd never took off.*

Johnny saw the fireball fading, but the low ceiling reflected the inferno so fiercely that it looked like the clouds themselves were burning up.

Wayside was a huge refinery. To blow that sucker they must have had someone on the inside. For the first time, he found himself admiring those fucks. This was war, and after the Persian Gulf with George the First he could respect warriors. He'd missed this kind of serious action.

Another sprint and he was by the back door trying to decide whether to risk a direct assault or slip in through the wood box. Wheelchair Wally had the use of his hands, so he could goddamn good and well use a gun.

He sized up the door. *Better move fast.* He kicked the fucker so hard the lock snapped and the jamb shattered like cheap china. The door slammed against a kitchen counter, and he saw Wally staring at him from ten feet away. Johnny aimed his .357 right smack at his nose.

"Move and you're a stump."

He edged closer, kicking broken crap out of the way, eyes on Wally, eyes on the corner behind him, ready for some asshole to come flying around it at any second.

But no one did. The sound of the TV rose to him now, a bulletin about a massive explosion in north-central Washington State.

And I'm in the eye of the shit storm.

"Who else is here?"

"No one."

"You lie, I'll kill you."

"I'm not lying."

"I want that fucking TV off."

"It's over there." Wally nodded at the remote on a short table in the living room.

"Go get it, and shut it off. *Don't* do anything stupid."

The TV fell dark.

"Now back up to me slowly."

Johnny stopped him a foot away with his free hand.

"Here's what you're going to do. You're going to roll back out there, and then we're going down the hall. We're doing this together and we're doing it slow."

Johnny crouched behind the chair, his gun right next to Wally's head, a perfect shooting position for searching the house—an office, two bedrooms, closets, and a bath. True enough, no one home.

"Back to the living room," he said, cracking the gun firmly against Wally's temple, right in the soft spot where it smarts like a son of a bitch.

"Don't do that," Wally said.

"You mean this?" Johnny whacked him hard enough to draw blood. "Or do you mean this?" He whacked him again, tearing more skin from the side of his face. "Don't fucking tell me what to do. That's rule number one. Rule number two is you tell me everything you know."

A few minutes later, wheelchair Wally's face looked nothing like the nice picture on the wall of him and his stumpy wife. He'd even tried to answer those questions that don't have an answer, like why Jerry Lewis is so fucking popular in France. Johnny threatened to put a hobo spider right on his nuts if he didn't come up with a damn good explanation.

But all laughs aside, Jerry Lewis was a control question. It let Johnny hear how Wally sounded when he really didn't know an answer. Made him believable when he started spieling about the tunnel and a certain barmaid who'd made off in it.

"Where's it at?"

Damn if they hadn't rolled right over it when they went down the hall.

Johnny kicked aside a shag runner and saw a piece of plywood set flush with the floor. Looked like the entrance, but any group shrewd enough to wipe out Wayside could blow off his face with a booby trap.

"Get out and open it."

Johnny dumped him on the floor like little Miss Green Thumb had dumped the bales out of the wheelbarrow. Then he kicked his sorry ass back over there and stepped away when Wally lifted it by a finger hole. Son of a bitch even hit the light switch for him.

He grabbed Wally's foot and dragged him back into the living room. Then he cuffed his hands behind his back and his feet to a leg of the wood stove.

"You don't feel shit down there, right?" He laughed. "I'll be right back."

He rushed out to the carport to make sure the dirt bike was gone and the other vehicles were still there. Check. Then he barged back in the living room.

"Don't dick with me. The dumpy one took off on the bike, right? And the other one went down there?" He glanced at the tunnel entrance.

"I'll tell you for sure, you cut me loose."

Son of a bitch can't move, he's bleeding, his goddamn socks are burning, and he's trying to play, *Let's Make a Deal*. With *me*.

Johnny grabbed him by the hair, pulled out a long pocket knife, and opened the blade with his teeth. Then he pressed it against Wally's throat. "I'll cut you loose. I'll cut you to fucking pieces right here. How'd you like that for a deal?"

Small shake of the head.

"I'm coming back to kill you if she's not down there."

"She is," he whispered.

Johnny pushed his head away and folded up the blade.

He smelled Wally's feet starting to burn and hesitated.

What the fuck, he's a cripple.

He cut the cuffs and dragged him into the kitchen, pulling off his charred socks and shackling him to the drain pipe under the sink.

"Merry fucking Christmas."

Johnny started down a wooden ladder into the tunnel with the smell of those goddamn socks on his hands. He brushed them against his pants and paused on the bottom rung to study the dirt floor. There they were, boot prints fresh as a nightmare.

Time to shut off the entrance light that Wally had thrown on. She could be staring at him right now. And then it hit him: The son of a bitch was probably sending her a signal when he put the light on.

I should have let him cook.

The darkness soothed him. It made him feel invisible, like the only light in the whole world was in his eyes, and his eyes could see through anything, even this.

But after moving no more than fifty feet a question began to nag him: What's a fucking tunnel doing down here anyway?

This wasn't mining country. Never was. And this wasn't a mine anyway. No rock, just dirt. To confirm what he'd been feeling with his hand, he flicked his penlight on the wall. Dirt and timber, that's all. And tall enough to stand in. He flashed the light on the floor and saw her boot prints still leading straight away from him.

He shut off the light and picked up his pace. He didn't have the answer to his question but he had a strong sense that he'd better hurry up and find her. *Yell at her*, he told himself. Forget this cat and mouse shit. Make her panic. See if you can get a handle on where the fuck she's at.

"Darcy," he bellowed. "I'm coming to get you, and even I wouldn't want to be caught down here with me. You hear? Even I wouldn't want to be caught down here with me."

Down here with me . . . with me . . . with me . . . echoed over and over.

*

Darcy started running, but on her toes, like she could move silently. But she knew better. Maybe he did too:

"I mean it . . . mean it . . . mean it . . ."

Racing into the blackest darkness she'd ever known, glancing off walls, stumbling, as scared of him as she was of flying off an unseen edge.

*

Johnny heard her, so he started running too. Not balls out, you never did that unless you had to. You wanted something left when you caught them, when you really needed your juice.

He'd no sooner found his rhythm than he remembered a bail jumper he'd tracked down three years ago. It'd been a real pain in the ass getting that guy. He saw his freaked-out face like the little shit's whole purpose in life had always been to give him the reason for the tunnel. But there was no comfort in the answer, not down here.

"Holy fucking shit," Johnny whispered, "she's heading for Canada." His legs pumped full bore, and his breath came hard and fast as bad luck.

*

Jesus, he's running. Darcy could hear him but she couldn't make out the real footfalls from the echoes, which made it sound like there were ten of him chasing her.

She didn't care anymore about the noises she made—he knew she was down there. She ran as hard as she could, more terrified of him now then of any hole or shaft she could fall into, fending off the walls with her arms, caroming through the darkness with her heart pounding like it wanted to beat her to death. Anguish squeezing out the last of her strength, his voice an iron brush on her back:

"*I see you . . . see you . . . see you . . .* "

Chapter 15

Sonya watched as a dozen children in bearskin coats lined up outside the kindergarten, a straw-bale building with softly rounded stucco walls and honey-colored cross beams. It rose near the copse of trees that separated the farm from the rest of the community, and was shielded from easy view by a row of towering poplars. *An ideal location*, she thought, because back here they wouldn't have to worry about the kids ending up in the river or hot pools.

But they did end up in the clinic. She couldn't shake the memory of those sick children, of Gwen shutting off her camera on the two occasions when they'd gone inside. The camerawoman wasn't here to shoot this little foray, either, which Sonya found particularly odd: not so much that she'd been left to walk over here by herself, but that Chandra and Akiah would pass up on an opportunity to show the world warm fuzzy pictures of her helping out with young kids. She'd look all but converted.

In marked contrast to the hospitalized children, these four-to-six year olds looked full of beans. They were singing *Home on the Range*; but they were giggling so much that they kept flubbing the opening line. As Sonya got closer, she heard why. They weren't singing *Home on the Range*. They were singing the Aboland version: *Om-om on the Range*, an improvisation the kids had come up with on their own, Sorrel said. The teacher looked at her pre-schoolers and kindergarten students with obvious pride.

"Okay, you Om-steaders, inside."

Sunlight streamed through three generous windows, warming built-in benches holding a rich collection of colorful pillows. Stuffed animals and fanciful wooden toys—dolls and hand-painted blocks and balls—perched on shelves shaped like stars, the sun, and crescent moons.

"When everyone gets settled, I have a surprise," Sorrel announced as the children seated themselves on a plum carpet in the middle of the room. She smiled warmly the whole time, her remarkably fair skin in striking contrast to her long, shiny black braids.

"Guess who's come to help us paint faces?" Sorrel asked her

charges in a big voice.

"You are." A boy with long black hair and chocolate skin pointed to Sonya.

"That's right. I've come to do some fun painting with you guys." Sonya found herself emulating Sorrel's playful tone.

"Would you save me too?" the boy asked her.

"Like Willow," shouted a bone thin-girl who had such short white-blond hair that she resembled a Q-tip.

"Sure," Sonya said, smiling. "But I don't think you're going to need saving. This is a very safe place."

Liar.

"No it's *not,*" challenged the girl with the short hair, who now sported a grimace to match her harsh haircut. "She almost got eaten *alive.*" She pointed to Willow, who stared at the floor, evidently uncomfortable with the memory of the cougar, or the attention, or both.

"Yeah, *eaten,*" two boys named Bodhi and Shalin shouted in unison, clearly delighted to indulge this possibility aloud.

"And last year," Q-tip went on, "A mountain lion *ate* my friend Starling." Words as big and bold as her blue eyes.

"I heard," Sonya said, at a loss for any other response. She looked at Sorrel. *Help me.*

"So you might have to save us." The chocolate-skinned boy crossed his arms: Argument won.

"If anyone needs saving, I'll be sure to do it. How's that sound?"

Good, to judge by the cheers.

Within minutes Sonya was painting a tiger on the boy's cheek. His name was Chakka, and he remained remarkably still as she finished dabbing the fine stripes on the skinny tail.

Sorrel sat beside her on the bench, drawing a dove on the forehead of a girl named Sheena. In half an hour they painted most of the class. Sonya scanned the room, wondering where Gwen was.

When she glanced back down, she was surprised to see that the last child in line was Willow. The four-year-old stared at the floor as she edged closer. A part meandered down the middle of her head, and there were freckles Sonya hadn't noticed before.

"Hi, there," she said. "How are you doing?"

"Okay." She sounded gloomy.

"Can you show me your eyes?"

Willow looked up, blinked rapidly, and sank her chin back to her chest.

"It's going to be hard for me to paint your face if you're looking down."

She tapped the bridge of her nose. "That's where I want it. You can paint it there."

Sonya asked what kind of animal she'd like.

"A butterfly. The Bread-and-butter fly. It will protect me."

"Ah," Sonya said, "I know which one you mean."

She painted a bright green and purple butterfly on her nose, using the bridge for the body and the sides for the wings. Then she turned her toward the window so she could see her reflection. Willow looked at herself for barely a second before tucking her chin in again.

"Thank you," she said slowly. "You are a good artist. You can paint me all the time."

After she walked away, Sorrel said softly, "She's been having some problems."

"I shouldn't wonder."

"We can't convince her that the mountain lion's not coming back to get her. She's been having terrible nightmares. Getting her to play outside is a real problem."

"But it's dead. She was with them when they carried it around on that pole."

Sorrel spoke in such a low voice that Sonya could barely hear her. "They found some fresh tracks. The kids don't know." She caught Sonya's eye. "That's why we need you here."

Said this as if to flatter her, but Sonya found it astounding. For this place and time, she—a *model,* for Christ's sakes, from downtown *Denver*—had a highly prized experience: She'd faced down a cougar. *Me, the great cougar spooker.* Unbelievable.

Sorrel's hand rested on her sleeve as she nodded at Willow. "It's just one new set of tracks, but it's like she *knows.* I see her staring at the snow all the time."

They watched her sit by herself and lift her eyes only to gaze at a gauzy fort that had been commandeered by the boys.

Sorrel walked over and stroked the girl's back as she talked to her. Sonya had been moved by how soft the teacher had been with the children, never yelling, cajoling them gently.

Had she ever been so gentle with Darcy? She doubted it. They were always struggling with each other, and with a father and husband who was a jerk. Then Darcy came back from L.A. and her adolescence exploded like a cluster-bomb, flinging shrapnel in every direction.

Sonya realized she might have offered these children more tenderness in the past half hour than she'd given her own daughter in all her years growing up.

Is that really possible?

No, she assured herself, *it wasn't that bad. You had great moments together.* But a wave of grief did overcome her as she recalled how brittle she'd been with Darcy, shouting at her when she was still a little girl, shoving her into her bedroom, spanking her, and thinking, no, *believing* she was a good mother, far more gentle than her own mother had been. But neither gentle nor loving enough, to look at the results.

*

Before the school day ended, the class drew get-well cards and shaped tiny clay gnomes for the children at the clinic. Sorrel said she'd deliver them after their classmates went home.

"I could do it," Sonya volunteered. "I don't mind." With her suspicion fully sparked, she wanted a second look at the clinic.

"No, I'll do it," Sorrel said, surprisingly curt.

"Her," said Q-tip, the girl with the short white hair, thrusting her finger at Sonya.

This kid's a pistol.

"Yeah, you do it." Bodhi pointed his finger at her too.

"Sonya!" his side kick, Shalin, shouted.

Now most of them were pointing to her and lobbying loudly on her behalf. In the midst of this commotion, Willow stepped forward and took her hand.

"I want Sonya to take my card and gnomie."

Sorrel relented, as if the girl with the butterfly on her nose deserved the final say for having survived the cougar encounter. But the teacher showed no comfort at this turn of events, which made Sonya even more curious about the kids in the clinic.

As soon as the parents started filing in, the children Sonya had painted took boisterous pride in pointing out that she had been their artist. She felt badly for Sorrel, having to stand in the shadow of the least maternal mom on the planet. But Sorrel sounded genuinely pleased to announce that Sonya would be helping out at the kinderhaus.

"She's great with the children," she told the parents with none of the reluctance she'd shown over Sonya's offer to deliver the cards and gnomes.

Sonya smiled gamely over the praise, feeling like such a fraud she wanted to run and hide. But before she could leave, Willow's expectant mom came up and took her hand.

"I just wanted to say that I'm so happy you're going to be working with the kids. Willow's crazy about you."

Sonya managed one more stiff smile before fleeing the kinderhaus.

*

Gwen sat by herself and stared at the silent TV screen in the underground production studio, waiting to hear if anyone would die. Waiting for the flames. Waiting now for more than an hour, feeling indicted by her own inaction. She could have emailed the Washington State Police, the FBI, even Texrefineco. But instead she looked blankly at the screen, at the bland anchors who knew nothing yet of a bomb and a massive refinery fire, and would never know of the hard-born beliefs that drive such desperation.

Her fingers were posed on the keyboard, but unmoving. *Like my conscience*, she thought, her childhood Catholicism kindled, as it often was, by a crisis, leaving her torn by the temptation to tell and the temptation to remain still, to hope and pray that salvation for the doomed and sodden life of the planet really did lie in a solitary act of silence, as it once had lain for her in a simple act of contrition.

She checked the clock on the computer screen. Less than ninety seconds. CNN's website bristled with the news of a suicide bombing in Jordan. She shook her head at the slaughter, as she had so many times in the past, before catching herself, gripped by the possibility that she now had common ground with blindly-driven killers.

She saw the refinery bomb as Terra Firma's own double-bind: the violence they'd accept to spread their message would become the violence that would destroy them. It had been easy to approve of Sonya's kidnapping—they'd intended her no real harm—but a bombing was likely to unleash the government's most ruthless response.

Ten seconds. She didn't need the clock anymore. She counted down, eyes moving from CNN's website to the TV.

Nothing, of course: a blank final second. Too soon for pictures, though she imagined the eruption of earth and steel and flames, the geysers of fiery gas scorching the sullied sky.

She wanted this screen, divided neatly as a compass, to make a believer of her again, to tell her that no one had died; but it was easier in these empty seconds to see Terra Firma's double bind burning them to death. To see fire fighting fire as it always had.

Minutes passed. She tried to remind herself of what Akiah had said as he'd climbed out of the studio, that we're all—

Orange and red flames stilled Akiah's words and filled CNN's corner of the screen. She looked over and saw that a bulletin had flashed on their website moments ago.

Now FOX. And then almost instantaneously the last two corners lit up with the same aerials. She saw it as a bird might have, or as a moth drawn to the glow of a cruel fire, borne on the currents of its own destruction.

She sat mesmerized as great balls of flame shot skyward and bloomed like furious red poppies, then dissolved into a haze thick as delusion. In the midst of this madness she recalled Akiah looking down at her from the ladder, and heard his final words in full: "We're all John Brown now, and this is our Harper's Ferry."

What made her cry was not that he was wrong, but that he might be right.

*

The clinic's walls and counters looked dull this afternoon with only the flat light of the dusky sky leaking through the narrow windows. The three young patients lay bundled under their sheets and quilts, drowsy as snow drifts.

Devaki, in her white turban, walked up as soon as Sonya entered. "Yes, you are here and why is that? Do you need more arnica? I will get it and you will take it with you."

"No, I'm fine. I've got some cards and little toys that their classmates made for them," looking at the sick children.

"Miss Sorrel, this is her job. Why is she not here?"

Sonya explained that, too, intrigued by Devaki's resistance, as she had been by Sorrel's.

"I'll just hand them out and leave, if you don't want me here for some reason."

"Why would I not want you here? Go, go." She snapped her fingers and stepped aside.

Sonya gave the children the cards and gnomes, describing how hard their friends had worked on them. Branch and Phoenix, the two boys, nodded lethargically at the drawings, mostly of snowmen and trees.

"Thanks," Branch managed, the circles under his eyes dark as his bangs.

Devaki hovered over Sonya, smiling (nervously, she thought) at the children.

"They are tired ones. You can see. They need to eat and get their rest. Come, you must eat your eggs and lentils," she scolded them. "This is most important."

Neither boy appeared capable of mustering a response, much less eating the modest plates of food on their wooden trays. Only Sylvan, brushing aside her thick braid, tried to eat. The effort appeared to exhaust her.

"How about if I help you?" Sonya offered.

"The girl Sylvan, she can feed herself."

But "the girl Sylvan" lowered her spoon and said, "Please," as if she'd been waiting for someone, anyone, to feed her.

Devaki watched Sonya spooning up egg and sat next to Branch. *To eavesdrop*, Sonya figured. *These kids are incredibly weak.*

"There you go," she encouraged Sylvan, who had just accepted a few bits of yolk.

"I know I have to eat to get better, but I feel so sick to my stomach."

"Maybe you shouldn't be eating. Sometimes you have to give your body a rest and—"

"No, the girl Sylvan she must eat," Devaki insisted. "This is important medicine for her."

"What's wrong with her?" Sonya said.

"Never you mind," Devaki replied, her voice rising as she spoke. "The girl Sylvan she needs this food. That's all I will say. The boys, too. Eat, eat," she said to Branch.

"This food specifically?" Sonya said.

"You ask too many questions. Feed the girl Sylvan and do not ask so many questions."

Sylvan fingered the fringe on Sonya's buckskin skirt. "I like the way it feels."

"Do you have one?" She'd noticed most of the little girls wearing them.

"Yes, but I can't put it on in here."

"Have you been here long?"

She nodded, an effort that looked draining. "A whole week. No, two."

"The girl Sylvan she does not know her days. Pay no attention."

I don't think so.

"When did your tummy start to hurt?"

"I think you should go. You give them the cards, yes, that's very nice, and the little gnomies. Now you go, Miss Questions."

But Sylvan took her hand. "Please stay," she pleaded softly. "My mama won't be here till later. Can't she stay, Devaki? I promise I'll eat if she stays."

Devaki affected a stern look. "Okay, okay, but only if Miss Questions stops her questions and you eat your food. You stop your so many questions?"

Sonya nodded. "I promise."

Sylvan ate, and now ran her fingers over Sonya's palm, tracing a line from above her thumb toward her wrist. She wasn't aware of what the girl was doing until she spoke up.

"What happened to your life line?"

"My what?"

"This one." She pressed Sonya's palm. "Your *life* line. It tells you how long you'll live. See mine," she held out her hand. "It's really long, but yours stops so soon."

Sonya placed no stock in palm reading, so she wasn't alarmed by what Sylvan had said and told the girl, who did seem upset, not to pay it any mind.

But Sylvan wasn't assuaged, and still looked troubled when Sonya hugged her and left.

Not five steps from the door she heard the gong sound for dinner, so she headed directly to the community center, spotting Edson a few yards ahead and hurrying up to him. Befriending him might prove as essential to her escape as finding skates and skis and other supplies.

He was visibly surprised when she linked arms with him, but he smiled when she asked if she could join him.

"If it's okay with Juno," she added.

Not that she really cared. After finding Juno in a threesome with Andromeda and Desmond, she figured the dogsled driver had no grounds to object.

"She won't mind . . . "

Lying. She could hear it in his hesitancy.

" . . . because she's out making a run with the dogs."

No, honest. But in a cunning sort of way.

"A run?" she said as they passed the tall torches burning on both sides of the community center entrance. "Where?"

"You *are* the curious one," he said, smiling again.

They settled at one of the large round tables off to the side. Sonya immediately felt more at ease there, less of the fishbowl effect than in sitting close to the front.

Andromeda waved when she saw her, but Sonya spotted hesitancy there, too, and wondered if she'd come over to reclaim her. But Andromeda turned back to her table, letting a few moments pass before whispering in Desmond's ear.

"So what was with that helicopter the other day?"

"What helicopter?" Edson said.

"You are such a bad liar," she said playfully, "which is one of your really nice qualities."

Talking in such a flirty manner came as a surprise to her as much as it did to him, to judge by the blush that burned in his cheeks and brow.

"So you saw it?"

"Sure, right before they stuffed me into a hole in the ground. We passed each other on the path."

"What hole? I've never heard anything about that."

She sensed he wasn't lying now, so as the kitchen workers streamed in with trays of roasted wild birds and vegetables, she told him about the underground prison cell.

"I had no idea, really. That's . . . " He shook his head. "I'm sorry." His eyes retreated to his plate and he began to eat.

The bird tasted repulsive, *far* too gamy. *But it's protein*, she reminded herself, and choked it down.

The mashed parsnips tasted much better, and as she spooned up the last of them, she asked him, "Why do you think they gave them that blanket?"

"What blanket?" he said too quickly.

Beneath the table she squeezed his hand, noticing his rough skin. "I told you, you're a lousy liar."

His eyes moved every which way. "They wanted samples, maybe?"

"Hair?"

"I guess, maybe."

"From that thing? The whole idea of a human hair blanket is creepy."

He took a breath, rested his wooden spoon on the table.

"It was Chandra's idea. Having all of us give part of ourselves for a 'protective covering.' That's what she called it. It's kind of a mystical thing with her." Spoken in the voice of a non-believer to a listener who only hours ago had heard Chandra dismiss the entire notion of a God. "That's why they sent it with Akiah and those guys when they went to get you."

"It was supposed to *protect* them? Don't you think that's kind of strange?"

He wouldn't go that far, only shrugged.

"You know what they can find in hair, don't you?" she said.

He eyed her closely, a steady gaze now. He knew. She was sure of it. Everything from his rough hands to his easy engagement with the outdoor world spoke of a man who understood rocks and minerals and the elements that can leech from them.

"Don't start saying that to people." After all his fidgeting, he spoke with a force that shocked her.

"Don't say what?"

"You know what I'm saying because I know what you're saying, and it's not true."

"How do you know it's not true?"

"Because that could never happen here. There could be all kinds of reasons for giving that thing away."

A human hair blanket?

Only one reason made sense to the Colorado-born-and-bred Sonya, who'd grown up with the lethal legacy of abandoned gold mines and the hazards that live long after they're closed: to test the blanket for a poison so powerful that it seeps from the ground into the blood, and from the blood into the hair. A poison that can leave you numb, nauseous, dizzy, and dead: Arsenic.

The kids in the clinic. Of course.

That's why they didn't want her there, and why Devaki had been insisting they eat. Sonya wasn't sure about lentils, but egg yolks were rich in sulfur, and sulfur helped your body purge the arsenic. As a child she'd heard about drugstores running out of sulfur tablets every time an abandoned gold mine was suspected of poisoning ground water.

One way or the other, you had to cleanse your system. Arsenic had been killing people and animals for the whole of history.

She pushed her empty plate away. Had she been eating it all this time? Drinking it? Was it in the air? Were Sylvan, Branch, and Phoenix the first to be poisoned in Terra Firma, canaries in the coal mine?

Glancing at Edson, she asked herself one more question: *Why are they keeping it secret?* The answer, she figured, was her. How could they ever convince her of the critical importance of Terra Firma if their frigid little paradise had been poisoned? Even they had to know that she'd never convert to their cause if their Shangri-la were a toxic wasteland.

But they were paying a hideous price—sacrificing their own health, and the health of their *children,* on the altar of their bizarre beliefs.

Double bind? Sonya shook her head. Worse than that. It was abuse of power. Abuse of children. Abuse of all they purported to hold sacred.

Chapter 16

I see you . . . see you . . . see you . . .

His shouts had faded but Darcy heard his hard footfalls and their sickening echoes grow louder with every step, which felt horrifyingly unfair: She'd never run this hard, blindly fending off the tunnel walls, stumbling, in terror of being tackled and taken prisoner.

The suffocating memory of his threat—Even I wouldn't want to be caught down here with me—drenched her with adrenaline as she raced into the deepest reaches of darkness, her limbs quavery and strangely uncooperative, her stomach a bubbling acid bath of chemicals ready to heave.

A bright line of light, narrow as a ruler and long as a door, appeared in the ceiling about forty feet ahead. She raced for it hoping for stairs or a ladder. Any way out of here.

Her focus grew so fixed on the light, on escape, that she shrieked with shock when he grabbed her and shoved her against the wall.

She almost collapsed, saw him smiling smugly in the dim glow as he reached into his jacket; but she pulled out her gun first. Using both hands, gasping violently, she pointed as steadily as she could, right at his face.

"Go ahead," she shouted between breaths, "say something now, you fucking asshole."

The bounty hunter.

The guy in deGenerate drinking Hurricanes. A lifetime ago. He had his hands up but he was still smiling. And he'd already inched to the side, beginning to block the faint light and her way out of here.

"No," she shouted. "Over there," using the gun to point.

"You don't want to shoot me," he said evenly, "'cause the way things are going in this case, you'll end up with a lethal injection."

Son of a bitch hadn't moved.

"Don't tell me what I want to do. Just move the fuck over there."

"Put it down." He said it like he was doing her a favor, and took a short step toward her, hands still up.

"Stop," she screamed. The tunnel echoed, Stop . . . stop . . . stop . . .

She'd backed up without realizing it, and he took another step forward. That's when she saw that he was on the verge of blocking out the last of the light.

"Back up," she yelled. "I know how to shoot this thing so just do what the fuck I say."

"I'm sorry, Darcy, but I can't do that. Here, give me the gun, darlin'."

He took a full step forward and she fired at his leg. The shot was so loud her hearing numbed instantly and she watched him crumple to the ground in silence. He lay on his side, gripping his thigh. Her ears didn't come alive with his moans for at least twenty seconds.

"You stupid fuck," she screamed, tears streaking her cheeks. "I told you to back up."

Her own moans rose above his, and she stomped her feet, repeating to herself, You shot him! You shot someone. Jesus Christ.

"Are you okay?" she finally shouted.

No response. He remained in a near fetal position, moans growing louder as hers subsided.

He's blocking my way.

She looked at the light streaming in about twenty feet away and wanted to run right over him, but didn't dare.

As her eyes dropped back down, she remembered that he'd been reaching into his jacket when she'd pulled out her gun. He probably had one too, and now he was lying so curled up in the shadows that she couldn't see what he was doing with his hands.

"Listen, I don't want to hurt you again but you got to give me your gun. Okay? Take it out super slow and slide it in front of you. Don't do anything fast. Okay?"

His moans morphed into a stream of pained profanity, but he did reach into his jacket, which made her thrust her pistol right at his head. "I mean it, please, slow."

"I'm getting it," he managed in a gritty voice, sliding the weapon out.

"Push it toward me, but don't pick it up."

He slid it several inches before his arm fell slack, maybe from agony.

She stepped forward, shifting the full weight of her weapon into her right hand. This didn't feel right. She'd always taken target practice with both hands. And the goddamn gun was shaking worse than ever. Shit.

Grab it. Two seconds, you'll be done.

But she refused to give in to impulse, instead lowering one knee to the ground, drawing so close that she could smell his pee. Must have happened when I hit him.

Alert to any movement, she curled her left hand around his gun and picked it up.

She rose as if she were slow-dancing with death itself before retreating two steps.

He'd gone back to hugging his leg, swearing in spurts.

Now she had to get him out of her way, but he'd balled up again and appeared no more likely to move than a big boulder plopped in the middle of a trail.

"Look, I've got to get you over there." Pointing with her gun again, this time at the wall.

His hand shifted. She thought he was trying to drag himself aside, but he'd pulled a pistol from an ankle holster.

"No," she screamed. "Don't—"

But he raised it, and she started shooting. This time she didn't stop, even after his gun fell to the ground.

The sound of the shots left her deaf. She stood there shaking, crying, stunned that she'd killed a man, and realizing it wasn't over.

You have to jump over him, she said to herself. You don't have any choice.

She stepped back into darkness before sprinting toward him, wretched with the fear that in her single airborne second he would come to life and snare her.

*

Commander McCarthy and his men rushed the back of the old ranch house, weapons drawn. They'd tracked the woman on the dirt bike to an exposed ridge and ran the copter right at her, forcing her to dump the Kawasaki at the last possible second to avoid getting speared by a strut. The crash pinned her right side under the three-hundred pound bike for an eighty foot slide through brush and gravel.

"You don't play chicken with a Huey," McCarthy said as his men scraped her off the bloody ground. Then they'd shoveled her swiftly into the bird, leaving her cuffed and guarded and weeping in pain when they'd landed a hundred meters behind the house.

Now McCarthy eyed the back door hanging cockeyed from a splintered jam. A breath later, he led his men into the kitchen, which looked looted. A handcuffed man lay on the floor by the sink, where another pair of cuffs bound his ankles to the drain pipe, Johnny Bracer style.

"Where are they?" he demanded as he signaled his men to secure the house.

"The tunnel."

"What fucking tunnel?"

"In here," one of his men hissed.

McCarthy raced around the corner, past an empty wheelchair, and saw the opening. He stared into the darkness, sniffing the air.

Seconds later he was back in the kitchen.

"Did the man go down there?"

The guy on the floor nodded.

"The girl, Darcy. She down there too?"

Another nod.

"Anyone else?"

"No."

"How long ago?"

"Five, ten minutes."

"How much of a lead did she have on him?"

"Three, maybe four minutes."

"That's all. You're sure? Don't fuck with me."

"Yeah, I'm sure."

McCarthy studied him. The guy didn't look like he had the strength left to lie. Then he noticed his charred socks and knew why: Johnny Bracer had softened him up.

*

Darcy scaled a ladder, pushing open a door like the one that had led into the tunnel. A single bare bulb burned right above her, lighting what looked like an empty shack: exposed two-by-four studs, plank floor, no windows.

She climbed out, pulled her gun from her pants, preferring its familiar feel to the heavier one she'd taken from the bounty hunter, and closed the door. No locks. Nothing. She was immediately seized with a nightmarish vision of the guy she'd shot, drenched in blood, dragging himself up the ladder. She wished like hell she'd taken his other gun too.

A note lay on the floor, written with letters cut from magazines, like the messages from serial killers she'd seen in gory movies. But these words proved reassuring:

Please stay here. Do not leave. We will come get you soon. Stick this note in your pocket.

She'd stick it in her pack. Her pockets were filling up with guns.

What pack? She looked around before realizing that she must have dropped it in the tunnel.

Well, that's that.

She wasn't going back down there for anything.

She jammed the note into her jeans and sat on the floor, aiming her gun at the door she'd climbed out of only moments ago.

*

McCarthy stationed one of his men by the back door, one by the front, and one by the cripple cuffed to the drainpipe. He led the other three down the ladder. He did not rush forward. Even with headlamps and automatic weapons, the tunnel felt damaging. He'd had this feeling once before, during a nighttime raid in the mountains of Pakistan, trying to grab bin Laden: as if countless eyes stared at him from the blackness, unblinking.

He spotted a knapsack and put up his arm to halt his unit. Moving cautiously, treating it like a suicide bomb belt, he studied the bulges and straps, but never touched them.

Cordite pricked his nose, and he directed his men around the suspicious-looking pack. No more than ninety seconds later drag marks in the dirt led straight to Bracer's bloody body, slumped on the bottom rung of another ladder.

McCarthy failed to find a pulse. His unit maintained a disciplined silence as he stared at the door in the floor above them. He figured Johnny had bled to death trying to climb up there, shot at least four times. Bracer had gone strictly by the book in calling off the tail. Sonya Adam's daughter had headed for Canada, and he'd tried to bring her down. But she'd got away. Or had she?

He stared at the door again, dearly tempted to smash it open, avenge this killing right now. He had history with Bracer. He'd *made* history with him, the kind that's quiet and cunning and leaves no trace. Let the brass ask all the questions they wanted to *after* he'd grabbed the girl. But he also had to decide whether to carry Johnny back across the border to where he'd been shot.

Tough call, but the only decision that truly gave him pause was whether to climb up the ladder dripping with Bracer's blood. Not that the blood bothered him, but he could face a serious demotion if he got caught carrying out an unauthorized military operation on Canadian soil.

*

Darcy saw a light flash up from underneath the trapdoor and thrust out her gun, aiming fiercely, shaking, breath catching, sweaty. Totally freaked. All in the first few seconds.

The light jerked away. She kept her gun pointed at the door. Really shaking now.

Then the light flashed again and she heard a creak.

Holy shit, holy shit, holy . . .

She looked around frantically, finding the door leading out of the shack about five feet behind her. Her head snapped back around when she heard another creak, loud as a cricket.

Get the hell out of here.

Slowly, she rose and backed up. In the next instant she heard two quick creaks.

He's right . . . under . . . there.

A *loud* creak. Any second that goddamn thing was going to open. The gun shook horribly in her hands, and *then* she was hit with the most troubling question of her life: Did she have any bullets left after shooting that guy?

As she stood there panicking, reaching into her jacket for the gun she'd taken from him, the door behind her opened.

She wheeled around and saw a young woman smiling beneath a huge knitted hat stuffed with dreads.

Darcy's finger flew to her lips to shush her. In the same instant she saw the red, six-pointed star tattooed on her forehead. The woman took her hand, and the two of them raced toward an old school bus idling in a wooded lot. It had been painted forest green, and in the light spilling from behind the curtains she scanned the white cursive on the side: *"The Ten Tribes of the New Apocalypse.*

We know where you're going, so come along with us."
The ten what?

No matter. At this point she'd have hitched a ride with Beelzebub.

*

McCarthy shoved the tunnel door open and stayed low, seeing if he'd draw fire. After a three-second pause, he rose up, leveling his semi-automatic left and right. He found himself facing a darkened doorway. Couldn't see a thing out there. Fiddle music, of all things, played in the near distance, drowned out by the groan of what sounded like an old vehicle pulling away.

He climbed down and ordered one of his men to photograph Bracer's body. The brass might want to show the world how an American war hero had been treated by these people.

"Then all of you carry him back to where he started from."

He snapped open his cell, moving quickly as soon as he realized he couldn't raise a signal, veering wide of the knapsack.

In the ranch house, he could finally make his call.

"The situation here is complicated," he said in one big breath. "First off, we need the bomb squad."

Then he gave them the really bad news about the girl escaping over the border.

*

The Jamaican driver turned his large, languid eyes to Darcy. His words sounded no less sleepy: "Sit down, outlaw woman, or you can dance, but you got to move from de door."

He brushed aside a purple paisley curtain hanging behind his seat, ushering her into a sudden kaleidoscope of wildly painted faces and fabrics and densely tattooed bodies.

A waifish man, wearing nothing more than his shiny blue pajama bottoms, played a feverish score on a fiddle, unfazed by the bouncing of the bus as it rolled off the wooded lot.

The woman who'd rescued Darcy was handed a bong with a sinuous stream of smoke rising from its bowl. She offered it to their guest, who declined, before drawing deeply on it. A hand, fingers on fire with tattooed flames, took the bong as the woman began to move to the music. Serpents of smoke escaped her nose, curling up around her face and swollen hat.

When the bus jumped onto a paved surface, she reeled into the arms of another bare-chested man atop a pile of pillows. He laughed and joined her in a circle dance swirling left, then right, and surging to the center, moving as one, like a flock of swerving swallows.

Two boys, no older than ten, picked up African drums and played with the fiddler, whose eyes were half-closed as his bow rose and fell furiously and his fingers flew across the strings. *God, he's beautiful*, thought Darcy, with the thickest blond dreads she'd ever seen.

Sticks of cinnamon incense burned in small ceramic stands. Darcy settled near one of them on a plush hemp pillow. Next to her an infant sucked hungrily at her mother's bare breast. Darcy saw that all the adults had the star on their foreheads. Only the waifish fiddler, who looked like he *might* be eighteen, and the boys and the baby had been spared the red ink.

The music played on, at times so frenzied that the fiddler's thin arms and fingers blurred before he slowed his bow so completely that each note arose with a sweet, fleeting identity, aching with such solitary sadness that Darcy's eyes filled as she listened to them fade, faint then fainter with the ineffable imprimatur of passing itself.

The tribe danced or listened to the music, but no one talked, not among themselves, not to Darcy. It was as if she'd already been accepted by a world graced with sound and motion and understandings all its own. She might have found their instant acceptance of her strange, but for the herb. Their eyes were as red as the stars on their skin, and she knew from her own experience that they were alive in the universe of immediate rhythms.

She was grateful for the music, the whirling movement. She didn't want to talk. She'd killed a man less than an hour ago, and felt the needling pressure of the guns she carried.

Only when the music stopped did she notice herself trembling. The fiddler lowered his instrument, his lean chest damp and shiny in the soft light from the tiny bulbs above. His eyes, blue as gentians, opened fully for the first time when he looked at Darcy and said, "We're the Ten Tribes of the New Apocalypse." His words had the ring of a pronouncement, perhaps the very language he'd used on stage or in a tent-camp revival for tribes grounded in beliefs older than soil.

"I'm Darcy," she said, turning to the others.

"We know who you are." An older woman with ebony skin and

wide white eyes had spoken. "What's the matter, child? You shakin' like a leaf in the wind."

Darcy gripped her arms and told them about racing through the dark tunnel, but nothing of the man she'd killed.

"Did anyone hurt you?" asked the woman who'd rescued her.

"No, they didn't get me," Darcy said in a near whisper.

The older woman leaned forward. "What happened to you, child?"

Darcy's voice left her entirely. She couldn't bring herself to say what she'd done in that tunnel. Her rescuer took her hand, and one of the men who'd been dancing took the other one. Everyone joined in a circle.

The fiddler looked in Darcy's eyes as he began to rock side to side. So did the others. Then he sang in a voice so pure it touched Darcy in a needful place she'd never known.

She didn't remember the words seconds after they were sung, but they possessed the simple eloquence of a hymn and brought out what could never have remained hidden for long.

"I killed a man in that tunnel. I shot him," she cried above the fiddler's clear voice.

But he didn't stop singing, and Darcy's confession hung in the air with the smoke and the distant whine of tires.

When the fiddler finished, the older woman leaned toward Darcy once more.

"You tell us, child. You tell us what you did."

"He was a bounty hunter," she began, describing how she'd shot him in the leg, and then had to shoot him over and over when he pulled out another gun.

"You still got your gun, child?"

She inched up her jacket to reveal the revolver sticking out of her pants. She also patted her jacket pocket.

"You got two of them?"

"I took his."

"You got to get rid of them. That's the devil's right hand. You know that? You tell Charleston," she said to one of the boys, "he got to stop when we get to the middle of the big bridge." She turned back to Darcy sounding as solemn as the song that had just been sung. "That's where you goin' to drop them guns in the deep water. And I got a story to tell you why. You hearin' me? You goin' to drop them guns?"

Darcy nodded. Her shaking had worsened and her rescuer drew her close.

"I got a uncle, he works the border. Ain't nobody talks about it but this is what they do. The Canadians, they see some people got some herb, they don't say nothin'. They just tell them people, 'You can't come in. You got to go back to the U.S. of A.' They don't give no reason. They just give a call to their buddies on the other side of the road. And over there, on the U.S. of A. side, they see a gun comin' in and they say, 'You got to go back to Canada.' And they don't say nothin' either. Don't let on about no gun. They just *give a call.*" She smiled.

"See, they workin' together, and they all cops at heart. They know they catch you bringing the herb into Canada, ain't nothin' goin' to happen. And you bring your gun to the U.S. of A., ain't nobody care. But you bring your gun to Canada? You can kiss your fantail good-bye. You hearin' what I'm sayin'?"

"I'm in Canada?"

"You are a smart one, child. You goin' to lose them guns like you never found them. And that bounty hunter man, don't you worry none about him. He was a bad one. We know all about Kodiak and Poughkeepsie. Their lawyers talkin' plenty about what he done to them."

"He did that?"

"Yeah, he sure was the one. Poughkeepsie and me, we go way back. So don't you fret about what you done to Bounty Man. We all war resisters but that don't mean we're pacifists. Not the same thing."

That's exactly what Darcy believed, but no one had ever put it so simply.

An hour later, when she stepped off the bus, her cheeks were damp as the river rocks far below. But she was glad she'd cried—the grief and tension had fled with her tears—and the cold air felt good on her moist skin.

A full moon shone on the water, and a thin layer of ice greeted her hands on the railing when she steadied herself to look down.

She pulled out the bounty hunter's gun and tossed it away without waiting. But hers came slowly from her pants. The day she'd turned eighteen she'd bought this gun, and every day since she'd thought of Keith the cop, how she'd find him and kill him and use his blood to wash away five days of rape and years of rage. But all she'd ever done was call the L.A.P.D. and make a report. Other calls followed—from them, from her, from a prosecutor—before they said that without any physical evidence or witnesses, they couldn't charge him.

She'd been holding her gun out over the river for several minutes when the fiddler came up beside her, bundled in a sheepskin coat. He took her arm in his slender hands, like they were siblings or lovers of long standing.

The older woman joined them, leaning close enough to speak in Darcy's ear.

"Don't need it now. I promise. You can let it go, child."

Darcy never heard a splash, but she knew her gun had fallen deep into the river and would never rise again. You could defeat the laws of man, but you could never defeat the laws of nature.

Chapter 17

Another meal, another plate of turnips and millet.

Sonya deftly slid aside a slice of turnip and spooned up the grain, promising herself that this would be her last lunch in the kinderhaus, or anywhere else in Terra Firma. Listening to all the crazy politics had been bad enough, but this was even worse—arsenic turned eating into a deadly game of dodge ball. She had to escape, and tonight she planned to do it.

As she finished, she couldn't avoid the hyper-vigilant eyes of Q-Tip. The gritty little girl with the white blond buzz cut had a real name, of course—Wenona—but "Tip" fit her so much better that Sonya had to quell the urge to use it aloud. More disturbing was Tip's ability to seemingly gaze right through her, as if her desperate plan were plain for all to see.

Sonya had lain awake last night wondering if she should just stand up at the next meal and shout, "You're all being poisoned with arsenic." But that would put her under greater scrutiny at the very time she planned to escape. Better to take off and come back with the cavalry. She wasn't sure how much good would come from shouting out a warning anyway. The Abolanders in the know, like Edson, appeared to be in denial.

Maybe, she said to herself now, *you can come up with a way to escape and warn them that some of their favorite foods are poisoned.* Fruits, nuts, and vegetables? Don't touch them; they were grown or gathered here, turnips chief among them. Wild game? Shaky, but you could at least *pray* that everything with feathers or four legs and fur had traveled from afar. Grains, like the millet? Fine. Bought from farmers in Alberta and Washington State. Eggs and lentils? She'd been quietly encouraging the kids to scoop up every last bite after discovering an Oregon address on the organic egg cases, and an impressive supply of organic lentils in fifty-pound sacks stamped Saskatchewan, Canada.

In the past two days she'd found out as much as she could about Terra Firma's food, and her snooping wasn't over yet. A casual stroll through the community center kitchen had revealed a great deal, and netted her a leftover bird that she'd added to her stash buried in the snow.

Talking to her housemate, Andromeda, about the food had proved less rewarding. Last night Andromeda had gone on about "our fine farmers who supply us with only the purest vegetables," drinking the group's Kool-Aid, as ever.

Sonya had apologized for no longer sharing Andromeda's table at meal times, saying, "It's been fun getting to know Edson better," implying with a certain look (honed for lingerie ads) the likelihood of longer, more meaningful absences. Her explanation provided both a benign reason for keeping her distance from Desmond, and an essential element of her plan to escape. And the specter of arsenic poisoning made bolting Aboland feel absolutely critical, not only to her well-being but to the children's. Just this morning Bodhi had been dragged off to the clinic. The adults were clearly at risk too, saved so far only by their larger size, which slowed the effect of the poison. But they could sicken at any time. Even die. She felt like she'd landed in Love Canal.

"Eat your vegetables, Sonya." Tip singsonged, looking peevishly at her plate, "'cause we don't raise 'em for the compost pile."

Parroting a parent, no doubt.

"You're so right, but my tummy's been feeling a little queasy the last couple of days."

"You having your monthlies?" she asked with the subtlety of a scrubwoman, drawing the attention of the others around the kid-size table, including Shalin, who'd been irritable all morning because of the departure of his best buddy, Bodhi.

Gwen tactfully shut off her camera as soon as Tip brought up the "monthlies." Charming expression.

"No, it's just—"

"Then eat 'em," Tip ordered.

"Now, Wenona," Sorrel turned to her most challenging charge, "if Sonya doesn't want all the yummy things that come from eating her fruits and vegetables, that's her choice. And when you grow up, you'll be able to choose too."

"That's not fair," Tip snapped.

You're so right, thought Sonya.

"Come on everybody, let's clean up so we can go skating," Sorrel said in her big voice, leading her crew to the kinderhaus' cooking corner.

Sonya did her dish duty. Then, trailed by Gwen, she exited the rear of the building, where a storage shed held rawhide balls, play ropes, wooden sandbox toys, and the skates and skis.

The children lined up eagerly, the bright afternoon sunshine highlighting their giggly excitement; but it was sparked by more than just the skating: Tonight the entire community would welcome winter with their annual spiral ceremony.

"The kids love it," Sorrel had told her. "The adults make a huge spiral out of pine boughs in front of the school, and then all the children light candles along it. It's very special."

Sonya planned to make it unforgettable.

The ice skates were nothing like the elegant white ones that had fired her figure skating obsession from age eight to twelve, when she'd competed in junior events and idolized Dorothy Hamill. A poster of the Olympic gold medalist had hung above her bed for years.

The Aboland skate, true to form, was a wooden platform fastened to a forged blade. Leather straps hung from the wood, presumably for cinching around their bearskin boots. A style more than a century old.

From what Sonya could see, the blades hadn't been sharpened for several seasons. She'd have to find a grindstone, having little doubt that Aboland had at least one foot-cranked model somewhere. A sharp blade would be critical on a long journey.

"Bodhi's really sick," Shalin said when she handed him a pair of skates. "We were going to play ice tag."

"He'll get better soon."

"The others, they're still sick," he said, walking away.

As they marched through Aboland to the river, Sorrel led them in a rousing rendition of *Yankee Doodle Dandy,* which seemed an odd choice to Sonya, given the politics of the place. But the children clearly loved it. Even Shalin came to life singing,

A real live nephew of my Uncle Sam, born on the Fourth of July . . .

Gwen captured all of it on camera.

About a hundred yards upriver of the hot pools, the children slid down a short snow bank with the abandonment of seals. Sonya, Sorrel, and Gwen took a more cautious approach.

Once on the ice, the teacher gathered the children around her. "Most of you know from last time that we have to stay far away from all the places where the hot spring comes in; but we're going to skate our big circle anyway to remind ourselves of where the weak ice is, and I'm going to lay these down again." She held up a branch about a yard long. "Sonya, would you hang back to make sure everyone stays together?"

"I sure will." Nothing like a burst of enthusiasm to keep suspicious eyes at bay, although not Tip's; the girl was glaring at her.

"Okay, let's put on our skates."

"Are you any good?" Chakka asked Sonya as she tied the leather straps around her boots.

"I'll see. It's been a long time since I've skated."

"She's fast," Willow said, as if they'd been skating partners for years. "I can tell."

Sonya had been a fast skater, but that had been decades ago on skates that even now would have been considerably more advanced than these thingamabobs, which looked filched from an ancient Viking museum.

The skates did prove surprisingly stable, if not fast; she could feel the dull edges dragging on the ice and vowed to hunt down that grindstone ASAP.

Sorrel had a determined style, clearly cramped by her armful of branches as she headed out on the wide reach. She set one down at each place where she paused with the gaggle to point out the darker, weaker ice in the distance, or the pools of warm water where offshoots of the hot spring entered the river.

"If you see that mist in the air," she reminded them, "that means warm water. What does warm water mean?"

"Danger," Tip snapped before any of the others.

"That's right, *real* danger."

After roughing out what appeared to be a half-mile loop, Sorrel asked Sonya to help her herd the children back together.

"Now you must remember that if you go near the water or weak ice you'll have to get off the ice for the whole day." Sorrel looked at each of the kids. "And if you break the rule again?"

"You're finished," Tip said with obvious satisfaction.

She's going to be a cop if she ever gets out of this place, Sonya thought. You can just hear it in her voice.

"That's right. No more ice skating for the entire year. This is very serious. So do we all know the rule?"

A lot of head nodding.

"Okay, you Om-steaders, what do I always say?"

"Don't have too much fun," several children shouted.

They were all smiling, even Tip.

"Do I mean it?"

"No!"

"Go!"

They skated off, scattering like minnows.

"Do you ever have to ban them from the ice?" Sonya asked Sorrel. She guessed that's what Tip had meant by, "You're finished." And she'd guessed right.

"I did last year. Bodhi, poor guy. I doubt he'll be a problem this year."

Sonya doubted it too, but for other reasons, now that he'd been taken to the clinic.

"See, as long as they listen, they're perfectly safe."

"You're stricter than I thought you'd be."

"They're our future," Sorrel said with feeling. "Nothing's more important than these children. Hold that thought."

She raced off and herded Chakka and another boy to safety after they'd darted outside the bounds. Then she skated backward to Sonya, eyes on her class.

"I'm not going to make them get off this time," she said. "They were playing ice tag and didn't even know where they were. They can be a little spacey at the beginning of the season. I try to be reasonable."

"Are there a lot of those weak spots on the river?" *The* question Sonya had been aiming to ask since Sorrel had started pointing out the darker, water saturated ice.

"Lots of them. Up and down as far as I've gone. Most of them are along the shore, but then there are these weird places where somehow the hot springs must get channeled out under the river. There's a lot of volcanic activity around here, so there are lots of hot springs. I remember when I first came here I thought moonlight skating would be so cool."

"You don't do that?"

"Well, I do it here because I know this stretch of the river; but I wouldn't dare do any distance skating at night."

A response so close to Sonya's plan that she feared the teacher had glimpsed it from her question.

"Would you get Noko? She's such a dreamer," Sorrel said before hurrying after Shalin, who'd found an ice-tag substitute for Bodhi to chase him out of bounds.

Noko? Sonya figured it had to be the short girl with her head down, idling right near one of the branches.

Sonya skated hard for the first time, relishing the momentary sense of flight between each effort. Without question, gliding across the ice would be her fastest way out of here.

For several seconds she let her gaze settle on Aboland, seeing it for the first time from the middle of the broad river. It looked brilliant and snug and safe, nestled among the mountains with the afternoon sun sparkling on the snowy rooftops. Smoke rose from the rock chimneys of the cozy cottages, and clouds of mist billowed harmlessly above the laundry. The community center sat at its heart, and in the distance she could just make out the poplars shielding the kinderhaus from sight. Then, in a jarring instant, she remembered that beyond the poplars and the school another stand of trees hid the barn and the farm and the tilling of this poisoned land.

She carved a turn that brought her in front of Noko, who looked up, startled. Now she recognized her, the child with frizzy red hair, freckles, and no front teeth.

"Hon, where you going?"

The girl looked around, bewildered to see that she'd drifted past a branch.

"I didn't *mean* to."

"I'm sure you didn't." Sonya put out her hand. "Let's skate back together."

As they started off, Sonya remarked on the smoothness of the ice.

"It's 'cause it froze really fast," Noko said. "One day it was water and the next day it was ice. Just like that." She pulled on Sonya's hand and looked up at her. "We *heard* it freeze. It made a funny sound, like *crinkle,* and my dad, he said that was the first ice of the year."

"Your dad's smart, Noko, and so are you."

The girl smiled as Sonya recalled how a river or lake could appear to freeze all at once because for weeks the colder, heavier water had been sinking to the bottom until there was so much cold, heavy water that it had nowhere to go, no way to escape the frigid air's final say. Nature changing in silence until suddenly it had changed for the season. Or for thousands of years, recalling all the talk she'd heard in Terra Firma about the death of the Gulf Stream and the birth of a new ice age in Europe.

Crinkle.

*

Gordon Basch had his own office in Washington, D.C. but he was up in New York to meet with James Lindon, the youthful-looking editor of *The New Yorker.* Basch had just passed the magazine's receptionist when a young intern hurried up to him, her brown eyes bright with excitement.

'This just came in," she said. "It's for you." She had to hold out the heavy parcel with both hands. "What do you think it is?" Eager, perhaps, to think that she might be delivering the next Abu Ghraib story to the famous journalist.

Gordon gently squeezed the package.

"It didn't feel like a bomb," she said.

"What? You felt up a lot of bombs?" He smiled. She laughed. "You're too young for that. Keep it up, I'm telling your mom."

Delighted by the attention, the young woman stared at him. "Go on," Gordon shooed her. "Go break a story."

He ducked into Lindon's office. The editor had been shanghaied in the hallway by one of the magazine's notorious fact checkers. Gordon rubbed his chin, a nervous habit, and carefully cut open the parcel. Spiral bound. Definitely CIA issue, if appearances meant anything. And "Top Secret" was stamped on the cover. But it looked thicker than the one on the podcast. And if that were true, then those hippies really had been trying to smoke out the Feds. Never would have happened.

No need for bluffing now. He turned aside the cover page. A *lot* of reading. A lot of science. A lot of calls and emails to try to make sense of the complex interplay of perilous factors coming to life on the northern tip of the planet.

*

Gwen left her skates on the river bank. Sorrel would grab them.

The class would be ending soon, and she couldn't use much video of Sonya skating anyway. Too many clues in the background. Even the shots of her in the school would have to be doctored carefully to make sure the children weren't recognized by relatives. She worried they hadn't been careful enough and that the CIA or the NSC or the FBI or some other alphabet-soup agency, pouring over every pixel in the podcasts, had come up with a telling lead. Aboland, this sweet spot of earth, air, and water, had started to feel conspicuous as a scar.

Akiah had been avoiding her, but Gwen had cornered him at breakfast and he'd agreed to meet this afternoon, suggesting they return to the community center.

As she walked past the houses, Gwen found it hard to believe that life in Aboland was going on as if nothing unusual had happened. Last night she'd watched the scary news reports feeding into the production room. The Texrefineco bombing had put the Feds in panic mode. More than two-hundred flak-jacketed, shotgun-wielding troops now encircled the White House, and the most scathing condemnations of Terra Firma were coming from their commander-in-chief, congressional leaders, and everyday citizens interviewed for news shows.

But no one was killed.

Gwen had been so relieved to hear this that she'd barely heard CNN's male anchor report that Texrefineco had received a fifteen minute warning. But she found herself paying plenty of attention when she heard that the Feds were saying that the explosion had been set off by an ANFO bomb, ammonium nitrate and fuel oil, the same explosive Timothy McVeigh had used in Oklahoma City. But he hadn't given a warning. He'd lit his goddamn fuse and murdered one-hundred-sixty-eight people, including nineteen children in a day care center. Gwen would never forget the photograph of the fireman cradling a dying baby in his arms. Or forgive McVeigh. If there had been anything, *anything* like that at Texrefineco, she would have been out of here *so* fast.

Last night's broadcast had moved on to other news, so Gwen had brought up CNN's website, reading that the reason for the attack had been made clear in a communiqué issued minutes after the explosion. It blamed Texrefineco for the grisly torture murder of twenty-two human rights workers in Nigeria, where the corporation had long colluded with death squads hunting down critics of the country's corrupt government. Its leaders were reported to have taken massive bribes from the oil industry.

The communiqué also pointed out that Texrefineco's pipelines in North America ran through aboriginal lands, expropriations long fought by First Nations people and environmentalists.

So Gwen had sat hunched over the laptop and felt her objections to the bombing soften in the slightest, but not enough to dampen her deepening concerns about the dangerous direction their campaign against global warming had taken, worries frankly exacerbated by the vituperation of Terra Firma by mainstream environmental groups. She'd looked back up at the television screen when CNN had showed clips from interviews with spokespersons for two organizations that she'd once admired: A woman from the Sierra Club called them "crazies;" and a bearded man from the Environmental Defense Fund spoke for about twenty seconds, but "demented" was the only word that Gwen remembered him saying. Then the anchor returned to say that Greenpeace had issued a one-word press release with their take on the Terra Firmans: "Lunatics."

As if all that weren't depressing enough, Al Gore had been interviewed live and called for lifetime prison sentences for anyone involved, including "those people who knew about this act of terrorism and did nothing."

Christ, he's talking about me, she'd thought.

Akiah was waiting for her outside the community center. The tall torches on either side of the entrance leaned forward with cold blackened tips, as if humbled by the bright sunlight.

He led her to a table beneath a banner celebrating weaving. *Nothing's unplanned with him,* she thought. He'd chosen the softest, most maternal of the trades to hang over their conversation. Not flint-knapping or blacksmithing or bow-making with their points and blades and blood.

No sooner had they sat down then he looked at her with those striking blue eyes and said, "We don't clear our conscience at the expense of the historic moment."

"Mao?" She really disliked the way he used his quiver of quotes, aiming each one like an arrow at the heart of an argument.

"No, me."

"You mean our guilt over the bombing?"

"*Your* guilt. We didn't set it off."

"Oh, come on, Akiah. You knew about it. 'Plan B,' as in bomb. The warning had us written all over it. And as soon as I heard it was a refinery, I knew *they* hadn't done it."

They being the shadowy coalition of Big Oil and secret government agencies always trying to ratchet up panic in their shabby war on terror. The recent history of the Mideast was fraught with fear mongering: WMDs, a mushroom cloud as a smoking gun, a President's ceaseless and carefully calibrated marketing of nuclear attack by people who lived in caves. The lethal list could go on *ad nauseam.* And probably would.

"It's a second front," Akiah said. "They tell *us* what they're going to do. We don't tell them."

"Who are they?"

"The ones we've been working with to get the daughter here."

"They're us, Akiah. Don't dance around this. 'People don't have to live here to be Aboland.' You said that, too. I remember. Your own words are catching up to you."

He looked at the ceiling, eyes trailing a beam to the wide circle of ash wood connecting all the spokes, conceding her point with a nod so brief that she might have missed it had she'd blinked. Then he looked back at her.

"But *they* took the initiative. *They* came up with the plan to bomb it. We couldn't have stopped them. Aboland's not an army. It's a prairie fire. The government will never be able to put it out."

"But they're trying, Ki. They're saying that anyone who even knew about it is guilty. And the damn thing is they didn't even need to set off that bomb to get her out of there. The tunnel was right below that house."

"But to get all that attention they needed to link it to us because we're the biggest story on the planet right now. They're driving home the point that Texrefineco is one of the most despicable corporations in the world. I'm not going to sit in judgment of them. Texrefineco should be on trial—for human rights violations. Someday they will be. Do you know they just kicked that Nobel Prize winner and her team out of Nigeria?"

"Well, that's an improvement. At least they didn't kill her."

"Exactly," he pounded the table, which echoed in the empty hall. "The *only* reason she's not dead like all the others is that the media spotlight is shining on Texrefineco and they'd rather play the victim than the murderers they are."

"How many did they kick out?"

"Three. That bombing saved her life. And her two assistants."

"Do we really know that?"

"*Yes we do.* They've killed all the others and burned down her house last week. She said herself that she expected to be killed. The only reason she's alive—look at me, Gwen—the only reason she's alive is that refinery was blown up."

Gwen had looked away because she wanted more than anything to believe that they'd played a part, even the small one of silence, in saving the Nigerian Nobel laureate from the death squads. The woman was a hero to her. She'd survived a disfiguring acid attack by her fundamentalist husband, enraged over her refusal to play the meek Muslim wife, and then had led the long lonely fight against the thugs who were running her homeland with the help of Big Oil.

"It's not enough to monkey wrench anymore," Akiah went on. "We're through playing games. Monkey wrenching's like tossing pebbles at the Great Wall of China and expecting it to fall down. 'Those who make peaceful revolution impossible will make violent revolution inevitable.'"

"You don't need to throw another Che quote at me."

"JFK. *JFK* said that."

"He talked a good game," she shook her head, "but he would have hated us too. So do the American people. They want to lynch us. They see us as *directly* responsible for the bombing. I saw the numbers this morning. Eighty-eight percent are condemning it."

"That's lower than I thought it would be. Think about it, Gwen. Ten percent actually support bombing a refinery and two percent aren't sure."

"But ninety percent *don't* want refineries blown up."

"You know your civil rights history, right?"

"Please don't compare us to Rosa Parks, not after this. I don't think I could take it."

"I'm not. We're not Rosa Parks. We're H. Rap Brown and Angela Davis and Malcolm X. We're John Brown too. We're mainstream America's biggest nightmare. We make all those moderates like Al Gore look great."

"Al Gore hates us. He wants to put us all in prison for the rest of our lives."

"That's exactly what we want. Don't you see? He's acceptable to them precisely because he *does* hate us. That's our role and we knew it from the start. You think Americans embraced Martin Luther King because they loved black people and couldn't wait to give them basic rights? No, they decided they'd better start liking him because they were scared shitless of the H. Rap Browns waving .45s in the background and screaming, 'Burn, baby, burn.' That bombing sparked the imagination of the American people. That's the fire we want. There's been an insane number of hits on the website, ten *million* documentary downloads. The Madison Avenue activists may hate us, but thanks to us they're reaching more people than they could have ever dreamed of."

She took a measured breath before breaking the brief silence. "The U.S. is saying we're somewhere in Canada, and that the Canadians can't be trusted to control their own borders."

"That's good, too, because it shows they have no idea where we really are."

"But now that guy from the gold company's been here. Sooner or later, he's going to put two and two together."

"I'm not so sure of that. We've been real careful. We've digitized everything on the podcasts. You know that. And it's not like we freaked-out over him coming. Everybody was cool, and there are other places like this. But Gwen, we've always known they'd find us sooner or later. That's not news. Whenever they do, the real negotiations begin."

"We hope."

"It'll be fine. And we'll be talking directly to the entire world."

"That just sounds scary as hell."

"Look, we all stood here," Akiah rose, looked around the huge hall, "and pledged to save the earth *no matter what.*"

"So you think that the community will accept that we've got supporters bombing a refinery?"

"It's not our role to accept or reject it."

"But we could condemn it."

"By staying silent, we saved three critically important lives. And we'll save millions more before we're through. Texrefineco's stock, by the way, actually rose."

"How'd that happen?"

"A cut in the supply of natural gas. Higher prices. And the market expects price gouging."

"They never lose."

"They can win all the battles they want on Wall Street, but we'll win the war out here."

She wasn't so sure. Terra Firma felt not only conspicuous, but vulnerable, far easier after the bombing to imagine a military attack killing everyone in Aboland than to envision the world suddenly saving itself.

*

Snow crystals sparkled on the field in the moonlight. Soon the children would begin to light the candles. That's when Sonya would have to make her move.

Pine boughs symbolizing the green life that survives the cold dark of winter had been spread in the shape of a spiral over half an acre in front of the kinderhaus. At the spiral's heart, a huge bonfire would burn at the conclusion of the ceremony.

Twenty-eight candles, one for each of the children below the age of fourteen, had been placed along the inside edge of the boughs. Each one "represents how life lights up the darkness," Sorrel had told her class earlier. The lighting of the candles would begin with Willow, the youngest of the school children. They were all lined up to the side of the crowd.

"It'll take a while," Sorrel had warned Sonya. "But it's very moving."

Sonya hoped it would take forever. She had tucked skates under her coat, and stashed skis and food and other supplies down by the river. She'd found a grindstone at the blacksmith's and had used it only a couple of hours ago. Clunky skates, but they'd move a little faster now.

She'd told Andromeda that she'd be with Edson, and Edson that she'd attend with her housemate, "because she's feeling like I've abandoned her." Playing one off against the other to give herself cover, as she'd planned for days.

In the press of Abolanders trudging to the school, Sonya had let herself fall behind until she stood at the back of the crowd, a mass of matching bearskin. She'd pulled her fur hat low on her brow, bundling herself in anonymity.

When Chandra held up a foot-long torch and said, "The

darkness of winter is the darkness of the world, and this," waving the flame slowly, shakily, "is Terra Firma," Sonya inched backward. She never saw Willow take the torch because she'd fixed her attention so wholly on the proud parents.

Only about fifteen feet separated her from the shield of poplars, but right now the distance felt more like a mile. Even with her first steps, she knew there could be no turning back. They'd discover the skates, then the missing skis, and throw her in the hole. And what would they feed her there? Nuts and dried fruit. Arsenic. She had to leave. Not only for her well-being but the health of all those children waiting to light a candle.

Her escape provisions were heavy on bread and rolls, and the cooked meats that she'd secreted away from meals and the community center kitchen, wrapping the food and burying it in her snow stash to preserve it. And despite her misgivings, she'd absconded with dried fruits and nuts too. If she finished off everything else before finding help, she'd run the risk of eating them.

They'd been a reluctant afterthought that had come as she skulked around the kitchen right after school, planning to plead hunger if she encountered the cooks. But it had been early for them, so it wasn't their busy sounds that reached her as she filled a cloth bag with dried blackberries and shelled nuts; it was the familiar voices of Gwen and Akiah.

She'd crept to where the kitchen door opened to the hall, cracking it enough to hear about the bombing of a refinery, and to catch Akiah's tacit admission of Terra Firma's indirect role.

I'm not surprised, had been her immediate thought. The reasons for escaping had grown only more dire: abduction, poisoning, and now bombing, an escalation that seemed to follow from its own impossible logic. The latest revelation made her all the more certain that she didn't want to be around for the repercussions. It was painfully easy to imagine the Abolanders' extremism costing them *and* their children dearly.

No one turned from the spiral ceremony as her dark form receded farther into the moon shadows of the tall, skinny trees. She needed but one final step to duck behind them. To her ears the snow sounded crunchy, screechingly loud, and she could not understand why no one had heard her. But fear magnifies the softest sounds and the wildest imaginings, and it wasn't until she reminded herself of this that her heart stopped racing.

Even so, her breath stilled as she took hold of a thin trunk, finally stepping from the shadows to the trees, melting away until she could no longer make out the crowd of adults.

Longer strides took her to the outer ring of houses. She found herself momentarily startled by Aboland's stark appearance as a ghost town, which it would surely become after the authorities came and rescued the kids.

At the river bank where the children liked to slide down to the ice, she dug out the skis and a pack she'd fashioned from an oilcloth and rope. Inside, she'd stuffed an extra pair of long underwear that she'd duped a laundry worker into giving her, a heavy wool sweater she'd borrowed from Andromeda, and a flint for striking a fire. Looking around, she picked out the tree next to where she'd buried her food, and in minutes carefully rearranged her pack to put the wrapped parcels on the bottom. Then she tied the skis to the pack and the whole ungainly ensemble to her back, cinching the rope firmly across her chest.

"Where are you going?"

She stopped moving, jolted by the voice. *Gwen,* she thought immediately; but the camerawoman had never sounded so harsh. Or young.

Oh my God. It was Tip, standing so close she could have touched her. Busted by a child she'd pegged for a wannabe cop only hours ago. The reality, after all her scheming and planning, felt crushing.

"And why are you stealing our skis? They don't belong to you. All this stuff is *ours.*"

For a shameful instant, Sonya wanted to tie her up and gag her, haul her off to one of the houses. Take the one or two hour lead that would buy her. But Tip would scream, or struggle so hard she'd get away. And Sonya needed more than an hour or two. She needed the night.

"I'm leaving."

"You're not supposed to."

Sonya struggled to remain calm.

"Do you know why I'm here? They forced me to come here. They took me away from my own daughter." She told Tip an abbreviated version of the abduction story. "Please, Tip, don't say anything." Reduced to begging a child. "Please just let—"

"Tip? My name's Wenona."

Shit. "Wenona, yes. I know that. I'm sorry."

Tip stared at her. "Why'd you call me Tip?"

Sonya froze.

"Why?" Tip repeated.

Oh, God. Grab her. But she couldn't do that.

"'Cause I like it. Wenona's a sissy girl's name. No one's ever given me a nickname. That's what it is, right? Like the other kids have but not me. But I'm not like the others," she added fiercely.

"Yes, it's a nickname." Doing her damndest not to sound wary.

"Can I come with you? They made me come here too."

"I can't do that, Tip."

"I *hate* it here." Her voice grew loud, shrill. "My dad's not here. And I know Christmas is coming and I want to be with him at Christmas."

Sonya took her hands, felt the bird-like bones through the girl's soft mittens.

"Listen to me, Tip. I'm going to come back with people who can take you to your dad. I'll be back before Christmas, and you'll be able to see him then. That's a promise. But it's not safe out there if you leave with me."

"You mean the mountain lions?"

She'd managed to put aside that threat during all of her planning; hearing it now prickled her skin.

Gently squeezing Tip's hand, she nodded. "And the cold. I want you safe and warm, and then I'll come back and you can leave."

Tip stared once more in her eyes, quiet quickly broken by Sorrel yelling, "Wenona? Are you out here?"

Sonya raised her finger to her lips. She needn't have. Tip tugged at her sleeve, pointed with her head that they should move upriver.

Sorrel called again, drawing closer.

"This way," Tip whispered. "She's coming here."

"How do you know?"

"Because she's found me here before."

She led Sonya along the ice as Sorrel's voice grew louder. They crouched behind a huge tree growing out of the bank.

"Wenona, are you there? You're not supposed to be playing out here at night."

Tip shook her head, refusing her teacher in silence.

They listened to Sorrel's voice grow fainter as she headed toward the houses.

"We need to get you back up on the snow bank," Sonya said. "And no sliding down it. I don't want you on the river by yourself. It's very dangerous."

"Who's going to help you if you fall in?"

"I won't. That's why I'm skating tonight with the moonlight."

"You could still fall in. It happened to a hunter last year."

"I won't. I promise."

"You promise a lot."

"I keep my promises too. Let's go back. I can't leave till I'm sure you're safe."

Nervously, Sonya led the girl to the snow bank hoping that Sorrel hadn't stolen back.

Tip sat down. "I want to watch you."

"But then you'll go? Promise?"

"I promise."

"Just one more thing, and I want you to promise me this too."

"What?"

"Promise me you won't eat any nuts or fruit or vegetables. The grains are okay. Do you know what grains are?"

"Like millet and rice and stuff like that?"

"Right. You can eat grains, and the powdered eggs and lentils, but don't eat the nuts and fruit and vegetables. Don't eat anything that grows here. It doesn't matter if it grows on the farm or it grows wild like the berries."

Tip's face grew pinched, like she was working too hard to remember. Then she crossed her arms.

"What's wrong with that stuff?"

"It's poisoned with something call arsenic."

"No, it's not. They wouldn't poison us. You're lying."

She sounded like she might start yelling. Sonya deeply regretted trying to warn her, before realizing that the girl had misunderstood what she'd said.

"It's not on purpose, Tip. The poison's in the earth, and it gets in the food that grows here. The adults don't know, either. I want *you* to tell them, too."

The girl's eyes opened wide, warming to the idea of such responsibility. Attention. "Okay, I *will.*"

"Tomorrow, when you go for breakfast, shout it out as loud as you can. Grains and meat, eggs and lentils are okay; but not nuts and fruits and vegetables."

Tip nodded, but Sonya thought the message was still too complicated for a six-year-old.

"Can you remember rhymes?"

I've got to get out of here. Still worried about Sorrel.

"I'm good at rhymes."

Sonya leaned over, thinking as fast as she could. "Let's try this: Eggs and meat, they're a treat. Lentils and grain cause no pain. But veggies, nuts, and fruit . . ." *What rhymes with fruit?* she wondered. She'd never been much of a poet. *Boot!* "But veggies, nuts and fruit, give them the boot. They have arsenic."

"Like rap," Tip said.

"Right, it's like rap. Can you say ar-sen-ic?"

Tip said the word carefully, then repeated the rhymes two more times, moving her body like a rapper. The child was no slouch.

Sonya hugged her, strapped on her skates, and began gliding backward, waving. At the last possible moment, when Tip would have disappeared in the darkness, she rose and waved back. Only then did Sonya turn and begin to skate hard, the moonlight milky on the vast, unwinding length of ice.

Chapter 18

A narrow stream of frigid air whistled through a crack in the back of the bus, stinging Darcy's cheek. She burrowed under the blankets she shared with the fiddler, and took a deep breath of the musk that still lingered from their lovemaking.

Someone a few feet away played Cat Stevens' *Morning Has Broken* on a sitar, each note roused from long beds of silence. She'd never liked that song, totally her mom's kind of crap, but after the night she'd just had it sounded fine as Ani DiFranco.

She opened her eyes on her lover, raising the covers for a flicker of sunlight stealing past the window curtain. His blond dreads trailed across his smooth chest and face. Darcy ran a finger over his arm as gently as she'd stroke a baby bird.

After she'd climbed back on the bus last night with her arm wrapped around him (the cold water far below the bridge forever silent with her secret), she'd settled behind the gauzy curtain that hid them still, and kissed him, unveiling a mouth as hungry as her own.

They'd fallen asleep only a couple of hours ago in a maze of legs and arms and pillows and covers, the motion of the bus as lulling as the aftermath of lovemaking itself.

How old is he?

Definitely younger than me. The peach fuzz on the top of his ear burned golden in the errant sunlight.

Though her rational side said that she'd just indulged in post-traumatic, battlefield sex, Darcy felt smitten *and* sparked, as if they'd been waiting all their lives to set each other off.

She kissed the hollows of his ear, let her breath settle, and kissed him again.

When the fiddler stirred, Darcy pecked his lips; and when he opened his eyes eager as ever, she plunged back into the warm bath of their smooth bellies.

As they lay satisfied and stilled by the first diversion of the day, Darcy asked his age.

"You older girls," he yawned, "you always get around to asking me that."

"Later, I'm assuming, rather than sooner." Darcy laughed

quietly.

The fiddler smiled, still sleepy with sex. "That's right, usually 'after the fact,'" highlighting those last words with a lilt that made her melt. "I'll be eighteen next week."

"So you're not even legal?" Darcy said with alarm.

"Of course I'm legal." He pulled her even closer. "This is Canada. I've been legal since I was fourteen."

"So I guess Terra Firma's in Canada?"

He gently nibbled her lips, "Not exactly."

*

She's up there. We're down here. Something's got to give.

A medicinal odor haunted the air as Commander McCarthy made his way past his squad, working on their laptops in the abandoned Washington County Medical Clinic. From the window he could see Canada, so close he could throw a rock over the border. He felt like lobbing a cruise missile.

The bomb squad had searched Darcy's knapsack and left its contents carefully arranged on a broad table below the window.

McCarthy pulled on surgical gloves and began to pick his way through her belongings for a clue, something that might indicate where she was going and with whom. He found nothing but junk, like her studs and earrings, bolts and rings.

And two Korans, which turned out to be only the covers; hidden inside the first was some book about global warming, and the second opened to The God of Small Things, a novel by an author with an unpronounceable name. Department of Defense would have to analyze it, but he paged through it now looking for underlining, margin notes, any kind of code. Twenty minutes later he hadn't found a thing. Ditto for the book about the weather. More junk, that's all.

Then he came across the Muslim get-up Johnny Bracer had told him about, which McCarthy found intriguing. Bracer had dismissed it as a disguise.

But why this disguise?

If that's what it is. McCarthy doubted the abaya was simply for show, reminding himself that if you walk like a duck and you quack like a duck, you're a goddamn duck.

He also went through all the tiny pencil entries and erasures in her address book to see if there was anything that might indicate

where in goddamn Canuck land she was heading. A name, address, phone number, something he could turn over to Canadian intelligence and say, "Go there. Do this."

That's what they needed up there, the step-by-step. His eyes rose to the window and he peered at the mountains, snow marching down their slopes in advance of the season.

Although to give the Canadians their due, they had livened up since the refinery explosion. They ought to. It was a U.S. refinery but that was their natural gas burning holes in the sky. Ninety-five percent of what we got of that stuff came from up there. Throw in the oil, and the Canadians were the U.S.'s biggest energy suppliers. Not Saudi Arabia, not Venezuela, not any of those places with whacked-out Wahabbism or crazy, Castro-loving leaders, but Canada, where they'd turned into hippie nation. Pot smoking, gay marriage, no military to speak of. McCarthy snorted. But it's a military they need right now, isn't it? And the only one they've got is down here on this side of the border. They freeload on the firepower. How long do they think they can get away with that?

"Got Welch for you." The youngest of his men, a twenty-five-year-old former Army special ops, handed him the phone. Welch was a Canadian intelligence officer.

"McCarthy here. What can you tell me?"

"We haven't found her yet but we've set up roadblocks on all corridors heading east, west, or north."

Had Welch just sounded a proud note? McCarthy found even the possibility defeating. He listened to the details, and gratefully put the phone aside.

Roadblocks? This was belts-and-booze-level garbage. What you use to catch people driving without seatbelts or DUI.

That's not what you do when you want to catch a terrorist for killing a U.S. government contractor, he wanted to scream at him. But he couldn't yell at these people. They don't like that.

Road blocks? Just hearing this made him want to march right up there and take over the whole goddamn investigation, which was what that senator from Oklahoma, Parsons, had been demanding on the Senate floor late last night:

"My friends in the intelligence community say that Canada's harboring those terrorists, and we're suppose to trust them?" McCarthy wasn't the least surprised that his considered opinion on

Terra Firma's location had been slipped to the senator, who'd then urged action to secure the northern border, "And if that means scraping a one-hundred-mile-wide strip from Halifax to Vancouver, then by God do it!"

Finally giving voice to what DOD had wanted all along: a nice fat no-man's land that they could scour like a greasy pan. Level it, fence it, surveil it 24/7. Parsons had fired-up his most ardent supporters in the packed Senate gallery by pounding the lectern and shouting a pointed reminder: "Don't forget that our good friends in Canuckistan were the same ones who protested when we were generous enough to put them under the U.S. Northern Military Command after 9/11."

For now, McCarthy had his men doing all they could on their laptops with three-dimensional, topographic studies of all of Canada's mountain country, a considerable undertaking. He'd assigned each of them a province and ordered them to scan every single mile for likely sites.

Road blocks.

They should have Black Hawks and Hueys and F-16s screaming up and down every one of their valleys. That's what the U.S. had been doing south of the border: recon from the air, the ground, and a massive commitment of analysts to pour over the data. They'd concluded that Terra Firma was not south of the border. That left Canada, and a rising level of impatience at DOD. Christmas was only three days away, and Central Command wanted Terra Firma shut down before they could release phony documents about methane in the Arctic Ocean. That could set off a real panic and scuttle an already sinking economy.

The clinic's antiseptic stink was making McCarthy sick. He stepped outside, saw wood smoke rising from a cabin across the way. Looked like the Unabomber's place. Hard to believe this town even had a name. Just a Shell station with a food court. Jo Jo's and steamed hot dogs.

Senator Parsons had finished his speech last night by calling Canada "a historical accident that must be fixed." That had set off quite a fury. This morning the State Department had been doing all it could to try to get him to recant, an effort that McCarthy figured was doomed to fail. The senator enjoyed a good frenzy. Always had. Not long ago, he'd even called for the execution of abortion providers. So maybe Parsons was nuts. But maybe he was right.

Something's got to give.

*

Are you ever going to tell me your name?" Darcy asked the fiddler as they rolled into a rest area.

"I'd really like to but names are scary right now. That's why we're not using them with you."

Not entirely true. Darcy had heard the wide-eyed ebony woman call the Jamaican driver Charleston; and someone else had referred to the woman who'd come for her at the cabin, who really did look like she could be the fiddler's older sister, as Albeni.

A relief driver tipped his Australian bush hat as she eased toward the bus's exit. She smiled back, stepped down, and stretched her arms gloriously to the sun.

The fiddler took her hand and they shuffled through fresh snow toward the bathrooms.

She ducked into a stall, shocked by its cleanliness. The commode was as white as the snow dusting her boots. And when she washed up, she faced a mirror, not a blank wall or square of stainless steel with a wavy, graffiti-streaked reflection.

Not that she wanted to look closely: too many days on the road.

The fiddler and Albeni joined her for the walk back to the bus, where Charleston was holding a CB radio mouthpiece. He'd just awakened and his eyes appeared swollen.

"Lead car says we got a roadblock three kilometers ahead. What we gonna do?"

The wide-eyed ebony woman stepped forward. "We have to put you in the box," she said to Darcy with no attempt to hide her concern.

"What's that?"

"It's safe. It's just no fun. Come on."

The entire tribe moved into action. The relief driver in the Australian bush hat pulled out a tool box lodged behind the rear wheel well. The women, including the mom with the baby, moved mounds of pillows and blankets and other belongings to the very back of the bus. The two young boys rolled up the carpet, and then rolled up the thick rubber pad underneath it.

Bush Hat handed Wide Eyes a power drill, and she started unscrewing a six-foot section of metal floorboards, revealing a

230

hidden compartment that had been built into the bottom of the bus. A powerful whiff of fresh cannabis arose from the opening.

"It's where we put the herb when we're movin' it around," Wide Eyes said. "That tunnel you were in, that's how we were gettin' it down to the States, but it's a done deal now. We already told 'em, 'Start diggin' another one.'"

"You think I'll be safe in there?"

Wide Eyes chuckled. "Go get the girl some blankets and a pillow," she said to the young boys. Then to Darcy: "You be fine."

*

The tech specialist had set up the video of Johnny Bracer's body on a plasma screen in what had been an examining room of the old clinic. Grisly stuff in high resolution. DOD wanted to release it to show "the ruthless execution-style murder of a courageous veteran and government contractor." That's what the colonel had told Commander McCarthy not ten minutes ago.

But McCarthy feared the possible blowback. He'd liked Bracer, thought he was first-rate all the way; but the ACLU chapter in Idaho was already screaming about him, though they didn't know his exact relationship to the terrorism task force, labeling him a "likely government agent who tortured our clients by burning and beating them almost beyond recognition." That was in a brief they'd submitted in federal court in Boise. They probably never would know his relationship to the task force . . . unless DOD released this. Why draw more attention to him?

It could get sticky in other ways, too. If the Canadians took a good hard look at the video, you never knew what they'd find. They might start saying Bracer was killed in Canada, and that his body was dragged back to the States. Then they might try to claim jurisdiction in the case. They were always getting touchy about border crap.

McCarthy watched the video again, a beautiful pan over all the wounds. His men had done an excellent job of propping Bracer up to show the bullet holes. The shooting looked brutal, which fit the spin. And if the Canadians got a taste of what had headed their way, it might shake them up. Not the military—they were way too pathetic —but the people.

"Psyops," they'd told him right before Gulf War I, "never stops."

Psyops. Short for Psychological Operations. So maybe DOD was right. Maybe it was time to beam these pictures north. If anything could, it *might* make them appreciate the threat crawling through their door.

*

Darcy started getting anxious as soon as she heard the drill driving the screws back into the metal floorboards. Sealing her up left no more than two inches of clearance for her face. She hated tight spaces, and this felt like a casket, which set off immediate fears of carbon monoxide poisoning. It *was* an old bus, and the cold air on her face this morning had whistled through a crack in the metal siding. *What if there's a crack in the exhaust system?*

All those stories about kids found dead in the trunks of old cars after trying to sneak a ride somewhere started to make her crazy. It was too easy to imagine the odorless fumes asphyxiating her. Once they were moving, she spent an intense minute trying to feel any leakage of air on her body. All she came up with was the spicy smell of herb. It filled her nose and kindled pleasing sense memories of the fiddler, which settled her fears until the squeaky brakes torched her nerves.

Voices coming from outside. Not loud but firm. Then she listened to the tribe stepping off the bus. The floor shifted again when two, maybe three people climbed on board. Heavier footsteps, like thick boots and big bodies. That's when it struck her that the tribe was really thin. Like they did yoga and fasted on green tea all the time.

She heard them singing a few feet away with a lone tambourine. Sounded like a hymn. Was that how they prayed? Maybe she ought to join in. She sent out a snappy *Our Father* to the all-powerful macho God of her childhood before catching herself praying to the patriarchy.

New footsteps. The floor creaked near her.

If they can smuggle pot, they can smuggle me. If they can smuggle pot . . .

As quickly—her panicky thoughts riding a toggle switch—she remembered an old Arlo Guthrie refrain:

"*. . . bringin' in a couple of keys . . .*"

Don't touch me, *please, Mr. Custom's man,* she said to herself.

The heaviest footsteps yet traveled the length of the bus and

232

then the length of her body, stopping, she guessed, right above her face. Her eyes opened wide but not a particle of light compromised the pitch.

She heard soft voices, made out nothing of note till she heard "marijuana." Clear enough to make her cringe.

The footsteps hurried away.

That's it. Now they're going to tear this place apart.

It sounded like a dozen of them were stampeding onto the bus.

Jesus, here they come.

But then a baby cried, close enough that Darcy heard her gulp for air, and the fiddler sang *"It's all over now, baby blue . . . "*

The bus started rolling away. So did the carpets and pad, and suddenly she felt like she'd explode if she didn't get out of there *now.*

But the drill still had to sound in each corner of the box before the cover finally opened to a flurry of hands reaching to help her. She grabbed the two that were closest and sprang out with marijuana twigs and seeds clinging to her hair. Like a Druid queen risen from the grave.

*

Commander McCarthy and his special ops officer sprinted across the landing pad at the Washington County National Guard Center and jumped into the seats behind the Huey's pilot and co-pilot.

Two large caliber bullet holes by the door had not escaped his attention, and he wondered where the bird had been hit.

Probably Baghdad.

The chopper rose rapidly as he slipped on his headset, relieved to be airborne after that old clinic. Smelled like death in there.

They headed straight for Canadian air space. It had taken two hours to obtain clearance, a purely *pro forma,* if frustrating, request. If the fugitive hadn't already melted into the vast Canadian land mass, the delay could have been defeating.

At this point, it appeared far more productive to search for a place where people lived, assuming the freaks at Terra Firma weren't holed up in caves (this wasn't Tora Bora . . .yet) than to try to find a woman traveling in an "old vehicle," the only description he'd been able to offer the feckless Canadian Welch.

But right before the bird had put down on the pad, his special ops officer had warned him that based on computer simulations of the country's thousands of mountains, looking for a small community like Terra Firma could prove problematic. For starters, there were so many valleys, broad benches, plateaus, and other land features "hospitable to habitation" that it could take months to search them all, even by air. "Canada is the second-largest country in the world," Special Ops had added, as if this were as big a revelation to McCarthy as it apparently had been to him.

To complicate matters even more, he'd pointed out that there were scores of settlements in the mountains up here: small villages, isolated farms along frozen rivers, handfuls of houses scattered everywhere, and known communes. In short, a mind-numbing array of suspect sites.

As the Huey reached cruising speed, the commander studied the terrain and saw why his officer had shared these concerns. The country was huge, hidden by snow, and—true enough—geographically indifferent, if not impervious, to simple scrutiny.

Still, this was a start. She was in Canada. So was Terra Firma. Mother and daughter. Americans. They'd find them.

But as he looked north to the rugged white ridges stretching toward the Arctic, he had to work hard not to become haunted by the snow-covered slopes of Tora Bora, and their broken vow to find a certain Muslim terrorist.

Tora Bora. Terra Firma.

It hadn't gone well over there, and so far little better could be said for the search here.

*

"Bulletin, bulletin, bulletin," Albeni laughed, looking up from her laptop as the bus climbed a freshly plowed road winding high into the mountains. "Something just came in from Terra Firma that you've got to see." She waved Darcy over to her pile of pillows. The fiddler and the others crowded around too.

"Is it my mother?" Darcy thought she'd probably made another podcast appearance.

"No, I'm sorry, it's not your mom. But it's pretty funny." Albeni clicked the cursor, playing a computerized cartoon of a sailing yacht, *The U.S.S. Big Oil*, crossing dark blue water while towering ice sheets calved in the background. "They're announcing 'The Race of Shame.' It's going to be the first sailboat race from

New York to San Francisco through the Arctic Ocean."

"Be nothin' but a big old sea soon enough," Wide Eyes said. "No jokin' about that. This'll sure get some attention."

"Listen to this," Albeni went on. "The joke is they've got ExxonMobil and the American Petroleum Institute sponsoring it." She scrolled down. "And the race slogan is 'Less ice. That's nice.'"

They played the video again, and after much cheering Darcy looked at the tribe and asked, "So where is Terra Firma? I'd really like to know where I'm going." She turned to the fiddler. "You said it wasn't in Canada."

"I said, 'Not exactly.' You get caught, we don't want you knowing."

"Well, saying, 'Not exactly,' makes it sound like a riddle."

Wide Eyes clapped and laughed. "Yeah, it sure is that."

The fiddler took Darcy's hand. "It's not that hard to figure out. Or you could just let it go till you get there."

But Darcy couldn't let it go. She even asked herself if Quebec had seceded from Canada, which could make the French-speaking province the answer to the riddle. But after a moment's hesitation, she realized that she knew better; she hadn't gone to the Denver International School without learning that much. She also realized that she had to ask a question that had been bothering her since the start of this trip:

"What was that explosion or earthquake or whatever it was that happened just before you guys picked me up?"

She'd stopped herself from blurting it out several times, suspecting the subject might set them off. Indeed, the silence that greeted her felt edgy, and didn't ease when Wide Eyes spoke:

"We don't know nothin' about that."

"If we can't tell you where Terra Firma is, we can't tell you about that," the fiddler said in a gentler voice.

"We don't know *nothin'* about that," Wide Eyes repeated.

Not another word was breathed about the explosion.

The final leg of Darcy's journey arrived sooner than she expected. As the bus putt-putted toward a six-thousand-foot-pass, the fiddler handed her a bearskin coat and thick, hand-sewn fur boots.

"You're going to need these. And here's a hat and mittens. We're going to be stopping right up here, and then we'll be snowshoeing for a while."

Charleston turned the bus into a pull-out at the summit. Everyone poured into the sunshine, so brilliant Darcy had to squint.

Albeni helped her strap on her snowshoes, and then hugged her good-bye.

"Thanks for saving me," Darcy said.

Albeni kissed her. "Anytime."

All the other members of the tribe hugged her too. Then Albeni, who'd posted herself back down the road, yelled "All clear," and Darcy and the fiddler scrambled over the snow bank, quickly snowshoeing down a long, gentle slope.

They trekked for almost an hour before entering a forest of snow-dusted spruce. Moments later they came upon a frozen stream and followed it downhill to a two-story boulder dripping enormous icicles. A short woman waited in its shadow by a dogsled. She waved at them, said her name was Juno.

"Are you ready to go?" Juno asked. "We've got a long trip ahead of us."

"I just want to say good-bye. Okay?"

Darcy drew the fiddler behind a screen of trees, kissing him passionately in the burning sunlight.

"I've got to see you again," she said. "I *have* to."

"Me too." Speaking almost in a whisper, he added, "My name's Kalidas. I wanted you to know. Everyone calls me Kali."

"Thanks for telling me. I really wanted to know." Darcy hesitated before saying, "Isn't Kali the goddess of death or something?"

"Different Kali. *Kalidas* means musician or poet. Don't go getting me confused with the other one. That could hurt," he joked.

"And *don't* you go getting that tattoo up here." She kissed his forehead. "That's too much." He'd told her that when they turned eighteen, all members of the tribe got inked.

But the tattoo didn't worry her when they kissed one last time. It was his life—and hers—that concerned Darcy now. They were living in the underground, and the bloodletting had begun.

Chapter 19

Step. Step.

Last night Sonya had chanted silently as she skated swiftly on the frozen river in the darkness. Visibility had remained excellent, the sky clear of all but a few clouds, granting the moonlight a wide berth.

She'd spotted mist rising from hot springs along the river banks often enough that she grew accustomed to the sight. Only once did she spy a column of moist air rising in her path, and she edged wide of the water with ease.

A moderate head wind had slowed her slightly, but cold as it had felt on her face she'd known that it was the same wind that had kept the ice mostly clear of snow. On every glide she'd looked around, searching for a structure or settlement, or roads skirting the river. Any sign of civilization.

Any sign of creatures too; even her thoughts were reluctant to concede the word *cougar*. Twice she thought she'd spotted a large, lurking presence on the riverbank far to her right. Both times she stopped to stare at the moon shadows, fearful of triggering a cougar's predatory instincts by appearing to flee. And both times she remembered the warnings in Aboland that they'd had a "plague" of the beasts because of winter's early start.

First light came as she skated around a long bend, a gray glimmer high in the sky that turned into a long tease, for dawn itself didn't arrive for almost two hours. She spied it on a distant snowy peak that awoke to the sun suddenly, as if a spotlight had snatched it from the shadows.

She figured that she'd averaged four to five miles an hour in the darkness, about twenty miles since she'd left Aboland. Tired, but not exhausted. Excited, but not unwary: dawn and dusk were the prime hunting times for mountain lions.

At least you'll be able to see them now, she told herself.

Not necessarily, she realized with a start as she neared the next bend in the river, astonished by the sight of a thick fog rolling right toward her.

In less than thirty seconds it shrouded her so completely that she couldn't see her mitten until she'd raised it within a foot of her face.

Don't move, she warned herself, worried about skating into a hot spring funneling under the river.

Her pack had grown heavier by the moment. *The sun will burn off the fog*, she assured herself. But how long would that take? Every minute whittled time from her night-long lead.

Nothing to do but take off her pack and sit on the cushy part. Wait it out. And try to put aside her fears of a creature that can hunt with its nose as well as its eyes.

*

Tip was rehearsing her lines as the breakfast gong sounded.

"I'm going, Mom," she shouted. Her mother was just getting out of bed. She always slept late. Sometimes during the day too. Tip didn't want to wait for her. Not today.

She threw on her boots and coat and raced to the community center, the whole way rehearsing Sonya's rhyme and trying out the word ar-sen-ic on her lips. She headed straight for a table up front.

"You got something to say, say it." That's what her dad had always told her. And she'd be seeing him *soon*.

Everyone was coming in. She saw Andromeda, the lady who rubbed peoples' bodies. She was looking around. So was her partner, Desmond. Twisting around all over the place.

Now Andromeda was pointing to Edson, the dog sled guy. Tip liked him because sometimes he'd give them rides. Andromeda walked over to him and leaned close to his ear. He shook his head. She looked around again, then ran back and spoke to Desmond.

Desmond said, "What?" so loud he made Tip jump.

He got up on his chair, asking if anyone had seen Sonya. Then he said it again, only now he was screaming, *"Has anyone seen Sonya?"*

He sounded really mad. But Tip told herself to not be scared. The center was almost full—what could Desmond really *do* to her? —and everyone was looking at one another. Very quiet.

Tip walked to the front of the hall.

"I got something important to say, everyone."

A few adults glanced at her.

Tip took a huge breath and screamed it out now: "I got something to say!" All eyes were on her now. So she began: "Eggs and meat, they're a treat, lentils and grain cause no pain, but veggies, nuts, and fruit . . . "

*

Sunlight whitened the fog, but it still looked thick as whipped cream.

Sonya searched the bottom of her pack for a cooked grouse that she'd wrapped in hemp cloth. *Rest and eat*, she told herself, *so you don't have to stop later.*

As she finished her meal, a distinct darkness appeared right before her eyes.

She rose to her feet, peering intently into the fog. There. Off to her right. Like whatever it was had begun to circle her slyly.

You know what it is. It's a cougar.

She turned too, trying to mirror the movement she imagined a few feet way. But she saw nothing. Then she spun around, as if sensing that it had crept up behind her. Still nothing.

Reddish nose. White muzzle. Blue eyes.

That's what she'd seen when she faced-down the cougar that had hunted Willow. And that's what she looked for now.

Was that a footstep? A thick pad on the ice? Goddamn it, she couldn't *see* anything, wasn't absolutely sure a creature was out there.

She raised her coat above her head to make herself look bigger, as she had with Willow's cougar. Minutes passed. Her arms began to ache. Sweat streamed down her face, and a cold breeze made her bare skin feel icy. But the returning wind also brought the promise of the fog lifting. *When it's gone, you'll see that there's nothing out there.* She had to believe this, standing alone on a frozen river in a foggy wilderness.

Her aching arms finally fell to her sides. Shivering, she pulled the coat back on.

The fog thinned in odd currents, like tunnels burrowing through the air. To her left she began to see ten, maybe fifteen feet; but to her right it remained opaque and pearlescent.

Behind her, the view extended barely a yard. Then the veil shifted, and she glimpsed at least forty feet of the frozen river before the fog thickened again, a merciless torment.

She began to feel crazy, claustrophobic, terrified of what she could not see *and* what she might face in the next instant. Time felt as mutable as matter, swelling with emptiness and filling with the void.

When a round of sunlight burned through the fog directly in front of her, she gave silent thanks.

But a moment later she would have sworn a long, tawny-colored tail flicked through it, convincing enough that she cried, "No," as if a predator would have heeded her panic.

The round of sunlight swelled, revealing only the blue pall of ice, leaving her to wonder, once again, what she'd really seen.

Now the fog began to pull apart like cotton puffs, opening up views almost as quickly as it had shut them down.

What? An hour ago?

Without warning, a helicopter passed, its *whup-whup-whup* right above her. She waved frantically and shouted before accepting that it could no more see her than she could see it.

But in the next sixty seconds the fog lifted, demonstrating the cruel caprice of these harsh environs, for the chopper had become a distant speck, a dust mote among mountains.

Sonya looked down, saw nothing but a river of ice. No cougar. No creatures stirring in the welcome stillness.

She relaxed and reached for her pack, spotting paw prints as large as her hands. Between the prints lay a two-inch wide impression in the fragile frost that coated the ice.

For several seconds the brute reality refused to register, hope squabbling with fear, before she recognized the line as the unmistakable track of a cougar's heavy tail.

The scant comfort she'd known seconds ago fled. Instead of a welcome stillness, she sensed a predator's stealth.

*

Tip's rhyme left the breakfast crowd jumpy with questions, a chaotic chorus that grew louder until Desmond silenced them by climbing back on to a chair and shouting, "That's just *bullshit,* giving vegetables the boot, and—"

Andromeda hushed him and rushed over to Tip.

"Who told you that poem?" she asked as dozens of Abolanders pressed closely.

"You know who. The ones you guys took away from her own kid, like you took me away from my dad. But she's going to go get him and come right back. And then I'm leaving."

"Sonya? Our visitor?" Sorrel slipped through the throng to

crouch beside Tip. "The nice lady who helps out in our class?"

Tip nodded with big head movements.

"Shit." Andromeda stormed away.

"Andromeda!" Sorrel snapped. "When did you see her, hon?" she asked Tip.

"Last night. I followed her down to the river where we go skating. She was escaping, but she told me all about the poison. She made up that rhyme I just told you."

Sorrel took Tip gently by the shoulders. "Look at me, Wenona. What poison are you talking about?"

"My name's *Tip*. She gave me that nickname, and that's my name from now on."

"Okay, Tip. Now what poison was she talking about?"

Oops. She'd forgot. "It's called ar-sen-ic. It's—"

"Wait a second," Akiah forced his way forward. "We've got to find out about Sonya."

He took Tip by the hand and waved over her mother, fleeing with both of them as the kitchen workers filed in with platters of food. The Abolanders drifted back to their tables, but few of them ate. They stared at the oatmeal and talked about arsenic, piecing together the rhyme that Tip had recited. The sick children in the clinic were brought up.

Debates broke out, soft disagreements until Desmond drowned them out again: "Can't you see what Sonya did before she ran away? *She* poisoned this place with lies."

Akiah burst back in the center. "Everyone assigned to search and rescue, report *now*."

*

Sonya had been skating around larger and larger patches of snow, but she couldn't avoid them any longer. She'd almost fallen twice.

She slipped off her skates and tied on her wooden skis, which weren't nearly as comfortable. The strap on the right one felt awkward on her instep, and the poles were pathetic: branches crudely shaped with no handgrips. At least the baskets near the tips looked functional: leather webs inside small, square wood frames.

She felt steady on the skies, but their primitive design made cross-country skiing a grind; and within half an hour the tendonitis in her right elbow flared up. It had been months since she'd suffered any symptoms, but gripping the pole sent sharp twinges down her forearm.

The ropes securing the pack branded her with their own misery, sawing away at her shoulders with every motion of her arm.

Her progress slowed and she perspired heavily, grimacing as the ski straps rubbed the skin on her right instep raw. Even navigating had become a challenge because the snow had deepened enough to make it difficult to distinguish the river from the land, forcing her to search for the humps that indicated the banks, or for trees that sometimes lined the edges of the ice.

As skiing turned into a wretched struggle, she grew reckless. She realized this and tried to steel herself to be extra careful, to make sure she didn't miss a road or building or any other sign of the civilized world. But even looking up made her head ache; the sun glared harshly on the snow, and she savored the rare shade of a shoreline tree.

The mountain lore that she could recall from her childhood in the Colorado Rockies had made her head downriver on the theory that skating upriver would lead to higher elevations, a harsher climate, and fewer people. Going upriver also raised the ominous possibility of coming across the gold mine. Desperation alone had driven her to try to flag the attention of the gold company helicopter; but if her strong suspicions about the arsenic were true, then the mining company might be colluding with her captors. They'd surely have ample motive for returning her to Terra Firma if covering up the poisoning meant protecting their profits, which seemed probable.

And it did seem likely that the arsenic had originated as a byproduct of gold mining upriver, if for no other reason than Chandra had appeared far too scientifically savvy to have established the community on a toxic waste pile.

But after forcing herself to look up countless times for any sign of human life, she began to doubt her decision. All she could see were endless mountains, a few marching all the way to the river. When the views did open, she squinted at rolling snowfields spreading into the blinding light of the far distance.

Not even a flicker of human activity until she spied a bridge arching over the river. Still a good half mile away, but she skied with renewed vigor, ignoring the aches in her elbow and shoulders, and the burning in her instep; heedless, too, of the threats that might be hiding in the shadows of the trees or in hot springs under the ice, now covered by three to four feet of snow.

When she reached the bridge, she took off her pack and rolled on to her back so she could quickly unstrap her skis. She wanted the damn things *off.* God, her instep burned.

After post-holing up the embankment, she grabbed a metal railing halfway up a snow bank that looked like it had been formed by road plows. She edged along until she could haul herself up, fully expecting to see at least two lanes of highway. But only unplowed snow appeared before her.

"No," she cried. "No."

She flung herself down and wept, eyes so blurry that she almost didn't notice the green highway sign on the far side of the bridge. The very top protruded inches above the snow, sparking a dim memory of Charlton Heston coming upon the head of the Statue of Liberty in *The Planet of the Apes.*

Though furious with frustration, she trudged to the sign and dug away the snow, relieved when she saw the tops of letters. *A town's right nearby,* she said to herself. *It'll say how close.* She looked across the bridge and saw that it led to a road that wound up through a canyon.

This isn't so bad after all. She could strap the skis back on, find a phone, and be done with the river, all of Aboland.

A bit more effort uncovered *Crescent,* and a few more swipes revealed *188 kms.*

How far was that? She wasn't exactly sure, but thought a kilometer was about a half mile. One-hundred eighty-eight of them sounded like an impossible distance on those skis.

She sat back, on the verge of collapse, before remembering that these signs generally listed more than one town.

Digging deeper, she uncovered a *2,* sickening when an *8* and a *9* appeared next to it. She never bothered with the name, unable to lift her eyes from the daunting distance.

Kilometers.

"I'm in goddamned Canada," she screamed, as if cursed by the sheer scale of the country, the remoteness suggested by the sign.

She pawed crazily at the snow, hoping for a town with a distance she could imagine skiing, but no more were listed.

She pounded the sign and sobbed. Then slowly she talked

herself back into moving.

You're no worse off than you were a half hour ago. Keep going. These are the shortest days of the year. Even shorter up here. You need the light.

She dragged her body down to the skis and pack and sat on the snow, fully intending to put them on. But she was worn out, hadn't slept in almost thirty hours, and curled up on her side. *Just a few minutes*, she promised herself.

In seconds, the bundle of black bearskin on the brilliantly white snow appeared as lifeless as the land itself.

*

Edson halted the dogsled in front of Chandra's house where the search team was gathering. Men and women stood with deerskin packs on antler frames. Wooden skis strapped to the frames poked high above their heads, and skates hung around their necks like they were overgrown children heading to the local ice rink.

With Chandra standing in the background, Akiah addressed them forcefully.

"Sonya *will* die out there if we don't find her. She has no idea of what she's getting herself into. Wenona says she skated to the right, which she probably thinks is downriver."

"Can we really believe that kid?" asked one of the kitchen workers. "Did you hear what she was saying about the food?"

"As far as Sonya goes, I think we can believe her," Akiah said. "Sorrel's been telling her that Sonya's going to die if we don't find her. But I still want a team to head downriver. She might have figured out she was going upriver and reversed herself. So let's not assume anything. Any volunteers for that?"

The soap maker and her apprentice raised their hands. Akiah dispatched the women and turned back to the rest of the search team.

"Edson's going to take the dogsled upriver. He'll make much better time than the rest of us, but I want everyone else to go upriver too."

He broke up the remaining eight members of the team into four groups of two, telling each pair to fan out on opposite banks as they moved along.

"Always look for her tracks on the ice. I've been out there and you can see them. Now if it looks like she skated over to the riverbanks, and you see *any* hot spring activity, you've got to look for signs of her falling in. Make sure her tracks go on from there. That's critical. We don't want to spend the next five days searching only to find out that she's dead.

"I'll be pulling up the rear." He eyed each of them closely. "Now please be careful, everyone. Remember, it's not just her life on the line."

*

A whup-whup-whup woke Sonya with a start. She looked up sleepily, and spotted another helicopter disappearing over the bridge. A second later it reappeared on the far side.

Swearing, struggling, she scrambled across the snow, lunging out from under the bridge as the chopper streaked onward. She shielded her eyes from the bright sun with one hand while waving wildly with the other. It wasn't the gold company helicopter. No lettering on the side.

She screamed at it, as if her anguish could be heard. A search helicopter, that's what it had to be, flying in the same direction she'd been skiing. Flying *away*.

But what direction was that? She wasn't sure anymore. It looked like late morning, with the sun off to her left; but there had been so many bends in the river that she wasn't sure what was north, south, east or west. It sickened her to think that all this time she might have been skiing upriver. Sometimes the sun had been on her left, like it was now; but other times it had been on her right. She felt discombobulated. God knows, she'd never had the greatest sense of direction. Without the GPS in her Lexus, she would have been lost half the time in *Denver*.

Another unnerving thought struck her: Shouldn't skiing downriver be easier? A downward slope, right? But those old skis would make any movement difficult. She glanced back at the "misery sticks" lying in the shadows. That's what some people called *good* cross-country skis.

She watched the chopper recede in the distance, scarcely believing they'd missed her, then looked back again and saw that the bridge that had shadowed the dark skis and pack had also shadowed her as she'd slept. In her bearskin, she'd been all but invisible from the air.

Why didn't you think of that? Why? Why? Why?
Because you were fried. Because you couldn't think straight.

She walked over to her pack, sat down and plundered the meager provisions. She tore off pieces of cooked grouse and made two simple sandwiches with the rolls she'd pocketed from meals. She washed it down with snow, feeling remarkably renewed in about fifteen minutes.

As she rose to her feet, she looked up at the bridge and considered following the road; but her head began to shake even before she consciously recalled the 188 kilometers to the nearest town. Besides, the helicopter hadn't been searching the road, it had been following the river. It might come back the same way. *If you'd thought about the shadows for a single second*, she said to herself in disgust, you'd be safe and warm right now.

Stick to your plan.

She strapped on her pack and skis with no idea of what she'd do at nightfall. She'd had vague notions of starting a fire with the flint, enduring the twelve hours of darkness *if she had to*. Mostly, she'd planned on finding her way back to civilization before then.

She had. But civilization had closed up for the winter.

By mid-afternoon she'd been skiing for several hours with no sign of the helicopter. Every motion caused pain. When she poled, her elbow throbbed. When she moved her right ski, the raw skin on her instep burned; she'd wrapped it in cloth but that hadn't helped. And no matter what she did, the ropes from her pack dug into her chest and shoulders.

But as she forced herself forward clouds began to gather, relief for her squinty eyes. Minutes later a snow-crusted dock appeared to her left. It drew her attention to a long brown building by the base of a mountain.

People, she thought. *There have got to be people there. They're shipping something.*

She took no more than a half dozen strides toward the dock before hearing the muffled sound of ice cracking under the snow. She stopped as suddenly as she'd started. Mist rose from a fissure to her right. A ghostly shape floated up from another one in front of her. The ice a few feet below her shifted, and the queasy sensation of floating turned into the terror of sinking. In seconds, water seeped into the firm snow, turning it to slush.

She tried to ski away, but her very first effort caused another crack to sound.

Instinctively, she lay down to disperse her weight, drawing up her knees so she could unstrap her skis. She also knew she had to quickly shuck off her pack because she was as good as dead if she slipped into the river with it cinched to her back. But every movement caused the surface to rock, and drew more water on to what felt like a tippy island.

She tore off her mittens and worked furiously to untie the ropes. Water rushed across the ice and snow and seeped under her coat and buckskins, numbing her neck and back all the way to her bottom.

Freed of her pack, she rolled on to her belly so she could inch toward the drier snow about four feet away; but the move drenched her chest and abdomen with the icy water, leaving her so frigid she shook almost uncontrollably.

Another crack sounded and the ice shifted right below her, horrifying Sonya with the vision of falling into a tiny hole in the Canadian wilderness.

She rolled twice in a panic, grabbed the firm snow by the edge of the sinking island, and pulled herself on to it, watching the chilly currents surge around her pack. Her skis floated on the skim that had settled over the snow. But what did any of this matter? She'd found a building. *People.*

She rushed to shore, toward the heat she imagined inside the tall, tan concrete walls.

Huge roll-up metal doors faced the dock. She beat on them to no effect, her hands unfeeling as clubs. Stepping back, she worried they'd closed for the day.

No, that can't be. It's winter. The days are short and there's still light.

She fought through drifts to the front of the building, a growing sense of doom shadowing each painful step. She found a locked steel door with a vertical window to the side, but no lights or any other evidence of human activity. Not even a shoveled walkway.

She refused to believe this, pounding savagely on the door, desperate enough to wake the dead.

Rushing—the minutes a grisly countdown—she dug for a rock to smash the glass, to save her from the drilling cold. She found a boulder about eight inches thick, picking it up with hands too numb to feel.

She hadn't the strength to throw it, so she rammed the rock into the window, staggering aside when she lost her grip and it bounced off the clear surface, almost smashing her foot.

Three more times she tried to break it. All she left behind were barely discernible scratches.

"It's like breaking into Fort Knox," she hissed, her breath whitening the air before she realized it might well be the gold company. And if it were—*Oh, God, no*—and her theory about the arsenic migrating downriver to Terra Firma was correct, then—*please, no* —she'd been skating upriver all night and day.

You idiot.

She swore violently at herself, for now, at the worst possible moment, she spotted a small sign—*Ascent Gold*—through the glass and knew she was right. Stunned, she stared at it, knowing that after enduring the most miserable torment of her life to escape *and* avoid the mine, she'd ended up right on its abandoned, poisoned doorstep.

Her swearing didn't stop until she turned hoarse; and then raw panic, sudden as a winter storm, overwhelmed her awareness.

Holy shit. What am I going to do?

Get your pack. Do it or die.

She stumbled back to the riverbank, finding boughs piled under a tree by the side of the dock. She grabbed a sturdy-looking length, stripped off the shorter shoots, and rushed back out, horrified to find the pack missing. Not even a trailing rope betrayed its disappearance. Her mittens were gone too. Only her skis remained, still floating above the submerged snow.

She poked the branch under the ice trying to find the pack, frightened she'd fall in but insane with the fear of not finding her food and extra clothes.

And the flint. My God.

She dropped to her knees and jammed the branch down as far as she could, now inching along the entire perimeter, never feeling more than the dreadful resistance of the depths.

Standing, shaking horribly, she began to shriek, as if a final madness might raise the pack from the dark water or ease the brutal pain breaking her body.

In the midst of these short sharp cries she thought to save the wretched skis, and this task—flicking them with the branch up on to the snow—reclaimed a measure of her mind. But she didn't retrieve them, though they lay dripping and freezing only a few feet away.

Her coat glimmered with a thin layer of ice, and the legs of her buckskins had stiffened too. With a deepening sense of horror she looked at the world that had received her, the endless trees and mountains and snow and ice and the shadows seeping down through the trees.

I'm going to die.

She thought of never seeing Darcy again, of never having the chance to reconcile with her daughter, and an agony as deep as childbirth wracked her, left her too shaky to stand for interminable seconds. Then she climbed back to her feet and told herself that this would be the worst of her suffering, when she was still aware enough to feel the unforgiving loss. She'd heard of people freezing to death and knew that soon she'd fall asleep.

In a daze she wandered to the dock and pulled herself up, standing in the late afternoon light as if she were expecting a ferry or a friend to pick her up. With tears streaking her cheeks, she looked at the mist rising from where the river had almost claimed her, and realized that if she'd fallen all the way in, her suffering would have ended by now.

As she beat her frozen hands together, she thought of the hot currents funneling under the river, the heat rising in those thick clouds. Warm enough to melt ice. Or save your life.

She forced herself to troll the bank for a hot spring. For how long, she had no idea. The shadows lengthened noticeably before she smelled the sulfur. It confused her because there had been no odor at the hot pools in Aboland. But this one appeared about fifty feet away.

Weeping wildly, she made her way to the blessed heat, swaying over the hot water, letting the mist coat her face like a warm cloth.

She dipped a finger into the pool, but she was too cold to tell the temperature. She felt only a dull ache, so she studied her skin until she grew certain that the water hadn't scalded her.

The ice on her coat crackled as she took it off. Then she shed the rest of her clothes and stepped into the spring.

It took only seconds for her to feel the sharp burning sensation of blood rushing back to her limbs, the same acute pain she'd known the few times she'd held her frigid hands under warm water. But this was most of her body throbbing, and it didn't stop when she jumped out.

Tears raced down her cheeks, but as the burning pain subsided she also wept with gratitude. Here was heat. Here was life.

Gingerly, she slid back into the pool; and as she began to feel her feet and fingers again, she gazed at the trees and snow that surrounded her.

Her eyes finally settled on her naked body stretched out as if she were basking in a spa. It was such a preposterous image that she started to laugh. She'd escaped all right, only to find herself marooned on this tiny island of warmth in a vast sea of snow and ice and winter-starved animals.

You're a real nature girl, Sonya. You've lost your pack with all your food and supplies and extra clothes. And your skis are still out there waiting to be buried under the next snowfall.

But she could not bring herself to rush out to get them.

Before dark.

Okay, she promised herself, *I'll do it before dark.*

After several minutes of staring idly up at the branches, she saw how the heat rising from the pool could dry her clothes.

She dragged herself out of the water and hung everything but the bearskin coat and boots from the tree, although moments later the boots joined the wool and leather laundry when she found them too frozen to pull on.

She had to retrace her route back to the river in bare, freezing feet, failing to notice the streaks of blood she was leaving in the snow until she returned with her skis.

A quick examination revealed a small gash on her right heel.

She flung the heavy coat over the branches and lowered herself back into the pool. Night was falling fast and all the shadows had vanished. She felt the first pangs of hunger and thought of the evening hunt.

Reddish nose. White muzzle. Blue eyes.

Scared now that the blood she'd left on the trail would lure a cougar the way a cut on a swimmer can attract a shark.

That's the least of your worries, she realized as the enormity of the Canadian wilderness hit her.

But seconds later the cougar threat felt close as a hot breath because the forest was no longer silent. Or had she only now noticed that odd scraping sound? Like an animal gnawing a bone.

What kind of noise had Willow's cougar made? She

remembered it hissing at her near the snow hill. But that had been when it was on the verge of attack. *What kind of noise do they make hunting?*

No noise, she said to herself, anxious from the darkening night, grateful for the rising moon. *No noise at all. It'll simply appear and pounce.*

She moved to the center of the pool, assessing the water as security. But this was no moat. No more than three feet of water separated her from the edge, and she immediately imagined a mountain lion springing at her, caring nothing for the trifle of water, not with flesh enough to feed on for days cowering a few feet away.

You're scaring yourself. Stop it. What did your imagination get you this morning? Fear. Incredibly useless fear. That creature never attacked.

Maybe because I stood up with my coat over my head.

She rose in the pool and saw that her size wouldn't intimidate a titmouse: only her upper body rose above the water. That's when the cougar crept up, at the very moment when she'd accepted her full vulnerability.

Reddish nose. White muzzle. Blue eyes.

And puffs of hot breath issuing from its mouth. Staring at her through those little clouds from five feet away, as if he, too, had passed a long hungry day on the trail of the only easy prey in the region.

God help me.

The beast was big, and its tail flicked back and forth. Its nose moved too, but only slightly. Then its eyes darted left and right, perhaps seeking an even easier path to its quarry. But as quickly they fixed back on her.

Sonya grabbed a hefty rock from the side of the pool. The cougar watched, eyes growing larger, then crouched and hissed, ready to spring. She hurled the rock as hard as she could, catching him flush on the face. The animal spun around, but didn't race away. It stared at the darkness, as if in the midst of this tumult it heard the wilderness whispering.

Sonya heard it too, the crunch of snow. Someone approaching.

"Watch out," she screamed. "Cougar!"

The animal never glanced back at her, peering at the trees as Edson emerged. He stopped fifteen feet away, glaring at the lion and lifting his arms to try to spook it. The lion didn't spook.

Sonya backed to the edge of the pool, grabbed another rock.

The creature crouched and hissed again, more loudly. A wild strangled cry rose from its throat and it sprang at Edson, like he was another male come to steal his meat.

The instant he leapt Edson pulled a knife from his belt, plunging the blade into the cougar's belly as it drove him down to the snow.

The cat landed on top of him. Its snarl sounded like a scream as it began to maul Edson. She threw the rock, striking the beast on its side, but to no effect. She threw two more, hitting the cougar's hindquarters, but the animal still gave no notice.

Edson stabbed the cougar at least three times, but the bloody blade had no more effect than his initial thrust.

The lion's head began to shake, as if its long teeth had found Edson's neck or face.

His hand faltered. She witnessed his futile attempts to push and kick the cat off, then saw him jam the knife into the creature's neck. The next second his hand fell from the hilt and lay limply on the churned-up snow.

But the cougar slumped too, collapsing on top of him. Its huge back heaved like a mighty bellows before the animal issued a nightmarish gurgle, deepened perhaps by the feral anguish of a great beast sensing the end.

"Edson?" she called out.

He didn't respond.

"Edson?" she called again.

You've got to see if he's alive.

But she could not lift her eyes from the cougar. The cat was still breathing, blood drooling from its fur like the thawed-out remains of life itself.

Powerfully scary seconds passed. The milky moonlight bathed the stricken bodies in a queer glow.

She rose from the water, pulling her wet coat from the branches and wrapping herself in it. Her feet began to freeze almost at once.

How are you going to do this? Drag the cougar off Edson.

You're not. Edson's dead, she told herself. Forget...

But she couldn't walk away. She'd never forgive herself if she didn't check. Yet the lure of leaving proved strong enough to offer its own rationale: *He* brought you to Terra Firma. It's his fault if he got himself killed by a cougar.

But you don't know that he's dead.

And he'd saved her life.

She wept with dread, couldn't bear the thought of touching that beast.

Her eyes landed on Edson's knife hand lying on the snow, and she thought of checking his pulse. An easy way out...if she could bring herself to get close enough.

As she inched toward him, the knife sticking out of the cougar's neck quivered with the animal's every breath.

She reached until she felt Edson's hand. The moment she did, the cougar dropped a paw on her arm, giving her the biggest fright of her life, nearly stilling her heart. But the paw did not maul her, and she felt only the heat of its pad.

Didn't matter. She scurried away, breathing so hard she thought she might convulse.

She looked around for a sturdy branch, finding one about six feet long, then poked the animal's hind end to check its condition. She had to do this. Her plan was too risky for a beast that could spring at her.

The cougar made a low-throated growl, but didn't move.

Emboldened, she placed the point of the branch on its shoulder and pushed.

It responded with such a guttural snarl that she jumped back ten feet. But again, it didn't move.

She forced herself to push harder. The cat's response weakened until it sounded like a death moan.

Now she'd worked up enough nerve to try using the branch as a pry bar. She wedged it between the cat and Edson, then worked her shoulder under it. Using the strength of her legs, she stood and drove the branch toward them. It bowed until she feared it would snap and send her sprawling across the animal.

But it didn't break and the cat rolled off slowly, coming to rest on its back.

Dark mats of blood stained its belly, and she saw more blood on Edson's chest, though whose she couldn't tell. His shoulder looked chewed, and the bearskin coat had been torn from his upper body and stomach. The buckskin had been shredded too, as if it were tissue paper, exposing ravaged skin and muscle from just above his groin to his neck.

She took his wrist, but failed to find a pulse. She sat back on her heels realizing she'd just watched a man and a cougar fight to the death. She also understood that she could leave in good conscience, take his dogsled and all his supplies and escape for certain.

She looked at his face. A two-inch flap of skin hung from below his right ear.

That could have been you.

Her head fell to his side and she clutched the remains of his bloody clothes, weeping from the horror of these woods, this river, the indomitable land that had swallowed her so.

When her sobbing subsided, she heard his heart. It thumped as clearly as any sound that had ever startled her.

She stared at him in disbelief. Not even a trace of movement indicated he was alive.

"Edson, talk to me. Please." She glanced at the cougar and saw it staring back at her. That paw moved again, and she jumped up, desperate for a weapon. But the paw stilled once more, though the knife handle continued to quiver eerily as the animal breathed.

Edson's eyes opened and he whispered, "The dogs."

"I'll take care of them."

"I'm hurt bad," he said.

"We'll get you out of here," realizing as she spoke that her words were fateful, her escape over.

"The sled," he managed. "Clothes for you. Medical stuff."

"I'll get them." But she felt less certain than she sounded because she was eyeing the cat. Did she dare leave Edson alone with that thing? Could it still hurt him? Kill him?

She poked it with the branch. No response. Poked it harder. Still no reaction. But Sonya felt an unexpected stirring in her own belly, real sorrow for the creature that would have killed her. Grateful only that it was male, a hunter in a hard land. Not a lioness leaving cubs to starve.

The dogs yelped piteously when Sonya stepped out of the trees. She dashed to the sled, and threw off her wet coat. Then she wrapped herself in a bearskin blanket, shivering hard, fighting spasms in the sub-freezing temperatures.

She quickly found the extra set of clothes and pulled them on. Even extra boots and socks. Abolanders always planned well, she had to hand them that.

The leather medical pouch lay in the front of the sled.

She rushed back, finding that the knife no longer trembled in the cougar's neck. A stillness had settled over the length of its powerful body.

Edson's eyes opened as she knelt over him. She worked gently to dress his wounds with salve and to stop his bleeding with wide strips of cotton cloth.

"I want to get you off this snow," she told him.

"I'll do it."

She laid out the bearskin blanket. Moaning, he pushed himself on to it.

"Broken ribs," he muttered. "Get a fire going. Long night. Don't want anything else coming 'round."

"Do you have a flint?"

"Matches. In the med kit." Every word a struggle, "By the river, dig down. Driftwood, old boughs. Leaves too."

Following his instructions, Sonya gathered up enough wood for the night and cleared a spot for the fire.

Nevertheless, she surprised herself when the flames rose. Not a little proud, too. *Heat. Life.*

With great effort, she carefully helped Edson move closer to the fire. "What about the dogs?"

"Feed them. Meat, bones in the sled. Don't get close. Throw them. They'll sort it out."

"What about you?"

"I can't eat."

By the time she returned from feeding the dogs, Edson had fallen asleep. She lay beside him on the bearskin to try to keep him warm, waking repeatedly to fuel the fire.

In the morning, he had her defrost strips of cooked elk in hot water. After they ate, she packed. Together they stood him up unsteadily. He stared at the cougar.

"Get my knife."

"What?" Surely he didn't expect her to pull it out of the beast's neck.

Surely he did: "I can't leave it. We should take him, too, but you'll never handle him on your own and I'm not fit to help." Still breathing hard, but speaking more easily now.

She had to yank hard on the handle to draw the long blade out, feeling the sucking grip of the animal's partially frozen flesh.

"In here." Edson pointed to a leather sheath on his belt.

He leaned on her all the way to the dogsled, then eased himself into it.

"I'm driving it?" she said.

"Yeah, now yell, 'mush,' and return the favor."

"Saving my life?"

He worked up a wry smile. "I brought you there in this thing; now you can do the same for me."

The dogs didn't need much guidance from her, sensing — most likely with their noses — the hot springs funneling out under the river well before she ever saw them.

A helicopter passed but Edson told her not to bother waving them down. "I'll make it," he said, apparently never considering that she had reasons of her own for wanting the chopper's attention.

She waved as best she could as the dogs raced on; but the bird never slowed, and she realized that if the crew were looking for her they'd never expect to find Sonya Adams running a team of dogs in the Canadian wilderness.

Edson didn't notice. He lay bundled in front of her.

The trip back passed quickly. They stopped a few miles from Terra Firma for the blacksmith and a farmer, one of the two-man search teams.

"I'll take over," the smithy said, anger tensing his voice when he saw Edson's condition.

"No," Edson said sharply. "She's doing fine."

They covered the last three miles in half an hour, pulling up to the snow bank where Tip had waved good-bye. A lone woman, bundled in furs, started toward them.

"Quick, get Devaki," Sonya yelled as she stepped from the sled. "Edson was attacked by a cougar."

The woman paused and said, "Mom? Is that . . . *you?*"

Chapter 20

For a moment Sonya could do nothing but stare at the hazel eyes peeking out from all that fur. Then she raced to Darcy as a camouflage painted helicopter buzzed directly overhead, so low that she felt the backwash from the blades at the same time that its shadow darkened the snow.

She hugged Darcy until her arms ached, the *whup-whup-whup* drowning out her exclamations of joy. She stood back to study her daughter, who smiled brightly at her in the sun.

"I can't believe this."

"Hi, Mom," she said softly, the Army helicopter's noise fading.

"It's *so* good to see you."

"You, too."

"And that," Sonya added jubilantly as she pointed to another military chopper streaking toward Terra Firma. "All this madness," she grabbed Darcy's hands and pumped them up and down, "is finally over. *Over.*"

Three other Army copters suddenly sprinted over the forest canopy, their growl growing like thunderheads.

"Hallelujah," Sonya shouted.

Two of the helicopters landed in the open space south of Aboland, whipping up snow spirals as heavily armed troops jumped to the ground.

"We'll get some help for him," she gestured to Edson, bundled in the dogsled, "and get *out* of here. And then you can tell me what the devil you're doing here."

But before they could move from the snow bank, two familiar faces appeared: Calypso, solid and broad, stood next to the hatless Akiah with his bone-handle knife poking out of his balled-up dreadlocks. Sonya could have gone a lifetime without ever seeing that again.

"Edson's down there." She held Darcy close to her side. "He needs your help."

Akiah seized her arm.

"It's *over,*" she shouted, trying to wrench herself free. "Don't you get it?"

"Get your hands off her," yelled Darcy.

Calypso picked up Sonya as if she were light as a leaf, slung her over his shoulder and started carrying her away.

She shouted and struggled to get down, looking back to see Akiah pulling her stunned daughter after her.

The sky darkened with more thundering helicopters.

Sonya screamed to no avail, so she began to plead silently to the assembling troops:

Hurry up and get in here.

*

Commander McCarthy had flown in on the first bird. They were still hovering, looking over the land, watching the deployment of his entire unit.

Terra Firma. No question anymore. What a bizarre mix of mud hovels and other Stone Age crap. Half-butchered animals hung from uprights. Skins on racks. Nature tooth and claw. Doesn't get much more primitive than this. Not even with the Mujahedeen in the mountains of Afghanistan.

Look at them jumping around like savages. The location had piqued his interest the moment he'd heard there was a settlement right on this stretch, of all places.

He'd sent in SRTV—Soldiers Radio and Television—to capture every second of the rescue. Producers, correspondents, crews. Alpha-omega coverage, enough to trump those goddamn podcasts. Hand Washington a *visual* victory for once. There'd be no Al Jazeera here.

The blades of his bird whipped up a blizzard as they landed on a slight rise about a hundred-seventy meters south of the buildings, if you could call them that. The snow settled to reveal increased activity in the compound, Terra Firmans running all over the place in furs, the men shaggy as Sonny Bono back in the day.

Yeah, well, I got you babe.

As he climbed out, Lieutenant Anderson hurried to his side with aerial photos on his cell of a large man carrying a woman, who was looking obligingly at the sky. A younger woman was running up behind her.

"That's our lady," McCarthy said. "And that's her daughter."

"Sir, should we intercept?"

"Not yet."

Going in directly could get complicated. Washington was working on that. And these people were shrewd and violent. They'd blown up a refinery, and the girl had blown away Johnny Bracer and never looked back. It was no stretch to imagine them ringing their compound with improvised explosive devices. McCarthy couldn't even think about heading in there until his men could clear it, or they saw some fur balls running around that open space. At this point, he wasn't about to risk a single soldier's life to get them. And Washington wouldn't countenance *any* casualties, considering the annoying "invasion of Canada" accusations that might come up. You'd think the Canucks would be grateful and shut up.

"I want our command center operational," he said to Anderson. "And make sure we jam any satellite signals coming from this place."

*

As soon as Sonya spotted the gold company's helicopter near Aboland's circle of homes, she feared Calypso would cart her off to the hole. But he carried her toward the community center instead.

Swarms of Abolanders hurried by them. They glanced up at her but they didn't waste any time staring. They looked scared, scurrying like *rats,* she thought, her attitude hardening with the first strong scent of freedom.

Calypso put her down by the entrance, right where a gaunt girl, no older than ten, pounded the bronze gong with a leather-padded club. The child looked worn out, panicked.

Calypso gripped Sonya's arm as Darcy ran up beside her, out of breath. He herded both of them in as Chandra said, "Quiet. Please be quiet," to the stirred-up crowd.

The elderly leader and everyone else pressed together on the north side of the inlaid mandala, which lay at the very center of the room.

Sonya found this strange, like the large space south of the mandala had become a no-man's land.

A few feet from Chandra stood a balding man in a red fleece vest. About sixty, Sonya guessed, but a tall, athletic, outdoorsy sixty.

Must be from the gold company. Too normal looking for this place.

"We have so little time left," Chandra said, "but it's critical that everyone stays on the Canadian side of the mandala. We can't say for certain that U.S. troops won't cross the border for us, but we can make certain that if they take us over here, they do so in violation of international law. Everyone knows their stations. Please go, but remember, under no circumstances cross into the United States."

Sonya stared at the mandala, astonished. *It's a border marker?*

"You create borders and borders create wars." That's what Akiah had told her.

Well, she thought, *you and your merry band might have done all you could to destroy a border but it sure as hell looks like a war is here now.*

*

McCarthy's troops were digging into the snow. Army green all the way. He didn't want them in camouflage white. He wanted them *seen,* for the very idea of resistance to die in the face of all this firepower. Gunships, rifles, cannons, RPGs, machine guns, all the tools and tricks to shrivel their dicks.

But the most important job—keeping *her* firmly in the crosshairs—belonged to the one weapon the civilians couldn't see: the drone. Armed with a missile and a lens. McCarthy's lethal eye in the sky.

This was Terra Firma's come-to-Jesus moment. *It's all over but the surrendering,* McCarthy thought. Not that they looked like they were about to do that. Even as they scurried they never veered into the half circle of houses on the U.S. side of the compound, which ended about a hundred-fifty meters from his troops.

Anderson hurried over. "Sir, we have a reading on that helicopter."

"Go ahead." McCarthy eyed it over there in Canada, behind the residences.

"It's owned by a company called Ascent Gold out of Calgary, Alberta."

A complication he couldn't afford to spend time unraveling, much less regret. Maybe Ascent Gold was in league with Terra Firma. Or maybe the gold miners were just in the wrong place at the wrong time. No matter, the bird had become a bogey, subject to a no-fly order, even if the owner didn't know it.

"Let me know if you get another visual on Adams or her daughter," he said to Anderson.

Not a minute later Anderson reported, "Sir, visual accomplished," handing him the binoculars. "Two o'clock. Mother *and* daughter walking toward a residence."

McCarthy studied them, then got back on the line to Washington.

*

"So it's real?" James Lindon, the dark-haired editor, leaned against the doorway.

"It's real." Basch sipped coffee. Mid-morning, and he'd been up most of the night.

"You're not getting set up like Rather with Shrub's National Guard Service?"

"No. I know where it comes from," Basch's red eyes fell to the report, "and nobody could phony up these numbers." The Pulitzer Prize winner had been running down hundreds of details from the CIA document. "Those hippies don't have the whole thing. No way. They would have put out the plans to mine the methane right away." It wasn't unusual for sources to provide a partial report, often to protect their role in leaking the material. Basch figured that's what had happened to the Terra Firmans.

"I've read something about the mining." Lindon hadn't moved from the doorway. He looked as tired as Basch. "As I recall, there's a real concern about releasing even more methane if you start tearing up the seabed."

"Exactly. There's been a little bit here and there, and some test drilling, but nobody's ever said anything about the fact that the companies are already tooled-up and ready to launch major operations, or that the government's approved their plans to start the mining. Man," Basch looked at Lindon, "the Canadians are going to be pissed. That's their goddamn land."

The editor shook his head. "The U.S. has been disputing that. They send warships through there all the time."

"They've been saying that once the ice melts, it's no longer Canada, but this is taking it to a whole new level. But here's the real irony: the companies plan to build their own goddamn compounds in the Arctic so that once temperatures reach 'unacceptable levels in the lower forty-eight'—that's how they put it—they can move their headquarters up there."

"Their own Terra Firmas?"

Gordon smiled but he didn't appear remotely amused. "Yeah, minus the furs and hippie-dippy bullshit. And a lot farther north. That's where the oil companies plan on hiding out for the next *millennium.* They want to mine the methane to eke out a few more decades of profits, and then when everything else really goes to shit they'll still be able to power their little Arctic paradise with it. It'll be one final feedback loop after all the others have done us in."

Lindon ran his hand through his hair. "You writing yet?"

"Nope. For now, we're going to have to scan this thing and post every last page."

"How many people you need?"

"Everyone," Gordon said. "And we've got to change the fonts." Each copy of a highly classified report like this had a different print type so that if it did get leaked to the media, the font could become a fingerprint that could lead government investigators back to the source.

"We'll change them," Lindon said. "How much more time do you need?"

"An hour, and then bring in everybody you trust."

*

Chandra stood at her door waving Sonya inside. "Come in," she said sprightly, as if this were a social call. Darcy, once more escorted by Akiah, followed closely behind.

"Please sit," Chandra said to all of them.

Exhaustion, rather than any desire to comply, eased Sonya into a chair. "We're here because you're letting us go, right?"

"Of course we're going to let you go. We sure can't hold you when we're all but surrounded. I expect negotiations will begin shortly. I would think that we'll be able to release you in a matter of hours, a day or two at the—"

"No, *now.*" Sonya jumped from her seat.

Chandra glanced at Calypso, who sat forward.

"Not now, Sonya. That wouldn't be safe. We need to negotiate your release and make sure everyone in Aboland is guaranteed humane treatment."

"I don't care about that. Officials from the United States are out there waiting for me and my daughter right now, for God's sakes. You grabbed me and you can let me go."

"You don't care? You don't care what happens to Wenona?

What about Gwen? Or Willow? Her mother's in labor right now at the clinic. And Edson? You saved his life. He's in there too."

"Along with all the kids you poisoned. That's a dirty little secret."

"It's no secret, Sonya. Everyone knows about it now. And we didn't try to make them sick. We're trying to make them better. They're taking sulfur tablets, and we've been bringing in safe food, which you must have known or you wouldn't have been able to teach Wenona that jingle."

"What do you mean everyone *knows*?"

"We told them last night, *after* we confirmed the arsenic poisoning with tests.

"And did Tip have anything to do with that?"

"Tip?" Chandra asked.

Sonya had to think of the girl's real name. "Wenona. I told her to tell everyone about the arsenic."

"That did create quite a stir, but we were already taking all the precautions that we could. We hadn't said anything because we didn't want people panicking. Robert Cunningham—you might have seen him at the center—had the tests done. He's from the gold company. They're having huge problems with arsenic."

Sonya tried to speak, but Chandra cut her off.

"Look, do you really want those soldiers racing in here? This can be done in an orderly way. Safely. We've planned for this moment. We know what we're doing."

"It sounds like you're planning to fight them."

"We're *not* going to fight them. That's absurd. Darcy, why don't you tell your mother what you told me."

"You've been *talking* to her?" Sonya said to her daughter. Then she realized her tone of voice wasn't helping. It already sounded like the start of so many of their arguments over the years. "I'm sorry, Darcy. I'm not mad. I just don't know what you're *doing* here."

"Mom, I got here last night. I came for you. I knew if someone had taken me, you'd have done the same. I couldn't trust the FBI. They treated me like a terrorist, and the whole government's been beating a war drum about finding you. You're huge news. There are stories about you everywhere. Mom—" a pleading tone now tinged Darcy's words—"it's not simple, what's happened to you. Not anymore. These people, they shouldn't have taken you. No way . . . "

Sonya nodded vigorously.

" . . . I *agree,* Mom, but you should know what they've told the world about global warming. They got a CIA report, and it shows that the government knows that huge amounts of methane are coming up from under the Arctic Ocean, and it could fry this planet."

It took Sonya a moment to remember the report that Chandra had shown her. What she grasped far more readily was that her daughter thought that the people who'd kidnapped her mother had done something worthwhile. Which was infuriating.

"So you think this is right?"

"No. No. Okay? It's wrong. Way wrong. But it's what it is. It's where we are now."

"Sonya," Chandra joined in, "we're going to release you. We were always going to release you."

"A year from now. Once I was convinced you were the one-and-only way and—"

A loud banging on the door interrupted her. Chandra asked Calypso to check on it.

Desmond stood there with a tall spear by his side. A red feather hung from the leather straps that bound the long flint point to the wood. He looked past Calypso, spotting Sonya. "You're not letting her go, are you? After she betrayed us?"

Chandra rose slowly from her chair, face filled with frustration. In these strained seconds it was easy, even for Sonya, to imagine that over the years Chandra had endured all manner of Desmonds, men and women always clamoring for simple answers and quick judgments, the trying followers who took their greatest pleasure in the punishment of others.

Chandra stood at the door, "I'm not going to discuss this with you right now. You've known what the plan was, just like everybody else. It hasn't changed."

"You *can't* let her go. She brought them here."

"I did not," Sonya protested.

"Please go, Desmond."

Chandra asked Calypso to close the door. Sonya's last glimpse of Desmond showed his face flushed with fury.

"So what happens to Terra Firma?" she asked as Chandra

settled back in her chair, "with all the poison around this place?" Thinking that if the Abolanders were forced to abandon their home, it made Darcy and her release even more likely.

"We have to leave," Chandra said bluntly. "The arsenic is going to keep coming down. It's from the mill tailings up at Cunningham's gold mine. That's right next to the Atami Glacier. You can see it from here. It's the big one that's twenty miles from here." Her eyes flitted to the small window. "Rising temperatures have been shrinking it, especially in the last decade."

As the freeze line moved up the mountain, she went on, the glacial melt started flushing out the toxic mill tailings, which had been frozen and stored safely in old tunnels and caves up there for most of the twentieth century.

"And all the while we were building below. We planned every little detail, but we didn't plan on global warming poisoning *us*. Our timing," she smiled grimly, "wasn't great for our health. On the other hand, it's a powerful message to everyone who doubts that climate chaos isn't toxic, or won't affect them."

"We're looking at millions of gallons of poisoned water coming down that mountain," Akiah added. "We're pretty sure now that it's in our wells, hot springs, soil. Everywhere."

"Mom," Darcy took her hand. "I know this is going to be hard to wrap your head around, but these people are the good guys."

"You don't know *what* they are," Sonya shot back.

Darcy's voice remained level. "While you've been in here, being treated okay, I guess, the government's been *torturing* my friends. They've locked up Lotus, arrested her parents, and made all of us look like terrorists."

"What do you mean, they've tortured your friends?"

"They tied Kodiak to a hot stove and they also burned a woman in the animal rights movement who did everything she could to help me find you. Their lawyers released pictures of them. It's horrible what's happened to them. Because the government was so sure these guys were terrorists. But it gets worse." Darcy blinked tears before dropping her face into her hands.

"What do you mean worse?"

When Darcy's only response was to cry harder, Sonya put her arms around her daughter. "It's okay," she murmured.

Darcy unveiled her wet face. "No, it's not. I killed a guy."

In the tightly contained seconds that followed, Darcy told Sonya about her encounter with the bounty hunter.

"The government's saying he was part of some anti-terrorism task force, but he's the one who did the torturing. He killed a man who was helping me. And then he came after me, Mom, in a dark tunnel. He was screaming he was going to get me, and he tried to pull out a gun. But they're saying I *murdered* him."

Sonya felt clubbed, hardly aware of the damp face now pressing against her shoulder.

Chandra spoke, nodding at the young woman. "Do you see why I'm saying we have to be careful? You don't want your daughter in the States right now. We want everybody, and that includes her, to leave here safely."

Sonya pulled Darcy closer, as much to comfort her as to squeeze the shakes from her own body.

*

McCarthy scanned the video surveillance in the command center, an insulated tent a good twenty meters behind his troops. The screens gave him every possible view of Terra Firma, but the only one that pricked his attention right now was the monitor showing the area immediately north of the compound.

Nothing but a big, wide stretch of Canadian snow. Not a single soldier in sight. No helicopters, no artillery.

Not . . . a . . . goddamn . . . thing.

Canada's got the most pathetic military in the world, he thought. *They've got all that gas and oil, and what the hell good does it do them? Where did all the money go anyway?* Their army made your average Somali warlord look like Patton. Invade Toronto and there'd be no resistance. You could take over the whole country with two squads and some hand grenades.

Ottawa said they were "on the way." ETA? Tomorrow morning.

And they wonder why we insist on securing the border. But what could you expect? They'd actually flown troops to war zones on commercial jets. They wouldn't accept our offer to move their men into position here. No, that might hurt their national pride.

McCarthy turned from the monitor. Unbearable.

They wouldn't let McCarthy's troops go in, either. Washington had been working on it, reminding the Canadian Prime Minister that post-9/11 his country was under the U.S. Northern Military

Command, in case the P.M. had somehow missed Senator Parsons' speech.

This is obscene, McCarthy said to himself as he walked out of the tent. *We've gone into Pakistan, Afghanistan, the Sudan, Iraq, you name it, anywhere we needed to wipe out terrorist training camps. We've scraped those killers off the streets of all kinds of countries, taken them where we could get answers fast. And now we're supposed to make an exception for a band of bombers and kidnappers who happen to be squatting on Canadian ice?*

He checked with Anderson. The drone had *her* location down to millimeters. She might *think* she's getting away, but that'll never happen. There were ways to neutralize your target without ever stepping across a border. "Announce the 'No Fly Zone,'" he told Anderson. "Do it for one hour. Make sure they hear it."

Suicide bombers come in cars, cabs, trucks, planes, jumbo jets. Next, they'd be turning up on skateboards and dog sleds. There was no reason on earth that they wouldn't come at you in a gold company chopper.

*

Calypso shepherded Sonya and Darcy back over to the community center. Chandra had asked them to wait there for the time being. *She clearly has no idea what's going on in here,* Sonya thought. Neither did Calypso, to judge by his startled reaction.

Desmond stood on a raised platform, thrusting his spear above his head like some tribal warrior while addressing a crowd that Sonya estimated as roughly half the adult population of Terra Firma.

" . . . planning to surrender," were the first words she caught. He followed with angry denunciations of "appeasement," and finished with a tirade against "any capitulation. *We* built this place, not Chandra. *We* can defend it."

"It's *poisoned,*" Andromeda said, standing only feet from her partner. "Kids are sick."

"She's right," Calypso agreed. "We can't stay here. We'll take the new land."

"What new land?" Sonya asked him softly.

But Calypso had his eyes trained on Desmond, and didn't respond. Darcy leaned over and whispered in Sonya's ear.

"That guy from the gold mine said last night they'd trade these people a thousand acres because they poisoned their land."

"And you believe that corporate bullshit? They know we're finished after kidnapping her," Desmond jabbed his spear in Sonya's direction. "We're all going to jail."

"No, we're not," Akiah said matter-of-factly as he entered the center and walked toward Desmond. "And stop pointing that spear at people. Only the ones directly involved in her abduction will go to prison. The lawyers say—"

"You've been talking to lawyers?" Desmond sounded outraged *and* incredulous.

"They say there's little-to-no likelihood that the people who are just living here will ever be prosecuted. And Canada would never agree, in their opinion, to extraditing them to the U.S. knowing they could be sentenced to death under terrorism laws there. The rest of us—" Akiah looked at Calypso—"we knew what we were facing right from the start. We never involved you, Desmond, so you can take the gold company offer."

"If I believed it. I'd be better off taking *her* to the Americans and taking the reward." He pointed at Sonya.

"That's not going to happen, either," Akiah said evenly. "Stop trying to divide the community."

"But he's right," a young man shouted. "Cause you're saying we're supposed to trust the people who poisoned us. That's crazy."

"No, it's not. They made a point of coming here to tell us about the arsenic."

"Yeah, when it was too late to do anything about it." Desmond pounded the base of his spear on the floor.

"'Too late' is after it kills you. It wasn't too late."

"So you're going to take the word of some filthy rich, gold-mining CEO that we'll get our land?"

"We're all about change, Desmond. We've all changed. You used to sell carpets. Remember all the toxins in that stuff? If we can believe in our own change, then we've *got* to believe that other people can change too. Otherwise, it really is hopeless. I think we should all take our stations."

Sonya was surprised at Akiah's calm and his effect on the Abolanders, including Andromeda, who followed him out of the center. But not all of them left. Half a dozen agitated young men were crowding around Desmond.

Calypso ordered them to leave, too, before leading Sonya and

Darcy to a table.

"Are we going to end up in the hole?" Sonya asked him. "Just tell me that much."

"No, those days are over." He stepped away, perhaps to allow them privacy.

The sound of jet helicopters continued to penetrate the thick straw bale walls. Nearly as loud were the screeching announcements about a No Fly Zone.

"I'm sorry, Mom," Darcy said above the noise. "I know you just want to go back. I didn't mean to complicate things."

Impulse control had never been her daughter's strong suit; but after hearing about her horrifying encounter with the bounty hunter in the dark tunnel, Sonya realized that she would have shot the man too.

"It was self-defense. You're innocent. We'll get a lawyer. It'll work out."

"That won't even matter. You hear the army outside, right? They're on the warpath. This is the biggest story since 9/11 and Waco. We'll be lucky if we live to *see* a lawyer."

"So what do you think we should do? Cast our lot with these people?" Sonya looked around the empty center. It appeared that the Abolanders had headed out to whatever their "stations" were. Battle stations? God, she hoped not. That's what she'd feared all along, that they'd do something stupid and get themselves and their children killed. And now her child too.

"No, I'm not saying that at all, Mom. I'm saying it doesn't matter. It's out of our control, and it's escalating in a really scary way."

Chapter 21

Commander McCarthy stopped the No Fly Zone announcements right on schedule, figuring that even the dead had heard them by now.

"Sir, the drone has a visual lock," Anderson reported, leading McCarthy to a black and white screen.

Seeing this was a relief. The target had evaded them for two hours.

"Sir, you can see that she's moving."

"Is the line secure?" The one to the Pentagon.

"Yes, sir."

With his eyes on the target, McCarthy started speaking to Central Command.

*

An FBI agent served James Lindon with a Federal Court injunction prohibiting publication of the "Top Secret CIA report: 'Methane: Global Warming and Global Security' because distribution would cause immediate, irreparable harm to the national security interests of the United States."

"This confirms it," Gordon said to Lindon as the agent left. Gordon had been slipped word that the injunction was on the way and had alerted the magazine's legal team, which crowded Lindon to get a look at the document. "Not that we needed further corroboration."

Lindon handed the injunction to Gordon, saying "These things have a way of following you around, don't they?"

Gordon managed a smile, and spotted the young intern standing a few feet away. He waved the injunction at her. "Now *this* feels like a bomb."

*

Akiah led Sonya and Darcy down a trail through the woods near the kinderhaus. Calypso walked behind them. The sky had clouded over, luring an early twilight. Sonya still felt shaken by her last glance at the soldiers and artillery massing south of the border.

A small clearing appeared, and Akiah opened a thick wooden door like the one that had led down to the hole.

"I know what you're thinking, but we're not going to lock you up," he said. "I just want you to know what the government's saying about you."

She climbed down a ladder into a small production studio, where she found herself standing shoulder-to-shoulder with Gwen. The camerawoman hugged her and introduced herself to Darcy. Calypso remained above ground, closing the door to the elements.

The studio walls were braced with wood beams and covered with planking, and the floor was concrete, heated like the cabins, with water from the hot springs.

Three open laptops were lined up on a table next to a single monitor with a four-way screen.

Akiah switched on CNN. Holiday wreaths hung in the newsroom behind a blonde anchor with bee-stung lips. She was reporting a news "blackout" on the U.S., Canadian border, "where Terra Firma, according to Pentagon sources, has been holding Sonya Adams."

A frowning photo of her—*Couldn't they have come up with something better?* Sonya thought—appeared above the anchor's shoulder.

"The Army's blacked us out, too, but we expected them to do that as soon as they found us," Akiah said. "We've always had contingency plans. Here, this is what we wanted you to show you. It's a CNN report that we recorded earlier. We want you to see how they're making you look now, because it's changing."

A rosy-cheeked, dark-haired anchor reported the recorded material, cocking her head slightly as she read, "Pentagon spokesman William Reilly says that Sonya Adams is likely a victim of Stockholm Syndrome by now."

The moment she referred to Reilly, he appeared on screen with a Department of Defense plaque in the background. He was a balding, middle-aged man with an intense expression. But his smooth voice offered no hint of anxiousness:

"Since one of our anti-terrorism units tracked down the terrorist encampment, we've retrieved routine satellite surveillance that shows Sonya Adams living there, a willing participant in many activities. Those photographs have been released to the American people . . . "

"*They* released them," Akiah intoned.

" . . . Some of them show her ice-skating."

The camera cut away from Reilly to black-and-white aerial stills of Sonya skating on the river from the morning when she'd helped out with Sorrel's class. But she found it peculiar that the pictures did not include any children.

"In other photographs," Reilly's voice continued off-camera, "she willingly takes off all her clothes to enter a hot spring. We've carefully blanked out the revealing parts of her body, although appearing naked among her abductors did not appear to concern Sonya Adams."

Now the screen did show others, including Gwen by her side.

Sonya felt herself burning with embarrassment as the camerawoman whispered, "And you were worried about *me* getting naked pictures of you."

"This is a real change in the coverage." Akiah pointed to the screen. "Up till now, the government's been showing you as a victim. Now they're saying, on the one hand, that you've been brainwashed; but they're also using words like '*willing* participant' and 'willingly takes off her clothes,' which are going to make you look a lot less sympathetic. And that's got us worried."

"Why?" she asked, still cringing at the screen.

Darcy shook her head. "She still doesn't get it."

"I get what you're saying," Sonya said. "But they have nothing to gain by killing me." Even saying these words, though, scared Sonya in a way that felt as foreign to her as it was frightening.

Akiah shook his head. "If they can make it look like we did it, or caused your death, they have *everything* to gain. A dead hero. A victim of 'terrorism.' Someone who will never contradict their story about us, which will be that we treated you cruelly, or turned you into a zombie who'd do anything we asked."

He turned off CNN. "We trust you more than they do, Sonya. We trust that you'll tell the truth when you get out of here. That you'll say we abducted you and made your life hell for a few days, and then treated you with respect and dignity. That we even saved your life. That's what they're really worried about. That you'll be a good, honest American."

"Then release me before this whole thing goes completely out of control."

"If we thought we could do that safely for everyone concerned, believe me, we'd be doing it right now. But the irony, as far as *you're* concerned, is that you're safer with us than you would be if we tried to turn you over to them."

"I don't believe that."

"Where have you been?"

"In this goddamn place."

Akiah winced—she'd never seen him do that—and raised his hands in apology. But even his conciliatory gesture made her wonder who was really manipulating her, the Abolanders or the government? Then, with a wince of her own, she realized they both were.

Sonya took Darcy's arm, horrified by where this left them.

*

McCarthy stopped checking the video feed from the drone after the target had dropped from sight. He wasn't worried. They knew where she'd gone.

"Sir, you want a laugh?" Anderson said. "Take a look at this."

He directed McCarthy's attention to a screen showing seven men practicing thrusts with their spears, as McCarthy himself had done thirty-one years ago in boot camp bayonet training. Only these goofballs were getting it all wrong, using an over-the-shoulder technique that left their torsos open to attack. You drove upward from your hips so you could gut the abdomen all the way to the ribcage.

Anderson smiled. "Sir, this'll make Grenada look like the Battle of the Bulge."

Maybe, but this spear-chucking crap might be a feint to draw attention from the real attack. *That's the biggest problem with crazies,* McCarthy thought. *You never know.* Are they really suicidal enough to come at you with spears? Or do they hold a much more deadly weapon?

Bet wrong and you just lost your life and the lives of your troops.

McCarthy had never been a betting man.

*

In the darkness outside the community center, Sonya could see dozens of bonfires on the southern end of Terra Firma. The military had chain-sawed dead pines, piled up their trunks and limbs, and set them ablaze. In the glow she saw a small cannon glinting, like

273

something on TV from Iraq or Afghanistan, and other artillery she didn't know by name. All of it looked deadly.

She and Darcy, still trailed by Calypso, entered the center, lit sparingly with table candles only, and made a meal of bitter nut butter and brittle crackers.

As they stood to leave, Akiah came in and asked them to "bed down" in the kinderhaus with Sorrel, three of the moms, and all of the children under the age of fourteen.

"It's the farthest place we can put you from the border, and probably the safest," he said to Sonya. "Plus, they could use your help up there tonight. Yours, too," he added to Darcy.

A minute later, his mother intercepted them as they stepped outside.

"Please don't do anything foolish," Chandra said to Sonya, "like trying to leave. There's a lot more in your hands right now than you might realize. We think once the Canadian army gets here we'll be able to start negotiations to get everyone out peaceably."

"You're having me guarded. How am I supposed to escape?"

The old woman smiled inside her fur hood. "But you'd upset the children if you tried."

Sonya pointed to the fires and the long line of troops. "That's what's going to upset them, not me."

"Right now I can't do much about them, but we can make the children as comfortable as possible. If you could cosset Willow, that would be a great help. Her poor mother's still in labor. She's having a hard time of it, and Willow still talks about how you saved her life. I also have to warn you that Wenona believed you'd bring her father back. She was upset when you returned without him."

"How's Edson?"

"Really beat up. Fifty-seven stitches. Devaki thinks he has four broken ribs. Devaki's been very busy."

Chandra took Sonya's hand in both of hers, their mittens a pile of fur big as a beaver.

"Sonya, thank you for saving Edson. You could have left him to die."

"No, I couldn't have."

"We might not have a chance to talk again, and I want you to know something: I like you. I'm surprised that I do, but I do."

*

McCarthy walked the perimeter. They had the border covered tight as a tank tarp. Night scopes made the darkness come alive, and the drone kept him aware of her constant whereabouts.

His only concern was the fog. The reports called for a thick bout of it tonight, and it was already drifting in. Not that those crazies would get anywhere near them. His men could pick them out in the dark, and they could sure as hell find them in the fog. They'd grown up playing video games and could aim with a screen just as fast as they could with a scope.

But SRTV wouldn't get any visuals with fog. And a victory without visuals wasn't what Central Command had in mind, especially when they had full control of the cameras for once. This would be an object lesson for terrorists of all stripes.

So they'd wait for the sun to burn it off in the morning. That was the prediction.

McCarthy had a few of his own.

*

By the time Sonya, Darcy, and Calypso had trudged to the kinderhaus, the night sky had clouded over and strands of fog were weaving a seamless white cloak over the trees and rocks and buildings.

Sonya found Willow sleeping soundly, hugging a straw doll and sharing a bearskin blanket with one of her classmates.

Sorrel came over, and in a hushed voice said that Tip was lying awake in the back of the room. Would she talk to her? The girl had refused to speak to anyone.

Sonya worked her way around the bundled bodies, but Tip turned to the wall as soon as she settled beside her.

"Hey," she said softly, "I'm really, really sorry I didn't come back with your dad. Do you know what happened to me?"

"No," the girl said sharply. "And I don't care. I want my father."

"I care. I care a lot about you, so I want you to listen while I tell you why I came back with Edson."

Whisper by whisper, she told the whole story. As she neared the end, she snuggled close to the girl. Tip neither resisted her touch nor relinquished herself to the embrace. But in the morning, when they awoke to the distant notes of a fiddle, Sonya found Tip holding her closely, and Darcy's sleepy hand on her hip.

"What's that music?" Tip asked.

"I think that's the fiddler." Darcy sat up smiling. "He's a friend of mine."

"What's that song he's playing?" Tip asked as she and Sonya climbed to their feet.

"It's called 'It's All over Now Baby Blue.'" Darcy stood too, pulling on her coat and walking toward the front door.

Sonya and Tip followed her outside, where great puffs of fog were pulling apart. Calypso appeared right behind them.

"Do you know what this is all about?" Sonya asked him.

"No." He shook his head as if to clear it. "It's not part of our plan."

Darcy turned back to them. "I've got to go see him."

"Who?" Calypso asked.

"The fiddler, Kali, with the Ten Tribes of the New Apocalypse."

"You're shitting me," Calypso said. "They're here?"

As they started through the thinning fog toward the music, Sorrel snagged Tip.

"I'm sorry, but it's safer here."

"I'll come back," Sonya said to the girl.

"You promise for sure this time?"

"I promise."

As Sonya, Darcy, and Calypso drew closer to the music, the fog turned into wispy swirls, and they could see smoke still rising from the bonfires a couple of hundred yards away.

And then, knee-deep in snow on the U.S. side of the border, they spotted Kali with his fiddle, the two young boys who'd played the African drums, Wide Eyes, and dozens of other people, far more than had been on the bus with Darcy. They were waving signs at the troops that were dug in about fifty yards from them.

Darcy shouted to Kali and moved toward him. Calypso grabbed her. Sonya reached for her too, realizing only then that she was stopping her daughter from crossing into the country where both of them had been born.

The fiddler shook his head at Darcy, bouncing his blond dreadlocks over his shoulders as he played. Only then did Darcy relent.

"Why's he playing that song?" Sonya asked her.

"I'm not sure. He played it once before, on the bus, when they had me hidden."

"What bus? What are you talking about?"

Darcy explained quickly, adding, "He told me the words, but the only part I can remember right now was something about the sky folding under you."

"Look at that sign," Calypso pointed. "There's some Christian Peacemakers out there."

"Who are they?" Sonya asked.

"They stand up to armies all over the world," Darcy said.

The fiddler finished his song and waved his bow at Darcy.

"How well do you know him?" Sonya asked.

Darcy took her mother's hand. "Really well."

*

McCarthy had been alerted to their presence an hour before that skinny gypsy had played his first note. The whole goddamn troupe had slipped in from the north, right through the fog. And the no-show Canadians hadn't been there to stop them. Now they were openly traipsing around on U.S. territory; but nothing was going down without the visuals, so he had to let the hippies prance and dance till the fog cleared completely. Wouldn't be long now.

It really did look like a circus. Sounded like one, too. There were sixty-three of them standing between the troops and Terra Firma, according to Anderson. It sure put to rest any worries about IEDs. There were even mothers out there with kids, one of them nursing a baby like it was a meeting of the La Leche League.

If we're lucky, he thought, *the ones in charge will make their move now that the fog's lifting.*

He'd no sooner taken comfort in this prospect when Anderson pointed to the screen. Not the drone's eyes, but one of their land-based lenses. A woman had positioned herself near the hippies with a camera, and she was pointing it right at his tent. Filming *his* troops. Making their own video record.

McCarthy nodded at Anderson. The commander never said a word. He didn't need to. The unspoken language of denial enforced its own code.

*

Christmas morning, and *The New Yorker's* top staff and legal team were sitting around a long conference table. The magazine's lead attorney turned to Basch. "I can tell you that no appeals court wants to convene today. That's not going to work in our favor."

The sandy-haired lawyer had been a Federal Appeals Court clerk when the Nixon administration had tried to stop publication of the Pentagon Papers by *The New York Times.* Almost forty years later, the same court would review *The New Yorker's* request to go ahead with publication of what the government now acknowledged was a top secret CIA report on methane in the Arctic Ocean.

"None of us should expect a quick ruling," the lawyer told them. "We're asking for immediate relief but I don't expect to get it. It is a day, need I say, that most people reserve for their families."

"Why would they lie? That's the part I don't get." A senior editor looked up from her copy of the court papers and took off her wire rims. "They had to know they'd get caught."

"They didn't know that," Gordon said. "Lots of stuff never gets out. If one person hadn't decided to risk everything by sending me a full copy, they might have gotten away with calling the report a fake. *One* person." He shook his head as if after all these years and all his exposés he could still marvel at the courage of a lone source.

"But still, to be caught in such a blatant lie," wire rims said.

"Hey, they're desperate," Gordon said. "The economy's tanking, and this is the *coup de grace.* They wanted to deny, deny, deny as long as they could."

"So we get to publish after they crush Terra Firma?" Lindon asked the lawyer.

"*Maybe* you get to publish. After the appeals Court, it'll go to the Supremes, and this is not the court Nixon faced. There's no Justice Douglas or Marshall sitting up there. You're looking at Alito, Scalia, and Thomas."

"Among others." Gordon stood, all of his attention on the lawyer. "Look, you're right, it's not the court Nixon faced, but what fucking universe do these people think they're living in? There's a million bloggers out there now. Do they really think that they can stop this story? By the time they shut down the ISP, that report will go viral."

"But *we* can't touch it," the lawyer said. "Not now."

*

The *Battle Hymn of the Republic* had just risen from Kali's fiddle when Sonya heard a cracking sound and turned to see Calypso collapsing to the snow beside her. One of Desmond's young supporters stood over him with a club. In the next instant, Desmond grabbed Sonya from behind and shoved a flint knife against her throat.

"It's all over. We're taking a reward for you and building our own damn place."

"You're out of your mind. They'll never give you anything."

"Yeah, they will. They'll work with anyone. They just want you."

But Desmond didn't push her toward the troops, whose guns faced them. Instead, he and two of his followers dragged Sonya and Darcy toward the helicopter. She caught a glimpse of Cunningham, the mining executive, at the controls with two Abolanders holding spears to his head.

Don't get in there. You're dead if you do.

But she couldn't break away from Desmond's fierce grip.

Then the softest *twap* sounded. She'd heard it before, but the noise still made no sense until one of the men holding Darcy fell to the snow, groaning and grasping an arrow in his arm.

Desmond swung Sonya around, as if to use her as a shield; but he'd swung her the wrong way, for another *twap* rose to her ears as an arrow pierced his calf, sticking out the other side of his buckskins. Desmond staggered backward, eyes wide with shock, losing his grip on her.

Sonya grabbed Darcy, and they stumbled away.

Desmond and the others dragged themselves to the chopper. As they climbed aboard, the big blade whirled faster and faster.

Akiah raced up, bow in hand, screaming, "No, don't." But the spears were still pressed to Cunningham's head.

At that moment, Chandra charged through the line of protesters and headed straight toward the troops, waving her arms.

*

McCarthy held the drone's joystick, watched the helicopter, and waited. That bird was singing, but would she fly?

She goes up, she goes down.

He'd seen them fighting over Sonya Adams and her daughter, the real crazies coming alive, trying to drag the two of them along on whatever the hell this was. A suicide mission? Looked like it. They'd taken over that helicopter with spears and knives.

One faction against another. That's the way it always was with these people. Baghdad, Beirut, here. They tear each other to pieces. And then they turn on you.

Chandra Daly staggered toward him. He looked at her in the flesh for the first time.

"Sir, bird's up," Anderson said, as if McCarthy could have missed the shaky lift-off.

How much rope would he give them? Just enough.

The helicopter started right at them, much as he'd figured. He could see the pilot, panic all over his face.

He knows.

Chandra Daly coming closer, too, the bird's shadow heading straight toward her. She was the head of this snake, and from the time they'd landed she'd been the drone's only target. He glanced at the screen, watching her in black and white, as he had for the past twenty-four hours.

He also saw her path and the path of the helicopter converging, as if it could have been foreseen.

Chapter 22

The helicopter exploded right above Chandra, a ball of flame so big and bright that the chopper's shadow dissolved in an instant, leaving Terra Firma's leader in the brutal spotlight.

For a blink, it looked like the burning chopper was suspended by strings in the sky. The incinerated men in the cabin shifted, herky-jerky, as a burst of flame shot upward so fiercely that it appeared to arrest the copter's fall. In the same moment, two huge blasts ripped out the sides of the craft, launching great chunks of the cabin.

Chandra had fallen to her knees, reaching toward the troops as the burning bodies and wreckage fell.

Pleading? Imploring?

Sonya would never know. As she stared, too stunned to speak or move, the flaming fuselage crushed the elderly woman.

Three more explosions followed so fast it was hard to tell them apart. Red and black mushrooms gushed into the air with a single *whoosh* that proved chilling and final.

Darcy pointed a shaky hand to the ring of houses, where the chopper's flaming tail section had smashed through a roof and a straw bale wall. The fire bloomed, as if of tinder, and leaped to the homes on both sides of it.

Noxious smoke from the melting helicopter swept over Sonya and Darcy. They staggered through the fumes choking, eyes burning, clinging to each other.

The Ten Tribes of the New Apocalypse and the Christian Peacemakers also scattered, but amid the screams and smaller explosions, the collapsing roofs and spreading flames, the *Battle Hymn of the Republic* arose once again from the fiddler.

Sonya and her daughter peered through the swirling clouds of smoke and saw Kali standing firm, a spectral figure against the backdrop of gunships and soldiers. As his hands moved, his eyes remained fixed on the troops he now faced alone.

He increased the tempo until the hymn's shrouded history surged. Then he turned as he played, pointing the scroll of his fiddle to the fallen, their bodies still burning.

With a start—notes still in the air—he rested his instrument by his side, raising his voice above the crackling flames to sing the long-neglected lyrics:

> *John Brown's body lays a-moldering in the grave*
> *"John Brown's body lays a-moldering in the grave*
> *"John Brown's body lays a-moldering in the grave*
> *His soul goes marching on*
> *He captured Harpers Ferry with his nineteen men so true*
> *He frightened old Virginia till she trembled*
> *through and through.*
> *They hung him for a traitor, themselves the traitor crew.*
> *His soul goes marching on . . .*

When he finished singing he returned to his fiddle, letting the notes linger like memory, mournful and slow. In the next instant, his arms slumped and he dropped his instrument and crumpled to the snow.

Darcy broke for him. Sonya yelled, "Come back."

But Darcy plunged ahead, screaming, "No, no," over and over till she fell to her knees by the stricken boy.

Blood spilled from a single hole in his forehead, where the red star would have been. But the ink had never stained his skin; only the blood marred his face and open, unseeing eyes.

Darcy raged at the troops, and as Sonya ran to her she saw that her only child bore a suffocating resemblance, in these resonating seconds, to the young woman who'd knelt in such open anguish by a fallen boy at Kent State.

Her daughter's grief sounded so deep, so primal, that Sonya wept her way through the knee-deep snow, shrieking "Don't shoot her. Please dear God don't shoot her."

She threw herself on Darcy, bundling her daughter in her arms, trying to protect her from the violence that had claimed the boy beside them.

When she looked up in fury, she saw five soldiers running toward them, and realized that she and Darcy had crossed the border.

She dragged her girl to her feet. "We've got to go back. We can't be here now."

Darcy appeared dazed, staring at blood on her bearskin coat. The charging men were less than forty feet away.

Sonya pulled her arm till she moved, and held her as they stumbled through the snow. The soldiers gained on them with every step.

Gulping air, exhausted, still crying, Sonya urged her daughter along.

Not twenty feet away, Akiah waved his arms, shouting, "Run, run."

The soldiers were so close Sonya could hear their boots.

Akiah started toward her, stopped, stared, and then dashed up, grabbing Sonya's hand and pulling her forward.

Darcy tripped, and Sonya's grip on her almost failed. Akiah spun around, seized Darcy by the collar, and the three of them, slipping and falling, lunged past the point where Akiah had been standing.

He turned to the soldiers, yelling, "This is Canada."

They never paused. Two of them peeled off toward Gwen, who stood to the side wielding her camera.

As the lead soldier leaped at her, Akiah drew the bone handle knife from his dreads and threw it, impaling the man's outstretched hand.

He yelped and fell, tripping his cohort.

Gwen ran away. So did Sonya and Darcy as the soldier gripped his wrist and stared at the crudely shaped handle protruding from his palm, the blade sticking out the other side, blood spotting the snow.

Akiah threw up his hands as the other three soldiers leveled their weapons at him.

Sonya and Darcy, sickened by smoke and thickening waves of fear, dragged themselves past the towering flames now consuming the circle of homes and the community center. They looked back only long enough to see the soldiers dragging Akiah to the line of troops.

A deafening *boom* snapped their attention to the center, where the roof, with its massive support beams, had just collapsed, raising a screen of furious red embers and a wild flurry of flames. The center's walls began to cave in, belching large plumes of black smoke

The roar of the helicopters grew louder as they crowded the

airspace above Terra Firma. Sonya thought of the kids in the kinderhaus, the only building other than the barn that wasn't burning.

As she and Darcy ran up the path to the school, streams of children—many without coats, hats, or mittens—raced out the door, shouting, crying, running away.

Oh, my God, Sonya thought. *What about the kids at the clinic?*
Sylvan and Branch, Phoenix and Bodhi.

She looked back, saw only the roaring circle of flames, and knew the fire had reached those beds.

Edson. Ventura. Her baby.

"You bastards," she wept, her eyes rising to the helicopters.

A child tugged on her coat. She found Willow staring up at her.

"Sonya?" The four-year-old looked scared. "Are you okay?"

Sonya wiped her eyes, crouched, and hugged her. She forced a nod for the child's sake. "Are *you* okay?"

Willow nodded, but Sonya knew better. Maybe Willow did, too.

Sonya called to her daughter, who was gazing at the destruction. Darcy appeared numb as she turned to them.

"Find Tip. Her mother's not going to be any help." *If her mother's still alive*, Sonya thought.

Darcy started after the children, then stopped. "Mom, isn't that her?"

She pointed to a frail figure huddling in buckskins by the kinderhaus door, staring at the helicopters racing toward her.

"Tip," Sonya screamed, "come here. *Now.*"

The child ran to her, terrified. Sonya opened her arms and held her along with Willow.

"Mom, what are we going to do?"

The fear in Darcy's voice brought Sonya to her feet. Everywhere she looked, smoke and flames fouled the air; and Abolanders ran aimlessly, many bleeding, blackened, screaming in pain, shock or fear.

"I've got to search that school," Sonya said. "There could be kids in there. Tip," she looked down at the frightened girl, "do you know where Sorrel is?"

"She took Shalin to the clinic. It was a long time ago. She never came back."

Oh, God.

"Take them," she herded the girls into her daughter's arms, "and go hide in those trees." She pointed to the leafless hilly forest that Akiah and Calypso had rushed her through on the way to the hole. "You'll be safer there. Wait for me. *Go.*"

As Darcy hustled the children toward the naked trees, Sonya ran into the kinderhaus shouting, "Is anybody here? It's Sonya," trading on whatever affection they felt for her to try to save their lives. No building seemed safe with most of Terra Firma in flames.

But right away she realized that the thunder of the helicopters and the distant screams would make it impossible to hear the soft cries of a frightened child, so she started searching under tables and the sink, inside the fabric fort.

She threw open closets, cabinets. No children. Hurrying back to the entrance before spotting pillows piled oddly under a shelf packed with stuffed animals.

She darted over and tossed the pillows aside, yet she still startled when she found Chakka, the little boy who'd had her paint a tiger on his cheek.

"You can't stay here," she shouted above the *whup-whup-whup* of a helicopter that must have been hovering right over the roof. "It's not safe."

An explosion that sounded dangerously close rocked the school and knocked a stuffed lion on to the boy. He jumped to his feet, and Sonya ran him out the door.

The helicopter was gone, but a huge fireball ballooned in the sunny sky to their left. *The barn,* Sonya said to herself. It looked as if a missile had been fired.

A cow lowed hideously, and she saw the creature dragging its legless hind end from the flames, leaving a bloody swath in the snow.

They ran toward the leafless forest, but didn't see Darcy and the two girls until her daughter rose from behind a snowy trunk lying on the ground.

"Soldiers," Darcy mouthed, pointing past her mother.

Toward the barn, Sonya realized.

"They were searching," Darcy said softly as Sonya drew closer. "They almost found us. What's that horrible noise?"

"A cow. It's really hurt. Follow me."

She hurried them up the trail that threaded through the skeletal trees and sharp shadows. The little-used path proved hard to climb, especially for the children; but she had them hold hands, and hauled them along, believing that every step took them farther from the violence.

A dark cloud from the obliterated barn drifted toward them. Sonya, thinking of the poisonous smoke and dust from the World Trade Center, had them stop and cover their faces.

While it passed they heard a single gun shot, and the cow no longer bellowed. As the smoke thinned to gray streaks high above them, they struggled toward a hummock.

Sonya led them to the entrance to the hole, brushed away the snow, and pulled open the heavy wooden door, guiding each of them to the ladder. Then she climbed down and closed it.

"This is scary," Tip whispered in the darkness.

"There are some candles in here." Sonya fumbled around in the cabinet and lit three of them, illuminating the bearskin blanket on the bench, the wooden cabinet, and the pale snaky roots hanging from the ceiling.

"What is this?" Darcy asked.

"This is the hole, where they locked me up."

Darcy looked around the tight space, her face smudged with smoke and soot. "It's like we're in a bomb shelter."

Sonya nodded, working hard to stop her tears. Here they were reasonably safe at last, and she could barely keep herself from falling apart.

These kids don't need that.

She opened the cabinet again, grateful to grip something solid, to try to still the trembling that had overtaken her. And the anger. The *outrage.*

"There should be some food in here." She found the nuts and berries. A few handfuls wouldn't hurt them, though she had no takers when she held up the bag.

Tip, in just her buckskins, was shivering, so Sonya wrapped her in the blanket and sat her on the bench.

"Mom, what the hell happened? Who was that guy who grabbed you?"

"Desmond. At first they housed me with him and his girlfriend. A little unstable."

Darcy shook her head and sat heavily on the bench, hugging

Tip, whose shivering had eased. Sonya sat Willow and Chakka beside her daughter and tucked the heavy blanket around the four of them. Tears were streaming down Darcy's cheeks.

Sonya touched her hand. "I'm sorry about your friend. He was very brave."

Darcy nodded, whispered, "He was." Her wet eyes glistened in the candlelight. "I'm never going back, Mom. I can't."

"You mean because of what happened with the bounty hunter?"

"No," Darcy shook her head. "I mean because of what's happening up there right now. What *they're* doing."

Ventura snuggled the bearskin around her neck. "Is my mom okay?"

"She's safe with Akiah." *There'd be a lifetime of hard truth for this child*, Sonya thought. *No need for it here.*

"And my new baby sister?"

"It's a baby girl, huh?" Sonya brought up her biggest smile, though all she could think of were burning buildings—smoke and screams and pain.

"My mommy was pretty sure. She said she had a feeling I was going to have a sister really soon."

Tip leaned past Darcy and tugged on Willow's arm. Sonya feared the girl's blunt honesty. But all Tip said was, "I'll bet she's a pretty baby."

Kind words, but it was the tears in Tip's eyes—and the gritty sensitivity they revealed—that turned Sonya away, choking on her own sorrow.

*

McCarthy no longer bothered scanning the screen. With that helicopter neutralized, he could concentrate on their prime mission: recovering Sonya Adams and her daughter. He had deployed a Special Forces unit to find them, the White House having just authorized a ten-mile border incursion.

McCarthy had no sooner issued that order when one of the screens monitoring news coverage caught his eye with a smoky, fiery scene that looked like it hailed from hell itself. McCarthy froze, stared closely at the video, astounded to see Terra Firma in flames.

"Where the hell is she?" he bellowed. "That woman with the camera? I thought we took her down."

"No sir, she escaped."

"Take her down *now.* "

Anderson's head was shaking. "Sir, look, that's not her. Or not only her. Those angles keep changing. There are a bunch of cameras out there. That's streaming video from a website." He pointed to a *www.attackonterrafirma.com* credit line running on CNN. A "Graphic Footage" warning appeared right above it.

McCarthy felt dizzy, like all the blood had rushed from his brain. He checked three other news channels—all of them were showing the same broken, burning bodies with the same warning. Graphic? McCarthy thought it looked like fucking Armageddon. New grisly scenes appeared every few seconds.

"Where are those cameras?" McCarthy lifted his eyes to the conflagration itself. His men had scanned every goddamn inch of this place, and the only camera they'd seen was that woman's. But Anderson was right: This was the work of a lot more than one woman with a camcorder.

"Sir, all the shots are aimed *at* Terra Firma." Anderson was studying the screens. "And they're all changing in the same sequence. I think these people secured at least five or six cameras to the trees. See, there," he pointed to a branch in the lower part of the video that had just started streaming, "that camera's not moving. They've got them set up for remote feeds that are going to that website."

"The satellite signals are supposed to be jammed."

"We did jam them. They've got them back up somehow. I know it sounds crazy, but maybe they've got land-based lines running out of here. "

"Take them out." McCarthy didn't want excuses.

"Sir, take what out?"

"The goddamn trees."

"All of them?"

McCarthy didn't answer. He'd started counting the rotating scenes. Eight of them. There were eight goddamn cameras out there, not five or six. Some showed buildings burning. Others had his men cuffing bloody and burned prisoners. Two kept returning to dead bodies, one smoldering. Another had a boy about three plopped down in the snow crying "Mama" over and over. A woman with a head wound lay next to him. You could hear the kid. Even with the screaming of the prisoners, you could hear him.

"Sir? The trees? All of them?"

McCarthy still didn't answer. He stared at CNN's coverage. Terra Firma was interrupting the streaming video to fill the screen with a website address: www.methaneglobalwarmingglobalsecurity.com.

Those fuckers had released it.

And the whole world was watching.

*

Sonya, Darcy, and the three children huddled together on the bench, terrified by the explosions. They'd shaken the walls and ceiling of the hole and rattled the wooden door so hard that Sonya feared it would blow open at any second.

Now, in a sudden lull, another ominous sound started creeping in. A sizzling, like the snowy forest was on fire.

She climbed up the ladder and opened the door a couple of inches just as the crown of a tree burst into flames. Cinders showered down in front of her, and branches crashed to the snow. She raised her head slowly, spotting flames all around her. The smoke singed her eyes, nose, lungs.

Sonya slammed the door, coughing, recovering only to grow tense with the realization that they were trapped by the burning forest.

Before she could take another step down the ladder, the entire roof of the hole thundered, bringing the snaky roots to life. She reached back up, testing the door to see if it would still open. Her stomach twisted when she couldn't budge it. Worse, it felt warm.

"What's wrong?" Darcy demanded.

"I think a tree's fallen over the door."

"Could we open it, if I helped?"

"Maybe, but we wouldn't want to right now because there's a fire up there."

"Are we stuck in here?" Darcy tossed aside the bearskin and stood.

"No." But Sonya sickened when she realized what that deceptively simple answer really meant.

Her daughter raised a candle and studied the door. "There's *smoke* coming from that thing. Is it burning?"

Sonya touched it. The door was getting hotter. She climbed

down, and though she tried to sound calm, she told Darcy they'd have to move the cabinet. "Fast," she emphasized.

"Why?"

"There's a tunnel back there."

"A tunnel?" but even as she spoke, Darcy helped her mother lift the cabinet away from the wall.

Sonya held a candle close to the opening, relieved to see the flame flickering. "Do you hear that sound? That's fresh air. It's coming from a hole way back in there. Akiah said it brings air from a long way off. If the smoke gets any thicker, we're going to have to get in there."

"Wait, that really freaks me out. I can't stand tight places. I had to squeeze under the floorboards of a bus."

Sonya nodded. "I feel the same way. But if it gets any worse, that's what we're going to have to do." She noticed the children rubbing their eyes. Tip started coughing.

"I don't think I can do that, Mom."

"Darcy, we have three kids here. We might not have any choice."

Darcy pressed the heel of her hand to her forehead. "How do we —" The door popped loudly enough to quiet her, and the wood started hissing as it burned.

"We've got to *move,*" Sonya said, fearing the fiery branches that could fall into the hole.

"Okay," Darcy conceded with a huge breath. "How do we do this?"

"I'm going to strip down to my long underwear." She looked at her lithe daughter. "Just to be safe, you better, too."

"Willow—" she crouched in front of her—"you're going to have to take off your coat and hat, mittens too. But all of you guys can keep your buckskins and socks on." She figured they were small enough to get through the tunnel with the extra layer. Poor Tip was still coughing.

She warned them that about twelve feet inside the tunnel they'd hit their first tight spot. "It's not bad, and once we're past it we'll stop and see what's going on out here."

"How do you know all this?" Darcy asked.

"Because I tried to escape through this thing. But we're not going to have to go as far as I went."

By the time they stripped down, smoke from the burning door had started to irritate Sonya and Darcy's eyes too.

"I'll go first. Willow, you follow me. Then Tip." A tough kid, and Sonya considered her the least likely to panic, so she'd put her farthest from the adults. "Chakka next. Darcy, you should come last. These guys won't need help," she said in a cheery voice, "but just in case you'll be right behind them. Now, you three—" Sonya corralled the children with her eyes—"you're going to have be plenty brave. We'll be taking candles and matches, but if they go out —" A loud crack silenced her. All five of them looked up to see the door glowing red.

"If the candles go out," Sonya finished quickly, "just listen to us. We'll get you all the air you'll need."

She crawled in with a lit candle, doing her best to force aside the horrors of having been entombed in here, coaxing herself forward with the strict understanding that the door wouldn't last much longer, and that they'd die if she didn't lead them to fresh air.

She felt Willow on her heels and heard Tip and Chakka say they were in. Nothing from Darcy until she shouted, "The door's on fire and it's breaking apart."

"Get in," Sonya yelled. "Willow, Tip, Chakka, *move-move,* make room for her."

Sonya squirmed to the low point that had stopped her initial escape attempt a few weeks ago, when she'd tried to squeeze through the tunnel in her bearskin coat.

"There's a lot of stuff that's on fire falling in the hole," Darcy called to her.

"Can you tell if it's the ceiling, or just the door?" *If it's the ceiling, we're really in trouble.*

"I think it's just the door. It's not like everything's caving in. A lot of smoke, though."

"I'm going under that low spot I told you about. Then everybody's got to do it as fast as they can so we can get away from that smoke."

"I'm too scared," Willow said from right behind her.

"Hold on to my foot," Sonya said.

The girl death-gripped her ankle.

Sonya pressed the side of her face to the cold rocky floor and slid through, eased by the bear grease she'd left behind when she'd backed out of here with Akiah.

Willow, Tip, and Chakka cleared it, leaving her right by the tight, twisting passage where Akiah had found her wedged in a near fetal position.

"You okay back there?" She could hear Darcy grunting.

"I'm just . . . getting through this tight spot. Tell me that's the worst of it."

Sonya let the question pass, holding the candle in front of her to see, once again, how the rock narrowed as it canted clockwise to a forty-five-degree angle, then disappeared behind the blind curve that had left her almost doubled over, trapped, and nearly mindless with fear.

She also saw that every surface still looked slick with the thick globs of grease Akiah had used to help her slide out.

The three children bunched up behind her, and she listened intently to Darcy's labored breathing as she worked her way along.

"How's the smoke?" she shouted back to her.

"I'm still getting some. It's like it was when we were back in that room. What's it like up there?"

"Better, it sounds like."

"My eyes are burning," Tip said. She hadn't stopped coughing since the smoke had seeped into the hole.

"Can we get to that air hole now?" Darcy started coughing.

"Sure. There's a section right here that'll be easy for the kids, but you'll have to be patient. It's really greasy, so you'll make it through just fine. And then we just have to crawl to the air hole."

"Okay, let's go." Darcy was coughing harder.

Inching forward, Sonya slid on to her right hip so she could see the wall as she moved along the section slanting up. The rock quickly closed to a few inches of her face.

While the grease helped slide her along, it also prevented her from getting any purchase. To advance, she had to press her hands, arms, and feet against the sides and shrug herself, like a caterpillar, up to the blind curve.

This worked until the curve bent her almost all the way over. Once she'd squeezed her shoulders in here, she found the space too tight to apply any leverage with her hands. As she struggled, she snuffed the candle.

The immediate darkness compounded her fear of being jammed

in here forever, frightening her so much that her breath quickened and she had to order herself to *slow down.*

Using the painful points of her elbows, knees, and hips, she took long minutes to wiggle out of this nightmare.

The crushing blackness made her frantic to relight the candle. The flame revealed a tunnel only inches wider than the horror she'd just revisited.

The two girls and Chakka passed through the twisty section easily, but moments later Darcy yelled that she was stuck.

"Listen carefully, hon. You've got to think of every part of your body as a loose link. I had to pressure the walls with my elbows and knees to move. Even my hips."

"It's so hard to hold on to anything with all this grease."

"It'll get your through there," Sonya said, hoping there was still enough left on the walls to help Darcy.

Ten endless minutes passed while they listened to her daughter struggle.

"God, I made it," they finally heard. "But how do we ever get out?"

"We'll get out. I promise. You breathing all right?"

"Better."

They crawled another thirty feet to the opening in the ceiling. Clear, cold air blew on them, and they all lay in the candlelight shivering.

"I'm really cold," Willow said.

Tip and Chakka said they were cold too.

"Let's all bunch together. Willow, you climb up around my legs; and Tip and Chakka, you guys squeeze together. Darcy, let's see if we can't get a little heat chamber going for them."

That settled the children, but Sonya had to take deeply measured breaths to fight a vicious panic attack. It swept through her system the instant she realized that *if,* for any reason, Darcy couldn't back out, they really could die down here, sealed in the earth forever.

No one even knows you're here. Not a single soul. And that fire could go on for days.

Akiah said there's another way out, she reminded herself, but the very thought of diving into that underground river triggered a paralyzing siege of fear. She tried to fight it off with the assurance that Akiah would tell the soldiers to rescue them. *When he hears we're missing, he'll think of the hole. If he's still alive.*

"Why you shaking your head like that?" Willow asked.

"I was thinking of the fire."

It turned quiet once more, and Sonya began to notice the sound of the river, realizing she'd been hearing it since they'd found the air hole. Then she smelled smoke, as inescapable, it seemed, as fear.

She had everyone back up a little so she could check the air hole. After less than a minute's exposure, her eyes began to water. But they were still getting plenty of oxygen.

What if it gets worse?

It *did* get worse, almost as soon as she thought that. A puff of smoke the size of a seat cushion enveloped her face, as if to suffocate her. She waved it away, but not the chilling sense of what could be coming in thicker, deadlier clouds in the next five minutes. Or five hours.

Tip began to cough again, and Sonya waited tensely to hear if the child would stop, as if this might be omen enough. Tip had been the first to cough from the burning door, and the first to cough in the tunnel. Up till now, they'd been able to move on. But where could they go? Not to that underground river. No child could survive going in that.

None of them spoke. It was as if they were praying, even the littlest ones, that their canary would quit coughing.

In the midst of this, Sonya heard the sound of the underground river growing more insistent, needling her nerves, raising the eerie memory of the wall of water that had raced by shiny and black in the candlelight.

Two minutes passed. The smoke became visible, a steady gray stream, then thinned. But Tip's coughing didn't ease, it grew louder. Sonya wanted to scream, "Stop." But it wasn't the girl she wanted silenced. It was that wall of water.

Darcy spoke quietly. "What are we going to do?"

Sonya stared at the opening above them. She couldn't bank their lives on it any longer. If it started drafting black smoke through the tunnel, they'd all end up in the river.

That'll kill the kids.

"You're going to stay with them," Sonya said to Darcy. "There's an underground river up here and I'm going to use it to get help."

"What? You're leaving us?" Darcy's fright set off Willow's tears again.

"It's a way to get help. I saw it last time. Akiah said a miner once fell in and it took him out of here." She'd spare Darcy the details about the miners who'd drowned.

"Then we should all go."

"It's not like that, hon." She couldn't elaborate. *Don't scare the kids.*

But one child sounded petrified:

"Mom, what are you saying?"

"That I have to leave you now. That I love you very much. That I'm going to go get help. And that I'm so sorry for every bad moment I ever gave you."

"No, don't go. I've got stuff I've got to tell you, goddamn it."

"You can tell me when we get together again."

"No, Mom, it can't wait. Dad's friend, Keith, that cop, r-a-p-e-d me. For *five* days. At his cabin. I . . . " But Darcy was crying so hard she could scarcely talk.

"Oh hon, I'm so sorry." Sonya actually moved to try to hold her daughter before the tunnel walls refused her. She collapsed against the cold rock, tears streaming as she listened to Darcy's sorrow rise above the rushing darkness of the river.

And still Tip coughed.

"I'm coming back, Darcy. I'm going to get help and I'm coming back, and we'll talk about it. Please know you're wonderful. And please know that I've always, *always* loved you. I'll be back with help. I promise."

It's what you say to your child, even if your child is twenty-three.

And if you're about to die?

Then you've told her you love her. You've said the right words, even if you've said them years too late.

"Can we see where you're going, at least?" Darcy asked.

"I don't think that's a good idea," Sonya answered.

"Mom, this is really danger—"

"No, it's not," Sonya said, breaking faith with her every fear; willing, if possible, to keep *all* the children calm as she herself sickened with dread. "Promise me you'll wait. But Darcy, if for any reason you need to find the river—you understand what I'm saying? —it's right up ahead. Just crawl forward. You can't miss it."

"I love you. I've wanted to tell you that since I got here."

"I love you too. With all my heart."

Sonya said good-bye to the children, handed her candle to Willow, and crawled until the downward tilt of the tunnel steepened.

When she felt herself sliding, she reached out with her hands; and when she touched the icy water an instant later, she balled up to protect her head as the current whipped her away, dragging her along the rough wall for the first few seconds. But even the battering of her limbs was lost to the shocking coldness. The temperature couldn't have been more than a degree or two above freezing, setting off a throbbing ache in her skull. But she suffered far worse when she swam for the air pocket that Akiah had described, and found the cavern filled with runoff.

Her eyes opened, searching, but found only a bottomless blackness, a netherworld never touched by light. Her thoughts moved too, counting *One, two, three . . .* the useless, heedless seconds passing like the empty hands of eternity, always reaching, never grasping.

Twelve, thirteen . . .

Lungs aching, tumbling like she'd been caught in a huge wave.

Twenty-one, twenty-two . . .

The pain in her chest was so severe, like the emptiness would snap her inside out, flood her lungs with water and claim the last of her life.

As she rolled in the frigid darkness, she reached wildly, feeling the pure hollowness of the cavern; but for one undying moment she was too numbed by the cold to register the air.

She burst above the surface, cracking her head on the rock ceiling. She barely noticed the gash as her lungs filled three times in rapid succession.

Almost as quickly, she raised her hands to protect her face, fearing that the fast-flowing river would smash her into a low-hanging rock.

Light appeared in the ceiling, the barest glimpse, as if a dim bulb had burned out and cast its last rays as a stain.

Her fingers, numb as they were, reached up and scraped ice. The frozen surface blued, as if the sun were fighting to find her; and the ceiling rose a foot beyond her outstretched hand.

A roar, louder than a football stadium, filled her ears as the ice whitened and the river swept her out of the earth and into the open. She looked down in terror and saw that she was riding a huge waterfall exploding into a pool at least six stories below.

I'm dead, were her last words before the waterfall drove her deep below the roiling surface, pounding her so hard that she thought she'd been battered against the boulders she'd glimpsed while falling. The violent pressure wrenched her arms, legs, head, jerked her sideways, and spit her from the pool into the churning river. Her eyes, widening with pain and panic, rose to see the water running white as snow before her.

She flailed her arms to keep her head above the rapids, frantic from the speed sweeping her forward.

A quarter of a mile passed before she could work her way over to the rocks and boulders lining the left bank, and another minute of savage struggle ensued before she could grab one of them long enough to haul herself from the icy flow.

She stood, legs shaky as a newborn calf's, like these were also her first steps in a new world; and then she immediately had to sit on one of the snowy boulders.

Blood ran from her hands and feet, and dripped from her head to her long underwear, blooming pink. Slowly, as her senses settled, she began to hope that she hadn't been broken in a critical way.

Her eyes lifted to the sky. Not a helicopter in sight. But far away she saw the smoke, as if rising from another age.

And now, much closer, she heard people. It no longer mattered who they were or the country they claimed.

She screamed.

EPILOGUE

Sonya Adams, *An Open Letter.*

I will never forget the massacre on Christmas day, the final horror of all those people dying. I still cannot talk about this publicly, but I will try, in my first and maybe only blog entry, to set the record straight about what happened on that terrifying day.

Let me start by saying that if there's any good to have come out of this tragedy, it would have to be the recent UN month-long session on global warming, especially with all the attention now getting paid to the threat from methane. The series that ran in *The New Yorker* spelled out the dangers that we're all facing much better than I can, but I do feel safe in saying that the pledges by almost all the countries of the world to clamp down on greenhouse gases immediately was great news. It gave me real hope, as it should everyone.

We are seeing a tremendous shift in attitudes. Even so, I hesitate to write the next few words. I know that there are people who will, once again, accuse me of being a victim of Stockholm Syndrome, or worse—an Abolander who was part of some bizarre conspiracy against our government—but I have to say that the Abolanders managed to achieve what most experts would have thought impossible: they actually focused world attention on the greatest crisis humanity has ever faced.

But they paid a horrible, horrible price. Those twenty-two dead men and women, so many of them young parents, should still be alive. The seven dead children should still have a future. If the nurse at Aboland hadn't evacuated their clinic right away, several more children and a newborn baby and her mother also would have died.

Christmas day was a moral outrage. I do not use those words lightly. I am still sickened by what I saw. I can't say enough about the citizens who are leading the fight to find out the role of the CIA and the U.S. military in this national tragedy. This national disgrace. It gives me some hope that senators and congressmen are using their powers to initiate and broaden investigations, including the ones digging into the role of energy companies in dictating U.S. foreign and domestic policies.

What frightens me, what should frighten all of us, is that the court martial of Commander Justin McCarthy and three of his frontline officers appears to be the sole result of the Pentagon's hasty investigation into the violence that it authorized. For once, can't the higher command be held to account for the blood that it spills so wantonly? We must demand this.

I'm going to take a moment here to repeat that what the Abolanders did to me was wrong, very wrong. They put me through a terrifying experience that almost ended up killing me, for Godsakes. But what I find so depressing, what I can't stop thinking about, is that the government's actions were so much worse. I don't see how anyone with half a heart can dispute this.

The Abolanders did not fire bullets. They did not fire missiles. They did not burn children to death in their homes. The government committed those atrocities. The government murdered U.S. and Canadian citizens, invaded Canada, tortured Americans, and from the start of their investigation violated universally recognized human rights.

So I cannot and will not cooperate with any prosecutions of the Abolanders. They've suffered enough. I will appear in court only as a character witness on their behalf.

I've taken another small step to try to set things right. I've added my name to a petition, signed by millions of people around the world, demanding that the U.S. government either charge Akiah Daly in open court with all the crimes that he's been accused of, including the bombing of the Texrefineco refinery, or return him to his home country of Canada. Like all of us, he should have the right to face his accusers in court and know the evidence against him, not simply be declared a terrorist and held in secret. We don't know if he's even in the U.S. or if he's been shipped off to one of those overseas prisons that we hear so much about. I can't even begin to fathom the stories linking him to Al Qaeda, and nobody else should either.

Now I'm going to address several rumors that have come up since the tragedy. I'll start with one that's actually true. Canadian troops did rescue me, my daughter, and the three children I took into that tunnel. They heard me screaming after I crawled out of that freezing river.

The Canadian soldiers were on a road right above me in a convoy heading to Terra Firma. If they hadn't been there I would have died from hypothermia, and Darcy and the children most likely would have died from smoke inhalation or drowning. There wouldn't have been anyone to sound the alert. They wrapped me in blankets, rushed me to a helicopter, and sent me up with four soldiers and their commander to try to find the entrance to the hole and the tunnel.

It took us about fifteen minutes before I recognized the spot. The smoke wasn't too bad because the forest wasn't as thick near the hole, thanks to a large outcropping of rock behind it.

The soldiers, wearing all kinds of protective gear and masks, went down on a cable to get Darcy and the kids.

My daughter was the first one out because she'd been the last to go into the tunnel.

The reports that Darcy requested political asylum as soon as she climbed in the helicopter are also true. But a wild cable news account of a so-called "firefight" between Canadian and U.S. forces was a complete lie. Here's what really happened.

Just as the last Canadian soldier latched onto the cable and started up from the hole, a member of a U.S. Special Forces unit came running out of the smoke and latched on right below him.

When the U.S. soldier got in the helicopter, he demanded that Canada release all of us to the United States.

The Canadian commander refused. He pointed out that we had been rescued on Canadian territory and that we were in Canadian air space. He also said that Darcy had requested political asylum, and that her request would have to be heard before she could be returned.

The U.S. soldier argued with the Canadians all the way to the landing area, where he was offered a ride back to the United States. He declined.

He was never held at gunpoint, which all of the cable news channels reported. The Canadians never threatened him. He never threatened them.

Darcy has settled in Canada while she awaits the outcome of her request for political asylum. That's also accurate. I've moved closer to the border to be near her. I'm taking a break from modeling, maybe for good.

I'm very pleased to say that the report that I'm about to become a mother for a second time is true. I've started adoption proceedings for one of the Terra Firma children, and she is living with me now. The reason for the adoption, though, is heartbreaking. The girl's mother died with eight others, including three toddlers, when the roof of the community center collapsed.

The child's dad (not a Terra Firman) and I talked, and he said he was unable to take care of her, which disappointed her deeply. But I'm eternally happy to have her in my life. She's an amazing girl with an unstoppable spirit and a hilariously sassy tongue, much like her older sister, Darcy, who also adores her.

Among the strangest rumors I've had to contend with was that I attended Chandra Daly's burial disguised as a funeral-home employee. A fuzzy photograph, supposedly of me standing by a hearse, appeared in one of the tabloids. It was totally fabricated. But those were real photos of me at the memorial service for all the people killed at Terra Firma. I'm not going to apologize for my attendance, despite the calls for me to do so.

I want to end this letter on a deeply personal note. It is my hope that what I'm about to say will put to rest the worst rumor of all: that I hate my country.

It's sad that I even have to say this, but I don't hate the United States, although it's true that I'm terribly disappointed with it right now. When I look at what happened on Christmas, I see what our country has been doing in other places around the world. The only difference was those cameras. They showed everything, and it was ugly.

It's bewildering to me at times to try to grasp what's going on, but I'm doing all I can to get informed. I'm reading more than ever, including books that Darcy recommends, and I'm talking to all kinds of people.

And you know what? Odd as this may sound, I'm starting to think we might be on the verge of reclaiming what's best about ourselves as a nation, which I'd like to think is a great sense of decency and caring, and planning for our children's future.

My daughter, it's true, doesn't share my optimism, and she's been vocal about this. She honestly believes we've turned a dark corner and will never recover. I can't let myself believe that, but I understand Darcy's feelings. The U.S. government tried to extradite her for a killing she committed in self-defense; and if a Canadian forensics team hadn't exonerated her, they'd have agreed to ship her back. Darcy might have ended up in a U.S. prison like her friends Lotus and Kodiak, for whom we're establishing a legal defense fund.

But we've been through terrible wars and terrible times before, and we've always managed to find ourselves again. I think we can this time too.

One more quick note before I go. I hesitate to even address this final rumor because it's so ridiculous that it's almost funny. But I know if I don't say something about it in this letter, people will assume that it must be another Terra Firma "fact."

Many of the Abolanders—Gwen, Ventura and her family, Edson, Andromeda, Sorrel, and others—have stayed in Canada, which has refused our government's requests for their extradition. These Abolanders continue their environmental work on small-scale, energy independent community living. To further their efforts, they have taken the offer of land from the Ascent Gold Company in exchange for dropping their threat of a lawsuit.

Yes, they plan to start rebuilding Terra Firma this summer.

Yes, they've received thousands of emails and letters from people who want to move there.

But no, *I* will not be joining them.

Voluntarily or otherwise.

Acknowledgements

I'll start my acknowledgements with the beginning of *Primitive*. Kevin Donald, an old friend, once told me the story of a model friend of his who almost boarded a plane for a non-existent shoot. Only a last minute telephone call to check on the supposed client prevented her from falling into the hands of the men who planned to kidnap her. I never forgot Kevin's story, and with different twists and turns it sparked the idea of Sonya's abduction.

I owe a deep debt to the late Don Shawe, who truly was a poet and a painter "far behind his rightful time," to borrow the words of another poet and painter. Don introduced me to aboriginal skills, and for all I know he coined the term "Aboland" as well. He was a master of expression, whether with a canvas or a sheet of paper, or when he rose before those who would rule us unwisely. I have your picture on my desk, Don, and your words in my head.

I'm also grateful to another old friend, Eric Burnette, for the idea of the "The Race of Shame," the first sailboat race from New York to San Francisco through the Arctic Ocean.

Eric also read *Primitive* in manuscript. I'm fortunate—and thankful—to have other friends and family members who did likewise. Let me begin with Mark Feldstein, a fellow author who spent many hours catching small and large concerns with one of the sharpest minds I've ever encountered. I was also helped greatly by others who read *Primitive* and provided keen insights: Kim Nykanen, Dale Dauten, Monte Ferraro, Darryl Santano, Tina Castanares, Christopher Van Tilburg, Linda Ellman, Tammie Andison, and Lucinda Taylor. In the eleventh hour, another old friend, Steve Saylor, weighed in wisely. Claire Dippel read an early, incomplete draft of *Primitive,* and also provided opinions that proved helpful. Paleoclimatologist Dr. Mel Reasoner offered helpful suggestions as well. My thanks to all.

Ed Stackler wielded his precise pen from the beginning of this book to the very end, and I remain—as always—grateful for his assistance.

Finally, I'd like to thank Deb Smith and Debra Dixon at Bell Bridge Books. I don't think this novel would have appeared without their heartfelt desire to see it in print. Deb Smith was a marvelous editor. Every author should be so fortunate.

Suggested Reading

There are many worthy books on the subject of climate change, or "climate chaos," in the words of the Abolanders. I'm going to note only the handful that proved especially helpful to me in writing *Primitive.* For a novelist, a resource book's value often lies in its highly idiosyncratic means of stirring the imagination, so what follows is in no way intended to diminish the considerable achievements of the many nonfiction authors who have contributed mightily to our understanding of global warming. It is a modest record of what moved me most.

In the novel, I mentioned by name the renowned biologist and paleontologist, Tim Flannery, but only alluded to his fine book, *The Weather Makers.* Although first published in 2005, it remains an important resource for understanding what is happening to our planet. My copy is highlighted, inked with margin notes, dog-eared, and revered.

Likewise, I found Al Gore's *An Inconvenient Truth* very helpful. I read it when it first came out because I doubted that his film would ever make it to the small mountain town that I call home. I couldn't have been more incorrect—or happier over my misjudgment: His Oscar winner ran for weeks on the only screen in town, and then came back months later for another run. I thought the film did an outstanding job of adapting his invaluable book to film.

Elizabeth Kolbert's *Field Notes from a Catastrophe: A Frontline Report on Climate Change* brought me, along with many other fortunate readers, into the lives of people already adversely affected by our warming planet.

I found Eugene Linden's *The Winds of Change* moving for a very different reason: it took me back to civilizations destroyed by earlier periods of stark climate change.

What's most astounding to me is the tremendous number of rich resources available to anyone interested in the subject of climate change. I'd suggest that everyone subscribe to Dr. Jim Hansen's email list, and catch *Democracy Now's* ongoing and aggressive coverage of global warming, along with so many other critical issues. Otherwise, it's a daunting task to recommend specific sites, blogs or books because there is so much valuable material within easy reach. I would urge readers to begin as I did, by firing up their search engines with two critical words: "Climate change."

Discussion Questions

Were the Abolanders justified in abducting Sonya?

How do you think Sonya was changed by her abduction and what she witnessed in Terra Firma?

Did your feelings about Sonya change as you read Primitive?

Likewise, did your feelings about Akiah, Chandra, Gwen, and other Abolanders change as you learned more about them?

Would you want to live in a place like Terra Firma?

Do you feel that Darcy acted wisely in searching for her mother by entering the activist underground?

How do you think the differences in Sonya and Darcy's values affected their relationship?

Darcy thought her friend, Lotus Land, was a hero for refusing to testify before a federal grand jury. Did you agree with Darcy? Would you refuse to testify to a federal grand jury under similar circumstances?

Why do you think Kodiak betrayed his fellow activists, and then turned his back on the deal he made with government agents?

What do you think of Sonya's comment about the attack on Terra Firma by U.S. military forces: "I see what our country has been doing in other places around the world. The only difference was those cameras. They showed everything, and it was ugly."

How do you feel about Sonya's refusal to testify against any of the Abolanders?

More Praise For Mark Nykanen's Thrillers

THE BONE PARADE

"Nykanen won an Edgar for television news coverage. That background shows. He has a great eye for description, and uses his narrator as a camera. Since his narrator is Ashley Stassler, a highly successful sculptor, that eye is highly trained and the descriptions are vivid and emotional...This novel has so many twists even the most jaded readers will stick with it."
— **The Globe and Mail**

"Nykanen's methodical killer [Stassler] shines as he feeds off the family's emotional breakdown from their captivity and body 'shaping.'" Stassler says, "'I give everything to my art. Everything.' Clearly Nykanen has followed suit. What results should satisfy anyone hungry for a clever psychological thriller."
— **Philadelphia Inquirer**

"A longtime television investigative journalist...continues his impressive transition to thriller writer with a harrowing serial killer tale in which the murderer happens to be a world-renowned sculptor of bronze works featuring families in distress."
— **Seattle Post-Intelligencer**

SEARCH ANGEL

"Nykanen is a master of knowing what scares us deep down...Words have power, and Nykanen knows their secrets. He knows how to take those marks on a page and shape them into something deliciously horrible."
— **Salem Statesman Journal**

"Takes you deep into Hannibal Lector territory... great page-turning escapism...Nykanen deftly alternates viewpoints as he goes deep into the nether regions of a killer's brain."
— **Lansing State Journal**

HUSH

"A well-crafted and sophisticated psychological thriller that captures in frightening detail the fevered inner life of a psychopath. Elegant and darkly powerful."
— **Vincent Bugliosi, author of Helter Skelter and Outrage.**

"*HUSH*...compresses a lifetime of experience with the criminal psyche into some 300 white-knuckled pages. It's a well-crafted psychological thriller that sets your teeth on edge and practically stops our breathing as it follows a serial killer/child abuser along a twisted path. There are not flights of magical realism here, no Stephen King fantasy; this is pure, realistic, well-written horror."
— *Eugene Register-Guard*

Breinigsville, PA USA
28 October 2009

226560BV00003BA/1/P